D0004541

~ A ~
SHARPNESS
ON THE
NECK

~ A ~
SHARPNESS
ON THE
NECK

Fred Saberhagen

TOR®

A TOM DOHERTY ASSOCIATES BOOK
NEW YORK

This is a work of fiction. All the characters and events portrayed in this novel are either fictitious or are used fictitiously.

A SHARPNESS ON THE NECK

A Tor Book
Published by Tom Doherty Associates, Inc.
175 Fifth Avenue
New York, NY 10010

Tor Books on the World Wide Web:
http://www.tor.com

Tor® is a registered trademark of Tom Doherty Associates, Inc.

Library of Congress Cataloging-in-Publication Data

Saberhagen, Fred.
    A sharpness on the neck / by Fred Saberhagen.
        p.   cm.
    "A Tom Doherty Associates book."
    ISBN 0-312-85799-3
    I. Title.
    PS3569.A215S46   1996
    813'.54—dc20   96-19126
                                          CIP

First Edition: November 1996

Printed in the United States of America

0 9 8 7 6 5 4 3 2 1

~ A ~
SHARPNESS
ON THE
NECK

~ 1 ~

The world abounds in mysteries. But some of the marvels which at first sight strike the observer as most impressive are susceptible to the most trivial explanations.

Allow me to offer an example. Charles Dickens, famed inventor of Christmas ghosts and Tiny Tim, when visiting Rome in 1845 chose to broaden his experience of the world by witnessing the beheading of a criminal. Afterward Dickens wrote: *A strange appearance was the apparent annihilation of the neck. The head was taken off so close that it seemed as if the knife had narrowly escaped crushing the jaw, or shaving off the ear. And the body looked as if there were nothing left above the shoulder.*

In fact, the cause of this seeming annihilation is perfectly simple. When the living muscles of the neck are suddenly cut in half, each end of each fiber contracts sharply, pulling with it the soft surrounding tissues, as well as the small, newly disconnected bones which had made up the spinal column. Tiny fragments are all one can expect to find of whichever vertebra lay directly in the path of the falling knife, which, at least in the classical French guillotine, is not only extremely sharp but as heavy as a small anvil.

* * *

Now that we have arrived in France, let me mention, parenthetically, a puzzle that I—I, Vlad Dracula—find somewhat harder to explain: In all the surviving bureaucratic paperwork of the Terror—I mean the French Revolution of the 1790s—in all the volumes of court orders, prison records, inflammatory speeches, in all the desperate accumulation of decrees and denunciations—the word "guillotine" does not appear even once. Newspapers, of course, are a different story. Charles-Henri Sanson, chief executioner and high priest of the device during much of that bloodstained epoch, as a rule called it simply *la mécanique*—"the machine."

I tell you that greedy and most fickle wench, *la mécanique,* consumed more blood in one year—nay, perhaps in a month, or even in a single day—than I in a whole century.

The long, broad stream of human history has cast up a hundred variations on the beheading device, from the simple headsman's axe or sword up through an infernal variety of complications. It seems safe to say that the one the world knows best is the eponymous child of Dr. Guillotin, who more than two hundred years ago, as a delegate to the French National Assembly, conceived his mechanical offspring, based on the latest humanitarian principles, in the course of an enlightened search for greater efficiency in terror.

The guillotine in its classical French form counted its first live human victim on April 25, 1792, in Paris, when used to dispatch a common murderer and thief, Jacques Pelletier. Some three years later, a steam-powered guillotine, intended to achieve the mass production of justice, was on the drawing boards—but by 1795 the number of beheadings, after averaging around twenty-six a day in Paris alone during the previous summer, had gone into a precipitous decline. The French Revolution, a monstrous child of oppression, was choked on blood and stumbling over bodies. To the best of historians' knowledge at the end of the twentieth century, that ultraefficient model of *la mécanique* has yet to be constructed.

Throughout a good part of the 1790s—those strenuous years which in France, at least, are never to be forgotten—Sanson and his sons and their crew (there was never a shortage of volunteers) performed their indefatigable labors, without benefit of steam, while elevated on a stage. Their Parisian theater of operations looked much like a prizefighters' square ring, and had the same reason for its existence: to provide a good view for a large audience.

The tall narrow frame of the guillotine, extending almost fifteen feet above the platform, was essentially composed of two stout wooden uprights a little more than a foot apart. The lunette at the bottom of the uprights consisted of two pieces of wood, each with a smooth, semicircular notch, that when clapped together formed a solid neckpiece pierced by a circular, neck-sized hole.

This hole was at the head of the plank bed on which the subject was placed facedown. The broad, single plank, painted blood red like the lunette and uprights, slid back from the upright portion of the frame, simultaneously tilting into an almost vertical position. First, as a rule, the subject's hands were tied behind his or her back. Then the man—frequently a woman; sometimes a child—who was to experience the full effect of the apparatus walked (or was dragged or carried) up to this plank, and was secured to it by broad leather straps encircling the waist and legs.

The plank was then tipped forward on its central pivot, bringing its occupant to a prone position. Now a precise adjustment by the machine's attendants, allowing for the subject's height—perhaps I should say for the total length when horizontal—positioned the chin in a nicely calculated way, to overhang the end of the plank by about three inches. The executioners, shifting their grip, slid the whole bed forward in its greased grooves, so that the chin of the occupant just cleared the lower half of the lunette. The upper construction of curved wood was then clamped down. A final adjustment, if necessary, was accomplished by tugging on the subject's hair, or on the ears if there was insufficient hair to offer a good grip. This part of the operation was not entirely without peril for the technician; more than one assistant executioner lost more than one finger due to premature release of the heavy knife above.

Let us now briefly consider that weapon, its cutting edge poised ten or twelve feet above the waiting neck. Attached to the top of the blade was a *mouton,* a piece of iron weighing some thirty kilograms, or over sixty pounds, intended to render more forceful the descent of the razor-edged cutter, which in itself weighed about twenty pounds. The impact of all this metal, falling usually on the fourth vertebra, tended to be decisive.

I can offer eyewitness testimony that it was Sanson's habit, each day after work, to bring home with him only the blade of the guillotine, without the *mouton.* His idea, that of a good workman, was to save the most delicate part of the instrument from rain and rust. Also there was some thought of discouraging curiosity-seekers from playing games with *la mécanique,* hurting themselves or some innocent victim.

Naturally Sanson, or more often one of his assistants, saw to it that the blade was cleaned very thoroughly before it was brought into his house. Those in charge also took care that the cutting edge, angled at about forty-five degrees from right to left for improved efficiency, was treated tenderly with file and whetstone to keep it sharp.

Up on the platform, when Sanson's shop was open for business, there waited wicker baskets also painted red, and made small and large, to receive, respectively, the heads and bodies of the corpses which were the finished product of all this industry and ingenuity. The baskets were usually kept half-filled with bran or sawdust, in hopes of making the cleanup easier.

*   *   *

How's this for a joke? Executioner to victim being dragged to the machine: "You don't want to do it? But it will only take a second."

Yes, I quite agree. But at the very height of the Terror, in the summer of 1794 (Year 2 of the now-almost-forgotten Revolutionary Calendar), one of Sanson's least intelligent assistants was wont to repeat this wheeze a dozen or a score of times a day. Of course each victim only had to hear it once; but after a few weeks it seemed that the fellow's own co-workers, tortured beyond endurance, were on the point of cutting their colleague's throat to shut him up . . . but I digress.

Where was I? Yes, there is one more point I wish to make about the guillotine, then on with the story, which I trust you will find fully satisfactory . . . Whenever, in these post-Revolutionary times, a full-size model of *la mécanique* becomes available—this happens somewhat more often than you might think—many people find something irresistibly attractive in the idea of trying on, as it were, that tiltable plank and even that lunette. (Few go so far as wanting to hear above their heads the speedy whisper of the falling blade.) Some of these enthusiasts are found among the adventurous elderly, sometimes they are young men, but for some reason the most susceptible to such temptations seem to be young women. All of them want to know: *How would it feel to lie down there?*

But it would have been hard to conceive of anything more remote from the thoughts of Philip Radcliffe and his bride of three months, the former June MacKenzie, on the late afternoon in the early summer of 1996 when those two young people encountered . . . no, not a guillotine, not yet . . . but their first vampire.

This particular drinker of blood made a first impression all sweet and girlish, with nothing at all in her appearance to suggest, at first glance, the true nature of her being—unless one considered the dark glasses, necessary armor against the day's last, relatively feeble rays of direct sunlight. She looked very young (though actually well over five hundred years of age, as I can testify through personal acquaintance) and was comely of face and figure. Her hair was curly, coloring on the dark side, more gypsy-looking than African. Wearing faded jeans, a man's shirt, and long silver earrings, she stood at roadside, one arm boldly extended, thumb up in the hitchhiker's time-honored gesture, flashing white teeth—none of them at the moment particularly pointed—as Radcliffe's convertible, slowing to ten miles an hour for a sharp curve on the winding, climbing, narrow western road, drew near.

The Radcliffes' kidnapping by the so-called undead took both of them completely by surprise. At the moment when they first came in sight of the young woman, there had been nothing on their minds more exotic than their choice of places, all hours of driving distant, where they might stop for the night.

But how could an even moderately adventurous young man, accompanied by a wife who invariably wanted to stop for injured animals, resist an attractive young woman standing at roadside at sunset, hitchhiking appealingly in an open area, typical of the western USA, where not even a single thuggish male companion could possibly be concealed? One could see the mountains rising, almost a hundred miles away, with not much of anything but distance in between. There was no broken-down car in evidence, to offer an explanation for her presence.

The girl at roadside came into the view of Philip and June just as the sun was on the point of disappearing behind the western mountains, on what had been till then a day of only minor surprises for the young couple. The youthful-looking hitchhiker was barefoot, a condition made more noticeable by her blood-red painted toenails. It seemed obvious that she had not been doing a lot of walking along the desert road in that condition.

Philip's intention had been to coast on past the waiting figure for a few yards before coming to a full stop. But the hitchhiker, as if afraid he was going to get away, darted into the narrow road right in front of his convertible, so that he had to slam on the brakes and curse violently to stop before hitting her. In the next moment, he had the impression that his car *had* hit the crazy woman; he thought he heard an alarming thump, and believed he saw her body propelled backward a yard or two.

June, her pale blond hair and skin in marked contrast to those of the hitchhiker, screamed and said something. Afterward, no one could remember what.

But in the next moment, it seemed that the impression of a heavy impact must have been mistaken, because the hitchhiker certainly was not harmed, had not even been knocked down. Almost before he had completely stopped, she was at the side of the car, reaching for the right rear door handle.

Certainly whatever had happened was not his fault, but Philip was half-convinced that his auto had struck her, and he couldn't refuse to stop and open the door for her.

Until that day, the young man would have given the year 1996 a mixed rating. Apart from the joys of his recent wedding, it had not been, for various financial and business reasons, among the very best years of his life. But on the other hand it was a comfortable distance from the worst. Career-wise, he thought it might very well be described as one of the riskiest of times, with the life of a computer consultant in a constant state of flux. But if you looked at the other side of the coin of rapid change, such an epoch was also the most promising.

Philip Radcliffe was twenty-six years old, and almost exactly six feet tall, broad-shouldered but rangy rather than massive in his build. He was blessed, or cursed, with a classically handsome face, which added to the impression of aristocracy. A shock of dark brown hair tended to resist all efforts at arrangement, lending its owner a romantic, windblown look.

Something in the young man's features or bearing, the look of his eye, the tilt of his head, along with the lack of styling in his hair, suggested the aristocrat even to people who had no clear idea what an aristocrat in the classic European sense ought to look like.

Having screeched to a halt, half on the road, half off, he opened his driver's door and started to get out of his car. But then he aborted the motion, slamming his door shut again. Because the young woman was already settling into the rear seat.

"Drive on!" his new passenger urged, slamming her door shut too—or at least thumping her hand on the flat panel. Radcliffe couldn't have sworn that she had ever opened the door, but somehow she was in. She gave a small but dramatic wave of one small hand, displaying long fingernails of the same color as her toes, and laughed.

June, twisting round her slight frame to look from the right front seat, gaped open-mouthed at the brazenness of this performance.

Philip, a trifle dazed by the rapidity of events, started to drive on. With automatic caution he reminded his new passenger to put on her seat belt.

His new passenger only drew in a deep breath, ran her fingers through her curly hair, and laughed at the idea, once more displaying her amazingly white teeth.

He snatched a couple of seconds from his driving to turn his head and look at her again. He said: "I thought for a moment that the car had hit you, back there."

The reply was breezy: "You don't have to worry about that."

Well, thought Philip Radcliffe. Usually he was quite firm in his attitude toward passengers, requiring that they all be belted in. But the laughter was like a jolt of reality. Illogically, seatbelts were suddenly diminished in importance.

Welcome a stranger into your car in America these days, and a sudden accident is one of the least of your worries.

"Where are you going?" Surely a reasonable and almost inevitable question to put to a hitchhiker.

"With you, Philip." And once more the dark-haired stranger laughed, this time more musically. She turned her head a few degrees from left to right. "Hi, June."

Phil was sufficiently disturbed that his steering, or lack of it, briefly caused the vehicle to wander back and forth across the road. The couple in the front seat looked at each other with stunned expressions, both of them wondering where inside the car or on it their names might be visible. But of course the names were not on display anywhere, and they knew it. The only reasonable explanation was that they knew this girl from somewhere. But no, thought Radcliffe—she was certainly not of the type that he could have forgotten.

For some reason he did not even notice that his new passenger was invisible in the rearview mirror; or perhaps, as breathers tend to do sometimes, he unconsciously suppressed the knowledge. Dangerously neglecting to watch the road, he turned his head to look at her. Numbly he asked: "How'd you know my name?"

"Somebody told me," she answered playfully, turning her face toward him. With the dying of the last sunspark on the mountainside, she slipped off the dark glasses, revealing warm brown eyes with nothing overtly amazing about them. "Better watch where you're going." Then, as an afterthought: "Call me Connie."

And Phil, even this early in the game, felt a secret pang of guilt at the impression this comely vampire woman made on him.

Not that any suspicion of her status, her subspecies if you will, had yet dawned on the puzzled young man. Neither he nor his bride had any clear idea of what a genuine vampire might be expected to look like. Apart from the enjoyment of a few old movies, they really had no thoughts on the subject at all.

But when the young woman smiled at Philip from between her heavy silver earrings, both observers understood immediately that there was something truly out of the ordinary about her.

Philip's job as a computer consultant, mainly helping companies to rid themselves of their mainframes in favor of smaller, relatively inexpensive hardware, involved a lot of travel. Begun with his wife three days ago in Kansas City, this trip had been designed with a combination of business and pleasure in mind. Already they had detoured considerably from the strict requirements of business, to do some sightseeing at Meteor Crater and the Petrified Forest/Painted Desert complex. They had visited Inscription Rock in New Mexico as well as the Very Large Array of radiotelescopes mounted on railroad tracks, and were regretting the fact that they had been unable to work the Carlsbad Caverns into their itinerary. They were looking forward to the Grand Canyon and, if they decided to stretch the trip a bit, Zion National Park.

The sun had at last dropped securely behind the western peaks, whose long shadows now entirely claimed the road ahead. Automatically Radcliffe switched on his headlights—and at the same moment felt the weight and balance in the car change subtly.

The second vampire to put in an appearance came a lot closer to looking the part, as it has recently been portrayed in films, even though he wore no cape nor displayed any obvious great fangs. The last beams of direct sunlight had barely left the car when he appeared, hatless, clad in a dark suit, sitting in the rear seat beside Connie. His entry was accomplished without the vehicle having stopped again or even slowed down, without either of the doors opening even for an instant. Radcliffe felt his presence, somehow, and heard him in the rear seat before he saw him.

This latest newcomer, who had arrived so incomprehensibly, seemed to have blown in like a cloud of mist, or dropped in from overhead like an invisible bird. He materialized as a rather serious-looking man of indeterminate age, though certainly not gray or wrinkled. This well-built stranger—lean body slightly taller than average, face dark for a Caucasian and rather handsome—reached forward, unsnapped Philip's and June's safety belts, one with each hand, and pulled both breathers unceremoniously into the rear seat as if they had been no more than four years old.

Somehow he accomplished this feat without breaking any of their bones, leaving any bruises, or even tearing any of their clothing. In the next moment the Radcliffes were flanking the stranger in the rear. He had one brotherly arm around each of them, holding them more utterly immobile than any seat belt. Had the vehicle in which they rode not been a convertible, top down, it would, according to the modern taste for economy in manufacturing, have offered barely room enough to occupy a seat let alone go changing front to rear. In that case, who knows what that forceful fellow might have done to get his kidnapping victims where he wanted them? But he'd have found a way.

The three adults now sitting in the rear enjoyed sufficient room because, in the same instant as the Radcliffes were forcibly transported rearward, the young-looking woman with the gypsy eyes had somehow transferred herself to the front seat, where she had already grabbed the steering wheel with one hand. Radcliffe hadn't really seen how Miss Gypsy had performed this feat of acrobatic stage magic, and he couldn't really believe it. But there she was anyway, now sliding neatly under the wheel and assuming all the chores of driving. So smoothly was this change of command accomplished that the automobile hardly hesitated in its forward passage, hardly wavered from its central position in the narrow road.

Almost before the Radcliffes had the chance to be alarmed, they were prisoners. Neither of their kidnappers had bothered to gag them, because neither cared in the least if the victims yelled.

June let out a wavering sound. It seemed not so much a cry for help as a recognition that crying for help would do no good.

No one paid her outcry any attention.

Fear arrived, for both victims, with a strong rush of adrenaline, but much too late to do either of them any good.

Philip Radcliffe thought: *Violent kidnapping is something that happens to other people, not to me. Not to us. Therefore, this can't really be going on.*

But it was.

"What is this?" His own voice sounded strange and awkward.

"For your own good," said the couple's new companion, who was now wedged in between them with an air of permanence, as if he'd been there for the whole trip. His deep voice carried some flavor of middle Europe. He sounded as if he were trying to be reassuring, and he gave Radcliffe's shoulders a fraternal squeeze.

Why am I letting this man restrain me with one arm? Who in the hell does he think he . . . Philip, at last energized by anger, willed himself to relax as a deliberate tactic—then in the next instant, struggled violently to be free.

More precisely, he *tried* to struggle violently—actually he could not move an inch. The single arm which pinioned him felt like a steel cable. The next step in his plan had been to punch the man beside him, or maybe slam him with an elbow. But any such heroics proved utterly impossible. Both of Radcliffe's elbows were being held immovably against his sides.

While Phil was trying to think of something to do next,

part of his mind took note of the fact that the young woman behind the wheel did not really seem to be concentrating on her driving. The car was going considerably faster now with her in control, but it seemed that the task was perhaps too trivial to hold her interest. She turned on the car radio and punched in one station after another until she came to a man on a talk show declaring loudly that there was obviously no chance of that other candidate, the wrong one, being elected in November. Voters would have to be crazy to pick that villain, declared the hectoring, annoying voice. Because of course if that scoundrel *should* happen to get in, America was doomed, and the children and grandchildren of everyone out there in the radio audience faced a future bleak beyond belief. They'd all spend the rest of their lives jobless but paying enormous taxes. Not only would they be buried in debt, national and personal, but half of them would be held hostage by domestic criminals or foreign terrorists.

"Turn off the noise," the man holding Philip immobile commanded harshly. (He had no wish to be mistaken for a hostage-taker, and might have allowed the radio to stay on if that word had not surfaced amid the babble. On the other hand, he might not.)

The girl in the front seat did not turn her head, and Philip thought she hesitated briefly, on the brink of arguing. But within a couple of seconds she obediently punched the radio off again.

~ 2 ~

June, writhing and straining, suddenly made her own effort to break free. But her first try fared no better than Philip's, though her struggle lasted somewhat longer. Phil on observing what his wife was doing gamely made another try himself, but their captor had no trouble at all managing them both at the same time, one arm to each. The dark-haired intruder sat through this interlude with a thoughtful expression on his lean face, and seemed to be waiting, like an experienced parent, for the kids to get the nonsense out of their systems.

June, gasping and tired, at last gave up, and breathed out a prolonged whine of frustration.

"Phil, *do something!*"

He grunted and strained again and muttered a few obscenities and oaths. But this time his heart wasn't really in it. He understood, as he sat waiting for his lungs and heart to slow to normal, that he might as well have saved his energy.

Glaring at their captor, June said: "I don't see how you think you can just come into the car and—and . . ."

"But I can." His voice was calm, infuriatingly parental.

"Depend upon it. Nevertheless, you have nothing to fear from me."

So, it seemed that they were well and truly kidnapped. Philip in the back of his mind was already running through a mental list of people who might be expecting to hear soon from either one of them. The list was short, and offered no comfort. The Radcliffes could be out of communication with the world for a long time before anyone else became alarmed.

After a few seconds of silence, the girlish-looking vampire in the front seat turned her head long enough to call back cheerily: "Call me Connie. And you're Phil and June. But you already know that." And she giggled.

"You may call me Mr. Graves," said the somber man who sat, apparently relaxed but watchful as a statue, between his captives in the rear.

"You're hurting me," June told him, in a tone of voice that suggested it was mainly her sensibilities which had been injured.

"My apologies," said Mr. Graves, sounding in fact not all that sorry. His voice suggested that of some Middle European diplomat with faultless yet not native English, and his dark suit did nothing to dispel this impression. He turned his face toward June. "I shall release you. But only on the condition that you must, for a while, accept my presence, and my guidance."

Evidently she gave some sign of her acceptance. Radcliffe, feeling like a fool in his helplessness, looked across and saw that his wife was now indeed free. She was rubbing her slender arms and shoulders, inspecting her wrists and hands, with a puzzled look, as if she were sure there must be someplace where she was really hurt.

Phil let out a breath of partial relief. "Put on your seat belt," he reminded his wife mechanically.

She pulled the strap into place, and snapped the buckle, in a kind of reflex action.

Graves had now turned his dark, compelling gaze to his

left. "Mr. Radcliffe, will you also ride peacefully beside me?"

"Doesn't seem like I have much choice," Phil gritted through his teeth.

"An intelligent observation," his seatmate observed.

The numbing grip relaxed. It was Philip's turn to rub his arms and shoulders, and to feel puzzled at the lack of damage. All that strength should have left something bruised or strained; but he felt only a faint tingling, like the aftermath of a good massage.

No one man, especially one so thin, could be that strong. It had to have been some trick . . .

"Please put on your seatbelt," the trickster urged him solicitously.

Radcliffe clicked the halves of the buckle into place. Then, summoning up his not inconsiderable courage, he demanded of his kidnapper: "And who the hell are you?"

"You may call me Graves," the dark-suited man repeated patiently. "Mr. Graves, if you are in a mood for formality. When we have reached our destination, we are going to discuss my identity more fully. It has a certain bearing on our business." For the first time he smiled faintly, showing a glimpse of white teeth.

Connie in the front seat turned her head briefly, glancing at Phil. Then she remarked: "He does look like him, doesn't he, Vla . . . doesn't he, Mr. Graves?"

"A definite resemblance," Graves agreed.

"Who do I look like?" Radcliffe demanded.

"You look a whole lot like a certain ancestor of yours," Connie remarked, over her shoulder. "One who lived about two hundred years ago."

Philip, his mind still numb, mental faculties staggering off-balance and scrambling through trivia to try and find a foothold, decided that Connie appeared to be about a decade younger than Mr. Graves, who had to be at least thirty. And she sounded like a native English-speaker, which the male intruder did not.

* * *

The man who called himself Mr. Graves had turned his gaze upon his male captive, and was studying him intently. Philip was the one, by all indications, in whom Graves was really interested. He didn't know whether to be pleased or not that June was being virtually ignored.

Connie, without looking round again, remarked: "Yes, this has to be the one that Radu wants."

"Really there can be no doubt." Graves was nodding slowly. "The resemblance is definitely there. The eyes, the mouth. Unusually strong, after so many generations."

"So I look like my ancestor?" Radcliffe's own voice seemed surprisingly loud in his ears. "Does this mean I inherit the whole fortune?"

Ignoring his comment and facetious question, the woman said: "I agree, as to that. And I have an excellent memory for faces."

June piped up: "So, you're taking us to someone called Radu?"

"Taking you to him? On the contrary!" Graves, turning his head to look at her, smiled in some private amusement.

Connie, her mind still off on another pathway, muttered musingly: "I wonder—to how many 'greats' should that ancestor of his now be entitled?"

June said: "Phil?" in a small, lost voice. But then she let it go at that. He looked past their kidnapper at her, and was vaguely relieved to see that she was bearing up, so far—and that she had her seat belt on.

Connie drove on for more than an hour, heading generally west and north, steering from one small road to another, never seeming to have the least doubt as to where she was going. They passed through no towns; here and there a lighted window appeared only in the distance, and other traffic was nonexistent. Phil kept formulating plans for sudden violence, for taking their captor by surprise—and giving them up. The attitude of the man beside him, the memory of that grip, were thoroughly discouraging.

Twice he was on the point of telling Connie to turn the headlights on, and twice he held back. Let her hang up the car on one of these roadside rocks, if she thought she could see in the dark—anything to disrupt the kidnappers' plan. But though the darkness deepened steadily, the driver proceeded unerringly and at the same speed.

Now and then she turned her head to smile solicitously at her victims. Meanwhile Graves spent most of the time sitting motionless, as if lost in thought.

Eventually, flicking on headlights at last, she pulled the convertible into what was obviously a prearranged rendezvous. A kind of rude driveway, no more than a set of rutted tracks, curved away from the thin road, leading behind a rocky outcropping to a building, some kind of abandoned shed, whose location effectively hid its presence from casual traffic. Here the deceptively flat-looking landscape had put up enough of a bulge to conceal till the last moment an isolated shed, surrounded by a small grove of trees. A dusty Suburban, two or three years old, was parked just beyond the shed.

As the car braked to a stop, Phil started at the sight of a small handful of masked figures, men and women, who suddenly appeared in the glare of his car's headlights, standing around the shed. Radcliffe saw with a chill that these people, dressed in nondescript clothing, were wearing rubber Halloween masks over their heads; ghosts and witches were represented, smiling, along with Frankenstein's monster, whose rubber features looked less happy. Radcliffe's uneasy attention took note also of a mummy and a werewolf.

So, the young man thought, with a sinking sensation. Numbers and organization proved that it wasn't just a couple of crazed acrobats who were doing this. He and June were somehow victims of a real, professional plot, well-organized if fundamentally crazy, based on some total misunderstanding of who he was. He now began to understand, or thought he did. Somehow these people had convinced themselves that Philip Radcliffe was as wealthy as his name suggested. Well, they were in for a jarring disappointment.

One of the masked figures opened the car door, and spoke in a friendly male voice. "Mr. and Mrs. Radcliffe, we're glad to see you. Please get out."

Others murmured assurances that they were not going to be harmed. Their spokesman handed June out of the car like a gentleman.

Philip, encouraged by the mildness of the reception, was shaking his head at them, raising his voice, trying to get in a telling word before things went too far. "If any of you expect to collect a ransom—"

"We don't," the masked spokesman assured him calmly. "Don't worry about that."

Philip had time to notice that the license plates on the Suburban were so obscured with dried spatterings of beige mud as to be unreadable.

Simple but clean toilet facilities were available just beyond the shed, in the form of a new portable chemical toilet of the type used on construction jobs.

There was an interval of waiting, with people standing. Nobody was smoking. Radcliffe supposed that would have been hard, with the masks.

While the kidnapped couple were being allowed a few minutes to use the facilities in turn, their baggage, including two or three backpacks and satchels, was transferred to the new vehicle. There was also some dirty laundry in a plastic garbage bag, and a small ice chest which now contained nothing but some cold, ice-melt water. All items were opened, with apologies, and inspected, before being loaded into the van.

"Oh, that's all right," June responded to the second or third expression of regret. Her nerve was up again, and so was her temper. "If you're going to kidnap us, what do we care if you search our baggage? I've been treated worse by airlines."

Rubber masks turned silently toward her. It was Graves himself who responded in a dry voice: "Your courage does you credit, madam. In fact, one would be virtually certain to be treated worse by airlines."

Not until Radcliffe's nervous gaze had fallen two or three times upon the waiting Suburban did he notice that its windows were shaded or heavily tinted. Riding in the second or third seat of that vehicle at night, a couple of kidnap victims would be able to see very little of anything outside except for passing headlights.

He kept trying to fight off moments of panic. Now might be his last chance to try to find out where he was, where they were being taken. Looking around him in search of a landmark, something that might later help him identify this location, Philip could see nothing familiar and nothing memorable.

The sun had now been gone for almost two hours, but the last glow of sunset still clung to the western sky.

Counteracting the prisoners' tendency to panic was the fact that all the kidnappers, masked and otherwise, continued to treat them with an incomprehensible, eerie courtesy. Radcliffe was several times assured that he and June would get their car back. He was allowed to see that it was being securely parked, its convertible top raised against possible changes in the weather, hidden partially inside the shed, which lacked one wall.

Before pulling out on the next leg of the journey, some of the masked people discussed a possible effort to erase the convertible's tire tracks from a long section of dusty road.

"The rain will take care of it," Connie remarked, as if to herself.

What rain? Philip thought. Then only moments later he saw the first flash of lightning, in the southwest.

* * *

Twelve minutes by Philip's watch after their arrival they were on their way again, the Radcliffes being transported by three of the masked folk in the new machine. Both Graves and Connie had been left behind, but not until Graves had assured both his prisoners that he would see them within a few hours: "Certainly before dawn."

Radcliffe thought he heard one of the masks murmur a question to another: would it now be necessary to tie the prisoners' arms and legs? The answer seemed to be no, but it was worrisomely long in coming.

The Suburban had seats for nine people, in a pinch, and currently six were aboard. From the sound of the tires, and the rocking motion of the vehicle, it was easy to tell that part of the trip was off-road, and a larger part on some secondary, unpaved route. Occasionally a piece of gravel pinged against the underbody.

This leg of the journey was longer than the previous one, lasting more than four hours. Gradually the area where rain was threatening was left behind. The victims had been allowed to keep their watches. Since their wrists weren't tied, they could look at them; but it did no good. With the windows of the vehicle darkened, it was hard to tell even the general direction they were now taking.

This time the masked driver used the headlights, and drove at a less alarming speed over the bad roads.

While they were under way, a couple of their masked guardians rode with the victims in the back seat, making reassuring comments, and from time to time engaging them in casual conversation. There were remarks about the weather and the baseball season. And about the coming election.

Radcliffe had little patience with this tactic. "What are you going to do with us?"

The people in masks were patiently reassuring. "Nothing that will hurt you. You will be required to stay for a time in a place where it will be relatively easy for us to offer you protection."

"Why?" Phil's was a ragged, anguished cry.

"It's a long story. Like I said, we're not going to hurt you, whatever happens. And you do need protection, depend on it. The thing is, we had to act first and explain later."

"Can't you at least tell us why?"

"I'd like to hear the explanation!" June challenged.

"You will, ma'am." The male voice was calm and courteous; it might have belonged to a good cop and not a kidnapper. "But from someone who can do a better job of it than I can."

From time to time Phil tried again: "We're not wealthy, you know. None of our relatives are wealthy. You think my company is going to ransom me? Hah! You're not going to get any money out of this."

The nearest rubber mask was nodding. "We understand that. Making money out of this is not our intention at all."

"Then what is?"

"Have a little patience. Everything will be explained."

"Why not explain it now?"

A hesitation. "Mainly because it'd sound too crazy. That's the truth. Mr. Graves had better be the one to do the job."

"Why?"

"He can do it more convincingly."

There came a mysterious interval in which some time was spent parked and waiting, evidently for a signal of some kind to be given from up ahead.

As if they were taking turns at trying to lay the groundwork for the task of explanation, which they foresaw would be long and hard, the guardians observed more than once that they had reached the couple barely in time.

"Barely in time for what?"

But of course that question received no satisfactory answer.

Graves after several hours' absence rejoined his captives and their guards. In the mystic grayness just before dawn, he stood waiting in the road, and boarded the vehicle when it pulled up and stopped for him. This time he climbed aboard in the ordinary way, moving with smooth agility.

The dark, mysteriously impressive man plainly did not care whether his victims saw his face or not. That was ominous when Radcliffe thought about it.

Having gone through his prisoners' pockets and purse, Graves said, in a tone of finality: "You are Philip Radcliffe." It sounded madly as if he were going to add: "I have a warrant for your arrest."

"Yes." In a way he was suddenly afraid to admit his identity, but with all the ID in his billfold, credit cards and such, it seemed pointless to try to deny the fact. Then, responding to what he was still convinced must be on his captors' minds, he repeated yet again: "But I don't have any money."

Philip's billfold, including the modest amount of money in it, was soon returned to him. "I am not interested in your money. You are not being held for ransom. You may as well believe me; what reason could I have for lying to you on that point now?"

Philip had been aware for most of his life, ever since he had grown old enough to be aware of such things, that some people after looking at him and hearing his name tended to assume that he was wealthy instead of moderately prosperous. Some even assumed he was immensely wealthy. He was at a loss to understand this, except that the cause had to be something in his name, or in his looks.

"All right," he demanded of his kidnapper. "If you don't want money, then what?"

"Believe it or not, our only object is to save your life. You are now in protective custody."

"If that's all it is, you can let us both go. I don't need to be protected." *Why do some of them take pains to hide their faces, while this man and woman don't care? Could the others conceivably be people I would recognize?*

The other appeared not to have heard that comment.

"You expect me to thank you? I didn't know that either of our lives were in any danger."

"You have put your finger on an important point. Your ignorance, through no fault of your own, is indeed something of a problem." Even as he spoke, Dracula kept looking over his shoulder. Consciously or not, he gave the impression of a man on guard against the pursuit of an opponent he obviously considered extremely formidable. "And whether you eventually express your gratitude or not is a matter of indifference. What I have sworn, I have sworn."

"What exactly *have* you sworn?"

"That you will be protected."

Radcliffe thought that over for a little while. The explanation seemed to be going in a circle. Trying to get back to practical matters, he asked: "Where are you taking us?"

"To a place where, for the time being, you will be relatively safe."

"We'll be safe at home."

"Alas, no." Slowly the dark, unmasked man shook his head. "Unfortunately that is not the case, for either of you. Not just now. But if all goes well, you should be safe at home in only a few days."

"Why do all your helpers wear masks, and you don't?"

"They are masked because you might, if all goes well, someday see them again. If you were to recognize them, an awkward situation could arise."

"But I'm never going to see you again?"

The other smiled faintly. "Probably not—but to me it is a matter of indifference whether you do. It will make no difference if you someday describe me and complain about me to the police."

"Oh, it won't? And to Constantia? If that's her real name."

"She and I, as you may have observed already, are different from the others."

"Different how?"

"That is part of the explanation to which you are entitled. But it will take time."

A little time went by before Radcliffe asked: "Safe from who? From what?"

"From a certain man, one who has vowed not only to cut off your head, but to drink your blood."

Radcliffe couldn't think of anything to say in response. Up front Connie, or someone else, was driving; he could see only the faint outline of a head. The vehicle roared on. Maybe they'd be lucky and a speed cop would pull her over.

June asked: "Is that the 'Radu' you mentioned earlier? And does he want *my* head too? To drink *my* blood?"

Their captor nodded solemnly. "I know him well, and he is quite capable of doing both. I would not be surprised to see that he had the guillotine all ready."

That silenced June for the moment. Phil stepped in: "You know this Radu. All right, who is he?"

"Someone I have known for a long time."

"How long?"

The other appeared to be considering his answer carefully. Finally he said, clearly: "More than five hundred years. Alas, he is my brother."

That put an end to all conversation for almost a quarter of an hour.

The sun was on the verge of rising when the vehicle at last pulled into a scanty patch of woods, between a pair of sandy hummocks, and rolled to a stop in front of a pair of small mobile homes. It was the kind of housing Radcliffe would have expected to see provided for workers at a small isolated mine—not that there were any visible signs of mining activity near.

Here two more masked kidnappers were waiting. The victims were bidden to get out of the van. By this time, both Radcliffes had recovered to some extent from the original shock, and each had begun trying to think of some way to escape from their kidnappers.

They got out of the van to smell a chill and dusty wind,

and find themselves standing in front of a small, dimly lighted mobile home. A few yards away, the shaded windows of a similar dwelling gave out a muted glow. The night was gone, the day was here, the sky still marked by a thin rising moon, and those stars bright enough to survive the early stages of the change. Mountains, ghostly shapes along the newly revealed horizon, loomed in several directions, the closest no more than twenty miles away.

Both little houses were set directly on the ground and appeared to have settled into their sites, as if they had been in place for some time.

A power line, looking out of place, came marching on its small poles across the desert.

A small, primitive landing strip was in view behind the buildings. A faded windsock hung limply. No aircraft were in sight at the moment.

Radcliffe and his wife were watched carefully but treated gently, like valuable objects, as they climbed out of the vehicle. While Mr. Graves watched the sky, as if suddenly interested in the weather, one of his masked helpers led Philip and June to the smaller of the two mobile homes.

"Come in, make yourselves at home. You're going to be here for a while."

"How long?"

"However long it takes."

The front door, which Radcliffe saw had been newly armored with a heavy grill—there were still scorch-marks from the welding torch—was held open for them. Somehow the professional workmanship that had obviously gone into the armoring was more frightening than almost anything else that had yet happened.

Inside, the structure was divided into a few small rooms, cheaply but cleanly furnished. The front entry led into a small sitting-room with an open door showing a small bedroom beyond. An archway on the opposite side led to a little kitchen.

"It's not fancy, but it's safe." The speaker, one of the

masked people, sounded almost apologetic.

Wandering numbly from room to room, Phil and June entered the small kitchen. On looking around, the newcomers discovered it was stocked with a surprising variety of food. The refrigerator held an unopened half gallon of milk bearing tomorrow's date, along with fresh fruits and vegetables, chicken and ground beef in butcher's wrappings, and a variety of drinks. The latter included half a case of premium imported beer, actually Phil's favorite brand, in twelve-ounce bottles. There were soft drinks in cans, a couple of varieties of bottled water. Breakfast cereals had been visible on the counter, along with a small assortment of dishes. Radcliffe took silent note of the absence of anything like a sharp knife.

The sturdy iron grillwork which protected the front door could be locked only from the outside; Phil supposed the same would be true of the kitchen door, if there turned out to be one on the far side of the structure.

Further inspection of the house confirmed that the windows, too, were all covered with heavy grills. Some thought and effort had evidently gone into making the place escape-proof.

At least the place looked clean and in reasonably good repair. The furnishings were new, or nearly so. An air-conditioning unit in the window waited silently, ready to deal with the day's heat when it came.

None of the masked people who were bustling in and out, carrying baggage and checking provisions, seemed to be watching the prisoners at all closely. Their baggage was promptly carried into the one small bedroom. Radcliffe, feeling exhausted, his mind wavering near hysteria, had the crazy notion that someone was going to expect a tip.

There was no mirror in the bedroom, but one in the bathroom, in the expected location over the sink.

"Phil, what . . . what . . . ?" June was whispering. She made a gesture indicating desperation.

He spread out his hands helplessly. "I don't know what. I don't know any more about this than you do."

Radcliffe and June had not long to wait before Mr. Graves came to speak to them politely.

"There is a videotape, which will explain much. You must watch it." He lifted in one pale hand a small black case which had been lying on the table beside the television and VCR.

"A videotape."

"Indeed. This will lay the groundwork for the explanation you very naturally demand. When you have seen it through, and considered its contents, we shall be able to talk to some purpose. Your many questions will be most swiftly answered if you will watch the tape."

"Wouldn't it be easier just to tell us?" June put in.

"I think not. A face-to-face discussion would inevitably involve arguments, demonstrations, a tedious business for which I will not have the time today, nor probably tomorrow. These hours I must devote to more important things." The dark eyes fixed on Phil. "You may place little value on either your blood or your life, but I have sworn a serious oath that I will save them both."

Phil nodded slowly. He knew the expression on his own face must indicate that he was seriously impressed. And indeed he was. *This man Graves is as nutty as a fruitcake factory.*

~ 3 ~

*H*aving thus sternly admonished his pair of prisoners, Mr. Graves, moving with the brisk pace of a senior executive who had important business everywhere, walked out of the little house, leaving the Radcliffes in the care of his masked assistants and Connie.

All of these continued their policy of referring to their leader, whenever he decided to return, June's and Phil's continued demands for explanations. The disguised ones oozed bland reassurances, and responded to questions by repeating Graves's urging to watch the tape.

Within a few minutes most of the masked guardians, as if seeking escape from the ongoing barrage of their victims' demands, had left the house. There remained on guard only one man and one woman, and this pair had discreetly withdrawn, like unobtrusive servants, into the small kitchen.

The two prisoners found themselves left alone in the small living room.

"All right." June's fear was being increasingly absorbed in anger. She sat down in one of the cheap armchairs, then immediately, too wired to admit weariness, bounced to her feet again. "Then let's take a look at the damned tape."

Her husband, who shared her mood, nodded. No other

course of action seemed likely to help them in the least. "It had better be good." He picked up the cartridge, noted that it was unlabeled, and loaded it into the VCR.

In another moment June and Phil were seated side by side on the sofa in front of the television. Philip picked up the remote control and turned on both machines.

When the tape began to play, Radcliffe's immediate hopes were dashed. The opening scene did not offer any dazzling enlightenment. It showed Mr. Graves, seated behind a table in what appeared to be the same room where the audience was now sitting, and looking earnestly toward the camera. Graves's image was dressed in what looked like the same dark suit in which he had carried out the kidnapping of the couple who were now his audience.

"Pay close attention," the taped image urged the two prisoners. "For I am about to introduce you to the man who has sworn to drink the blood of Philip Radcliffe." A pause. "And to cut off his head."

That last line was followed by a longer pause, which Phil thought must have been calculated, scripted, for dramatic effect. Certainly it got the full attention of the small audience for whom it was intended.

Mr. Graves's image on the TV screen looked into the camera, speaking quietly and unhurriedly. He admitted at the start, with disarming casualness, that he had not been present at many of the events which he was about to relate. "But there is enough information to reconstruct certain important scenes with a high degree of reliability."

Mostly he spoke while looking directly into the camera, but now and then dropped his compelling gaze to some scribbled notes on the table before him. The earnest tone of the presentation put at least one of the audience in mind of a speech from the Oval Office.

As the first minutes passed, the keen attention of the audience began to waver, and they looked at each other unhappily; the session began to seem an ordeal by nonsense.

Already the very gentleness and consideration in minor matters with which the Radcliffes were being treated had begun to arouse in them suspicions that the whole kidnapping might be a monstrous joke, perpetrated by some of their supposed friends.

"Junie, is this all a gag?" Philip hissed, at a moment when he thought he would not be overheard. "Some kind of a gigantic . . . *put-on?*"

June looked back at him in quiet desperation. "I don't know. The thought crossed my mind, too. But who do we know who'd do a thing like this?"

Despite the inroads of weariness, even with hysteria not far away, it was difficult to think of anyone.

The tape played on.

Philip and June sat side by side on the cheap sofa, holding hands most of the time, frequently exchanging looks but seldom comments, not knowing whether to laugh or cry. On the small screen the videotaped image of the man who seemed their chief persecutor was now well into what was evidently going to be a long narrative of the past.

And it wasn't working.

It was not that the speaker raved or rambled. No, he spoke coherently and calmly enough. Having got a brief introduction out of the way, he began the body of his story by recalling another year that, like 1996, had once been called the best of times and the worst of times.

Still, Phil and June were looking at each other in dismay; far from offering any reasonable explanation, the story seemed only to confirm that they were in the hands of hopeless lunatics.

The scene opened (according to the narration of the thoughtful, dry-voiced image on the screen) in the city of London, in the year 1790, just as the Revolution and its Terror were taking over across the Channel in France. Months earlier, the Bastille had fallen to the Parisian mob, and in that country all titles of hereditary nobility had been abolished. King Louis XVI and his queen, Marie Antoinette, were prisoners of the new government in all but name, though still clinging, tenuously, perilously, ambiguously, to some pretense of authority.

"The very year," observed the image of Graves on screen, "of the death of Benjamin Franklin—who, as I am sure you know, Mr. Radcliffe, is your own ancestor." The dark eyes looked into the camera . . .

Yes, he, Philip Radcliffe, had known that about Franklin. He had been well aware, at least, that it was an old tradition in the Radcliffe family. But what connection could there be between randy old Franklin and the craziness of Mr. Graves and his associates two hundred years later? If the ancestral Franklin really had something to do with their behavior, maybe he, Radcliffe, could talk them out of it . . . but with the best will in the world, it was hard to concentrate under these conditions of captivity. Radcliffe fidgeted on the sofa, moment by moment expecting one of their deranged kidnappers to come in and say or do something outrageous. Nothing of the kind happened, but he kept looking for it all the same. And June, beside him, was in no better shape.

On top of the other craziness, the watchers soon found themselves being intermittently distracted by what looked like technical difficulties; sometimes the image of the man on screen turned transparent, colorless, and strangely insubstantial. Then again, for intervals of several seconds the man and his clothing, along with the pen or pencil that he was holding in his hand, disappeared altogether. Meanwhile, all other objects in the picture, including the narrator's table and chair, remained rock-steady.

"Why is the picture doing that?" June whispered.

"I don't know." Philip looked around again, as he did on an average of once every thirty seconds, to see if anyone was listening. "Maybe that's someone's idea of really super special effects, that are certain to impress us."

"But all this stuff he's saying about vampires and oaths doesn't make sense . . ."

"Shh. I know, but listen . . ."

Twentieth-century Philip and June, seeing and hearing Vlad Dracula's version of Philip's ancestor's adventures of two hundred years ago, tried to convince each other that it would afford them some clue to the madness of the people who were holding them prisoner.

Guardedly keeping an eye out for any of their captors, who were maintaining a steady though relaxed presence in the other room, Radcliffe and his bride exchanged a few terse comments. The implication had been that they would be left undisturbed while they watched the tape, and so far their kidnappers were holding to that plan. None of the masked figures appeared to be observing them at all closely. Now neither Connie nor Graves had been heard from for a considerable time . . .

Beside Phil, June made a small noise, like a young woman caught in the grip of an unpleasant dream. His attention jerked back to discover his wife staring at the screen in apparent fascination.

"What is it?" Phil demanded.

She had paused the tape, and now gestured nervously toward the frozen image on the screen. "*What* did he say? I thought he said that someone, the man in the coffin in the London cemetery, had had his head cut off before he was buried . . . but then his head and body somehow came back together again?"

"I heard the same thing."

"Let me rewind, run that bit over again."

They did so. But instant replay proved to be of little help. The words spoken had been correctly heard, but that fact brought no real enlightenment. Neither watcher could derive from the tape much more than seeming confirmation that the narrator, the creator of this tale, had to be a madman.

The voice of the storyteller was calm, the sentences and thoughts coherent. But overall, the picture he painted was growing more and more disturbing. This so-reasonable voice detailed horrors, and more than horrors: a fantasy of survival in and beyond the grave, of centuries of life—or of extravagantly and grotesquely transformed existence.

The kidnapping victims looked at each other, each thinking how exhausted the other looked. At first there seemed no possibility of swallowing the story—long-lived vampires, grotesque and monstrous mutilations—as fact. But the narrator plodded on, implacably. *All these things were true,* he seemed to be saying, with calm infuriating arrogance. *Take it or leave it.*

After half an hour or so, Philip and June, uneasy and unable to concentrate, decided it was time to take a break, and stopped the tape. Outside, the day was heating up, and they turned on the small window air conditioners with which their prison had been provided. They went to make themselves their first meal in the small kitchen. As they entered, the pair of masked guardians who had been sitting at the little kitchen table got up at once, and with some murmured politeness withdrew into the living room.

The prisoners looked at each other and shrugged.

"What'll it be?"

"Let's do breakfast."

A few minutes later the two of them were seated, conversing in low voices over toast and coffee and bowls of cereal. Minds whirling, they tried to analyze what they had heard and seen so far.

"He's mentioned Benjamin Franklin two or three times, as if he were really relevant. All right, so you have a family tradition that your great-great-however-many-greats-grandfather was Franklin's illegitimate son. But why does that give these jokers the idea to kidnap *us*?"

"I don't know." Phil looked around and lowered his voice.

"Believe me, I can't see any possible connection. Our Mr. Graves is evidently an utter lunatic."

"Better not let him hear—"

"I won't, I won't. All right. The only thing to do, when we've finished our little snack here, is to go back and watch and listen. Go over the whole thing this time. Even if it's crazy, it's likely to contain some kind of clue as to what these people really want."

"All right. Back we go. We'll humor them."

The Revolution, the biggest and bloodiest one in the memory of the Western world, had taken place in France. But Graves in his taped narration had chosen to begin his story with certain events which were taking place at the same time in London . . .

. . . It was around midnight, on a night of comforting and concealing fog, a chill damp night after a chill spring day, when young Jerry Cruncher and a couple of his comrades, industriously plying their illegal trade, were approaching in a spirit of enterprise a fresh burial, during the course of which the official diggers had disturbed a number of ancestral interments in the churchyard soil. No one in the Year of Our Lord seventeen hundred and ninety could fairly be blamed for this; generation after generation of burials had already left the ground beneath their feet a thick mosaic of human bones and coffin remnants.

Less than a dozen hours ago, on the previous afternoon, the newest member of the silent majority had joined these centuries of Londoners, one more necessarily wedged in among old coffins, bodies which had lain in the earth for decades, some for a hundred years and more, disturbed only by the occasional new arrival.

The latest crew of excavators, three in number and totally unofficial, arriving well after nightfall, felt themselves securely alone. These entrepreneurs moved their lantern down into the excavation as soon as it was deep enough, and they made no unnecessary noise, but worked away briskly, soon forgetting any fear of discovery. A single hour of hard digging in the freshly loosened dirt achieved great progress. As they began their work they had deliberately toppled the modest-sized new headstone away from the grave, where it soon lay half-buried under the mounting pile of newly upturned earth. Had Jerry been more imaginative, he might have wondered if the worms in this particular store of dirt were getting tired of being alternately dug up and reburied.

The drifts and shoals of flowers that had been deposited at graveside by weeping relatives during the afternoon were quickly tossed out of the way at midnight. But their blooms, not having had time to fade, were still dimly visible in the softly focused light of the single lantern, and two busy shovels were well along in building new piles of earth. Jerry and his mates had taken off their coats and thrown them aside when they began to dig.

Today's new grave had been sunk to an extra depth, somewhat below the traditional six feet, in the futile hope of foiling just such an expedition as the one now under way.

The broken, worm-eaten boards of the coffin had symbols of true power carved on them—ancient signs that Radu Dracula had understood, in the brief glimpse he had of them before he was put inside—but which his discoverers did not begin to understand.

Of course he should have thanked Jerry and his coworkers for the rescue. But to give thanks was never Radu's way.

"Wot in th' 'ell? Where's she gone, now?"

One of the diggers called down curses on their bad luck—which was in fact much worse than he suspected. The first touch on the afternoon's fresh coffin had sent it shifting and falling from its designated resting place, sliding down another three or four feet into an unexpected cavity created by the decay of much earlier interments. Jerry and his two companions were surprised; but as an *habitué* of such environments, I can assure my readers that the circumstance is not particularly unusual.

Ever deeper delved dogged Jerry and his determined colleagues. But the more the short-lived, breathing intruders discovered, the greater the depths to which they probed into this unexpected trove of splintered wood and rotten bones, the more they were impressed, and the more their greed for treasure was aroused.

" 'Ere, we've struck some kind of pit. Bring another light, I say!"

. . . and Jerry, when he was holding the second lantern closer, looking into the accidentally broken coffin (not even the oldest of the two or three the diggers had disturbed), saw that which confirmed his first vague impression. He beheld the body of a white-haired man of saintly and ascetic mien, who had obviously been claimed by death when far advanced in years. But his corpse was in a startlingly, even unbelievably good state of preservation.

For a moment young Jerry Cruncher, never too swift of thought, was convinced that what lay before him was actually the fresh body he had come to steal. But for a moment only. According to his information, today's interment had been a woman, and there could be no doubt that the body before him now was no female, as beautiful as the long hair, slightly curly, and finely chiseled features were . . . the clothing on this strange one was almost a century out of date, decayed and discolored. But still it originally had been of the finest quality—you could tell that by the persisting fineness of lace, and by the buttons, which were of pearl and ivory.

And though the cloth had decayed, had fallen prey to rot and insects, it seemed that the flesh had not.

Holding his lantern closer, the young graverobber caught the glint of what certainly must be a valuable ring, glinting with both gold and jewels, on one aged finger, and if his eyes did not deceive him, there were even two ostentatious rings on the same hand . . . mere costume jewelry? In this bad light it was hard to be sure, but he thought not.

And only then—such was the intensity of his focus upon profit—only then did Jerry note that the body's head lay divided from the torso, the two parts of the body separated by a narrow strip of wood running athwart the coffin. This fact struck the discoverers as remarkable indeed. The disjunction was not merely an effect of decay, or of the jostling of the old box by more recent burials. No, it had obviously been accomplished deliberately before interment; the coffin had actually been constructed in two compartments.

What Jerry was seeing seemed to him impossible to interpret, to invest with meaning. Vaguely he assumed that the man had been beheaded for treason. At the moment no other reason came to mind for such a grisly act. Though the punishment was still on the books in His Majesty's courts, and no one had yet removed the last dried traitor's head from Temple Bar—its empty sockets still peered into the office windows of Tellson's Bank, where Jerry sometimes served as errand boy—he hadn't heard of any such event in recent years.

Jerry, going single-mindedly after those gleaming rings, gripped the headless torso and took hold of the stiffened arm in its crumbling sleeve. It occurred to him, even as he reached into his jacket pocket for his clasp knife, that the arm in his grip ought not to be so stiff after so many years, nor ought it to be so rounded with firm flesh. The depth of this burial, and the presence of at least one layer of rotting coffins in the earth above it, indicated that it must have lain undisturbed under the dirt for a period at least equal to a long human lifetime.

The dead hand on its rigid arm somehow resisted, passively but very effectively, the removal of its jeweled and golden rings. The longer and more closely Jerry looked at those small circlets, the more he would have sold his soul to have them. The gleaming treasure so concentrated his attention that he was hardly aware of the body and its strangeness, except as an obstacle that stood between himself and instant wealth, to be overcome.

Jerry's two colleagues were drawing closer to him, one on each side. The one on the right grunted: " 'Ere! D'you s'pose them rocks are real?"

No one bothered to answer.

The graverobbers were on the verge of a serious falling out over this tremendous treasure, not realizing that the current possessor of the gems was going to have something to say regarding their disposal. For a long moment the two men glared warily, suspiciously at each other. Then the moment was past, and they agreed it would be daft to fight. Here was enough treasure, and far more than enough, to enrich them all.

But over the next few minutes, it was borne in on both of the intruders that the beheading, and the compartmentalized coffin, were not at all the strangest things about this find. The state of the body augured that this had to be a fresh burial, while the condition of the coffin, and the clothing, testified that it could not be.

And the very strangest oddity of all was this: How could a body actually have been buried with such a cargo of wealth? In Jerry's experience, the people in charge of burials, except for close relatives temporarily deranged by grief, considered that gold and gems belonged to the living and not the dead. But that was not Jerry's problem now; the carelessness of those long-dead workers was his good fortune.

"Real? By God, we'll soon find out."

Methodically one of his companions opened the blade of his clasp knife—he had to retrieve it from the pocket of his discarded coat—and started trying to cut one of the old man's fingers off. Jerry took hold of the dead arm to steady it. The steel was sharp—its owner made a point of keeping it that way—but what should have been a simple task proved amazingly difficult to accomplish. It was as if the skin and flesh could not be permanently severed, they closed as soon as the penetrating blade had passed . . .

The sensation of an independent movement in the arm that he was holding went through Jerry like an electric shock.

~ *4* ~

*E*re! Wot—?" Jerry's chums were stuttering and mumbling in amazement.

Before their eyes, and hardly more than an arm's length away, the wooden casket was collapsing around its occupant. The pieces of wood, the planks and plates and partitions making up the coffin, which for decades had enforced compartmentalization inside that silk-lined receptacle, had badly rotted over that span of time in the damp earth. Under the strain of sudden movement, they had now broken loose from each other and fallen free. They were no longer capable of maintaining a separation between the occupant's head and body.

The diffuse beam of the lantern showed how the free hand of the headless body in the coffin—the hand not occupied with being robbed—went groping for the gray-haired head, found it, and pulled it into place.

Jerry, beyond astonishment, stood gaping like a fish in air. The two pieces of the long-dismembered corpse had somehow got themselves back together.

One of Jerry's fellow despoilers, watching, sat back on his heels, pointing with his raised right hand and muttering incoherently in horror and disbelief. The other stood as silent as a statue.

Unbelievably, within the grave, the head of slightly curly hair—a lustrous, luxuriant white—was now turning of its own volition on the reconstituted neck. The withered, regal face came more fully into view, the long-lashed eyelids quivering and opening at last. For a moment Jerry viewed the impossible sight with sheer relief, because it proved that he was only dreaming. But even as the thought crossed Jerry's mind he knew it was ridiculous.

The lantern light shone full upon a pair of eyes of glassy blue. The expression in them was only half-conscious—no, not even half, but now they had actually opened and were anything but dead. They moved in their sockets, and slowly achieved a focus. Their gaze was shiny and moist in a way that suggested some warm emotion, like that of one awakened from some pleasant dream.

The pale, withered hand, whose bejeweled fingers had successfully resisted the robber's sawing with the knife, shot out and closed with unexpected power, with the tenacity of death itself, upon the intruding hand and wrist of the unfortunate graverobber.

Jerry went stumbling forward, to the aid of the man who was down deepest in the pit, when the latter cried out for help.

The body in the coffin was garbed in once-rich, now worm-eaten fabric, antique clothing that crumbled, spitting free its loosened buttons with the motion of the unspoiled flesh within. That entire pale-skinned body now moved, stiffly at first, as if almost paralyzed, then with increasing ease and speed. The once-fine silken lining of the coffin, now mottled with decay and mold, tried to stretch and crumbled, too.

It was at this point that the taller of Jerry's associates turned away and fled, running in silent, deadly earnest, in superstitious terror. The sight of the white hand gripping his comrade's wrist had been too much.

Jerry and his remaining colleague, a man named Smith, were at the moment too stunned to try to run. Then, with a tremendous effort, Smith managed to wrench himself free, a feat made possible only by the fact that his coatsleeve tore away in the corpse's grip.

Even as Smith went stumbling back, the undead hand grabbed Jerry, who had remained too paralyzed to move.

The other man, possessed by a fatal loyalty, or terminally afflicted with common sense too strong to let him believe what he was seeing—or perhaps simply too stupid and unimaginative to be much daunted even by a vampire— picked up a shovel and started pounding on the thin and ancient-looking arm emerging from the coffin. His aim was accurate. The impacts were startlingly loud, as if the man had been beating on a solid beam of wood.

Still, the only immediate effect of this effort was that a second white hand, as if energized by the assault, emerged from among the cracked boards and took effective action, catching the pounding shovel on the third try in a grip that proved as relentless and remorseless as that of Fate itself. The shovel was wrenched violently from the hands of its breathing wielder and thrown aside.

All this, from the moment of the old coffin's sliding into the deep pit until now, had happened very quickly. The pounding feet of the man who had run away could still be heard, but in a few more seconds the sound faded into darkness and patchy fog.

Somewhere, in the city that now seemed so far beyond the cemetery wall, a dog was howling in abandon.

Jerry was still held by one wrist. His remaining comrade appeared to be free, but did not run away. Nor did Jerry struggle. Slowly the bodies of both men slumped, until they were sitting on the ground. It was as if they were held in place by a combination of greed and amazement, subtly aided by an hypnotic influence which neither breathing man could recognize for what it was.

Presently the inhabitant of the coffin, twisting his body

slowly from side to side, and now displaying a touch of uncertainty in his movements, had got himself entirely free of
the splintered wood. Now he was sitting up. And now he was
crawling, the warm blue gaze in that decrepit face fixed on
Jerry, his teeth, which were very white and at the moment
very pointed, displayed in a friendly smile.

Deep in his throat Jerry was making incoherent sounds.
Just when he was on the point of springing to his feet again,
he was stunned and half-paralyzed by a gentle-seeming
stroke, almost a caress, as the hand he had been trying to
butcher for its rings released his wrist and rose to stroke him
on the cheek. A moment later the same hand fell on his ankle
with a wrenching grip, to pull him even closer with nightmarish ease. Then the hand let him go for a fraction of a second, only to re-establish its grip upon his neck. There it left
an impression that filled his arms and legs with pins and nee-
dles.

Satisfied that Jerry was temporarily deprived of the
power of movement and of speech, the thing from the coffin
reached out and took hold of Jerry's remaining colleague.

Too late, and ineffectually, the man began to struggle.
Then he screamed: a faint, half-breathless, inarticulate
sound. The sound was not a conscious utterance, but only the
result of the breath being crushed entirely out of his rib cage
by arms almost skeletally thin, but far stronger than those
of any breathing human.

No blood had yet been visibly spilled, though now a great
deal was being drained. The helpless, dying man was being
dressed like a fowl, by a butcher who set a very high value
on the avoidance of carelessly spilled blood.

And soon the two pale hands, working together, had
wrenched off one of the living arms that a minute ago had
been swinging a shovel at him. And now at last there came
a spray of red, quickly cut short as Radu's mouth closed over
the pumping artery.

* * *

... and a little later, after a timeless interval of unconsciousness, Jerry Cruncher opened his eyes to see that the man who had been buried (his hair that had been white was now luxuriant and raven black, growing on a head as firmly fastened to his body as Jerry's own—How could he ever have imagined that the head had once been separate?)—that man was chewing to pulp much of the soft tissue of Smith's body, his white teeth crushing, splintering the bones. The man from the coffin was straining Smith's blood through his mouth to swallow it, spitting out the gruesome residue, murmuring and puffing a red froth of satisfaction ...

The white face, marked with only three almost microscopic spots of wasted blood, turned in Jerry's direction. All the signs of age had disappeared, subsumed in a glorious and vital youth.

Jerry, his body no longer physically pinned, but his mind effectively paralyzed, was compelled to watch while his companion's life was drained away, his body efficiently emptied of blood. All he could think of was that his own turn would be next ...

But the blood of one stout man had evidently been sufficient to take the edge off decades of hunger.

When the mouth of the thing from the coffin was no longer too busy taking nourishment to speak, there issued in a whispery rasp from its dry lips elegant words, sentences, in a French that was highly literate but almost barbarous in its antiquity. When Jerry only stared with lack of comprehension, the French was followed by a kind of English closer to the speech of Shakespeare than to that of the wretch who had come intruding with his shovel.

The voice grew more dry and ghastly with every word it uttered. *"Come here to me, young man. Come here."*

"Uhh ..."

"But wait. First ..."

Radu, standing now, free of the last coffin-fragment, methodically hand-scooped earth to bury the ghastly, unrecognizable remains of Smith at the bottom of the hole from which his own breathless yet undying body had so recently emerged.

Then, still standing up to his ragged knees in loosely piled dirt, he turned to the other graverobber. Jerry was considerably younger, and much handsomer, than either of the other two.

"Come here."

Again, the victim had no choice.

"What year . . . ? What is the Year of Our Lord . . . ?"

This time Jerry willed himself to spring to his feet and run, and nothing visible held him back from darting away in flight, leaving the horror behind; but there could be no possibility of help within a hundred yards, the distance of the nearest portion of the cemetery fence. Nearer than that were only grass and darkness, trees and tombstones. And the confident attitude of the thing from the coffin assured him that he had no chance to get anywhere near that fence by flight.

What year? Unable to do otherwise, he muttered an answer to the question.

Meanwhile waves of horrible fear were washing over him, blending with a luminous, sickly, and all but irresistible attraction. It seemed to Jerry that his body was moving and acting on its own, independent of his will. He sidled closer to his undead captor and whimpered unconsciously, like a timid pup. He shivered as if with electric shock when the pale hand fell on his arm.

There was already a delicious anticipation in the shiver, a reaction no more controllable than that produced by a dousing in cold water.

Sheer food-hunger had for the moment been satisfied; in the far more delicate blood-draining that now ensued, there was a kind of love.

Smoothly and almost effortlessly, with a look and a touch and the murmur of a few soft words, Radu seduced the young man who had tried to despoil his body. The breathing youth was handsome, or at least made that impression on the vampire, who had been underground and dreaming nightmares for more than eighty years.

Before climbing out of the pit, Radu scraped up and gathered, from where it lay mixed with the wreckage of his coffin, the essential native earth that Vlad had seen to it was there to sustain his life. He bundled the earth into a piece of cloth that had once been Smith's coat, and put the bundle carefully under his arm.

Then Radu, like an insect newly emerged from his latest chrysalis, resumed his coupling with the young man, strengthening himself further and weakening his breathing victim.

Presently the two began to walk together toward the cemetery fence, and the murmuring night-sounds of the great city that lay beyond.

Before the sun had worked its way up into the cloudy sky to brighten London, Jerry Cruncher had come home to the room he shared with his girl, bringing with him a man she had never seen before, and who introduced himself to her as Mr. Shade. Jerry, looking unusually pale, seemed both pleased and put on edge by the newcomer.

"Who is he, then?" the girl whispered to Jerry when they had a moment to themselves.

"Never you mind who. I'd say the fewer questions you have t' ask, the better."

She was intrigued to receive the attention of the handsome stranger who had now attached himself to Jerry.

But she was somewhat surprised when the suave newcomer almost at once pulled her to the bed and began to bite her throat. And she was even more surprised—though now her head was spinning in a haze of pleasure—when Jerry, responding to Mr. Shade's gesture of invitation, shed his clothes and climbed into the bed with them.

She'd never thought that Jerry was the kind of man who did such things with other men . . . but at the moment noth-

ing mattered but what was happening to her. Pleasure unbelievable, delight that she had never imagined until now . . .

Gradually, in the hours and days following his fortuitous release from his drugged, nightmarish sleep, Radu satisfied
himself that Vlad was nowhere in the immediate vicinity of
the cemetery. Indeed there was no evidence that his hated
elder brother had ever visited London at all, but instead had
entrusted his younger brother's transportation and burial
there to someone else.

The one who had been buried, freed now from unbearable dreams of hell, granted an escape from his coffin, knew
basically what he had to do in these circumstances. He had
played a very similar role in other scenes very much like this
one, several times before, in other centuries—and so began
the lengthy process of warily, methodically, ruthlessly, patiently learning and working his way into the changed society into which he had emerged.

Over the next few days he gave attention to his speech
and wardrobe, bringing both up to date, equipping himself
to move when necessary in both the highest and the lowest
strata of society.

For a whole month following his latest emergence from a
coffin, the pallid and handsome vampire spent most of his
daylight hours drowsing indoors, in one poor room or another
in the neighborhood of Hanging-sword-alley, Whitefriars,
where Jerry Cruncher lived. The revenant, breathing only
when he felt it necessary to get wind to speak, closed his nostrils against stench and tolerated ugliness and noise.

Ah, to be able to admire himself in a mirror! But that
pleasure was permanently denied him. The eyes and faces of
admirers were the only looking-glass he could ever use.

He kept his eyes open for the man who had run away in terror from the graveyard, and managed to learn his name from
Jerry. But that man was gone from his old London haunts,

vanished as if . . . yes, as if the earth had swallowed him.

Few men loved luxury more than did Radu, but few could be more patient in assessing the right priorities. In present circumstances, luxury could wait.

By night, now almost every night, he strengthened himself with the blood of youth, seeking and attracting both sexes to his couch. Coolly he gave thought as to who among these breathing folk, and how many, he should begin to recruit to his cause.

During this period he drowsed and daydreamed away many a daylight hour. But he did not really sleep at all. What Radu Dracula's soul demanded now was not rest—he had had enough and more than enough of that—but vengeance. Retribution, overwhelming and exquisite, on the man who had put in him the ground. Upon his elder brother. Upon Vlad, who had been, for most of the last three hundred years, true head of the House of Drakulya.

Through all the nights during the next several months, through all the long days of that time, during hours when bright sun made even shaded rooms uncomfortable, Radu's eyelids were seldom closed for more than a few moments consecutively. In that epoch he spent most of his hours lying in one cheap room or another, listening to the noises made by breathers enacting their wretched existences around him. Now and then he enjoyed the blood of one or another of the youthful, savory bodies who could be so easily persuaded— with a few words, a tender look, a gentle touch—to yield to his embrace.

But there were many hours when he was quite alone, resting wakefully in as dark a room as he could find, clinging to the bagful of his native earth he'd salvaged from what his buriers, determined that he should not die, had provided for him in his most recent grave.

Time and again, on gray or sunny afternoons, he caught himself beginning to drift into trance, and with a start and a shiver of fear he fought himself free from the soft entanglement. Then he would arise, and pace the cramped room for a time, pushing sleep away as if it were his deadly enemy. His sufferings during the long slumber so recently concluded had immeasurably deepened his terror of nightmares. Thanks to his brother, he had had enough of helpless, abandoned sleep to last him for the next ten centuries.

And what else had been done to him? Could he be sure that his personal beauty had not suffered? Again and again Radu yearned for the help of a mirror, even knowing as he did how useless such were to him. Then he would thoughtfully finger his own neck where the skin, its youth renewed thanks to his recent heavy feeding, had now grown seamlessly back together. He could tell, from the way that breathers looked at him, the things they said to him, that they thought him no more than seventeen years old, and as gloriously beautiful as ever. Well, in a way he was fortunate. Mutilation at least he had been spared. The torture and dismemberment that Vlad had inflicted upon him in 1705 might have left permanent scars.

Radu looked forward with keen anticipation to meeting his older brother again. He craved a carefully planned meeting that would give him the opportunity of surprising Vlad. Dear Vlad, who had arranged to have him put under the ground. Had beheaded him and beaten him as punishment, had drugged and hypnotized him into decades of dreaming hell.

Dear old Vlad, who would not really be expecting to encounter his younger brother in one piece and above ground again. Not now, not for many decades yet.

Radu knew from long and bitter experience that trying to revenge himself upon his brother was not a business to be lightly or impulsively undertaken. When he had succeeded in such efforts in the past, it had been only after careful and thoughtful preparation. Therefore he now postponed any plans for fresh revenge until he should have established himself in this unfamiliar world of the late eighteenth century—

which was considerably changed in many ways from the city and the society of a hundred years earlier. Radu had been on fairly familiar terms with the London of a hundred years or so earlier, so that the city's vast expansion in the interval had not left him entirely disoriented. A number of familiar landmarks, parks and monuments and palaces, were still helpfully in place.

Observing the size to which the metropolis had grown in both area and population during his recent extended sleep, and taking note of the relatively frantic pace of activity now occuring the newly revived vampire could not escape the conclusion that the world was changing faster and faster as the centuries whirled by—soon it would be absolutely dangerous to sleep for more than a few years. The scope of transformations accomplished in even a few decades would render the new world unintelligible.

Dear old Vlad. There was so much, so very much, that Radu had to thank his brother for.

$$\sim 5 \sim$$

S till the gypsy-looking Connie and the darkly handsome Mr. Graves boldly displayed their faces, while their less flamboyant associates continued to wear masks in the prisoners' presence. These disguised underlings, or some of them at least, evidently shared living quarters in the larger mobile home, a few yards from the smaller unit that served as their victims' prison. Looking out through one or another of their own barred windows, the Radcliffes could see them always scrupulously masked, occasionally coming and going at the larger house. Their victims decided that the place must be crowded if it housed them all.

Having a second breakfast, largely because of the speed and simplicity of preparation, had been the Radcliffes' first choice when they once more got around to dealing with their hunger. During the meal they kept expecting to be interrupted by one of their cheerful guardians, but that didn't happen. The only sign of the kidnappers' continued presence was an occasional murmur of muted voices from the other room, where the guardians had gone when their victims occupied the kitchen. No one sat with Phil and June, or stood over them, while they ate their cereal and toast, drank their juice and coffee.

By the time they had finished breakfast, subtle changes in the muted sounds from the other room suggested that a different pair of kidnappers had relieved the pair originally on duty.

Occasionally the mask of one of their overseers in the living room could be seen turned toward the kitchen, but no one bothered the prisoner couple. When they had finished the brief meal, they were left, still without direct supervision, to wash up the handful of dishes and utensils.

Several times since they had been lodged in this prison, it occurred to Philip to wonder if hidden microphones and even cameras might be recording his and his wife's behavior. He whispered his suspicions to June, who shook her head and looked helpless. He made a close-range inspection of the cheap battery-powered clock on the kitchen wall, and of the dully ordinary electrical outlets, without observing anything suspicious. Maybe the feeling was paranoid, but he couldn't entirely shake it.

After mechanically cleaning up the remains of two breakfasts, both prisoners found themselves exhausted. The kidnapping had dragged them through a long and sleepless night after full day of vacationing. They glanced into the bedroom, where the single small bed looked inviting, but agreed that there was still no possibility of being able to sleep.

Alternatives being severely limited, they went back into the living room for a second session with the tape. The current pair of masked attendants took themselves unobtrusively out of the way.

June threw herself down on the little sofa and nodded at the machine before them. Her face was pale, her voice unnatural with stress. "How much more have we got to go?"

Philip popped the reel out of the VCR and peered into it through the little window on one side. "Looks to me like we've watched about an hour so far; about five hours of tape left on the reel, but I can't tell how much has content."

"Let's give it another try. Maybe there'll be some magic revelation."

"Don't hold your breath."

When they tried fast-forwarding, stopping at intervals to sample content, it was soon plain that they had more than an hour of material to look at. Viewings taken at random spots along the tape indicated that the next two hours or so, like the first, consisted of nothing but Graves, sitting behind his table and talking, sometimes reading from his notes, to the camera. It was a daunting prospect.

Meanwhile the prisoners continued to be faintly cheered by the accumulation of bits of evidence that their kidnappers, whatever they thought they were up to, had some genuine concern for their victims' physical comfort. They continued to be allowed perfect freedom of movement within the few rooms assigned to them.

There came a moment when one of their captors, hovering tentatively in the doorway, suggested that they might enjoy a supervised outdoor walk. Hats of the proper size were available to guard them from the desert sun.

Still Radcliffe could not entirely free himself of the tantalizing suspicion that the whole kidnapping performance might be nothing but a grandiose joke. It was impossible to know what expressions the guardians were wearing behind their masks, and much of what Connie said could not be taken seriously. But the suspicion of a hoax withered rapidly when Graves dropped in to call. This man at least was in deadly earnest.

Half an hour after the Radcliffes finished their breakfast, Mr. Graves was back, looking somewhat worn, and older than before. He gave a token knock on the door with one knuckle of one pale hand before putting a key to the grillwork and letting himself in.

The chief kidnapper was still conspicuously maskless,

but now had armored his pallid skin against the desert sunlight with a broad-brimmed hat. Urbanely he inquired how Philip and his lady were settling into their new lodging.

Radcliffe got up from the little sofa to stand with folded arms, confronting him. "You were going to tell me your real name."

The other looked at him in silence for a few moments, then said: "For the time being, 'Mr. Graves' will still do."

"Is the real name really the one that the tape suggests?"

The dark eyes glittered. "What do you think?"

Radcliffe started to speak, hesitated, and finally shrugged his shoulders. "Have it your way."

"I intend to do so." Graves nodded agreeably. "Now let us speak of other matters which are awaiting our attention, all of them of much more direct importance for your future welfare than my name."

"What are those?" June demanded.

Graves helped himself to a seat, and with a sweeping gesture invited his guests to do the same. "Have you now watched the entire tape?"

"We've got a good start on it." Philip considered complaining that the tape was boring, and overall poorly done. But then he thought better of it. "Just tell us this, are we being held hostage? Until someone else does something you want, or—?"

Their kidnapper was shaking his head emphatically. "Nothing like that. You are not hostages."

"Then what—?"

"I have no time just now for a long discussion. That is why my colleagues and I invested a large amount of time in preparation, making the tape for you to watch." The dark eyes burned at Radcliffe, and he got a sense of patience beginning to wear thin. "I strongly advise you to watch it."

"All right," said Philip in a small voice. At the moment he was overwhelmed by the feeling of being a small child, foolishly stubborn in his rebellion.

In another moment he and June were once more side by

side on the cheap sofa, facing the small television set, and now Graves turned it on, along with the adjacent VCR. After another moment of grim silence, he put on his broad-brimmed hat and stalked away; they heard the jail-door clash of the grillwork slamming shut behind him.

Over the next hours and days the unmasked couple appeared and disappeared, usually one at a time, sometimes together, generally at night. How that oddly matched pair might be spending the bulk of their time, whether they remained in the area, or where else they might go and for what purpose, remained a mystery to their prisoners. Always, when they wanted to come in, they tapped at the door first, demonstrating at least a pretense of courtesy. Once Connie, who seemed determined to be different, came in through a window on the side of the building where there was no door.

Constantia—as Graves preferred to call Connie—was more often than not observable somewhere in the vicinity of the mobile home. Though Graves was certainly not given to shouting orders or enforcing discipline, Philip continued to be certain that he was in command. All the others, including Connie, did as they were told.

As soon as Graves had again stalked out the door, doing his impatient executive bit, squinting against the desert sun even with his whole face shaded by his broadbrimmed hat, the captives began a second session with the videotape. But this try lasted only about five minutes.

At that point Philip and June, both pretty well worn out, fell asleep sprawling fully clothed on the sofa, leaving Graves-on-tape to deliver his vital lecture to closed eyelids and unhearing ears.

When they awakened, several hours later, they rewound the tape, which had long since spun to its conclusion, as thoroughly ignored as most television screens at any given moment. Then they took turns showering in the little bathroom, and dressed in fresh clothing from their bags, which had remained unopened since being brought in.

"Looks like we may be here for a while," June sighed.

"It does." That was a depressing thought.

Once more they were impressed with their captors' eerie thoroughness when they opened drawers and saw that some spare clothing, of medium quality and in the proper sizes, had been provided. Men's and women's jeans and T-shirts, and a change or two of underwear and socks. Even gym shoes and moccasins. Radcliffe tried on the larger pair and looked at June soberly. "They fit."

One of the female masked guards knocked tentatively on the bedroom door and asked permission to come in. She seemed satisfied when told that the provided clothing fit. "Good. We weren't sure we'd be able to bring your own things along."

"Thanks," said Philip, bemused.

"Told you, we're not out to do you any harm. Did you watch the tape all the way through?"

Philip wanted to yell that he wanted to hear no more about the goddamned tape. He considered saying that he had watched it—but then decided not to make false claims. There might be some gem of information buried in the video that he would then be assumed to know.

At last he fell back on the truth. "Have to admit that we gave up on it again." He didn't admit how quickly the collapse had come. "We were falling asleep on the sofa. Now that we've had a little rest, we'll try again."

The rubber mummy mask nodded solemnly. "You'd better watch it. Really. Think about the ideas it presents. Nothing else is going to make sense until you accept that." And the watcher strolled away.

June was trying on the women's shoes. "Phil. They fit. Everything fits. They even know our sizes."

Radcliffe could find nothing to say.

Hours passed, while Mr. Graves and his cohort kept on persistently trying to brainwash Radcliffe into accepting their mad tale. As Graves himself was absent most of the time, the others continually urged Philip to absorb the story from the videotape. This was a persistent but patient effort, and no one pretended to be surprised that Radcliffe considered it mad. They cheerfully acknowledged that he would need some evidence before he gave it credence.

Eventually he and June, fully awake, did see the tape all the way through.

No, this wasn't any joke. Whatever the original motive, duration and intensity had taken it out of that category. Some kind of a crazy cult, then, even though these people were missing the aura of fanaticism that Radcliffe presumed all hard-core cultists must exhibit. And they had worked long and hard and skillfully to get the Radcliffes in this position. But still neither victim could imagine what they hoped to accomplish by their kidnapping.

Approximately at sunset, Graves was back.

Phil was ready to confront him. Things couldn't go on like this. "Mr. Graves, you said it isn't ransom you people are after."

"Correct."

"Then what? I mean, what do you want from me?"

"Again I must ask you: Did you watch the tape all the way through?"

Philip drew a deep breath. "Dammit, we have. We've seen the whole thing. It's quite a story, I'll give you that. I'll also admit that we've learned some fascinating details about the French Revolution. And we're up to date regarding your theories on some other subjects."

"So. Your reactions? Conclusions?"

"Okay, let's discuss. On the tape you keep talking about someone who bears my name, and is evidently supposed to be my ancestor. There's a kind of family tradition about him, and I can't prove that anything you say about this other Philip Radcliffe is wrong. But I still don't see what all this has to do with June and me being—"

Graves's voice had suddenly acquired a sharp bite. "The tape is not solely or even chiefly concerned with the French Revolution. Do you agree?"

"Well . . ."

"The tape presents an incomplete history of that epoch, but it does much more. That is the whole point of its existence. The historical relevance of that material to your own situation is its *raison d'être.*"

"The business about vampires. One of them in particular, who's out to get my family, for some reason. Yes, of course I understood that."

"Yes, of course. 'For some reason.' " Graves mouthed the words as if they tasted strange. "Evidently you understand the message of the tape, but you do not believe it."

"I . . ."

"It seems to me that you are remarkably more stupid than your ancestor of two hundred years ago—and you, madam?"

June was adrift in anger and confusion. "Well . . ."

"I see." Graves, as if confirming some unfavorable estimate, nodded at them both in turn. "Instead of wasting my time on tape, on attempting a reasonable, logical approach, I should have listened to certain of my advisers, who . . . but never mind that. It is too late to change our approach now.

"Your reaction to the business about vampires, as you call it, has been to turn off your brain. Instantly you recognize the serious discussion of such a topic as a symptom of madness, and your own minds are still locked closed." Graves uttered a small hissing noise, a disturbingly reptilian sound. "Well, at least you are watching the tape. I still have no time to argue with you. No energy to waste on demonstrations. Pray watch it all over again."

He turned his gaze on June, and she nodded. "We will," she breathed.

"Good." Graves's look softened somewhat. "I realize that

you find yourselves in a difficult situation. But once you accept the essential information the tape contains, your own position will be much clearer."

Once more he faced Radcliffe. "To answer your question, we want nothing that will be harmful to you, believe it or not. Quite the opposite. I insist that you accept my protection until I have reached an accommodation with my brother."

"The one who wants to drink my blood."

Graves nodded.

"So where do we go from—Never mind, I know, you're going to tell me to watch the tape to find the answer. Everything I really need to know is there."

Graves, smiling faintly, continued nodding.

"Just tell me one thing first, okay?"

Graves raised an eyebrow, a gesture of unstudied elegance.

"How do you hope to reach this accommodation? Is your brother coming here?"

"That is one possibility, but I think a faint one. And if he does not come here—then I must seek him out." It was plain that Graves was not looking forward to the prospect.

"You'll seek him out. Then what? You'll talk to him?"

"I shall try to do so." The speaker paused, staring into the distance. Then he added, as if speaking more to himself than to Radcliffe: "And he will doubtless try to kill me."

"He will? Why will he do that?"

"I should have thought it obvious, to one who has now heard and seen the story on the tape."

"All right," said Philip vaguely. He didn't want to spell out his objection that a concocted story, a crazy lecture on a videotape, was one thing, and real life another. "And when this man, your brother, tries to kill you, then you in turn . . . ?"

The other shook his head. "No, I shall not try to kill my brother. I am forbidden that."

June had been watching and listening to the men in

silent fascination. Philip, shooting a glance at her, found what he saw disturbing.

"Really?" he asked Graves. "Forbidden how?"

"I have sworn an oath. Even though killing Radu now would be a relief, I think, for all concerned. My task is somewhat more difficult, though not impossible."

As soon as Graves had departed, Radcliffe turned to Constantia, who had just come in. "I don't understand this at all." That wasn't strictly true. He had come a long way, he thought, toward understanding. *Believing* was another matter altogether. "What did he mean, 'I am forbidden that'?"

The gypsy girl looked wistful. "It is a matter of oath-taking and honor with him, you see. He can fight his brother, and even inflict serious damage on him. But he cannot kill Radu."

"I still don't get it."

"Few in this age could possibly understand."

The furnishings of the small mobile home included a table-drawer stocked with paper and pencils, and a small collection of books, from popular novels to science, math, crossword puzzles, and chess problems.

Even with all the lights turned on, the little house could hardly be called well-lit at night. But in one or two places there was light enough for comfortable reading.

The windows were all neatly shaded or curtained, and the prisoners were encouraged to keep the shades drawn after dark. The small-unit air-conditioning purred on with reasonable effectiveness, though it was somewhat noisy. Here in the high desert, the temperature dropped sharply after sundown, and the cooler could be turned off and windows opened for a breeze.

One of the masked people, in what sounded like a kind of afterthought, warned both prisoners never to invite any strangers in.

June and Philip thought that a strange request. They looked at each other and shrugged; it would cost them nothing to agree.

"You've got the doors locked anyway, the windows barred."

"Even so."

"All right. No strangers get invited in. How long are we going to be here?"

That question received basically the same answer as before. "I hope that in a few days matters will be settled, one way or another."

On the kitchen wall there hung a 1996 calendar, the handout of some charitable organization. June had turned to the proper month, and started to check off the days since their arrival.

Radcliffe wondered who might have been living in this house yesterday, or last month. The place didn't appear to be brand new, just well cared for. But whoever it was seemed to have left no clues behind.

The previous tenants, whoever they might have been, had evidently done without a telephone. But once or twice Radcliffe saw his masked and breathing guardian, standing at a distance out of earshot, speaking calmly into a cellular. Some forethought had obviously gone into this plan.

The TV was connected to a satellite dish. On the evening of their second day in the mobile home, between intervals of exhausted sleep, Phil tuned in to the news, with some vague hope of discovering that the Radcliffes had been reported missing. Well, if they had, there was no way the TV newspeople were going to let the world know about it. What scanty factual content there was had trouble finding space between political attack ads, and consisted almost entirely of political soundbites, alternating with the usual courtroom scenes, celebrity scandals, and a peculiarly outrageous murder in a remote part of the country. Sure, the news would be delighted to report a missing man and woman—as soon as someone provided them with a good videotape of his mutilated corpse, or at the very least a roomful of sobbing relatives.

Graves, choosing that moment to pay another brief call on his prisoners, happened to observe the broadcast as he came in. The chief kidnapper seemed to Radcliffe a little tired and a little more philosophical—also a little more human—than before. He commented that supposedly your neighbor's grief was almost as entertaining as your neighbor's blood . . . Radcliffe didn't want to pursue that line of thought.

"Have you now seriously considered the content of the tape—as it applies to you?"

"I still have trouble making that application. Maybe it's partly because I don't care for the special effects."

Graves looked his puzzlement.

"I mean the way your image flickers, comes and goes."

"Ah." The dark man's face cleared. "That was not calculated. It is because of mirrors, you see."

"Mirrors?"

"I am told that inside the type of video camera which we used—I am not really familiar with the technology—there are mirrors, or rather some analogous electronic device." He frowned lightly. "But I earnestly urge you to disregard the special effects, as you call them. What does concern you vitally is the content of the tape. Are there any questions you would like to ask?"

"When can we go home?" Phil demanded promptly.

Graves looked at him. "I meant, about the content of the tape."

"If you'd let us take the tape home," said June, "we'd watch it very carefully."

Graves stared at her flatly for a long moment. Then he said: "If I were to tell you that you may go now, and had you driven to your automobile and released—would you jump at the chance to simply go, and after reporting your adventure to the police, attempt to resume your normal lives?"

Radcliffe tried to look as if the question deserved serious consideration. So did June.

"We wouldn't necessarily report anything to the police," Philip said at last. "We haven't been harmed so far, and . . ." He let his words trail off, because he could see it was the wrong answer.

Graves was looking at him with an increased contempt, though no real surprise. "I had hoped that by now you would have come to a better understanding regarding your situation. You must be made to realize that what you tell the authorities after your release, or do not tell them, may be of some importance, but it is not the main point."

"What is the main point?"

It seemed that Graves, confronted with such stupidity, was mentally forcing himself to count to ten before he answered. The reply when it came was mild enough: "Let us go into the house, and watch the tape together. Certain sections of it, at least."

"All right."

"The mirror in your bathroom is perfectly functional?"

"As far as we can tell," said Phil. For some reason he could feel his scalp beginning to creep.

"Good. I shall stand in front of it, and you will have the chance to seek my image in its bright, well-lighted surface."

But that demonstration was not to be, not then. Interruption came before it could take place.

One of the masked people came and stood in the doorway and made a cryptic sign to Graves, who announced that he was called away.

June and Phil silently thought of possible trickery.

The live man turned in the doorway to deliver his exit line. His voice ate at them like the voice of doom: "Perhaps my plan was wrong in its approach, but there is no help for that now. You must not only watch the tape, you must ponder seriously its contents, and accept the truth that it reveals. I cannot compel you to believe the story on the tape. But you must know it, well enough to discuss it intelligently with me, next time we meet."

Phil wanted to tell the man that he was crazy, but the words choked in his throat. His wife beside him was nodding helplessly. "We will," she said.

~ *6* ~

Within two weeks of his emergence from underground, Radu made his first foray outside the boundaries of the metropolis of London. At first, moving across country only after dark, he went no farther than a few miles from the East End of London, where he had hidden the precious supply of his native earth that had sustained him for almost a hundred years.

Only now, when he began to travel, did he fully appreciate the scale of the changes in human society and achievements which had come about during his last sojourn underground.

As weeks and months went by, he extended the scope of his explorations. Visiting by night certain ships out of the thousands which were engaged in the unending maritime commerce on the Thames, scraping secretly through holds and bilges, he augmented his perilously thin supply of his homeland's hospitable soil. He also made sure of several earths he had earlier secretly established in Britain. Evidently Vlad had never located these deposits, for they were still usable.

He had also to establish new earths, of the soil of his homeland, as that seemed prudent. He had to, if possible, re-establish some network of allies among the European vampire population. At any one time, near the end of the eighteenth century, there were probably not more than a dozen *nosferatu* active on the whole continent.

In this same period Radu, establishing sporadic contacts with British vampires, began also, in his way, to make discreet inquiries about me. His family name was known to them, but, as he discovered to his delight, they tended to confuse him with his brother, who seemed never to have visited Britain.

Within a month he had convinced himself that Vlad was certainly not to be found in England. The elder Dracula was known to the local *nosferatu* only by reputation.

Radu could begin to relax a little.

At that time, in the early summer of 1792, I was still in a state of blissful ignorance regarding the fact that my brother was once more prowling above ground.

Other matters, which, as far as I could tell, had nothing to do with Radu, were claiming my attention. It was in Paris, in the cemetery of the Church of the Madeleine, on one particular summer night, that I participated in one of those meetings that turn out to be of great consequence to the persons involved, though at the time none of them are conscious of the fact.

The reason for my presence at that time and place was very simple: I had been resting in one of my earths nearby.

Even at this late date I do not care to be more specific about exact locations. Enough to say that I reclined not in any ordinary grave. But the reader may visualize several possibilities, e.g., crypts or accidental cavities in or under the church itself, or one of the other buildings nearby. Certainly it was in a location which I believed was likely to remain undisturbed, at least for a long time. Somewhere, even now, a reader is guessing that it might be in some ancient monument. Well, that might be a good guess. Or how about this one: under a path or road? But never mind.

A light of unwonted brightness shone there, from a lantern hanging on the stub of a tree branch. It was, though I did not yet understand the fact, one of the new Argand lamps, invented in England a bare ten years earlier, which derived from their burning oil about ten times the light of old lamps of the same size. And by this light, the forms and features of two women were revealed, both of them intent upon some task whose details I could not yet make out, but of whose basic nature I felt immediately certain.

In that year, and through much of the madness that followed through the next few orbits of the Earth, the Parisian guillotine's victims were commonly hauled, after decapitation, to the cemetery of the Madeleine. But in the year and month of which I speak, their numbers were increasing only gradually, and sometimes whole days went by without a single accused aristocrat or traitor losing his or her head in the name of Liberty.

I had been asleep for several days, oblivious to what was going on in the breathing, waking, workaday world only a few yards from my hidden fastness. But my first sight of this new digging, the broad trench ten feet deep, obviously intended for mass burials, stopped me in my tracks. Such excavation suggested either an epidemic or the near approach of war. A faint odor of corruption was perceptible despite the scientifically enlightened attempt at thorough burial.

Listening carefully, I could hear no cannon. That, I thought, suggested pestilence as the most probable cause.

How little did I know.

I decided that a brief examination of whatever bodies had been buried in the trench would be the quickest means of gaining the information that I sought. And indeed one glance, more or less over the shoulders of the two women, was sufficient. They were all adults, and mostly men. Most were fully clothed, though coats and hats were absent. And they were all without their heads; and I suddenly understood just what kind of an epidemic had begun to ravage Paris.

The new government had adopted the guillotine in April of that year, the same month in which Revolutionary France found herself at war with Austria and Prussia. The introduction of the new machine was viewed as an idealistic gesture. Away with the hideous and prolonged tortures which in the past had been the common means of capital punishment! The age of humanitarianism had arrived. No more would those condemned to death be broken on the wheel, drawn and quartered, or have their flesh torn with red-hot pincers—modes of punishment still very much in style across the map of European civilization. In France, simple beheading had formerly been reserved for aristocrats, but now everyone in the newly classless society could enjoy its benefits.

Let me assure the modern reader that it is not my intention to single out the French as particularly brutal. The last execution for witchcraft in England had occurred as late as 1685, when Jack Ketch, whose name came to stand for all of his profession, hanged Alice Molland in Exeter.

In 1790 in England, the penalty of burning to death, inflicted for a variety of crimes, had finally been abolished— for women. And hanging, drawing, and quartering was still on the books as the prescribed punishment for treason.

Also there is testimony that as late as 1790, the heads of executed traitors were still to be seen exhibited on Temple Bar—staring eyelessly in through the north windows of Tellson's Bank, which stood adjoining. (One version has it that they were two officers of Prince Charles's army, decapitated in the old, inefficient, and haphazard way, by the headsman's axe or sword; another, that they were veterans of the Jacobite rebellion of 1715.)

But let us return to that fateful night in 1792, in the cemetery of the Church of the Madeleine, the burial ground of Revolutionary freedom. I was aware that the place was guarded, at least sporadically. The sentries were under orders from the Committee of Public Safety, to prevent grieving relatives

from attempting to retrieve the mangled bodies of their loved
ones. As one might expect, a little bribery allowed such re-
coveries to take place fairly often—the fewer bodies, the easier the gravediggers' task. And, as it happened, no guards
were anywhere in sight when my fateful meeting took place.

Still unaware of my presence, the two women kept working away under their bright light, right at the place where
the latest crop of bodies had been dumped. A new section of
trench was dug almost every day, laborious spade and shovel
work. Then the section excavated on the previous day was
filled in on top of the latest crop of bodies—then usually only
two or three, sometimes as many as half a dozen—after they
had been hurled carelessly into the pit and sprinkled with
lime. Still, as I have already remarked, there was only a
trickle of dead flesh as yet, foreshadowing the floods to come;
sometimes a day passed without a single beheading.

The elder of the pair of workers, whose age I judged at
a youthful thirty, was sitting on a chair or stool, not knitting
but holding a raw-necked head, a fine example of Sanson's
handiwork, face uppermost in her lap, which she had protected with a piece of canvas.

In my experience it had been invariably only the worst,
blackest sort of magic which brought its practitioners into
cemeteries to perform rituals at midnight. What little I had
seen of such behavior was not only evil but amateurish, a de-
fect which confirmed me in my determination to avoid the
business as thoroughly as I could.

Gradually I drew closer to the busy pair. I wondered if I
should call attention to my presence with a gentlemanly
cough.

I had been standing in thoughtful observation for almost a minute before the younger woman looked up and saw
me there, standing in the fringes of the bright light of the Argand lamp. For some reason it did not strike me until later
that this modern technology argued against the magical explanation of the women's presence, which I had so unthink-
ingly assumed. Also, for would-be sorcerers, the pair seemed

remarkably unconcerned about an idler who stood by and watched.

"Good evening, citizen." By now the older worker had observed me too. There was nothing frightened or uncertain in either woman's manner. If this was satanism, it had grown bold indeed.

Both of the women were obviously hardened to their work. And the elder, as she worked on, informed me that they were there by order of the Convention.

Is the Revolution dabbling now in magic? I asked myself; but did not bother to voice the question aloud.

While the woman of thirty kept talking to me, mostly banalities about the weather and the price of bread, her hands kept busy with what was, as I thought, some kind of would-be magical hocus-pocus with the freshly severed head in her lap. Illumination from the bright Argand lamp bathed the sallow skin, the half-exposed teeth (somehow their whiteness was surprising, suggesting health), gray lips, and matted hair.

Meanwhile her younger assistant, who so far had paid me little heed, was digging methodically through the grisly pile of stiffened, chilling flesh, inspecting and discarding, one after another, the heads that she discovered. A few she chose and put down on the ground in a row, sluicing them with water from a pail to wash away the earth and blood from their faces, to get a better look at them. At last she seemed to find a head she definitely wanted, and set it aside, with a little murmur of satisfaction.

Meanwhile the older woman worked on. Her skilled technician's fingers, dipped in what appeared to be clear oil, carried on a deft anointing of the skin of the dead face which she was cradling. I caught the dim flash of a small needle in the lamplight. The eyelids had already been sewn shut, just a little tuck in each would do, and now the lips, which at one corner of the mouth still tended to sag open.

Deftly her young fingers smeared a thin layer of clay over the fringe of hair around the.dead face. The man, whatever his name, had been clean-shaven, rather handsome, with a receding hairline.

"That's good," his attendant muttered to herself. "The less hair the better; it only gets in the way."

In the way of what? I wondered, but indolently did not pursue the question.

The younger woman, straightening her back, remarked: "They say the beard keeps on growing after death."

I looked at her, and found her comely. But at the moment I felt no great hunger. Casually I observed: "They say many things which are not so."

Though I lingered near the women, I was not watching their work very keenly. The scene, with its ghoulish pair, reminded me of my first encounter, hundred of years earlier, with Constantia, who as a mere breathing girl had been aching to try her hand at witchcraft, not at all afraid to turn up some supposed wizard's grave. Also of several other episodes, involving would-be witches and magicians, which I had observed down through the centuries. Long ago I had realized that not one in ten of the folk who thought themselves adept in those dark practices were actually in contact with any powers beyond those generated in their own sick minds.

The two women now before me seemed perfect examples of such self-delusion. But at least their magical paraphernalia struck me as unique. They were using a device of a good size and shape to fit into a hatbox, containing some kind of blocks, screws, and clamps to grip a detached human head and hold it in place, face uppermost, upon one woman's lap, while she and her fellow technician worked.

I assumed, without giving the matter any real thought, that the decorations on the hatbox were some kind of amateurish magical symbols.

Only one face, the dead one, that of some poor breather who would breathe no more, was in full light, while the live countenances of the two women remained in shadow.

*   *   *

What would the attitude of the Revolutionary authorities be toward witchcraft, satanism? The question was seldom asked openly but there can be no doubt that those fanatics were generally against black magic; the devil no less than God was a rival authority, jealously demanding allegiance. Another dreadful superstition. On the other hand, he would have offered an ally against all churches, synagogues, and mosques.

I have sometimes wondered whether it might have been some hint, or even stronger indication, of that darker worship showing itself among his colleagues, which induced Robespierre to formulate his cult of the Supreme Being—but that was to come later.

Whose face were the women working on? It was only logical for me to satisfy my curiosity by asking. They murmured something, being evasive; I did not press the point.

After a thin coating of oil had been applied to the subject's face, it was time for the plaster of Paris, the latter swiftly mixed in a handy bowl or basin.

They had recently been working on a woman's head, which now lay discarded and forgotten again, and the process suggested some ghastly beautician's work. Thinking back a century or two, I recalled having seen breathing women subject themselves to mudpacks and the like.

To me the younger of the two breathing women, who had not spoken a word to me as yet, was the more attractive and therefore the more interesting. Though her face remained in shadow, as seemed only fitting for one engaged in black magician's work, darkness gave no protection against inspection by a vampire's eyes. Hers was a striking face that stayed easily in my memory. As did her voice.

But at the time, my thoughts preoccupied with other matters, I didn't even bother to learn her name. That would come later . . .

"I have no need to ask what you are doing," I remarked. In this, as we shall see, I blundered seriously on the side of overconfidence. I thought I knew essentially what was going on, though some of the details were unique in my experience, strange enough to make me curious. Whatever thoughts I had of the two women in that hour were confined to the universe of magic, and of evil. In my defense, I can only plead that ascribing such motives to whomever I encountered in that place, and at that time, was a natural mistake.

She was unperturbed by my question. "We have perfectly valid business here, citizen. Have you?"

"It is the business of my life."

"Your home lies near here?"

"Very near." I gestured vaguely. "It is at most times a peaceful neighborhood."

~ 7 ~

Generally the Radcliffes' masked guardians spoke to the gypsy girl with an air of wary respect. One or two of them called her Constantia, while others more casually used the name of Connie; the woman answered indifferently to both names. A few minutes after her master, Graves, had completed his first visit, she dropped in on the Radcliffes uninvited, apparently with nothing more complicated in mind than a simple chat. None of the breathing, rubber-masked guardians were quite so intrusive, but continued their self-effacing ways.

Later on the first day of the Radcliffes' confinement, Connie once more entered their quarters approximately at sunset, and remained until the two prisoners, who had had only a couple of hours of sleep out of the last thirty-six, showed unmistakable signs of giving way to exhaustion.

She gave them a sly, suggestive wink, and said she knew that they were on their honeymoon. No one tried to explain that they had passed that stage several months ago. And on the second day, Connie was in and out at intervals, along with several of the masked attendants.

Connie, when bidding the couple good night on their first evening in the makeshift prison, had assured them that they would enjoy undisturbed privacy in the house until morning. They could latch their doors, front and back (" . . . and your *bedroom* door too!"), and Mr. Graves wouldn't mind. In fact he preferred it that way. Barring emergencies, no one would intrude on them.

To Philip it seemed silly to try to lock out the jailers—the hardware available to defend the prisoners' privacy, unlike that which kept them in, was cheap and flimsy, no doubt original equipment with the mobile home. But, he thought, why not at least make the gesture, show that they wanted to discourage intrusion as much as possible?

So now, as on their first night here, Radcliffe, with June trailing after him (they were rarely out of each other's sight now), went around latching all the doors and windows. As he snapped the last catch shut, he told his wife: "At least we'll hear them if they break in."

"Right." Barring tricks, he couldn't help thinking, and secret passages. A few days ago, a mobile home with secret passages would have seemed a crazy idea. But a lot had happened in the last few days, and everything else about the situation was crazy, too. Neither of the Radcliffes wanted to remind the other that they still hadn't figured out how Graves had gotten into their car while it was in motion, even if the convertible top had been down . . .

Stumbling through the house, on the verge of falling asleep, Phil and June halfheartedly discussed the possibility of taking turns standing watch through the night. As they were trying to decide who would have the first shift, exhaustion intervened, putting an end to the discussion. This time they at least made it as far as the bedroom where both, fully clothed except for their shoes, slept like the dead until daylight.

On awakening, Phil quietly unlatched the bedroom door and looked out into a silent, sunlit house. Then in his stocking feet he tiptoed through all the rooms. There was no sign that anyone had even looked in on them during the night.

In a few minutes, Constantia appeared. As in their previous daylight encounters, she was wearing her dark glasses, and this time, in deference to the day's full desert sun, had put on a broad-brimmed hat. Despite the growing heat, she was also wearing a kind of jacket, fringed in cowgirl-western style, with a high collar.

June was polite with Connie, but spoke to her more frigidly than she did to Graves when he took his turn at dropping in. Phil didn't have to ask to know that his wife did not like the woman at all.

This morning, as usual, Connie was ready to talk on a variety of subjects. Frequently she chattered, though what she said did not always make sense to her distracted hearers, especially when she harked back to events they had heard described on the tape as having taken place in a previous century. But today Connie tended to lapse into periods of moody silence.

These usually began when she was looking at Philip Radcliffe. Connie would occasionally begin staring at him in a vaguely, unconsciously hungry way. The impression she gave, to June at least, was of a woman pondering whether she ought to seduce a man.

And in this case first impressions were exactly right.

After locking the door of the Radcliffes' domicile behind her, Constantia strode like a moody teenager, scuffing the earth with her fancy, rode-lady cowgirl boots, the few yards to the other mobile home, where she opened the unlocked door and walked right in. A small group of guardians, giving their heads a rest from rubber masks, sat tiredly talking in the small living room; their voices fell silent briefly as Connie passed.

She made her way down a narrow hallway to the door at the far end. There in the smallest of the small bedrooms, a chamber heavily shaded and darkened, but already growing warm because it lacked a window air conditioner, Vlad was lying on his back on a folding camp bed, just about to go into a brief trance and get some much-needed sleep.

The dark man, stretched out on his plastic bag of earth, roused himself long enough to ask his long-time friend and occasional associate how the two prisoners were doing.

Connie, shifting to a language so old and rare that no one else in the Western Hemisphere was likely to understand, reported that they seemed all right.

Then she added: "The young man is quite attractive—at least I find him so."

Vlad raised himself on one elbow, the dry earth crackling in the plastic garment bag beneath his body. "May I remind you, my dear, that this is business?"

"Of course." Connie's lower lip protruded, somewhat sulkily. She no longer appeared to be seventeen years old. Not quite fifteen, actually.

"You also found his ancestor quite attractive, two hundred years ago. And we both remember what came of that infatuation—do we not?"

"Of course, Vlad."

"Of course. The result was difficulty. Unpleasantness. We are not going to have a similar *contretemps* here, are we?"

"No, Vlad."

"No, we are not. Now I require some rest." And with a breathless little groan he stretched himself once more at full length on the crackling earth.

Letting herself quietly out of the darkened bedroom, going to the adjoining chamber where her own plastic bag of earth lay ready to afford her her daily rest, Constantia in the privacy of her own thoughts continued toying with the question of whether or not to begin the affair with Radcliffe. Now Vlad, for one of his fussy, honorable reasons, had flatly forbidden any such thing. And if she disobeyed him, his reaction, if he ever found out, was not going to be pleasant.

June read the other woman's behavior more accurately than Radcliffe did, and June was not very good at concealing her feelings about anyone.

Once June had called Phil's attention to Connie's behavior, he took notice of it, and the way the gypsy girl looked at him started to make him nervous. But he didn't want to admit the fact.

After Connie had gone rather sulkily out into the heat of the day, the two prisoners, alternately sitting in the living room and hunched over the kitchen table, talked things over in whispers between themselves. They agreed that Mr. Graves in contrast to Connie seemed a perfect gentleman—when he was not actually in the act of kidnapping people. He was also considerably more frightening.

Radcliffe said to his wife: "You know what the truly scary thing about these people is?"

"I can think of several."

"What I had in mind is that there are long stretches when what they're saying and doing almost seems to make sense. Or is it just me? Am I getting brainwashed? Junie, I tell you, minutes go by, even hours, when everything they tell us seems so reasonable, and they don't sound like crazy cultists. I mean Graves has a way of putting things that makes them sound convincing. But if you listen close and think about *what* he says . . . especially on that tape . . ."

June was frowning. "Do you think that all this—all this about vampires and so on—can be only *symbolic*? I mean that we're not meant to take it literally?"

Phil thought about it. But he didn't have to think very long. "No. No, I don't think that at all."

While cleaning up the remains of another snack—so far the milk and cereal were holding out—the pair conferred between themselves. Now, with several hours of sleep behind them, it seemed at least possible that they would be able to think clearly about their situation, and maybe attain some useful insight.

But anything of the kind eluded them, at least at first.

"Phil, what are we going to do?"

"I don't see what we *can* do, except watch their silly tape over and over again, and play along with their ideas. Next time we see Graves, we'll have to tell him we've seen the whole tape and we understand it. We're ready to have discussions with him and believe anything he tells us. Meanwhile we look for a chance to get away, though it doesn't seem likely that they're going to give us one."

This time they watched the whole tape, almost three hours of content, all the way to the end, in one continuous session. It was a sobering experience, but when they had completed the chore, they still didn't know what to think. Except that Mr. Graves might know a lot about a great many subjects, but he was no ball of fire when it came to making a media presentation.

Just sitting around and waiting quickly became unendurable. Radcliffe, when he felt reasonably sure that no one was looking, stalked through the house, quietly testing the locks and heavy bars on both doors, then examining the grillwork on all the windows. He discovered no weak points. The only real result was that now, having proven to himself that he was in a small and doubtless not fireproof building with all the exits locked, he began to feel a touch of claustrophobia.

Once or twice, during the morning and afternoon of their second day of confinement, the two were invited out, by two or three of the masked monsters, for a walk. On these occasions they were always closely watched.

June was nagged by the idea that there might be some significance in the identities of the individuals portrayed in the masks most of Graves's assistants had chosen to put on. They were plastic or rubber creations that covered the entire head, Halloween-costume imitations of various imaginary monsters of the Hollywood variety. Both prisoners got the impression that there were more masks than people, suggesting a deliberate attempt at preventing identification, for the same people didn't always wear the same mask.

June could not entirely rid herself of the idea that some deep meaning might be found in the individual choices, and she began to jot down little descriptive notes on all their jailers. Then she decided this was a bad idea, tore up the sheets from the note pad, and burned them in the sink. Phil saw the assumed identities as purely accidental.

Then June turned away from the sink with a quick motion, almost a little jump. "Something just occurred to me."

"What?"

"We've seen Frankenstein and the Wolf Man, right? And the Mummy, if I'm interpreting that funny-looking one correctly. I mean the one who looks like a bad case of sunburn, peeling."

"Right. Plus a whole lot of others who I have no idea who they are. So?"

"Well, it just occurred to me—Count Dracula is missing."

Connie appeared more restless than usual the next time she showed up, around noon on the following day. The gypsy-looking girl made little or no effort to conceal the fact that she found it definitely boring simply to sit around all night and all day, especially when she was forbidden to taste this young breather's blood; she thought there ought to be some fun in this kidnapping business for her.

Then the gypsy girl wistfully asked June how her hair looked. Even as she asked the question, she was twisting the dark curly strands around her finger, pulling them forward while she frowned up toward them with her eyes crossed. "It's not really long enough for me to see."

"Why don't you go and look in the mirror?"

Connie only giggled, as if the idea were somehow painful.

By this time Philip and June had had the idea of vampires thoroughly drummed into their heads by the videotape. Now June asked their visitor point-blank if she was a vampire.

Connie answered simply that she was.

The other woman pursued the point. "And when Mr. Graves on the tape talks about a woman named Constantia, who is doing all these things in France, two hundred years ago . . ."

"Oh, he means me. Oh yes, absolutely." Connie smiled, a cheerful conspirator. "Not that *everything* he says about me on the tape is necessarily strictly true."

The captives, not knowing how to respond to this declaration, looked at each other. It sounded to them like this girl really believed what she was saying.

"If you're a vampire," Radcliffe proceeded cautiously, "is there some way you can demonstrate the fact—I mean short of actually biting someone and drinking blood?"

"I could, sweetie. Oh, it would be very easy. But Vla . . . Mr. Graves doesn't want me to do anything like that yet."

Nervously Connie looked around. June was staring at her in an unsettling way. She was also afraid of Vlad's anger, and admitted as much to the prisoners.

Spontaneously Connie added, in the manner of one impulsively giving good advice: "I wouldn't make him mad at me, if I were you."

Graves had never uttered any threats, but Radcliffe found himself in full agreement. "Is he really five hundred years old?" he asked on impulse.

"Just about." Constantia smiled; her look had undertones of wickedness. "I'm *years* younger than 'Mr. Graves.'" This time she pronounced the name with more than a hint of mockery.

"Oh?"

With a giggle she delivered her punch line: "Not a day over four hundred and eighty."

June and Phil had gathered from the tape, where the identification was strongly implied, that Mr. Graves and the story character called Vlad Dracula were supposed to be one and the same—now and then Graves, narrating on tape, even slipped into the first person without appearing to notice that he had done so. But like any rational breathers at the end of the twentieth century, the couple had been resisting the idea.

Radcliffe wasn't ready to give up on the subject. "How old is he, then? Really?"

"Oh-oh!" Her long lashes flickered at him flirtatiously. He couldn't tell if the gesture was serious or self-mocking. "You haven't been really studying your videotape, or you'd know."

"That's not true, we have been watching it. I mean really." He looked at June for confirmation.

June nodded vigorously.

"Not the whole thing." Connie was dubious.

"Yes, really." June added her assurance to her husband's. "We've seen it now from beginning to end."

Their visitor shook her dark-curled head, marveling. "You see it and hear it, but you don't believe it." Now Miss Gypsy was about to pout. "We went to a lot of trouble to make that tape. I ran the camera most of the time."

"I didn't know."

"Well, I *did*. And I know some folk who'd give a million dollars to have it. Even to know half of everything that's on there. You're being given it for nothing and you won't even take it seriously." Now she was really pouting. Maybe, thought Radcliffe, she was perturbed because she thought the tape mentioned her only in a slighting way.

June was following another train of thought. "Who? Who'd give a million dollars?"

The girl in silver earrings smiled. "Some people I know. Men and women who study things like this."

"Like what?"

Connie's smile took on a different quality. "*You* know. So, you want me to go and look in the mirror? I will, if you come along with me. But maybe I'd better ask Mr. Graves first if it's all right."

Once or twice when Radcliffe and Connie were out of earshot of the others, the young man, belatedly becoming aware of the attraction Connie felt for him, began hinting to persuade Constantia that it would be to her own benefit to help him and June escape from these crazy kidnappers.

Connie answered playfully at first. He was just too cute and she wasn't going to let him go—things like that. But when Radcliffe persisted in being serious, the woman blinked and her face went sober. For once she was entirely serious, and her face, while still as unlined as ever, just might have been a hundred years of age. "You don't know Mr. Graves."

"No," he admitted after a few moments. "No, I don't guess I do."

~ 8 ~

*I*t may help the reader to an understanding of my relations with my brother, to be told that centuries ago I adapted a version of the Golden Rule to serve as my guideline: since the early years of our ongoing quarrel, I have striven to do unto Radu before he does unto me. So far, being slightly older, considerably stronger, and totally untroubled by any fear of consequences, I have been successful in the great majority of our clashes.

But I regret to report that as yet there is no end to our conflict in sight. Sometimes I wonder: What would our father have thought, had he known the true nature of the burden he had placed on me, of responsibility for my brother? Had Father imagined that it might possibly continue for five hundred years and more?

No, I simply cannot imagine the paternal reaction to such knowledge. My mind simply boggles—as, I am sure, father's would have done. To the best of my knowledge, my esteemed parent had never even the least commerce with vampires—though he must have been aware of their existence. I cannot imagine the supposition crossing our father's mind that either of his sons, let alone both, would ever become vampires—certainly he himself had never been granted that wondrous transformation. Or perhaps he had deliberately declined it. I should not like to think that of my father.

Still, an oath is an oath. It was put to me as a matter of personal and family honor, and I as a dutiful son accepted it unquestioningly on its own terms.

Having survived a serious altercation with my younger brother in 1705—remind me to tell you, sometime, the full story of that remarkable encounter—having survived that, as I say, and having firmly reasserted my proper position as head of the family, I considered what course of action to take next. Honor, as we have seen, precluded my having the scoundrel put to death outright. But at the same time, duty and prudence alike required some drastic action.

The best compromise I could arrange with my conscience required devious and difficult arrangements. In the end, as we have seen, I had Radu put underground, alive (well, more or less alive. Just enough, as it seemed to me, to meet the minimum requirements of my pledge to our father.) in one of the quieter churchyards of London. The length of his confinement under these conditions was to be left to chance.

When I gave orders to certain reliable associates of mine, specifying in some detail how Radu was to be transported and put away, I had thought I might look forward to as much as five hundred years of peace. But alas, even though my orders were carried out with remarkable fidelity, that was not to be.

Whilst making the arrangements for this burial, I, as the responsible older brother, considered whether it would be somehow possible to arrange to be notified whenever my younger sibling should be awakened. But I could discover no way to make any such arrangement reliably, and in any case I was not really sure I wanted it. I have resolutely declined to spend my life looking over my shoulder.

The news of Radu's revival—first in the form of a rumor, and then in independent confirmation—reached me in the summer of 1792. Coming decades before I expected it, it struck me with a forcible shock.

Certainly I was disappointed to discover that the fiend was already above ground and prowling again; the punishment had not endured for even a hundred years. Oh, with any luck at all my younger brother might easily have remained inert, only groaning now and then in nightmare, for another fifty years or so. But though disconcerted I was hardly at all surprised. Luck was something that seemed usually to flow in my younger brother's favor.

No doubt you are already thinking that simply condemning a vampire to a long trance must not in itself qualify as punishment. And you are right—there must be additional conditions. Sometimes putting the subject in a trance deprives him of the opportunity to do something above ground that he badly wants to accomplish. For example, achieving the seduction of a certain breathing person, or persons. And there are other ways of arranging matters so that his long and enforced sleep is far from pleasant.

Here is one such possibility: Trance, as we know, is essentially a kind of sleep, and sleep is often stalked by dreams. A nightmare-filled catalepsy, which endures for a hundred years or more, is not at all the same as a long peaceful slumber. The specific details of the nightmare we need not go into here; I have no wish that my readers' own slumbers should be disturbed.

Does it seem to you that such an experience would inevitably drive its victim mad? If you think so, you do not know Radu.

As I started to explain above, before I wandered somewhat off the point, my arrangements for Radu's burial in 1705 included having his head cut off before he went into the coffin. This operation of course was performed, as I am sure you realize if you have kept up with me this far, with no intention of killing the dear boy outright. I made sure that his short-ening was accomplished by a steel blade, with nothing in the least wooden about it. (In a later chapter we will have fur-ther occasion to contemplate the fact that if a vampire is decapitated by an irresistible force borne in metal—the very description of the guillotine—then the head and body are de-cisively severed, but not killed.)

Yes, it is virtually impossible for metal to inflict deadly harm upon a *nosferatu*. Yet massive force, such as the tra-ditional guillotine is designed to apply, can achieve a sepa-ration. Under proper conditions each component of the maimed body could be counted on to survive for a long time, and if the two parts were left where one might come in con-tact with the other, they would inevitably get back together. On the other hand, if they were separated inside their coffin by a wooden barrier, I felt perfectly confident that they—he—could survive indefinitely, howbeit in an incapacitated state, until the barrier was breached, inevitably by time, or sooner or later by the inadvertent action of gravediggers legitimate or otherwise; and the two parts could roll and claw them-selves together . . . thus, Father, did I ease my conscience with regard to my oath to you. I had not killed Radu, whose head and body would someday reunite.

With a wish to keep the whole business as thoroughly out of sight and mind as possible, I caused my brother's mor-tal parts, vitally dismembered but still undead, to be con-veyed into a distant land for burial. This tactic put a broad girdle of the sea, twenty miles at least of salt, tide-flowing water, as a barrier between Radu and his homeland—and, as I had thought, between him and most of his breathing min-ions of that century. My oath required, of course, that a por-tion of our native soil sufficient to enable him to survive be buried with him. The logistics of it all were every bit as hard as you might think.

I relied upon hypnosis, aided by a judiciously measured dose of a certain peculiar substance left over from the Bor-gia pharmacology (at its most productive three hundred years earlier), to make sure that my brother was properly entranced. His mind was programmed, as it were, to experience a number of unpleasant dreams, or more precisely one dream only, repeated and repeated.

As for myself, my long immunity to fear in waking life has left me, ever since my childhood, proof against nightmares in the life of sleep. Radu therefore could not hope to impose upon his elder brother the same punishment of bad dreams that I inflicted upon him.

Of one thing I could be entirely certain: Radu was going to be terribly angry when he awakened after experiencing such a penalty. Constantia thought it necessary to warn me of the fact. But I shrugged, and reminded her that when my errant brother got out of his partitioned coffin, he was going to be murderously angry anyway, at me and at the world. Homicidal animosity was his ordinary state. And I could not make his state of mind my chief concern. Even had it been possible for me to disregard my oath to our father, simple justice required that he be punished for his misdeeds. Of course with authority came responsibility. Chastisement, sometimes severe, was not only permissible, it was sometimes required under the terms of my promise—with the proviso that any correction always stopped safely short of capital punishment.

Have I forgotten to mention that a beating with a wooden cane was also part of the just punishment inflicted? I had employed that method several times, on earlier occasions, and had gained no permanent advantage thereby. At each impact, my cowardly brother screamed unashamedly with pain and fear—the beating naturally took place at a time when his lungs were still connected to his mouth, and the nerves of his spinal column to his brain. At intervals between screams (well, he knew how I detested screams, and I am sure he meant them to annoy me!), he sobbed that he had seen the light, and was now determined on reform. Even had that claim been true—and I knew better than to believe it—it would have had no bearing on the justice of the ongoing punishment.

The chronic difficulty which I faced was that the culprit would heal with great rapidity from any physical punishment I might inflict—anything short of the ultimate and forbidden sanction of the great true death.

In any case, I found the news that Radu had returned to the world in 1790 vexing, to say the least.

Mentally reviewing my available options in dealing with my younger sibling, I found that they were, as before, severely restricted by the vow our father had extracted from me as an adolescent.

Father had been satisfied, even pleased, by my willingness to pledge my honor in the cause of duty.

Following my own version of the Golden Rule, I thought that for my own sake I had better locate Radu, if that was at all possible. Before he located me.

I confess that I began the effort with no methodical plan. For a time my chief hope was to run across some lesser vampire who might give me a clue as to where Radu could be found. Still, I more than half expected to discover my brother himself gloating over fresh corpses, the day's harvest of Sanson's guillotine. Of course the blood so prodigally wasted there would be stale, chill, clotting, well past its peak of flavor and nourishment. But there would be in what was left a tang of despair, of ultimate fear. It was suffering, and the evidence of suffering, that attracted Radu more than blood.

Actually Radu could tell, by the shadings of flavor in the blood, that some of these condemned had gone to their doom tranquilly, at peace with the world that was about to eject them. Or at least he had convinced himself that it was so.

In 1792, beginning a methodical attempt to locate my younger sibling, and knowing his penchant for cities, the bigger the better, I thought I could not do better than to spend some time in Paris, then indisputably the greatest metropolis of Europe. I had not visited France for some time—there is something in widespread and oppressive poverty that depresses the spirit of the onlooker.

During the last decades of the eighteenth century it had appeared to me, as it did to many another observer, that a great social upheaval impended in France. Since 1789 I had been convinced that something of the kind was imminent. I think my claim as I make it now is not mere hindsight. A society of such archetypal injustice and widespread desperation was doomed to fail. The monarchy was stupid and inert, oppressive accidentally and lazily rather than efficiently. Everyone who had eyes to see and ears to hear, and who thought about the matter at all, must have seen that the old world was straining and struggling to give birth to something new. But until the fall of the Bastille in 1789, and the virtual imprisonment of the king and queen which soon followed, I, and many others, had not bestowed on these phenomena the attention they deserved; we *nosferatu* tend to believe that politics and social structures among the breathers have only marginal effect upon our lives. The truth is that I viewed the impending cataclysm rather smugly as regards its effect upon myself.

How wrong I was.

The sprawling palace of the Tuileries, and the extensive gardens adjoining, lay between the Rue de Rivoli and the north bank of the Seine. A year or two before I came to those gardens looking for my brother, they had been a favorite strolling place of the French king, Louis XVI (who was always much more interested in his hobby of locksmithing, and in hunting, than in politics), and his queen, Marie Antoinette (an unhappy Austrian spendthrift, who never quite understood anything that was going on). Often the royal couple had been accompanied on these walks by their two small children.

But in France those apparently tranquil days were gone, never to return. Of late the royal family had not been much seen by the public, except on the several occasions when their privacy had been invaded by an angry mob.

That August morning, unpleasantly warm and humid, found me not in the best of tempers; I had been out since around midnight, looking for Radu as usual, and had prolonged my search well into the hours which were counted by sundials. Throughout most of that summer I had spent a great many of my waking hours trying to locate my brother, and with Radu on my mind, what sleep I managed to obtain tended to be very light indeed.

Wearing my customary daytime costume of broad hat and a flowing cloak, making my way uncomfortably through summer sunlight from one spot of shade to the next, I gradually progressed along the edge of the vast garden of the Tuileries.

On the tenth of August the traditional function of the place as a parade ground for fashionable strollers had been violently pre-empted. This time the mob was vastly greater than before. There had been cannon fire, and a fierce fight with the Swiss Guards, mercenaries who were more loyal to the French crown than the French themselves were turning out to be.

From a distance of thirty yards or so, I observed, with disapproval, that the spot I had chosen as my next observation post was already occupied. There beneath a chestnut tree stood with folded arms a lone male figure with a bearing at once youthful and military, though at the moment in rather shabby though well-cut civilian clothes. Here was one man not trying to emulate the Revolutionary prototype of the *sans-culotte*—no red cap or huge mustache or workman's *carmagnole* jacket for him.

This young man, whose bearing and attitude suggested an army officer in mufti, was sheltering on the fringe of the park surrounding the besieged palace on that bright, hot August day, in the very spot where I had determined to establish my observation post. I could not tell whether he had noticed me or not; his attention was intensely concentrated on the events taking place in the broad garden space before the palace of the Tuileries.

The Swiss Guards had looked magnificent in their uniforms of gold, white, and red. And they had fought well, until betrayed by the catastrophic ineptitude of their commanders. And now the fight as such was over, and they were being slaughtered by the mob.

As I discovered later, my instincts were not at fault. Only a little earlier, Brother Radu had indeed been gleefully observing the slaughter in those green and pleasant gardens, and even playing some small part in it himself. And he intended to come back. It was hard to believe that the simple smell of human blood carried on the evening breeze would not have attracted him. There were gallons of blood for the taking, from bodies only freshly dead or still barely alive. Having selected the site of my ambush, I waited for a chance to seize him unobserved.

But I was not the only one in the neighborhood who had determined to have a good view of the horrors, while staying far enough away from them to escape direct involvement. Two of us at least had exercised a canny skill in picking out the perfect vantage point for observation.

At first my accidental companion and I regarded each other with considerable suspicion; but it was after all fairly obvious that we both were interested in seeing what was happening, and neither of us minded to take part.

Nor was either of us given to wasting time in hand-wringing or uttering expressions of dread and loathing. Each for his own reasons had come to the conclusion that he would not attempt to interfere with what was happening upon those sunlit lawns and miniature glades, and that was that.

But we could hardly fail to acknowledge each other's presence somehow. Presently the short fellow and I began a conversation.

"Permit me to introduce myself."

That day I decided to call myself Monsieur (the day was still two months away when all in France were commanded to claim no title but that of Citizen) Corday. That name had not yet become infamous in republican circles, nor famous among monarchists; young Charlotte, who bore it, was not to murder the Revolutionary enthusiast Marat for almost another year.

—but I digress.

"Napoleon Bonaparte, major of artillery," my new acquaintance replied briskly, acknowledging my apparent worthiness with a small bow.

I responded with a similar gesture. "I assume, major, that those Swiss fellows being slaughtered across the street are not—? But no, forgive me, of course they could not possibly be under your command."

I thought that a deep fire indeed had suddenly kindled in his eyes, when he perceived what I was on the verge of suggesting: that any soldiers for whom he was responsible might find themselves so outnumbered and disorganized in the face of the enemy.

This forceful little Major Bonaparte spoke some Italian, but generally conversed in French, accented by his native Corsican dialect.

Once we had opened a conversation, he seemed glad to have an audience for his professional military grumbling about how the Swiss, given proper leadership, ought to have won.

Continuing a desultory conversation with the fellow, I heard him speaking his French and Italian with traces of an uncouth Corsican accent (which at the time I was unable to identify as such), traces that grew stronger when the man became excited, as he certainly did on the night when we first met. His physical stature was unimpressive, though his poise and energy made him seem bigger than he was.

He told me, with an absolute conviction, just how effective a dozen cannon would have been—no, even as few as four or five—only a few hours earlier, in repelling the mob's assault upon the palace and its grounds. He spoke as one assuming an inarguable right to hold a professional opinion in the matter. I soon discovered that my new acquaintance had been in recent months an officer at the front, defending a confused and beleaguered France against an Austrian incursion. Anyone who might doubt my veracity regarding this encounter is advised to consult the history books, which now and then do get things right. It's well documented that Major Bonaparte watched the August 10, 1792, massacre at the palace of the Tuileries from a safe spot—but our spot was not all that safe, nor did he ever stand, as is sometimes claimed, in a shop window.

I can testify—if anyone in my readers' century has lingering doubts—that Napoleon Bonaparte had a very convincing way about him; before I had been with the man five minutes, I was wishing that I had been able to employ him as a general in my old, breathing days, when the command of armies had been one of my chief concerns. Then, as he talked on, my own viewpoint gradually shifted; in another five minutes I was wishing that I could have served in some army under his command.

He told me that he had been in Paris since May, chafing at the delays of the new bureaucracy (at least as capriciously stupid as the old) while being considered by the National Assembly for one post or another, and I believe he mentioned that he was staying at the Hôtel de Cherbourg.

Still, my senses were by far the keener, and suddenly I raised my head. "But it appears that the action is moving on." The bulk of the distant mob was again in motion, fitful and mindless, like a swarm of bees, leaving a litter of mangled bodies in its wake. "Are we to follow?"

He surveyed the scene, hands clasped behind his back, then nodded decisively. "There may be something of value to be learned. If you will follow me, M'sieu Corday?"

~ 9 ~

My new companion had a way of putting questions that made them more compelling than direct orders from any ordinary man.

And I had no reason to decline the invitation. Stubbornly I remained determined not to leave the vicinity of the palace as long as the instinctive feeling persisted that my brother was somewhere nearby. So much spilled blood would have drawn him almost irresistibly, I thought, were he anywhere within miles of the scene. I felt sure Radu was somehow involved in the slaughter going on across the street. Or, if not actually on the scene as yet, he was likely to show up at any moment. I resolved to stay, even if this meant having to risk some sharp discomfort from the sun. If necessary I could get through the remainder of the bright day with the help of my hat and the garden's numerous trees, a great many of which were still sufficiently intact to offer shade.

They were no longer as numerous as they had been, many having been hacked down to satisfy the general appetite for destruction. The gunfire had been desultory for some time, and eventually died away altogether. But the screams of bloodlust and of terror continued sporadically, hour after hour for the rest of the day and even, with lesser frequency, into the night. The Swiss Guards had quickly ceased to exist as a fighting force, and now, for the short balance of their miserable lives, found themselves ideally situated to play the role of victims, scapegoats for several hundred years of oppression in a country few of them had even seen until six months ago.

At this point I believed it possible that the king and queen of France remained in the palace and were hiding with their two children somewhere within that labyrinth of corridors and rooms. Most of the people in Paris still thought so, and earlier in the day most people had been right. But later, by the time I arrived on the scene, the royal family, opting for a kind of protective custody that almost amounted to arrest, had gone to join the Assembly.

As we began to follow the mob, I asked Bonaparte if the royal family were still in residence, and he declared decisively, on what basis I never learned, that they were not.

When I inquired of him, tentatively, if he was a monarchist, he smiled and remarked: "France is less suited for democracy than a good many other countries."

And once Bonaparte felt sure that I was something of an unreconstructed monarchist myself, or at least no agent of the new regime, he related the story of the day's earlier events, as he had been able to piece it together.

In the early morning of that same day, King Louis had felt sufficiently confident in the loyalty of his troops to call them out into the heavily fortified courtyard of the palace for a review. The Swiss Guards cheered him boldly, but the Parisian National Guard, present in greater numbers, were in a sullen mood. Now and then a cry of *"Vive la Nation"* rose from their ranks.

Only a few hours later, serious fighting had broken out.

Napoleon had been able to identify a few of the individuals who played key roles in the day's events.

There was the Marquis de Mandat, commander of the

loyal National Guard—an organization of doubtful loyalty to say the least; there was George Jacques Danton, Revolutionary leader with a massive presence and a booming voice, given to intimidating military commanders; there was the brewer Santerre, and others, each leading his own militia, or some segment of the faceless Mob . . . all in all, there was much confusion. The Swiss Guards were first ordered to fight, and then to fraternize—and then fighting broke out again, after many of the Swiss had apparently discarded their weapons.

I was really not much interested in the political, or even the military, details; we vampires tend to take the long view in such matters, thinking that political trends tend to average out over time, while the more fundamental wellsprings of behavior flow on regardless.

But the young major of artillery who shared my observation post was, unlike most officers of his rank, extremely keen on politics. Also he was obviously in need of someone to talk to. He was not really much upset at the fact that people were being slaughtered; in his chosen profession, that was bound to happen all the time. Human lives were the raw material of his art. But Bonaparte found incompetent leadership in any field intrinsically offensive. Watching that protracted butchery in the gardens, his attitude was that of a great musician being forced to endure a floundering, utterly maladroit performance.

I do not suppose that even Louis, incompetent leader that he was, intended anything like a slaughter of the only loyal supporters he had in sight. No doubt his only thought, in scribbling an order for the Swiss Guards to lay down their arms, was some muddle-headed idea that further loss of life might thereby be prevented . . .

Perhaps it had been the very fact that the Swiss were beginning to retreat that provoked their attackers to such a brutal onslaught. A group of rebellious soldiers from Brest, called *fédérés,* fell in the slaughter along with the loyal guardsmen, simply because the rioters could not distinguish their red uniforms from those of the Swiss. A few who had realized what was happening shed their uniforms in time and got away.

Napoleon and I were afforded the chance to observe some of the high points of the protracted slaughter. But these we endured impatiently, I waiting for some indication of my brother's presence, and Bonaparte thirsting for some event, some sign, that would lend political and moral significance to the whole. Alas, neither of us were afforded any real satisfaction.

On that afternoon the Swiss Guards virtually ceased to exist. They were hunted down by jackal packs of rioters and practically exterminated. Rioters too weak or cowardly to risk an actual fight followed the death squads and stripped and mutilated the fallen. A few arms and legs were actually cut off. Much more popular, as usual, was the trick of slashing off the genitals and stuffing them into the mouth of the same or a different body. (Why *is* this such a favorite ploy, down through the centuries, of breathers who are struggling to be as bad as they can be, and who doubtless each time believe they are being inventive?) In all, some six hundred of the Swiss perished.

Later the events of August tenth were called by Robespierre (who, I am mortally certain, was not on hand to see them) "the most beautiful revolution that has ever honored humanity."

But let me not get ahead of my story. On that August morning, I had not yet met Robespierre, or any of the other leaders—past, present, or future—of the Terror.

Much of the beautiful profusion of shrubbery in the garden had by now been trampled down. There were dead bodies, hundreds of them, piled and scattered under the stately chestnut trees. Some were those of Revolutionaries, part of the ragtag force which had launched the first assault, blown to rags and fragments by the few cannon blasts the Swiss got off before they were ordered to cease firing. But most of the dead were the Swiss Guards. Many of these had been stripped and mutilated, and were strewn about like toys after a children's party. A bonfire had been started, fueled by shredded uniforms and other debris.

As the center of mob activity spasmodically shifted, the outer courtyard and the surrounding gardens were soon occupied only by the dead and a few feebly active wounded. My colleague and I relocated our observation post as well. My thought was that the best place to look for Radu was wherever the most acts of violent dismemberment were taking place.

As for Napoleon, he was no more interested in blood for its own sake than a farmer is fascinated by acres of topsoil, or a sailor by tons of water; but he remained very curious to see how the whole business was going to turn out in political terms. And if there was one thing Bonaparte could not comprehend, it was the utter failure of leadership on the part of royalty. It was all that such people had to do with their lives.

At one point, I remember, Napoleon turned to me and took me by the arm. "If I had been king this morning . . . or if you . . ."

And his words, his manner, conferred upon me a great gift, a sense of glorious comradeship, of goals attainable that were worth dying for, which he seemed to have the means of bestowing, whether or not he was fully conscious of what he gave. It was as if I heard a ghostly trumpet call. "There we agree, my friend. The situation at this hour would be much different."

And we moved a little closer to what was left of the action.

"What fatheads!" he cried. "How could they have suffered this rabble to get close enough to stab them with pitchforks? It would have been perfectly easy to mow down the first four or five hundred with cannon. The rest would still be running."

By this time half of the fierce afternoon had burned away, and I had at last been rewarded by a glimpse of Radu from a distance—wearing a mustache, a red hat, and a few other items that must have been intended to constitute a disguise. But I was fatally familiar with that face—and I could have done much better at concealing my identity from him had our positions been reversed.

I did not think that my brother had caught sight of me, and I hoped that he, absorbed in his enjoyment, would be completely unaware of my presence. It might be possible to take him by surprise . . .

I felt I had once more to trust my survival to the lesser shade of hat and cloak—even though the lowering sun was beginning to come in under my hatbrim—to catch up with the man and get a better look at him.

I invited Napoleon to come with me; I thought Radu would be less alarmed by the sight of a pair of unknown figures approaching than of one only. My brother would be thinking that I would almost certainly be coming after him alone. Also I had begun to be fascinated by this breathing major.

But Bonaparte declined, saying brusquely that observation had become very difficult, and he had business elsewhere. We exchanged the informal salutes of a silent farewell, and he separated himself from me before I actually entered the palace.

As I drew nearer, I moved along the fringe of the mob of victorious rioters. Some were holding pikes from which depended ragged bits of red uniforms and other, gorier trophies. Now I took note of how the walls of the palace had been scarred with musket balls and grapeshot.

As I entered the building through a wide-open servants' entrance, I was greeted by a loud crash of crockery in the huge kitchen adjoining.

I poked in my head and looked around. Inside, everything had been turned topsy-turvy. Everyone was grabbing whatever he or she could manage to grab, some serious about gathering booty, others seeking only souvenirs.

Looking down into the wine cellars I beheld a hundred

soon-to-be-drunken revelers jostling and fighting with each other, each determined to have the first choice of the King's best wine.

Standing at the foot of the great staircase, I looked up at an unstained expanse of marble. It seemed strange to me then that this one area should be entirely free of death, and I have no explanation for it now.

Pink cupids, secure in niches among their rosy clouds, looked down with wide, uncaring eyes from the high, plastered ceilings. Their expressions did not alter when now and then a new scream echoed from the mirrored walls.

I moved on, pausing at intervals to look and listen, my feet despite vampirish reflexes occasionally slipping and sliding in a mixture of wine and blood which anointed the floors of tile and polished wood. Boldly I proceeded into the palace, and then strode through one suite of rooms after another.

It was as true then as it is now, that when a man of robust appearance walks as if he had a right to be where he is, few are going to challenge him.

The main hallway had been newly redecorated with blood, here and there still fresh enough to be bright red.

Up the stairs and into the chapel. Here, as if they had been brought as offerings in some profaning black mass, the dead were piled. The air sang with hungry flies. Some indecipherable mess, oozing blood, had been dumped onto the high altar; in the rear, the organ had been smashed.

No living soul besides myself was present. It seemed to me that I had entered one of those times and places on this earth where the existence of Hell is foreshadowed, as it were, beyond any reasonable doubt. And those are the very places and the times where one is well-advised to seek Radu.

Here and there a few candles were simply burning in their holders, flames wavering no more than usual with drafts, their light glinting on a thousand facets of silver as if this were a dinner party. I wondered who had lighted these tapers and set them out, and wondered more that no serious fires had yet started.

In the front of the chapel a well-dressed man was standing in the pulpit, blowing on a horn, and it took me a moment to realize that he was imitating the Angel of the Resurrection. In front of him had gathered a small applauding crowd.

(Radu, where are you?)

But my esteemed sibling was nowhere to be found.

I looked and listened carefully. Some inner sense kept nagging me that Radu was not very far away. And in a long life I had learned that it was usually wise to trust my inner senses.

Now and then some scream of special shrillness burst out loud enough to be heard above the background roar—in my experience, Hell is seldom silent. Fresh cries of agony burst forth when some poor wretch who had been hiding was discovered and dragged out to death.

Two unarmed men—who yesterday, to judge by their clothing, had both been laborers—were fighting tooth and nail, sobbing and gasping in their rage, over a hoard of small coins spilled on the floor from God knew where. Might this trove have represented the eight-year-old Dauphin's childish exercise in greed? Now neither of the robbers was able to pick up a single sou without the other striking it from his hand.

Hundreds of vases, dishes, pieces of statuary, vast mirrors had been smashed to fragments. Half a dozen young girls, part of the invading mob, were haggling and quarreling over the remains of what might have been the Queen's cosmetics.

Their voices rose in fishwife clamor, and they seemed on the verge of hair-pulling and of blows.

In rapid succession I visited the Council Room, and then the Billiard Room. It was the same story everywhere, some apartments ruined and deserted, others still crowded with the many bodies of the Mob, staying near one another as if they feared that separation could cost them their vital madness.

In the dining room, one man, happy with his day's work, was eating jam with his lady friend, the two of them laughing as they smeared the red stuff on each other's faces. Another, enacting the role of a servant, laughing like a madman all the while, was handing out neatly folded napkins to his unwashed comrades and delicately filling their wineglasses. Someone had been using the table linen to clean and test the sharpness of a bloodstained sword.

Well, no one was going to be washing and mending these tablecloths tomorrow. All that I heard and saw assured me that any servants who had not joined the mob were going to be murdered as the lackeys of aristocrats.

Other people were methodically smashing plates and glasses. A very young but ugly woman had bared her breasts, and was dancing wildly on a table to music that she alone could hear. A man with a pot of honey and a spoon in hand stood in front of her, trying to attract her attention.

I pushed on, having forgotten for the time being my recent new acquaintance outside. Now and then someone bumped into me, took a look into my face, and moved on. I patiently proceeded.

Here was the doorway to what I realized must have been the Queen's private suite of rooms. The way was partially blocked by a row of dead bodies wrapped in sheets and blankets. Such a neat enshroudment must have taken place earlier in the day, when some tidy-minded members of the household staff had still had time to worry about the dead.

Inside the Queen's rooms, more women of all ages were ransacking the wardrobe of Marie Antoinette, trying on hats and bonnets. Nearby stood a piano, violently bereft of ivory keys, steel strings pulled out and broken. A bust of the young Dauphin, which must have been on the piano, now lay on the floor, chipped and soiled.

Poor Marie Antoinette! Not that I ever met her, but I doubt she meant anyone any harm, no more than her husband did. There is no shred of evidence, you know, that she ever really said it: I mean of course the famous quote about letting the poor eat cake if they could find no bread.

> *Ah! ça ira, ça ira, ça ira,*
> *Les aristocrates à la lanterne . . .*

So it goes, so it goes, so it goes. To the nearest lamppost with those damned aristocrats, and hang them high. The ragged chorus dissolved in incoherent noise. Other musical instruments had been smashed also.

(Radu, where are you? Surely you, as inevitably as the million flies, will be drawn to this scene.)

"Hey! You, there!"

The roar of triumph had come from behind me. I thought that the voice of Satan was in that noise. Turning, I beheld the speaker. He was advancing on me, a massive, archetypal figure in a red cap, clad in the rags and wooden shoes of a homeless Parisian, wearing the apron of his trade and waving a butcher's cleaver. Having established eye contact, I raised my eyebrows and slightly shook my head, trying to convey the idea that it would do him no good to pursue me further.

Normally when I attempt to communicate an idea of this kind I am successful. But not this time. Try to be kind, as folk in the twentieth century are wont to say, and see where it gets you. The man with the cleaver was all enfevered by the carnage surrounding him; he had me cornered, and plainly he was determined not to be cheated of his fun. No doubt in my hat and cloak I did look like some simpleton's idea of an aristocrat attempting to disguise his appearance.

My righteous butcher, armed with unshakable faith in his own strength and aflame with revolutionary zeal, was at least correct about one thing: He had me cornered, as it was still daylight. Denied the choice of disappearing into nothingness, or of turning into some four-legged or winged beast, I had no really convenient option other than to stand my ground.

As the cleaver slashed toward my head, I plucked it from his grip and threw it away. A moment later I had seized one-handed the neck of that great cockroach and, with bone-cracking force, smashed his surprised face into the elegant wall paneling.

On that afternoon in that particular palace no one paid much attention to a little more blood here and there. In fact, I had thought that no one in the rooms nearby was paying any attention at all, or I would have chosen a less dramatic method of pest eradication. My meatcutter's body slid easily down the wall and blended into the similar litter on the floor. Briefly I considered claiming his red cap as the spoils of war, to serve me as protective coloration. But alas, it was already too late for that.

Unhappily my disposal of this vermin, which might well have gone unnoticed amid the general uproar and carnage, had instead attracted the attention of several additional aristocrat-hunters, no less eager than the first. They were now shouting at me from an adjoining room. These folk I hoped to be able to avoid by retreating into the upper levels of the palace, where I expected to find mostly servants' rooms.

Kind fortune discovered to me a narrow stair, formerly a path for unobtrusive servants, which went up inconspicuously within the thickness of a wall. I took this path, and no one immediately followed me. For a minute or two I was able to hope that my pursuers would be distracted, but so determined were they that at last I judged it wise to climb out of one window and up a more or less sheer wall into another one, following a route that few if any breathing opponents could have managed, and none at all if they were carrying weapons.

Things were going on much the same upon the floor above, except that there were fewer people. On impulse, throwing open the doors in a large cupboard in hopes of discovering one of Radu's breathing helpers, I found instead first one terrified servant of the royal household and then another, a pair who had been hiding from the mob. When I appeared they were convinced that their last hour had come, and began entreating me in the most disgusting terms for mercy.

Bah. I shut their whimpering, howling faces and stinking bodies—they had already soiled themselves in fear—back up inside their closet. Whether they ultimately survived or not I have to this day no idea, but I suppose their chances were rather good, as the hunters were more interested in me.

Once or twice in my prolonged and convoluted passage through the ruined palace, I had observed signs which it would have been possible to interpret as evidence of Radu's passage, things to indicate that he had proceeded me along this route, stopping to take his debased pleasures where and when he chose. For example, here and there a body showed evidence of more than ordinarily fiendish torture. But with atrocity on every hand, it would have been difficult even for him to distinguish himself in this company.

I had just begun to feel that my stubborn pursuers had given up, when one of them again caught sight of me in the distance, down a long vista of corridor, and raised a cry. I cursed and dodged out of sight, but here they came after me again, pounding on door after door and pausing at a couple of locked ones to break them down. These artistic palatial doors were not stout enough to require a great deal of effort. Five years ago, only madmen had dreamed of a mob that would one day be treading these exquisitely parqueted and tiled floors, seeking the blood of the oppressors of the poor.

Fortunately for my patience, and for their own lives, none of those now looking for me ever quite managed to catch up. But neither was I successful in picking up the trail of my own quarry.

*   *   *

Thus it was that I, Vlad Dracula, spent the waning hours of that memorable afternoon barricaded in one of the highest rooms of the palace. From that sanctuary, up near the roof, I contemplated the beauties of the sky and waited for nightfall. Meanwhile I listened to distant music and laughter, screams and curses.

> *Ah! ça ira, ça ira, ça ira,*
> *Les aristocrates à la lanterne . . .*

Before the last verse of the day's last performance of the *carmagnole* had faded into silence—a silence very like that of the grave—I had time to contemplate at some length the strange behavior of the human race.

At last the sun went down, and my nature underwent its usual diurnal change, which allowed me to make my escape by flying out a window. It was pure joy to put aside for a time the outward form of humanity, and to abandon my small, winged body to the enveloping peace of the upper air.

~ *10* ~

After my futile attempt in August of 1792 to come to grips with my brother at the palace of the Tuileries, I departed from Paris, called away by matters which have little to do with the subjects of this chronicle. Suffice to say that for a year or more I was traveling, mostly out of France. Of course during this period my closest blood relative was never far from my thoughts, and now and then news reached me, indirectly, of some of his activities. Apparently he had chosen to remain in France, drawn like a moth to the Revolutionary flame. There was a report that Radu had taken to frequenting lunatic asylums, recruiting disciples among some of the inmates.

Not that the folk outside those walls seemed a great deal saner. Six months after the Tuileries, in February of '93, all of Europe learned that Louis Capet, formerly king of France, had been guillotined like a common criminal.

In July of that year, the Revolutionary propagandist Marat was assassinated, made a martyr in the eyes of his fellow enthusiasts; he was stabbed in his bath by Charlotte Corday, whose pretty head was separated from her body by Sanson a few days later. On 16 October, Marie Antoinette followed her once-royal husband to the scaffold.

By the time of my return to Paris in the spring of 1794, when I was once more free to concentrate upon my problems with Radu, the French Revolution was entering its most acute phase. The infection known as the Terror was building to its most feverish height, before it reached its sudden climax in the Revolutionary month of Thermidor.

One of the events which drew me back to France at just that time was the news which had reached me concerning a gathering of vampires, which was soon to be held there.

Simultaneously with word of this gathering there came to my ears an indirect communication from Radu. His emissary proposed, in his name, that we two brothers should take advantage of the conclave to discuss a truce.

Treachery on Radu's part was of course the first idea that sprang to mind when I received this news. Yet at the same time—perhaps I was tired—I allowed myself to toy with the idea that it might after all be possible to come to some agreement with Radu, to reach an armistice if not conclude a peace. Foolishly I allowed myself to be tempted by the notion that my brother and I might be able to coexist, however uneasily, in the world.

Constantia too had evidently been invited to the gathering, or at least had learned about it, and for old time's sake she found a way to let me know.

A hundred years earlier, the protracted feud between the brothers Dracula had been the subject of much gossip in the small community of European *nosferatu;* now the subject was waxing popular once again. In general our colleagues found it vastly entertaining, if now and then a little worrisome.

One or two of the newer members of the club, though they had recently met Radu, had never heard of me at all. Or they had heard vague tales of Prince Dracula (the peak of whose international fame, literary and otherwise, still lay far in the future) but took it for granted that Radu was the only member of the family to bear that title, the only Dracula still alive (or "undead," if you prefer), and had always been the only one of any importance.

Radu had been giving intense consideration to the problem of recruiting people, preferably people of proven capabilities, to help him defeat his brother. In the end, as far as I could piece the facts together, he thought it best to try to intrigue them with the idea of a kind of hunt. He seems to have described the upcoming effort as a kind of sporting event—it would be fun, and not very dangerous, to track down the cowardly Vlad (whose reputation, he assured them, was based on falsehood!) and torment him or kill him. How well Radu succeeded in this effort we shall see.

I may digress for a moment to remark that now at the time of writing, as the twentieth century jitters unpredictably toward its close, the study of vampire populations still offers a fertile field of investigation, though (I admit we ourselves are partly to blame) facts are often hard to come by. An investigator of a scientific turn of mind might endeavor to calculate our probable longevity in terms of half-lives; in using that word I am not speaking of some supposed twilight existence of the undead, but adopting a scientific concept which is most commonly applied to the heavy nuclei of radioactive atoms. A population of such atoms is said to have a half-life of one thousand years, if its numbers are diminished by fifty percent after the passage of that measure of time. And in the Europe of two centuries ago, I now compute that the half-life of the *nosferatu* as a group was more than two centuries.

Certainly the scholarly movement, which came to be known as the Enlightenment, sweeping across Europe in the last half of the eighteenth century, had brought some decline of belief in our existence, at least among the self-considered intellectual elite—though not nearly as great a falling-off in supernatural terror as was produced a century later by the widespread adoption of the electric light.

* * *

While still perhaps two hundred yards away from the small group which was already gathered for the meeting, I could recognize the voice of Radu. No mistaking it, though he was speaking quietly and his mellow tones had not graced my ears for many decades. My flesh crept—no, I am not a total stranger to that sensation—with a premonition of evil. I listened, paying close attention, as I drew nearer. My brother was engaged in telling a small assembly of our colleagues his version of our family history—a lively chronicle in very truth, though perhaps not as extravagant as his tales would have made it—in an effort to enlist their support against his brother.

The answers given by the group were skeptical and not particularly enthusiastic. Only one of the other voices was that of a vampire I had met before.

Nodding to myself, I paused before joining the small assembly, to take thought, weighing the several possible ways in which its members might react to my presence, which to some of them would be totally unexpected. Much would depend on how much progress Radu had already made in winning them to his cause. And then, having made some preliminary decisions, I moved forward again.

Certain students of our miniature society have wondered why I appeared at this secret gathering of vampires in the traditional clothing of a French priest—wearing a black soutane, which is a cassock, along with the traditional buckled shoes and a black broad-brimmed hat. My reasons for this choice of dress were personal; I did not explain them to anyone at the time, nor do I consider it my duty to account for them now. It was not the first time I had worn such an outfit, and several explanations have been suggested, among which the reader may take her/his choice. The simplest may be that a clerical identity made certain things easier when one moved in society—or at least that was how things had worked in France before the Terror got under way in earnest.

Others have speculated that Vlad Dracula was wearing a cassock and a black priest's hat on that night as a gesture of defiance, simply because the Revolutionary government had forbidden such apparel, at the same time as it required all priests to take an oath of loyalty to the new government.

There is even one quite romantic, chivalric interpretation, to the effect that I had disguised myself as a priest in the hope of giving a certain real priest, whom I knew to be a worthy man, a better chance of getting away from his *sans-culotte* pursuers, who were determined to deprive him of either his sworn loyalty to God, or of his life. I can imagine those unfortunate fellows discovering, too late to help them, that they were chasing down Vlad Dracula instead; and like a varied assortment of rascals before and since, they were not to profit by the exercise . . . but the reader may take his choice.

I did not really expect to be challenged when I arrived at the meeting, but I was.

Even as I neared the door, I was formally commanded to present some ancient password to a young vampire-sentry.

"Who told you of our gathering?"

The question was asked in tones of a childish suspicion, and from one of my age and accomplishments it deserved no answer. I tilted back my head and raised two open hands toward the sky, like one calling upon the heavens to witness some phenomenon beyond mere human comprehension.

Though my vampirism ought to have been obvious enough to any of my colleagues, I did not necessarily consider myself slighted by the fact of being challenged—it was part of an old and honored ritual. I had an ample supply of passwords, in many languages.

For several minutes I had already been aware of my brother's presence in the small group ahead. From where I now stood, I could hear six beating hearts but only one set of breathing lungs.

Shortly before I entered the room—a chapel long-profaned, though only recently abandoned by its breathing owners, located a level or two above the ground floor of the ruined castle—with all my senses tuned to full alertness, I became aware that the breathing lungs were small organs working shallowly and rapidly. Their owner was at the far end of the chamber, behind some angle of stonework and as yet invisible to me.

I gave the password almost absentmindedly, without making an issue of the challenge. My attention and my thoughts were now focussed almost exclusively on my brother.

Each of us solemnly assured the other that he was looking well.

As I made my entrance, the group of five or six vampires, men and women, young and old, was deep in discussion; this came to an abrupt halt, and I suspected its subject would be likely to affect me directly. I did not need to hear much to know that Radu was actively attempting to enlist their aid in his war against his brother.

A silence fell.

Quietly I entered the darkened room, and Constantia, rather proudly as I thought, introduced me to the small handful of those who had known me only as a name. I was glad to see my old companion—in her breathing days my lover—present at this gathering, though I knew better than to depend on her for any support in a crisis. The former gypsy girl was in fact one of the senior members of this group, though she looked as young and beautiful as ever.

Constantia had come to the meeting dressed up in a long gown of rich fabric that had certainly never belonged to peasant girl or *sans-culotte*. She wore it with a natural grace.

She alone among those present, besides Radu, could testify absolutely to my true identity. She had in fact been present at my first emergence from my first grave—another story I have told elsewhere.

"Vlad Dracula, Prince of Wallachia."

All the group save Radu and Constantia were strangers

to me. I had the feeling of one who had neglected his social obligations and fallen out of touch. Constantia introduced the others, one by one, and I bowed slightly at each name. They were of a wide range of ages, and some bore names I recognized. It was not exactly the sort of gathering I had been hoping for; there were none I would have chosen for my associates.

To Radu I remarked: "You appear to have rested well since our last meeting. Did you enjoy a satisfying sleep?"

"I feel quite refreshed, thank you," Radu responded. "Quite energetic."

"Would it be impolite of me to inquire how all this energy is going to be employed?"

The stone-arched room before me was high and narrow, not big enough to accommodate many more than the lord of the manor and his immediate family at their devotions. Though partially roofless, on that night it was by breathers' standards very dark, which mattered little, because none of those on hand for the meeting needed much light to see. In that old room, redolent of remembered prayers, the very walls still reeking faintly of old incense, the eyes of a breathing human would have picked out only ghosts of illumination entering by the tall windows, where only fragments of stained glass still remained, making an irregular rim and corners.

Down in the empty cellars and across the occasionally moonlit floors of the old house, rats and mice went scurrying here and there, going about their murine business, accepting vampires as one more fact of life, no more and no less incomprehensible to mice than so many breathing farmers, or tax-collectors, would have been. And spiders, progressing in their eight-fold strides so swift and light that even I needed to strain my ears to pick them up.

And there, standing in the midst of the little gathering, was my beautiful, beautiful brother, beautifully dressed for the meeting in silks and furs, in the style of a century long gone. As our eyes met at last, Radu stood silent for a moment, trying to be aristocratically impassive, and almost succeeding—but I could see that he was afraid.

Was he on that evening a little taller than I, or a little shorter? I find it difficult to remember. In the course of his adult life, Radu has been both. As usual, more slender. Quite young in appearance, as always. Almost always. I sometimes think that Radu would rather die than let himself be seen in public with an aged face, gray hair, or wrinkled, sagging skin at his throat and on the backs of his hands. In vampires these phenomena tend to come and go, largely dependent on the vagaries of diet, and to me they are generally matters of indifference.

In this company of our peers—if that is the right word for them—neither of us felt quite secure enough to move decisively against the other.

Radu faced me solemnly. "Vlad, we have been enemies long enough."

I took time to gather my thoughts before replying. "What do you propose?"

"We are brothers, after all. I have sworn an oath to give you no more cause to hate me."

"You? Have sworn?"

"Upon our father's grave," he proclaimed in a clear, convincing voice, meanwhile raising his right hand. "There is nothing that I hold more sacred."

"Bah! I doubt that you even know where it is."

He looked nobly sad. Chagrined at this rebuff, but still determined to make himself my friend. "I suppose it's only to be expected that you would not believe me. Nevertheless, I have sworn."

My brother's face was no longer disfigured by the mustache I had glimpsed at the Tuileries on the tenth of August. He would not choose to wear that appearance in this company, nor did I choose to mention our near-meeting then. Nor, of course, was he wearing now either the red cap or the *carmagnole*.

It so happened that I was now the one in disguise. On seeing me, one of Radu's friends made some harsh jest about the soutane, asking when I had taken holy orders, and a little later inquired whether I intended to say mass.

I gazed at him steadily. "I dislike jesting about sacred matters."

The vampire who had spoken fell silent, blinking, not knowing what to make of that dead-serious reply.

"Vlad has had just cause to be upset with me." Radu was musing aloud. His demeanor was that of one inclined to be forgiving. "In fact I sometimes fear that he might even nerve himself one day to make a serious attempt upon my life." Radu turned to our peers and colleagues, wistfully inviting their understanding.

"Do not tempt me," I growled softly.

Throughout the course of this dialogue, our peers and colleagues were looking at me thoughtfully, and I could see that most of them were not quite able to reconcile the figure I presented with the one they had been forming in their minds, based on Radu's description.

"So, this is the famous Prince of Wallachia?" one demanded suddenly.

Having answered that question with regard to myself, if I thought it deserved a straight answer, I now repeated it, turning it on Radu.

"Thou knowest who is famous and who is not."

My brother, it gradually became clear to me as I listened, had been telling these potential recruits to his cause that *he* was the one who had nailed the turbans of the sultan's envoys to their heads. (Remind me to tell you about that, another time). He, the prince who had so thoroughly terrorized the potential criminal elements that a merchant's bag of gold could lie untouched in the streets all night—but that story I have told elsewhere.

At least Radu had been making those outrageous claims before I arrived. Constantia, who had been listening to them, knew better, and Radu of course realized this; but he also knew that she was not going to contradict him.

The subject which had been under discussion before my arrival was soon taken up again: the recent shocking events of the Revolution, and how the profound changes taking place in the breathers' society were going to affect their lives. Opinions were divided on the probable effect of these attacks upon the Church. The consensus was that almost any change was likely to be for the worse—a truer, more spiritually active church would not be a good thing for the villains in the group.

One of them wondered, with a languid laugh, whether under the new regime aristocrats among the *nosferatu* might be called to account for drinking the blood of the unwilling. I had gathered from the speaker's previous remarks that he was planning a dreadful vengeance on his peasants, who in their ignorance were congratulating themselves on having, as they thought, burned the lord of the manor alive.

Eyes of divers colors, set in a variety of pallid faces, turned in my direction. Some, no doubt, were not impressed with what they saw. Well, it was not my purpose to appear impressive.

One asked: "And what does our most recent arrival have to say upon the subject?"

I was reluctant to comment on the Revolution, except to say that the lower classes were not without rights—as long as they chose to exercise them.

"How do the Americans put it now—we are all 'endowed by our Creator with certain inalienable rights'? In this the peasants of France are remarkably like everyone else. Including us."

My words were met with a largely uncomprehending silence.

~ *11* ~

From the moment of my entry I had been aware that the company had already been enjoying some refreshment. The remnants of some *hors d'oeuvres* were in fact scattered about, as I soon noticed: fragments of a few small human bodies, quite freshly dismembered, none more than three years old. When the bones are young enough and tender—so I am told—chewing by certain ruthless and discriminating connoisseurs extracts from them an essence composed largely of the blood-manufacturing cells which they contain.

One of the infants' lifeless bodies was in plain sight, and still recognizable for what it was. The soft, small bones had been crushed between vampires' teeth and sucked dry. The floor was stained by a few small drops of fresh blood, wasted by some careless gourmet.

The delicate peak of flavor, as I have heard from vampires who pride themselves upon their epicurean tastes, begins to fade into a steep decline almost instantly at death. For the true aficionado, only the cells of the living body will do.

Constantia, catching my eye, shook her head slightly in a gesture of almost prim disapproval. Knowing my own poor opinion of such cannibalistic behavior, she desired to express her sympathy. Politeness, or her idea thereof, had perhaps kept her from stating any forceful objection, beyond merely declining to partake, when the recent snacks had been brought forth and offered round. I did not think it altogether beyond the bounds of possibility that she might have been persuaded to join Radu and his colleagues in their appetizer. For my own peace of mind, I never questioned her on the matter.

But, as I have already indicated, the supply of treats was not yet exhausted. The single set of operating lungs, whose presence I had noted upon arrival, now sharply drew in air, filling themselves for a desperate effort. A small heart raced. There was a stir of motion in a far corner of the long room. The child who was to be the last *hors d'œuvre* (she had hardly blood enough to provide the main course for such a gathering as this) was a small girl of five or six (thoughtfully provided by Radu? One of his colleagues thanked him for the treat), who had evidently been kept immobilized, by hypnotically enhanced fear, at the far side or end of the room.

It was soon quite clear to me that the child had mistaken my black-garbed figure for that of a priest—her eyes must have been quite well adapted to the dark by this time. She uttered a cry of desperation and came running barefoot, in her small ragged dress, to clasp both arms about the waist of the deceptively familiar figure of the newcome vampire, appealing to him in a shrill wordless cry for help.

Naturally this outburst attracted the attention of the company. One of Radu's less mature companions giggled, as a normal human might at some bizarre behavior on the part of a dog or cat; the rest reacted only in an abstracted way, even as their attention might have been drawn to a chicken bursting out of some breather's kitchen and scampering a half-winged progress across the floor. Even Constantia, I could see, was no more moved by the victim's anguished effort to escape than she would have been by the squawking of some barnyard fowl.

But I, Vlad Dracula, regarded the event quite differently. The longer I lived, the less it seemed to me that human children and chickens ought to be considered on the same level—regarding human adults I am not always so sure—and I felt constrained to honor such an appeal. Even if considerations of honor could have been set aside, the innocent but ardent contact awakened in me something that had been sleeping, perhaps for centuries. No doubt it may surprise some of my hearers now, to reflect that there had been a time when Prince Dracula's own offspring had embraced him so.

The others, except for Constantia and Radu himself, both of whom had known me for centuries, were much surprised to observe my reaction.

Listening to Radu talk, one might assume that he had never been a father. Of course I knew that, in a biological sense at least, that was not true.

Besides, though I would not have chosen this time to force a confrontation with Radu, I was not going to retreat from one. And it crossed my mind that, even leaving aside all considerations of honor, to postpone indefinitely the devouring of this particular little girl would be quite certain to irritate my brother immensely. So much for attempting to reach an accommodation.

With this in mind, I lifted the desperate child gently into my arms. Her hands clutched at my black robe briefly, but as her head came down upon my shoulder I could feel the small body express, in a long shudder, the end of its capacity to struggle. In the next moment its muscles all relaxed, in a total surrender of consciousness to exhaustion. Small mind and childish body had done all that they could do, to achieve their own survival.

My peers—if that is not too generous a term for them—watched this act in silence.

Meeting one curious set of eyes after another, I remarked: "I see now that all the talk about a truce was foolishness, and I do not intend to remain here long. Is there any business under discussion here that might affect my future welfare? If so, it would be courteous of you to let me hear it."

The members of the group exchanged looks among themselves. But as a group they could not agree upon an answer; and as individuals they were silent.

Now I concentrated my gaze upon Radu. "No doubt my brother will let me know if any important decisions on such matters are taken after my departure. His welfare and my own are very closely bound together."

Receiving no better reply from Radu than from the others, I turned to leave.

At that point another vampire, one of the younger men who did not know me very well even by reputation—in fact the one who had originally challenged me—moved to block my way.

I turned an inquiring gaze upon this human obstacle, and I have no doubt that my dark eyes expressed a keen and compassionate interest in his welfare.

The youth—my interlocutor's age was certainly under a century—was not easily deterred. "Where do you think you're going with our snack? If you are hungry, there are rats in plenty to be caught." Of course the implication that I fed on rats—which I would not dispute; I strive for a balanced diet— was meant to be insulting.

"No doubt you are mistaken, m'sieu. Your snack is probably scuttling around in the cellar at this moment, on six legs. But it is not an insect that I carry here, nor even a chicken or a rat. It is a human child. Perhaps you remember the existence of such a species. The girl, as you saw, desired to place herself under my protection. I have accepted the responsibility."

The stripling who confronted me looked over his shoulder as if inviting some comment on my speech. But none of the others, including Radu, had moved or had any comment to make. They were watching prudently to see how he might fare.

At last he faced me again, his limited intellect laboring to find a suitable rejoinder. Eventually he came up with: "What is that to me?"

I shrugged. I was cradling the girl in my left arm, and my free right hand dangled loosely. "It need not mean very much to you at all. But as to that, the choice lies in your hands."

He shook his head. Honor and logic and responsibility were all alien concepts to this man. It was as if I had been addressing him in Arabic or Swahili; all he could gather from my speech was the elementary fact that I opposed him.

He raised his voice a little. "I say the morsel you have there is ours. What do we care about what responsibility you accept or—?" and, even as he spoke, he began to reach out an incautious hand.

Since my words had not sufficed to obtain passage, I judged this a good opportunity to test how efficiently I could administer a minute dose of one of the less subtle Borgia potions, and what its effect would be upon the nerves and bones and bloodstream of one of the lesser *nosferatu,* such as he who stood in my way.

The nail of my right forefinger was suddenly an inch longer than it had been an instant earlier. Its sturdy thickness, and the sharpness of its point, were quite sufficient to let it stab through garments and through flesh, to scrape bone, and probe toward a certain nerve.

The fact was that before coming to the meeting, I had prudently equipped myself with a few vials of the dear Lucrezia's favorite chemicals (almost three hundred years in storage had rather mellowed them, but hardly decreased their potency), thinking they might come in handy the next time Radu and I should meet.

I had wanted to make sure, also, before using them on my brother, that those venerable toxins were unlikely to kill a vampire. No use trying to test it on an animal—no animal had the mental and spiritual power to attain the *nosferatu* state.

My knowledge of anatomy was precise. The one who had found the concept of responsibility so utterly alien managed a shrill cry for help as he went staggering and slumping back, knocking over an item or two of the room's sparse furniture in his uncontrolled passage. He drew a shuddering breath, as if preparing to cry out again, and then he fell down heavily. He was kicking and writhing aimlessly, but I thought he probably would not die.

No one was rushing to his defense.

Critically I regarded his twitching form; for more than a decade I had been endeavoring to find a suitable opportunity to test the stuff, and I was well satisfied with the result. He would survive—I thought. It is not so easy as all that to stop the *nosferatu* heart.

Then I swung my gaze back to the others. I like to think that there was an engaging twinkle in my eye. "Does anyone else have anything to discuss with me?"

But all my remaining hearers had drawn back a step or two, and all were silent.

Radu, standing in their midst, began an urgent, almost inaudible muttering, trying to excite them into taking some group action to stop me. But his efforts were unavailing. After the demonstration they had just seen, they were too cautious—as was, of course, Radu himself.

My small companion and I remained unmolested as I climbed aboard my horse. We had proceeded on our way for a hundred moonlit yards or so, and I was sure that no one had yet followed us, before I whispered to her: "It seems that you had fallen in with some folk there who were no better than they should be."

Of course I really expected no response, and there came none, save for a tighter clutching of the arms. The girl still slept. Swift, light breath puffed against my cheek. Her tiny maiden's heart had slowed, its rhythm re-entering the normal range for a breather of her age and size. Now moonlight showed me the presence of a pulse just at the deep curve of her throat, under skin unbroken as yet by any fang-marks. I examined her minutely to make sure. There had been as yet no sampling of this treat.

I touched her throat just at that spot myself, but with my lips alone. And having done so, I sat back in the saddle, pondering the mysteries of my own heart, which I was far from understanding.

We rode on our way unchallenged, and within a quarter of an hour arrived at a country crossroads, the intersection of two rutted moonlit tracks beneath which I could dimly sense the ancient graves of two of my own kind. Long ago the true death had established its claim upon them.

Around us the panorama of farms and villages and woods was quiet, town folk and peasants alike slumbering and dreaming, some quite peacefully. It might have been some calm land in a fairy tale, dwelling in peace, yet to hear from its challenging monsters and rescuing prince. How fortunate those good people, if they could tell one from the other!

But now I judged it was time for me to wake my companion, a task I accomplished as gently as I could. When her bright eyes were open, I asked: "Do you know, little one, which way your village lies from here? Your house?"

After the child had inspected the three roads available, omitting of course the way that we had come, I was rewarded with a pointing finger.

When we had proceeded in the indicated direction for perhaps another quarter of a mile, I judged it safe to stop at least briefly.

At this point I dismounted and sent my horse away, relying upon a certain knack of communication with animals that I enjoy. I intended to regain the animal later, but meanwhile it would create a false trail to deceive the one (at least) who, I expected, would be impelled out of sheer vindictiveness to follow me.

But something far more important, namely my oath-taking, had now been brought into the situation. Vital to me, because I am what I am. And of great significance to Radu, because of what it meant to me.

The child had become a pawn in the deadly game we brothers played, but she was still a child. And I realized that in putting on the garments of a priest I had accepted a certain responsibility.

"What is your name, little one? Come, you are safe for the time being, you can tell me." The question kept her from falling back to sleep. Gently I rocked her, as her mother might have done. Yes, I have told you that I have been a father; and you might consider the incontestable fact, strange as it may seem, that I was once a child myself. My manner and voice were as soothing as I knew how to make them, and the immediate cause of terror had been left behind. I thought that the speaking of her name might be of some assistance in my seeing her to safety, and causing her trail to vanish.

Around us the night was very quiet, the loudest sound a gentle susurration of insects. The path behind us was untrodden, at the moment, by anything more dangerous than a mouse; the air above the fields and forest flowed undisturbed by the flight of anything larger than a bird or natural bat.

With a little more coaxing, my small client produced a distinct word: "Marie." It was so softly breathed into the night, I needed vampire's ears to hear.

"A pretty name indeed. And where am I to discover your house, Marie? Your Mama and Papa?"

Another whispered name. Presently we moved on again, in the direction of that village.

When we had reached what I considered a safe distance from my deranged colleagues, I exerted some hypnotic power to ease the child's mind of the most corrosive residue of fear, the memories of what had already happened to her, so that her agitated trembling almost—almost—ceased, and the nightmares that would otherwise have soon arrived to murder months of sleep were drained of most of their capacity to hurt.

A quarter of an hour later, I felt confident that she had regained her essential sanity, and was almost beginning to feel at ease within the circle of my arm, though of course terror had established a foothold that years of peace would be required to eradicate. By now we were within the boundaries of the village, just outside her house. A neighbor's dogs were moved by my close presence to begin to bark, but from a distance I tranquilized the yapping pups, so that after a brief outburst only a querulous whine went trailing into silence.

To expunge from my small client's inner mind and soul the whole burden of fear associated with the incident would not have been wise, even had it been possible.

And after taking thought, I removed from around my own neck a certain holy medal, marked with a cross (Ah, are you astonished yet again? Remember that in my breathing years I did endow five monasteries.) and other symbols, and having this hidden virtue: of making the wearer impossible to locate by any of the darker arts—remind me to tell you the story, sometime, of how, in a vastly different time and place, I had happened to come into possession of such a thing of virtue—and hung it on its silken cord around the child's neck, athwart those silken veins and gently pulsing arteries. No doubt, I thought, her parents would soon take notice of the addition, she would tell them that the priest had given it to her, and they would suffer her to retain it.

But having come so far, Marie was reluctant to leave my guardianship—to cross, alone, the last few yards of darkness before the door of the small peasant house. That building's windows were glowing with late lamplight, and its interior was wakeful with the murmur of anxious parental voices, disputing between themselves in prayerful agony as to whether there was anything to be done now to try to regain their missing child.

She still felt safer clinging close to me than running to the house. But this condition lasted only until we were close enough to her home for her to hear the voices. Then without another word, she suddenly let go my hand and darted forward, raising a wordless cry. Cries of relief, soon turning to anger, came out of the abruptly opened door and glowing windows. There followed the sound of a sharp slap, and a child's outraged scream. Parental voices were bellowing their hoarse anger and relief.

By that time I was already in full, silent retreat, four-footed in wolf-form, and many yards away. My thoughts were already turning back to my problems with Radu.

But not entirely. For a long time afterward, I could still feel on my right hand, in a kind of tactile afterimage, the grip of five small fingers.

~ *12* ~

I was soon to learn, the hard way, that my brother—who proved much better-organized than I had given him credit for—was rather skillfully arranging an intense vampire hunt, for which purpose he had recruited both *nosferatu* and breathing helpers. The former included some of those who had been in attendance at the meeting.

Very few people in the world had ever been able to do a better job than Radu of frightening and bullying people—and I am thinking now of the kind of people generally considered to be terrifying characters in their own right. But it is fortunate for me that he himself was hunting elsewhere when one of the party of his allies, under lesser leadership, had success.

Radu mercilessly drove his adherents, playing on their own fear and bloodlust, to track me down, then to take me by surprise, if possible, while sleeping in one of my French earths, and to kill me on the spot without allowing me to regain consciousness.

The second-best alternative, from the hunters' point of view, would be to harry me out of the earth and then dispose of me aboveground.

Of course their task was facilitated by the fact that I had given away my talisman, possession of which would have greatly reduced their chances of locating me by magic. But their job was made more difficult by the fact that Radu himself was prudently staying home.

Later, Constantia told me that as soon as she became aware of this effort, she had tried to warn me but had been unable to locate me in time. Also, according to her account, she had undertaken to organize countermeasures among the vampire population who did not like Radu. But I am afraid that her attempt must have been rather tentative.

She frankly admitted also that she was terribly afraid of Radu, and to try to ingratiate herself with me harked back to those long-ago days of our first meeting, when I had been a most junior and uncertain vampire and she a breathing gypsy girl.

I smiled at the memory, and nodded. "As a girl you were delightful, but as a magician you were . . . shall I say, not among the most effective I have ever met."

Ever proud of what she considered to be her magical powers, she responded with a gamine's grimace. "I have learned something over the years."

"No doubt you have. Tell me, Constantia, my little gypsy—what is the great attraction of the truly dead for the seekers of occult power? In cemetery after cemetery I have seen . . . but never mind."

Unlike the breathing populace of France, unlike the rest of Europe for that matter, our little community—if that is not too strong a word—had among us no First, Second, and Third Estates. Nobility, clergy, and commoners were all represented in our ranks, and among these disparate components something like a rudimentary democracy had taken shape long before Paine or Jefferson or Franklin made their first political statements—centuries before Marat and Robespierre and their ilk worked fanatically at forging their nation's bondage in the name of Freedom.

There is an analogy: Aristocrats are to the common people as vampires are to breathers. Both small, exotic groups might be said to live by sucking the blood of the mundane majority. And both offer the masses in return a certain entertainment value, if nothing else.

There are differences, of course; all analogies limp, as the Germans used to say. Vampires expand their membership by more or less active recruiting; it is much more difficult to pass from serfdom to aristocracy, where membership is jealously guarded.

After having seen the little girl safely inside her parents' cottage, and having satisfied myself that for the time being the child was as safe as she could be, I moved on through the peaceful night—thirty miles or more, traveling for the remainder of the night—before coming to the hidden earth I had been hoping to find. This sanctuary lay, in the form of a body-sized cavity at a depth of some six feet, under a patch of open ground in a pasture. I had not visited this spot for many years, and alterations in the growth and the very existence of nearby trees made it necessary to rely upon sightings of certain landmark rocks to determine the approximate location.

I was pleased to find this lair undisturbed, and before dawn could seriously inconvenience me, I sank into the rich French soil to enjoy a thoroughly deserved rest.

When I lay down, I was no longer garbed as a priest, but in a costume which would probably have caused any chance observer to take me for a hunter or gamekeeper. With the exception of a practical and quite mundane hunting knife, I bore no weapons—I have to this day a chronic dislike of firearms, though as a breathing soldier of the fifteenth century I was no stranger to the operation of the antique matchlocks, which were then the best technology could do.

It was, and still is, part of my general policy to conceal supplies of clothing, money, and any other vitally important items, wrapped in oilskin, in or near most of my earths. Exactly how many of these hospitable nests I had then, or possess now at the time of writing, is not a subject we are going to discuss. Inspecting these arrangements at least once every few years, and renewing them when circumstances warrant, is part of the housekeeping of every prudent vampire.

In every year of my life there have been some days when I have behaved prudently—and there are many other days on which I at least like to think that I am doing so.

And then there are those days when the idea of prudence never enters my mind. I must admit that there are years in which these latter form a definite majority.

The hunting skills, magical and otherwise, of Radu's people proved keener than I had anticipated. And I had given up my anti-location talisman to small Marie.

One of Radu's search parties, consisting of three of his breathing associates and two *nosferatu,* one of the latter a woman, used magic and other means successfully to track me to my temporary lair, arriving there some six or seven hours after the ground had received my grateful body in mist-form. That they succeeded in taking their quarry by surprise was largely a matter of luck.

Only one of these people—the practically fearless, comparatively youthful vampire whose courage had already been rewarded with a serious injury—had been among the group I met at the deserted chapel in Radu's presence. No member of that gathering, with the doubtful exception of Constantia, had actively come over to my side.

The leader of this particular search party—the very man I'd dosed with Borgia poison—still suffered from a sore shoulder and a half-useless arm, besides a few more general, systemic side effects. By the time he caught up with me, he had recovered sufficiently to enter the lists again, and was burning for revenge. Not only for the physical hurt, but for having made him look a fool.

* * *

Either of my two vampire-enemies who were present could have assumed mist-form to enter my sanctuary without digging, but hunting a dangerous quarry by that method has its own frightful perils; and neither of the *nosferatu* who had come out against me had quite the stomach for any such tactic.

Having successfully located their quarry through magical or near-magical sensitivity, they took up tools and weapons with eager, trembling hands, ready to enjoy a triumph but fearing at every moment to provoke and alert the monster underground. By this means they dug and scraped away the first two or three feet of age-packed soil, using tools they had brought with them, or had stolen nearby. Then, unreasonably afraid that their noise and activity would rouse me prematurely from my trance, they tried to impale me with wooden spears, screaming as they thrust down at me through the last two or three feet of earth.

The remaining layer of soil was hardened by having lain undisturbed for many decades, but it failed to muffle the louder scream of mingled rage and agony, which now went up to them in answer.

I owe my life to their fear—and to the fact that my potentially strongest opponent still suffered a weakness in one arm. The assault failed by being launched prematurely, before they had dug deeply enough to be sure of my exact position, and too tentative.

Having thus brutally been made aware of the presence of mine enemies, I dragged myself awake as rapidly as possible. The process occupied only a few seconds, much less than it would have taken ordinarily, but under the circumstances it was still almost fatally slow. Long enough for my enemies, stabbing blindly into the ground in a frenzy of overconfidence, to inflict another wound or two.

I was struggling, trying to fight back, even before I was fully out of my resting trance. Fortunately no more than two of the ten or more spear thrusts into the dirt had actually struck me. Clawing my way up out of the earth, spurting blood and spitting mud between bared fangs, I cursed my own overconfidence, lack of prudence—call it what you will—that had caused me to underrate my brother's ability to mobilize a force against me and to overrate my own power to terrify and subdue the opposition.

Wounded, with only one arm fully functional, I erupted savagely in man-form out of the temporary grave, raging and showering loose dirt in all directions.

Even still half-asleep, before I was completely up out of the earth, I used my hunting knife to good advantage, slashing a breather's Achilles tendon and thus bringing one opponent down.

Shortly I sustained a belaboring with wooden weapons which deprived me of this handy knife. But moments later I was gripping in my right hand the fire-hardened point of one spear I had already caught and broken off. With this weapon I quickly disposed of one more of my attackers.

Exactly what reaction my foes had expected of me when they provoked me to come roaring up out of the earth, I do not know, but evidently not the berserk fury of this counterattack. No mere breathing human possessed a fraction of the speed and strength required to face one of the *nosferatu* in open combat. I make no idle boast when I assure the reader that, had they not taken me by surprise, no three or four of them would have been able to stand against me for a full minute.

My strategy was to concentrate my efforts upon one of them—ideally the most dangerous, he of the poisoned arm—and quickly put him out of action or drive him away.

Knowing the best strategy and being able to achieve it while under multiple attack are not the same thing.

The small grove echoed with the savage impacts of wooden weapons. One after another, these went splintering away. Blood spattered violently upon the nearby trees, and winged little breathing things, and running things, went clamoring out of our way.

After making a good beginning to the fight, I was forced to endure a long moment or two in which I could do little more than sit, almost helpless. They might have finished me then with spear-thrusts, but they delayed a little. And that little was too long.

They stamped and wheeled around me. Fortunately for me not all of them were skilled in personal combat and they got in each other's way, their wooden spears and clubs clattering against each other, saving me from further immediate damage.

A turning point came when I was able to seize my remaining breather attacker by the ankle, and by main force throw the man off balance.

I fought my way to a standing position, only to be seized and dragged to the ground again by the desperate effort of my opponents. Kicking viciously at every ankle I could reach, I shattered several bones. In a moment I had again regained my feet.

My enemies might have chosen to abandon the struggle at that point, but instead were incautious enough to stand their ground and try to finish me off. One factor in their calculations must have been that they still dreaded their master more than me.

There is a peculiarity of vampire combat that I have seldom heard remarked upon: that one never gasps or pants with exertion. Physical weariness ensues at last, as it must in all living things, but not because of lack of oxygen. One must resort to other means to gauge the weariness of one's opponent, or ally. Even when one is mortally wounded, the voice ordinarily remains full and well-controlled. Only emotion, and not the need to gulp for air, may cause it to break chaotically.

When the broken fore-end of my captured wooden spear was broken once again, this time into uselessness, I fought on with my bare hands and, toward the bitter end, with a succession of small logs or fallen branches. Stones, born of the ancient earth but as lifeless as brass or steel, tended to be no more effective than those refined metals.

At this point, with only three of my original five assailants still on their feet, the breather turned tail and ran away in terror. Evidently the thought of what Radu might do to him was not enough to make him face me any longer.

One might, in emulation of Samson of the Old Testament, use an animal skull or one of the long bones as an effective weapon. On occasion I have found the skulls of horned cattle to be quite formidable tools of combat against my own kind, but unhappily none were within reach. My own talons and fangs tended to be effective.

My opponents on that day were neither the least nor the most skillful or brave that I had ever faced. The mere fact that their entire band had not yet broken and fled testified to their basic nerve and competence. They endeavored to get me between them, but I foiled that tactic by getting my back against a tree.

In a brief pause, before the next stage of our fight began, my *nosferatu* enemies bragged to me of Radu's cleverness and power, and that they were sure they had chosen the right side in our prolonged conflict. They taunted me with the damage they had already done to me, but I could hear the hollowness of fear in everything they said.

The man I had almost killed in the old chapel boasted to me that he personally had tracked down the small peasant girl after all.

The words came out quite clearly: "She was a tasty morsel." And he licked his lips.

My reply was also enunciated with precision: "Molesting the child was a serious mistake. I made it clear to you that she was under my protection."

Having issued that indictment, as it were, I paused, the better to concentrate on the next exchange of blows and thrusts. One as experienced in combat as I was could sense a difference in the air. My confidence that I would survive this encounter was growing fast, and that of my opponents waning with reciprocal speed. "But you have committed an even greater error just now, in telling me what you had done."

I was far from convinced of my opponent's truthfulness in making such a boast—but whether I believed it or not made no difference in my determination to finish the speaker off.

In the end I was forced to believe him, for he produced convincing evidence, in the form of the very talisman I had given to the child—and his trembling hand now held it out to me in a dying, taunting gesture. I snatched it away from him before he could fling it out of reach.

And then, having disposed of his last ally, in my rage I did the very worst that I knew how, in the very limited span of time available, to the pain-nerves in his guilty hand. His shrieks were deafening, but they soon ceased.

So, it was not by means of magic that he had tracked her down. How he had done so I never learned. But alas, Radu and others might have known the child's village, even her house, before they kidnapped her.

At least I had regained the talisman, and I hastened to hang it around my neck. Now Radu and whatever force he might raise next would have to pursue their hunt for *me* by non-magical means alone—which restriction, I thought, would probably not deprive them of success.

Verily I would have been gasping at that moment, were my body at all dependent upon air. Swaying, I looked about me at death and destruction. The only one of my foes who was still alive was he who had earlier taken to his heels, and was by now a mile away.

Radu's people had achieved—at considerable cost to themselves—at least one minor victory, freezing me in man-form all through the remainder of the night. Then when I came to consider the matter, I thought that they might have won much more than that; truly it began to seem to me then that my wounds were likely to prove mortal.

*   *   *

My first instinct for survival after the fight, as I clutched at a tree branch for support, was to seek sanctuary by changing form; but I realized in time that my chance of getting through a day in mist-form would be zero instead of only vanishingly small. I could recall how more than one old colleague of mine had perished, changing into mist-form when seriously hurt, and being blown to nothingness by a mere passing breeze.

I thought that in wolf-form I was not likely to fare much better. A wounded man might obtain help at a farmhouse, might find some place indoors to shelter from the sun. A wounded bat or wolf would certainly not. Aerial flight, and also the speed of a four-legged run, were going to be denied him, at least until he had had some chance to rest and heal.

Looking at the red ruin around me, I scorned to refresh myself with the blood of any of my breathing attackers. One reason was that doing so might have made it easier for my enemies' magic to follow my trail. Another and perhaps stronger reason was that my pride had soared with the heat of combat, and I assured myself that I was not *that* hungry.

Remembering the man who had chosen to run away, I told myself that even in my wounded condition I would have had a good chance of running the coward down. But the effort would surely have completed my own exhaustion, and I thought there was nothing of much importance to be learned from him—from the beginning I had felt no doubt as to who had put the attackers on my trail—so I chose rather to concentrate instead upon my own survival.

It was fortunate that I did so.

I experienced a well-earned satisfaction at having survived Radu's initial attack. More than that, I congratulated myself upon having won the first skirmish, diminishing the numbers in the force that was now arrayed against me. Still, as I surveyed my prospects for survival with fearless—no, not courageous, that is something else—realism, I thought that they were not good.

I meditated—quite uselessly, of course—upon the fact

that I might have started to recruit an army, or at least a posse, of my own, once I knew that Radu was again above the ground. Perhaps, I thought, I should have done.

In whatever time and place a *nosferatu* lives, the willing help of at least one intelligent and understanding breather can be of tremendous benefit. I foresaw that I would seek such aid from someone soon—if I lived long enough. I was not without friends, in France or elsewhere. But calling for help was usually the last alternative I considered when in trouble. Earlier I had vaguely reassured myself with the thought that I had friends—but it was my own fault now that they were none of them on hand.

Swaying with weakness, and temporarily prohibited by my injuries from changing shape, I made what plans I could.

My appearance at this time must have been truly ghastly. Never had I less regretted my inability to use a mirror. I had a great lump on my forehead, not to mention a torn flap of skin hanging over one eye. With trembling hand I held the flap in place, until it began, very delicately and tentatively, to heal there.

Listening, sniffing the breeze, even though I was denied the keener senses of the wolf, I thought I detected certain evidence that more of my enemies, though still miles distant, were gathering, swarming, on my trail.

Of course it would have been mad, suicidal, for me to go back to sleep in the same earth. If one band of my enemies had found it, the others could do so also. And now the whole area around was trampled, strewn with the debris of combat, flesh and blood, bits of wood and cloth and bone and metal.

Our struggle had been a prolonged one, and not much of the night was left. I had no choice but to retreat at once, and in man-form—never mind that I was still oozing, dripping blood, leaving a trail that would be child's play to follow. I would have to cover as much ground as I could before the dawn, then take whatever chance Fate offered. I tried to bind up my most heavily dripping wound, where someone's spear had gone skewering deep into my side, but soon I abandoned the attempt as hopeless. One arm was almost useless, and my usable hand was shaking uncontrollably.

I could certainly be thankful now, with my berserker combat frenzy ebbing, that I had not been foolish enough to attempt a pursuit of my surviving attacker.

Similarly I had to abandon the idea of improvising some kind of sunshade to protect my head and face when dawn overtook me, as it seemed it inevitably must. My eyes in particular would be at risk, but there was nothing to be done about that now.

Slowly I called up a mental map of the entire province, trying to decide which was my nearest earth, which the least likely for the enemy to have discovered.

The mental image of the map as it took shape was scarcely reassuring. There was only one real possibility of survival, a sanctuary in the cellar of an antique farmhouse, which unfortunately lay more than a few miles from my present location. To reach it before dawn in my present condition would to say the least present a considerable challenge.

Doggedly I let go my hold upon the branch and began to walk; and only as I did so, provoking in myself gray tendencies to faint, did I begin seriously to doubt whether I would make it as far as my sanctuary.

Feeling as clumsy and vulnerable as any breather, I trudged on. I was possessed of one tiny advantage, in that I was heading west, the dawn at my back and still perhaps two hours behind me.

Fortunately the sense of being still pursued grew no stronger, no more immediate. I knew in my bones that I was too weak to stand and fight again, even if next time I should not be so badly outnumbered. The slow draining of blood and vitality inexorably took its toll. A single determined breather with a wooden club or spear could probably have finished me when I began to flee the dawn. But of course I would make an effort, if it came to that.

More than once on that terrible trek I heard a howl in the distance, the sound carrying from miles away, and wondered if my enemies were using hounds to hunt me down. Ordinarily I might have been able to turn the hunters' own dogs against them, even at a distance.

I had managed to slow my blood loss to a trickle, then to stop it almost completely. Alas, that "almost" was likely to prove fatal. My increasing weakness was binding all my powers ever more closely to me, diminishing their range.

Dragging myself from the support of one tree or fence-post to the next, I at one point considered trying to rest in some cave where a group of vagrants had taken shelter. But I quickly rejected the idea. If I could enter the cave without an invitation, the more dangerous of my pursuers would be able to do the same.

Hunted through the darkness before dawn, aware to the minute, almost to the second, of the approaching sunrise that was almost certain to prove fatal, I considered taking shelter in someone's mausoleum. But again I would be helpless if any of Radu's people overtook me there.

When in ordinary health, I might easily enough have passed a day and night and a second day above ground, given reasonable shelter from direct sun. But in my wounded condition, the healing power of my native earth had become a grim necessity. At last, with dawn relentlessly about to break and only one possibility of help within a hundred miles, I limped, wounded and bleeding, toward the dwelling which, cold calculation informed me, represented my last chance.

It would not have surprised me in the least to find this last hope denied me, my earth defiled, or rendered useless by being kept under watch.

The last quarter of a mile took me almost half an hour to cover.

It would not have surprised me at all to discover, in any

of these last breathless minutes before sunrise, Radu's smiling face looming out of the early morning mists ahead. My brother might have somehow learned all my secret sanctuaries. Certainly Radu would want to be in at my death if he possibly could, would give almost anything for the chance to observe my pangs of dissolution, and taunt me on my way. Perhaps at the end he would have dragged me into a tree's shade so that the killing power of sunlight should not have its way with me too swiftly. But no Radu appeared. The fugitive's last chance was not yet quite foreclosed.

And now the little farmhouse on its hill had come in sight. But there had been an ominous change—an enlargement of fairly recent vintage—in the building since I had seen it last.

Long ago indeed, in fact as far back as the early seventeenth century, I had foresightedly established, in the building which had then occupied this ground, one of a small number of emergency spare earths. But now very little of that original old stone structure still remained, and what was left of it had been enlarged upon, incorporated into what was now a much larger manor. Some might have called it a chateau.

Sometime during the decades since my last visit, a new generation of breathers had made the place their own and taken up their residence inside. One or two of them at least were in there now. If I listened I could hear their voices. They were a man and woman talking freely to each other, conversing in good humor, if not necessarily in the way of lovers; I could hear their careless laughter, and their four breathing lungs.

From my throat there issued, without any conscious intention on my part, a horrible growling, too low a sound for any breather at the distance of the manor house to have detected it.

There was no way that the Prince of Wallachia was going to be able to force his way into that or any other house against the will of those who sheltered there. No way today to claim his shelter unmolested. Not that my honor, in any case, would have allowed me to take on the role of thief and brigand, stealing from the innocent.

From somewhere there came back to me the image of small Marie, the sound and smell of the child's exhaustion and her terror. Now it was Prince Dracula who had sunk into impotence. If Marie had been at hand, he would have tried to lean his weight on her. Feeling as feeble as any breathing babe, he was going to have to ask for help.

~ *13* ~

*P*hilip Radcliffe stood on the landing of a curved, stone stair inside the centuries-old farmhouse, close beside the embrasure of a window pierced through the thick stone wall. He was at that moment gripping an antique candleholder in his right hand, holding it close beside the wall, trying to get a good look at the stone surface near the window. The wall at that point was practically featureless, but the young man was frowning lightly, squinting his eyes at the memory of something there.

Meanwhile his free hand was resting in a brotherly fashion on the shoulder of the young woman who stood beside him. She had been gazing out the window, and now spoke, breaking a brief silence. "It's almost morning."

Radcliffe and his fair companion had spent part of the preceding evening strolling through the house with lamps and candles, studying certain portraits of his ancestors, in his mother's family, which were still hanging on the walls. Now and again, as here, they discovered only empty places where those remembered pictures had once hung.

Not that tracing a family tree had been their chief concern. "It seems we've talked the night away." Radcliffe's

French was lightly accented, but almost good enough to allow him to pass as a native of this province.

"With eighteen years to catch up on, it's no wonder we've a lot to say to each other."

Last night no one had bothered to close any shutters above the ground floor, and now all the windows were open to welcome in the burgeoning light of dawn. The two young people picked up their wineglasses from the broad stone windowsill, touched them together, and once more sipped the excellent wine, from a cellar even older than the house itself. From this window they enjoyed a good view of the impending sunrise, brushing now with light the highest trees of a distant hilltop. The surrounding country showed a wild character, its narrow, fertile valleys cut apart by wooded hills and ridges. This was a region mostly of small isolated farms, and, as Radcliffe remembered, much ranged by hunters. No one around here was likely to be much surprised by the sound of dogs baying on a trail.

An acquaintance of the Philip Radcliffe who would be kidnapped in 1996 would have noted a definite physical resemblance between him and this man who shared his name and was his ancestor. But the hair of this earlier Radcliffe was darker, almost black, and he was not as tall as his descendant. Also, the appearance of the Philip Radcliffe who would never see an electric light was made more interesting by a facial scar, the relic of a tavern brawl during his student days in Philadelphia. And by light smallpox scarring.

Philip frowned, raising his candle again, letting his eyes rove up and down the curve of stone wall that embraced the stair. He was sure he could remember an assortment of old ancestral portraits on this wall. He mentioned the thought to Melanie, and she agreed.

"And just here . . ." He had turned away from the window, and his two hands were making parallel gestures at the blank space. "There hung a picture of an old man . . . my mother's grandfather? I seem to remember her telling me that."

Melanie Romain, daughter of the local physician, a young woman of striking features, rough hands, greenish eyes, in turn raised her glass to Philip. "But you couldn't have been more than six years old—seven at the most; I think I was only six when your mother took you to America. Oh, how I cried!"

Melanie's dress was politically correct for these revolutionary times, in that it was several years out of date in styling, worn and fraying at the hem. But that correctness was strictly an accident. She certainly had not the look or manner or speech of a peasant, or of one of the urban *sansculotte* women. But whatever her social status under the old regime or the new, her roughened hands showed that she had been no idle lady.

Last evening she and the American visitor had shared a frugal meal and some excellent wine by candlelight. For the past twelve hours or so, Radcliffe had enormously enjoyed the pleasant company of the young woman he remembered as his childhood sweetheart.

The game of memory had occupied the couple, off and on, during much of that time.

"Do you remember . . . ?"

"Of course. But do you remember . . . ?"

And they had discovered that their political opinions, along with the other ways in which they viewed the world, were very much alike. Both fiercely supported the recent American revolution—though Melanie had never visited America—and loathed the *ancien régime* of France, with its rigidity and divine rights of oppression. Melanie's attitude toward the new government in Paris was entirely shaped by the fact that it had arrested her father, who stood in daily danger of losing his head. Radcliffe was sympathetic, and had high hopes that such an obviously terrible mistake could soon be rectified. "From what I remember of your father, he is an unlikely candidate to be involved in political activity."

"No man less likely, I should think."

Radcliffe put down his candle, and raised the wineglass

he had let stand on the window's broad stone sill. "To true liberty."

"Gladly will I drink to that."

"And to your father's in particular, and to his health—may they have realized their mistake, and set him free yesterday, or the day before."

Melanie sipped again. But the expression on her face was not at all optimistic.

The illumination entering through the windows was still faint; dawn had not yet entirely won the battle for the eastern sky, and they had brought only the single lighted candle with them when they climbed into this miniature tower.

Yesterday Radcliffe had passed through the doorway of this house for the first time in many years. His destination was Paris, and he was nearing the conclusion of a journey from America that had taken him through England (though that country had now been at war with France for more than a year) and across the Channel on one of the many smugglers' boats, which plied a profitable trade.

This modest manor house was in bad condition now, having been largely neglected for more than fifteen years, since shortly after the time that his mother had taken him to the New World.

Almost all the servants, along with the majority of peasants from the nearby village, had fled the estate years or months ago. Some had run away in terror; some had been caught up in revolutionary fervor, determined to join with the enemies of their former master in attempting to destroy him.

Last night, sometime around midnight, Philip had sent to bed the two people he had found residing in the house on his arrival: Old Jules, a former servant whom Radcliffe remembered fondly, and Jules's granddaughter, a girl of fourteen or so. It seemed that the chief reason the pair had occupied the place, despite the Revolutionary fever which had swept the countryside, was that they had nowhere else to go. Both Jules and the girl had, as if by some instinct, resumed the role of servants when he had arrived and identified himself. Both were now asleep somewhere in the downstairs rooms, and from time to time Old Jules's snores were faintly audible.

Since Radcliffe's arrival yesterday the old place had engulfed and enchanted him with a dream-like half-familiarity. He supposed such a reaction was only to be expected, for he had last been here at the age of seven. This stair, like all the rest of the house and the few outbuildings which had survived, was strangely shrunken in size from the images that existed in his memory.

Almost all of the people he had known here as a child were gone now. Jules had been able to give him detailed reports on some of them. But none of the changes in house, or lands, or other people, were nearly as fascinating as those which had taken place in Philip's childhood companion.

Melanie Romain had arrived yesterday evening, curious about a report of a stranger at the house, and all through the night the two had sat and strolled about talking. With each passing hour they'd grown more and more enchanted with each other, though they hadn't put that into words as yet.

Philip's plans had not included any interruption of his travels, and he was now eager to resume his journey to the metropolis as soon as possible. He now thought he had an additional and even more urgent mission to perform when he reached Paris. But even his plans for his journey had changed since yesterday evening. The good news was that Melanie was going to come with him; the bad news was the reason for her journey.

One of the recurrent themes of their nightlong conversation had been the story of Melanie's recent travels from city to city, seeking out one revolutionary hero or authority after another, pleading with anyone who she thought might possess some influence, to come to the aid of her father. Dr. Romain had been arrested a month ago as a suspect.

"Suspect in what crime?" Radcliffe had asked in puzzlement when Melanie first tried to explain her father's predicament to him.

She explained. "Suspect" had now become, in the language of the Revolutionary tribunals, a category of criminal all to itself. The Tribunal in Paris had recently decided to dispense with the ritual of presenting evidence, since everyone knew that the accused were guilty.

"What madness!"

"Indeed." She sighed, and her greenish eyes went distant. With her only surviving parent facing the executioner, the intervals in which she could forget, laugh, think of something else, were short.

In fact, Philip Radcliffe at this moment would almost certainly have been repacking his few belongings preparatory to setting out for Paris if Melanie hadn't shown up last night. Her presence had created a serious disruption of his plans, but in fact he was only vaguely conscious of it.

Philip and his young visitor had already discussed his mother, who was still alive, across the sea in Martinique. And about his mother's affair with the great Benjamin Franklin. "I stand before you as living proof that that occurred."

And Melanie, from the happy days of her childhood, vaguely remembered Philip's mother. "She is a gracious lady, and I am glad to hear that she still survives."

And why his surname was Radcliffe.

Philip, having been in France now for more than a week, had already been challenged several times and forced to defend himself against accusations of spying for the Austrians, or for Pitt, the treacherous prime minister of England, by proclaiming himself the natural son of Benjamin Franklin.

Franklin had been and still was highly esteemed in France, and Radcliffe had mixed feelings on observing that his father's portrait, usually with fur hat and bifocal spectacles (his own invention), appeared on all manner of objects.

Philip had already seen the familiar face on snuffboxes and chamber pots.

The story of Philip's paternity was quite true, and fortunately he had documentation in the form of a worn and dog-eared letter from his father, who had died in Philadelphia in 1790.

"For all the years he spent here," he remarked to Melanie, "Father never did master French well enough to feel confident writing it, though he could read and understand the spoken word with some facility."

Radcliffe now pulled from an inside pocket the oilskin packet in which he was carrying this letter, opened it and showed it to his companion.

She murmured: "I remember . . ."

"But I forget, did you ever meet my father? I suppose you might well have done so. My mother's often told me that he visited us here, but I have only the vaguest memories of him here, or none at all."

"Then I suppose," said Melanie, "that I was too young also."

"Yes, of course."

The first meeting with his father that Philip could remember had not taken place until he was half grown. Then, after Franklin's return from Europe in 1785, he had seen the esteemed gentleman more than once in America. Franklin had acknowledged his relationship to young Philip, wished him well, and offered to use his influence to help him obtain legal training, if that was his wish. Philip had interrupted his apprenticeship at law to undertake this journey, and his half-resentful attitude toward the old man had mellowed into a sincere liking.

Radcliffe was also carrying a letter sent to America by the revolutionary firebrand Tom Paine, inviting Philip to call on Paine if he should come to Paris. Paine was an old acquaintance, if not exactly a friend, of the young man's father—in fact Benjamin Franklin had once been widely credited with the authorship of Paine's famous political pamphlet, *Common Sense*. Phil also had in his pocket another letter that he hesitated to show Melanie; his elders in Philadelphia had impressed on him that the message he was carrying to Paine was something of a diplomatic secret.

Nor did Phil want to raise Melanie's hopes regarding her father only to see them dashed again. But he seriously thought that he, armed with the letters of introduction he was carrying, might well be able to exert sufficient influence upon the revolutionary authorities in Paris to be of some use to her father.

According to the young woman's description of the course of local events over the last year, typical of the turmoil which had swept through most of the country, some kind of rural mob had gone through a show of seizing this estate, in the name of the People. Melanie of course had not been on the grounds at the time, or even in the village. The intrusion had taken place months ago. The mob had made a drunken, abortive effort to burn the place down. But the house was constructed mostly of stone, and a timely rainstorm had put out the fire, so only minor damage had resulted.

Actually the chief culprit in the matter of damage, as far as Radcliffe could see, was only neglect, which over the last several years had somewhat ravaged the house. Still the structure was basically intact. It seemed very doubtful, though, that anyone in his mother's family would ever have a claim on the place in the future.

That was too bad, in a way. Philip would have enjoyed a leisurely return, in some peaceful future, to the house and lands that held so many happy memories. On the other hand he was perfectly ready to admit that the local peasants, whose blood and sweat and lives for countless generations had been invested in this soil, had a far better claim on the place than did he or any of his family.

*   *   *

The two young people remarked to each other on how swiftly the night had passed while they had done no more than talk and sip a little wine.

Several times during the course of their nightlong conversation, Radcliffe had asked Melanie what she had been doing all the time he had been gone. He had yet to receive anything like a full or detailed reply.

Melanie continued to be vague in her answers whenever the conversation touched on her personal life. When pressed, she said she had been away to school, but seemed reluctant to provide any details.

"So," said Philip, drawing a deep breath and ready to try again. "Now you've heard all about me. I do believe I've told my entire life story several times over in the course of the night. And I've learned from you all about the state of things in France—and about what's happened to your father. But it would please me to hear of happier days—how you spent your time before the great upheaval. How long did we decide it must be since we last saw each other—? Yes, eighteen years. I'm twenty-five now, and you're—twenty-four? Of course. So we must have been about seven and six when we last played together."

"Yes, 1776—that was a big year for revolutions," Melanie commented, smiling. Her companion could not help noticing that she had once more evaded the question.

When he continued watching her in silence, she added: "My life would make a dull story, I'm afraid—until the Revolution started. Since then all lives in France have been exciting." She mentioned that she had spent some time working with her father, the physician. "Until he was arrested."

"I am really so sorry, Mellie." The old childhood nickname had come back effortlessly. "I remember the good doctor well. At least I think I do."

Again she sipped her wine. She had consumed several glasses over the course of a whole night, and so had he, though not enough to have had any noticeable effect on either party.

Melanie, while visiting in the village yesterday, and at her wits' end as to where to turn next, had heard that someone was occupying the house again. One reason for her visit had been to warn whomever had come here against the local republicans, or Jacobins, who committed desultory acts of terror.

From the moment she had heard of the reported stranger, she said now, she had wondered whether he might possibly be her old playmate.

She had driven out from town in her father's light carriage. Greeting her at the door, Radcliffe had at first not recognized her—nor she him.

"Yes, Mademoiselle, how may I be of service?"

"To begin with, it will be safer for you to call me *citoyenne*—but stay, M'sieu, have we perhaps met before?"

The couple had spent the night in each other's company, under conditions of deepening intimacy, though as yet there had been only casual physical contact between them after a kiss of greeting at the moment of recognition. They were beginning to fall for each other in a serious way. They had, as it turned out, a very great deal to talk about.

"And what do they say that you must do, this local Commune, or Committee—or whatever is the latest name they give themselves?"

"They call themselves the Committee of Public Safety, having adopted the same title as the men in Paris who last year proclaimed themselves our new masters. You will be wise to treat these local people with politeness when you meet them, but here they have nothing like the power of Robespierre and his gang in the city."

She was looking out the window again. "It appears that we are going to have a visitor."

Vlad Dracula, dragging himself along, struggling to stay on his feet—more than once slipping to his knees and fighting his way erect again—had almost reached the house. This would have been the moment for dogs to rush out barking, but it seemed there were no dogs. If they had come, he was ready, thinking he still had the power to quiet them.

The harried fugitive, staggering with fatigue and loss of blood, had fallen from sheer weakness several times during the last half hour. He knew that he would not survive the first minute of full sunlight under these conditions, not even the slanting, early morning rays; such shelter as he might find under a tree or in a hedgerow was not going to be enough in his condition.

Seen at close range, the building's dilapidation was all the more apparent. Obviously the house had been neglected over a period of years, but it had not deteriorated to such a degree that a man could expect to find a hole large enough to climb through. As far as the visitor could see from where he tottered, doors and window shutters remained intact.

When he saw a trace of smoke rising from the chimney, he knew that some chance existed that he might be invited in.

It was not in his nature to give up. He approached and knocked on the door.

Inside the house, Radcliffe had earlier seen to it that his primitive firearms and other weapons were loaded, and was keeping them within reach. His armament included two pistols which Old Jules had kept hidden away, so they had not yet been confiscated by any Citizens' Committee of Public Safety.

Philip now checked the pistols' flints and made sure the weapons were loaded and primed. The couple looked at each other, and exchanged whispers. This could very likely be the rural *sans-culottes*.

Holding a loaded pistol in each hand, Radcliffe called out: "Who's there?"

Old Jules had awakened and was standing beside the

door, watching Radcliffe for instructions while gripping an ancient sword.

Melanie on hearing a knock at the door had calmly hefted one of the big meat knives racked in the old stone kitchen.

The male voice from outside sounded weak but clear. "Only a hunter. I am lost, and seeking shelter."

In the east, to which I had my back, I could now sense the sky-glare brightening relentlessly, belaboring my senses with its urgent warning. Behind that silent augury there burned the unshielded furnace-fury of the Sun, relentlessly advancing just beneath the shoulder of the slow-spinning Earth, ready to sear and blast my life away.

Radcliffe put down one pistol to open a small judas hole in the door. "Who's there?" he called out once more, sharply.

The man outside called out again in a ragged voice. From what Radcliffe could hear, he was claiming to be a lost hunter.

Peering out suspiciously, Radcliffe could see the self-proclaimed hunter, a lone, emaciated figure swaying on its feet, supporting itself with one hand against the wall. As far as Philip could tell, the man was unarmed, and for a moment the American thought that he was drunk. The morning sky now shed enough light to make it plain that all was certainly not well with him. He was wearing a hunter's garments, but they were torn, stained with blood and earth. Considering also his pale, almost skeletal, face, he looked more like the quarry than the hunter, in fact like a man who had been buried alive, and Radcliffe muttered as much in English under his breath.

He glanced at Melanie, who at the moment looked surprisingly like a sheltered young woman who might consider fainting. Taking her turn at the peephole, she started to say something, then was silent. Firmly she nodded. The doctor's daughter had not lost her instinct to show mercy, to help the underdog.

Moving back a step, Radcliffe picked up a pistol from the table and checked the priming and the flint. Then, holding the weapon ready, he gestured for Old Jules to unbar the door.

~ *14* ~

When the heavy wooden door swung open, Melanie got her first close look at the man leaning against the wall just outside. She drew a breath and started to speak, but the words were never uttered. Under the stranger's gashed forehead, his dark, tormented eyes briefly met hers, before both people looked away.

"Are you alone?" Radcliffe asked.

The pale-skinned, almost skull-faced figure drew a soft breath. "Very much so." His French was precise, but Radcliffe, who had absorbed the language at his mother's knee, could hear traces of some foreign accent, one that he could not identify.

"I see you have had an accident," said Philip.

"One might call it that."

"Well, come in, man, don't just stand there—but stay, do you need help walking?"

"I think not." And even as he spoke, the stranger displayed a surprising burst of strength, lurching forward as if his life depended on the advance, and he dared not risk delay. This effort carried him for two or three short steps, just enough to bring him through the door, where he halted, leaning against the wall again, as if in the last stages of exhaustion. He had the used-up look of a man who had just run a long distance. There was one notable anomaly: He did not appear to be gasping.

And only now, when he moved forward, was the extent of his wounds, and their number, obvious to the onlookers. A drop of fresh blood fell to the floor.

"Let us help you, sir!" Radcliffe cried.

A brief nod in reply.

Radcliffe pulled one of the stranger's thin arms over his own shoulder and put his own much better-nourished arm around the other's waist. Meanwhile, Melanie had come up behind Radcliffe and was staring past him toward the visitor. The young woman did not speak, but slowly lowered the weapon she was holding.

Once more the stranger's gaze rested on Melanie, and now for a slightly longer time; but his eyes were almost vacant, and there was in them no sign of recognition.

The old servant Jules, watching, almost unconsciously made the sign of the cross. A moment later his granddaughter Marguerite imitated his action.

The very first direct rays of the morning sun came grazing through distant treetops to strike first upon the whitewashed outdoor wall, and then the very lintel of the door.

The visitor, momentarily left standing alone just inside the entry, had managed to get his body entirely in shadow, but still he winced and seemed to shrink within himself. Behind him Radcliffe was pushing the door closed, blocking out the direct sun. Old Jules, at a nod from his master, secured the portal with a bar.

Oblivious to most of this, the supposed hunter was trying to gather what strength he had remaining. He took off his hat and said, in a low rasping voice: "You had better bar the door behind me. Admit no one."

"We have already done so. Are you pursued, then?"

"Not to my knowledge. But it is only fair to warn you that I may be."

Philip and Melanie exchanged a glance. Each would

have described the man before them as certainly aristocratic.

Radcliffe growled: "Damned Jacobins. Republicans, they call themselves. Bandits, I call them—are they close on your trail?"

"I think not," the victim repeated patiently. "But it is possible."

"And by what name shall I call you, sir?"

"My name is Legrand." A year ago the name Corday, that of Marat's assassin, had acquired attention-grabbing connotations.

Philip muttered hasty introductions, then, assuming his uninvited guest to be a persecuted aristocrat, impulsively swore that he would never give the man up to his enemies.

He was not really sure what was available in the way of beds and couches in the house; Radcliffe had not yet had a chance to try any of them for himself. But Vlad, once the freedom of the house was granted him, ignored any suggestions along that line. Instead, he groped his way, weakly but unerringly, as if the location of his goal were somehow clear to him, back through the house to the kitchen, then past the kitchen into a kind of ancient storeroom, to the spot where his cache of native earth had been buried so long ago. He could feel its presence beneath him. His undead bones perceived a certain radiation, like that of fire-warmed stone on a frozen night. With a groan he lay down there, right on the stone floor, directly over this hidden source of joy.

Even on the brightest summer days the light back here would always be dim, with the room's one small window on the north side and covered by a heavy wooden shutter.

Blessed relief flowed through all his ancient vampire bones, coursing in what remained of his blood.

Lying for the moment with his eyes closed, oblivious to the curious stares of those who had befriended him, he thought: *Let me lie here all day unmolested, shielded from the blasting sun, and at least I will not die before nightfall.* He would remain too weak, though, to do much more than survive. Unless he could find nourishment.

Dracula's host, a long way from perceiving the fugitive's peculiarities, offered his strange guest first bedding, and then food—though of course it never occurred to him to offer sustenance of the only kind that would have been of real benefit.

"Again I must ask you—would you not prefer a bed?"

"I tell you no." The voice, though somewhat stronger, was still no more than an agonized whisper. "If you would truly help me, let me be as I am."

"Very well. At least you had better let me see to your wounds." And the American wondered if his guest might be delirious.

But his next speech sounded entirely rational. "If you wish." Pause. "I thank you for your help. There is no doubt that you have saved my life."

The servant who had been sent for water and bandages now returned, and Melanie, the physician's daughter, with Radcliffe's somewhat awkward assistance, undertook the job of binding up the patient's wounds.

Weak as their bearer was, these had started to mend already, so to the uninitiated they appeared to have been made several days ago—but they were not as far restored as they would have been had not the spearpoints that made them been poisoned.

She muttered, uncomprehendingly: "This looks as if you had been—*gored,* by some horned animal. Or stabbed with a sharp stick."

The victim had nothing to say about that. There were other spots where his pale skin looked bruised and swollen, as if he had been beaten with some blunt object.

Melanie, who had been her father's frequent assistant in medical emergencies, firmly and naturally took full charge of the job of washing and bandaging, in which she had both skill and experience.

Radcliffe watched her working on the gash in the visitor's right side. "Ugly gash," she muttered. "I would think it needed stitches, and the one in your forehead too, but already they seem halfway healed. How did you get them? It must have been days ago."

"Would you believe I suffered a hunting accident?"

The American shook his head. "Not without a considerable effort. Were you hunting with spears and swords? And you said that you might be pursued."

In reply the victim only grinned, stretching the taut skin of his face, making it even more skull-like.

They offered him various items from their modest supply of food and drink—Old Jules's granddaughter had made delicious soup—but the patient firmly declined. Even in his condition, he could be very firm. When pressed, he rinsed out his mouth with a mixture of wine and water, then spat out the red stuff violently.

After sunset came, the main event of the evening, as far as the weakened, hunted vampire was concerned, was the return of the doctor's daughter. Melanie was accompanied by the servant girl, who was carrying a lantern, a jug of water, and some soup. Even at midday the room remained very dim.

The servant girl paused in the doorway, while Melanie, advancing across the room, knelt down on the stone floor and murmured softly: "Is there anything I can do for you, Citizen Legrand?"

"You and your husband have done very much already. You have saved my life." The victim's voice was stronger than his deathly appearance suggested.

For some reason Melanie thought it necessary to make the situation clear. "He is not my husband."

The visitor only looked at her, and again she felt it incumbent upon her to explain.

She sat back on her heels. "Philip and I are friends. We knew each other as children. Philip is an American now, but he was born here on this estate. The land is—was—in his mother's family. Before she took him to America, he and I often played together in this house, on these grounds . . . that

was almost twenty years ago . . . so we are old friends."
Pause. "That is all."

"Ah." And something in her listener's eyes seemed to
alter. "I think that 'Radcliffe' is not a French name."

"Philip was telling me about that last night. His mother
married an American called Radcliffe years ago, and her
young child took that man's name."

After a moment's pause she added: "Philip's natural father was Benjamin Franklin."

Almost any resident of France would have been interested at the mention of the late American celebrity, who had
lived in France for so many years, and the wounded vampire
was no exception. His low voice murmured: "Now that you
mention it, our host does bear a certain resemblance to
Franklin, around the eyes."

"You were privileged to meet the great M'sieu Franklin,
then?"

"Once, years ago, I had that honor . . . and how is the
elder statesman now?"

"I regret to say that he died four years ago, across the
sea in Philadelphia. I am surprised you did not know."

"It is the world's loss." A thin arm bent and straightened
in an elegant gesture. "One falls out of touch with many
things."

With the situation now a little clearer to both Vlad Dracula
and Melanie (though in fact each still labored under a fundamental misunderstanding), the kneeling woman at last slid
closer and reached out to inspect the patient's bandages. At
her gesture, the silent young girl who had been hanging back
in the doorway now brought the light closer. The patient made
no effort to sit up, and to examine him the doctor's daughter
was compelled to sit right down on the stone floor, which she
did with a natural and very non-aristocratic movement.

But it was an awkward position in which to try to work,
and in a moment she asked irritably: "Can you not sit up?"

The patient shook his head slowly. "At the moment, you must believe me, I am vastly more comfortable, and even stronger, as I am. Healthier, lying flat on this stone floor, whether you examine me or not. It may seem strange to you, but it is so."

"Come, though, at least turn over a little and let me see." At first glance, she could tell that the main bandage over the ribs had loosened notably, as if the man could have lost weight over the last few hours. The physician's daughter, a briskly persistent nurse, looked under the bandage, then blinked her eyes at what she saw. "*Mon Dieu,* but you heal fast! There is a notable difference from just a few hours ago."

He grunted. "At times in the past, when I have been injured—others have told me that I heal with great rapidity."

There was a persistent hesitancy between them, and at last the young woman, having pulled off and thrown away the patient's bandage which was no longer really necessary, decided to deal just as firmly with the other matter, the one lying unmentioned and unresolved between them.

Sitting back on her heels again, running a hand through her long hair, she announced briskly: "Citizen, I think that we have seen each other before."

Once more settled in the unlikely looking position that gave him greatest comfort, he blinked at her benevolently. "That is possible. Perhaps we shared a dream."

"No." She shook her head, being firmly practical. "You must know what I mean, and it was not a dream at all. This morning, even while you still were standing outside the house, I recognized you. We met in Paris, one night near midnight, at the cemetery of the Church of the Madeleine, the place where the bodies from the place of execution are brought to be buried."

"Yes, I am familiar with it."

"We had a very strange conversation in that cemetery, you and I. I still remember it pretty well, though it took place a year ago, or even more. I was there with my cousin, my teacher, Marie Grosholtz."

The man on the floor did not comment. He waited, as if withholding judgment.

"You came upon the two of us while we were at our work there in the churchyard, and you startled us."

"For that I apologize."

"You are forgiven. But the good God knows what you must have thought that we were doing. With the heads." Melanie tried a little smile, which brought no response. "You made a strong impression on me."

He watched her, steadily.

She drew herself up a little and tried again. "From certain remarks you made at the time, Citizen Legrand (I think that then you may have given us a different name), I understood you to be completely convinced that my cousin and I were up to some . . . that we were cutting up dead bodies in the pursuit of some kind of black magic. But I want to tell you that was not the case at all . . . and it occurs to me that now, meeting Citizen Radcliffe here with me, you may believe he is also involved in that sort of wickedness. But the accusation is not true of either of us. I can explain."

Slowly the supine man shook his head. "I make no accusations. You may have noticed that I offer no reason for my own presence in the graveyard."

Melanie Romain looked at her patient—if it was still possible to call him her patient—carefully, studying him for the space of several breaths. Then she said: "I do not think you were there on any business of witchcraft either."

"Certainly I was not." There was more than a touch of asperity in the answer.

And somehow, without either party seeming to be fully aware of the fact, he had taken her hand in both of his, and had absently begun to stroke her wrist, a procedure to which she made no objection—indeed, she hardly seemed to notice.

Then abruptly he released the hand of the young woman, saying: "And it is all one to me, whatever the cause may be for your unusual interest in the bodies of the dead."

Meanwhile the young servant girl, who was still faithfully holding the light, had inched a little closer, and a little closer still. She continued watching in silence, fascinated. Her gaze had become locked on the dark eyes of the man lying on the floor, who was taking no notice of her at all.

Melanie too was gazing intently at the visitor, and now she shook her head decisively. "I see you do not believe me, M'sieu Legrand, when I protest my cousin's innocence and mine. But I tell you no, it is not what you are thinking. Some deluded folk may still believe that bits of flesh and bone cut from rotting corpses have magical value, but to me that is all superstition. Did I say anything to you at the time, to give you the wrong impression?"

The man who reclined on the floor shook his head again. Once more he raised himself a little on one elbow, and his voice strengthened. "It makes no difference to me what you said then, and I have told you that I require no explanations now. You and your cousin Marie may dig up all the dead bodies in the world, and play games with all the loose heads— my only concern is that nothing you do will bring harm to our host. I now owe my life to M'sieu Radcliffe. I heard him swear to defend me against my enemies. In my time I have heard many men swear many things, and I believe I can tell which ones mean what they are saying. I can do no less for him in return."

Melanie blinked. "But I have no intention of harming him."

"Good. Then you will readily comprehend that he should not become involved in any dangerous graveyard operations—whatever their object." Legrand's voice suddenly sharpened. "Is he connected with such matters now?"

"No!" The young woman was quietly vehement. "He knows nothing about my cemetery work."

"Good. And I think it will be well if he remains in ignorance . . . you see, from this day forth I am bound to take a strong interest in the welfare of Monsieur Radcliffe. It has become a matter of honor for me. So I should like to have your assurance that you, whatever your other interests may be, will do him no harm."

For a moment the young woman appeared confused. Then she shook her head in silence, but quickly and eloquently; the gesture indicated, as convincingly as any words, that doing any damage to their host was indeed the farthest thing from her thoughts.

The wounded man let himself sink back, so that again he lay flat on the floor. For the moment he was satisfied. And he was very tired.

And also his need of nourishment was growing steadily stronger.

As his two visitors were leaving him to his rest, his gaze flicked restlessly from Melanie's back to fasten on the enthralled eyes of the servant girl. The girl's bare feet were barely moving, and it almost seemed that she did not intend to leave the room at all.

Whatever the sources (in fact there were more than one; but we need not go into details) of the good red food that over a matter of a few hours became available to the vampire, the strengthening effect was immediate and strong.

Radcliffe, when he saw his guest again early the next morning, blinked at the remarkable transformation. This hardly seemed like the same man who had staggered up to the door at the point of death. Health and vigor had been amazingly restored; in fact the visitor actually appeared to have grown younger overnight.

"You are feeling better, then, M'sieu Legrand?" the American asked, thinking even as he posed the question that it was obviously unnecessary.

The lithe figure, in its stained and tattered clothing, bowed. "Very much so, thank you. Thanks to your hospitality. This evening I shall be on my way."

Vlad Dracula, in conversation with his brave host, declining to share the last of the wine, mixed with some local well water—the fact that it was now breakfast-time was a good excuse—referred again to his passing acquaintance with Radcliffe's father, Benjamin Franklin.

The two men then exchanged some admiring comments regarding the great man, and Dracula repeated some of the conversation which had once passed between himself and Franklin.

With my strength restored, slightly more than twenty-four hours after my arrival, I prepared to depart. It was a cloudy day, and from the stock of clothing left to molder in the house's wardrobes I borrowed a broad-brimmed hat and cloak. From the stable I took a horse, which I paid for generously, in gold coin.

To Radcliffe I extended my hand and said: "Chevalier, I owe you my life." Then, thinking that Radu and his people were very possibly on my trail, with murderous intent, I added solemnly: "I advise you to leave this house promptly, and not to return at any time soon."

"I am no chevalier, but an American."

I accepted the correction with a slight bow. "Still, my suggestion stands, M'sieu Radcliffe."

"You give me good counsel, which only confirms my own plan, which is to depart for Paris within the hour. As for what you think you owe me, I would have done as much for anyone." Then the American paused to think about it. "Almost anyone," he amended.

"Nevertheless, Philip Radcliffe, I shall not forget the debt."

We shook hands firmly.

And I bowed to the young lady, Melanie Romain, who had come downstairs and out into the dooryard, to see me off. She looked a trifle pale, and serious. I thanked her gravely for her help.

I felt a natural kinship with the aristocracy. But I quite agreed with Radcliffe that if this French aristocracy cared nothing for the welfare of the people they ruled, and ignored all the people's problems, they had only themselves to blame for the Revolution.

We shook hands once more and I took my departure, after gracefully declining a last suggestion that perhaps we would be better off traveling together.

When they had watched their visitor out of sight, Philip said to the lady standing beside him: "A strange man."

"Very strange," she agreed thoughtfully.

Meanwhile, Old Jules's granddaughter, who had come out to gaze after the visitor's departing form, raised one hand to touch the scarf which, Philip noted, she had put round her throat, against the morning chill. She had found it somewhere in the house, he supposed, and maybe it had once been his mother's. But let the poor child have it now; she certainly deserved something for her loyalty.

Yes, Marguerite was looking a little pale this morning, though otherwise cheerful and well-satisfied enough. She was humming a little song as she went cheerfully about her voluntary chores. Radcliffe decided that he had better pay her a little something, besides the scarf, before he left for Paris.

~ *15* ~

After doing his best to provide their mysterious wounded visitor with all the help that he was willing to accept, Philip Radcliffe had found himself a decent-looking bed, not too dusty, in one of the upstairs rooms, and had slipped off his boots and thrown himself down. His plan was to rest for perhaps half an hour before making final preparations for an early resumption of his journey to Paris.

He awakened in the late afternoon, feeling that he had slept for hours. Guilt at his tardiness was ameliorated by an accompanying practical conviction that the sleep had been essential.

Travel and nervous strain had left him more exhausted than he had realized. After a good sleep, the problems of the world, even those of Revolutionary France, looked considerably less formidable.

He awoke to find Melanie in his room standing over his bed, looking at him with what he thought was a strange expression.

"I thought I heard you stirring," she said. Vaguely Radcliffe noticed the servant girl, Marguerite, hovering in the doorway.

Melanie, her impatience showing, half-apologetically

urged her new companion to start for Paris. They could cover a considerable distance before nightfall.

"Of course." He sprang up, feeling vaguely embarrassed and apologetic, and looked around for his boots. He rubbed his eyes. "Did you get any sleep?"

"Not a great deal. But I think enough. To be able to talk for a few hours with an old friend, a sympathetic listener, was perhaps better for me than sleep."

He went to the window and drew a deep breath. There had been rain, and the whole world now smelled clean and new.

In the glow of approaching sunset, Old Jules and his grand-daughter were preparing some kind of meal, consisting largely of eggs and bread and a little cheese. There was also some honey; evidently the bees were on the job. Jules said the pond had been yielding fish, but he'd had no luck there today.

Radcliffe, accompanied by his fair companion, took a last walk upstairs and down through the old manor house, and looked around.

Again it struck him: How the house seemed to have shrunk since then!

Carrying a loaded flintlock pistol, and looking warily about him, Radcliffe walked out into the farmyard, and took note of the absence of any livestock worthy of mention.

The current de facto master of the house wondered about his strange, and strangely injured, guest. There were things about the man that Radcliffe did not understand. The bandages Melanie had applied yesterday had already been discarded today.

They found the discarded bandages, the ones Melanie had thrown away last night, when she saw that they were no longer needed. There was surprisingly little blood on the cloth—only a faint brownish stain that vanished mysteriously on being exposed to sunlight.

"Did you wash these, Marguerite?"

"No ma'am." The girl sounded surprised at the question. Who would wash such rags? Her eyes were sleepy, and her thoughts seemed to be elsewhere.

One of the responsibilities his mother had tried to charge Philip with, when she had heard that he might be visiting the old family estate, had been to do what he could for some of the old family retainers, or at least to see what might have happened to them.

Radcliffe had left Philadelphia with some idea of perhaps being able to evaluate this property. But once he had been confronted with the reality of Revolutionary France, any such plans were quickly forgotten. Obviously the lands and what was left of the buildings were worthless under these conditions. What they might be worth in the future, or who was going to possess them, seemed impossible to guess. And the old family retainers, with the exception of Jules and his granddaughter, were dead or gone away.

Not that he had forgotten for a moment his main purpose in coming to Europe and to France: He was charged with carrying out a particular and confidential mission for the fledgling government in America. More precisely, for one of its leaders—Washington himself.

Radcliffe now hinted at something of the kind to Melanie. Once in Paris, his duty would require him to see Tom Paine, and communicate some message to him.

Tom Paine, the English-American internationally honored in revolutionary circles, was now (along with Washington and others) an honorary citizen of France. Lately Paine had even been made a member of the Convention, the ruling legislature of the new French government that called itself republican. The man who had been king had been beheaded, more than a year ago, despite Paine's suggestion that Citizen Louis Capet had better be exiled to America, where he could learn the truth about democracy and the nature of republican government.

Radcliffe tapped his pocket, in which he was carrying, besides his own written invitation, a sealed letter addressed to Paine.

The sealed letter was in fact a private plea, from Washington himself, couched in diplomatic language, urging Paine to stop making an ass of himself, and sever his connection with the crazy men who were generally giving the idea of revolution a bad name, and were irritating the English unnecessarily.

Melanie simply nodded. No intelligent, politically conscious Frenchwoman needed the identity or importance of Tom Paine explained to her.

God knew, Philip didn't blame the peasants of France for revolting. Not after all the stories of starvation and maltreatment he had heard in the short time since he had arrived in the country. Many thousands had gone hungry, millions had been treated like animals under the old regime. But during the few years since the fall of the Bastille, the new stories of mass beheadings and worse were deeply disturbing. Surely human rights and justice were not to be established by turning into savage animals. Humanity ought to mean more than finding a new and painless method of capital punishment . . .

Philip continued trying to gather information about the political situation from old Jules, as well from Melanie. Radcliffe hadn't been in Paris for many years, having come directly to the estate from some seaport town, after a surreptitious landing in a small boat on the beach.

"In Paris, things will be different." His voice sounded confident, though he could no longer feel sure of that.

"That may be, Citizen." The old man, who had probably never in his life been more than two or three miles from where he was born, let alone to the big city, scratched his head, sounding dubious.

Philip clung to the idea that he would have much less reason to worry about his own personal safety once he had reached the city. Here in the countryside, barbarism reigned.

But in Paris he would be respected, given a hearing, as an American and an acquaintance—perhaps he could even claim to be a friend—of Paine.

In short, discounting rumors to the contrary, and thinking that the latest stories from the capital were probably exaggerated, Radcliffe clung to a belief that in Paris the Revolution would not be conducted by backward peasants. It would be, or at least could be made to be, more reasonable, more enlightened. There would be, there must be, some sane authority to whom it would be possible to appeal. It was out here in the hinterlands that people had turned utterly into savages.

When Philip asked Melanie when she had last visited Paris, her replies were somewhat vague.

"I seem to remember your father telling me, once, that the Romains had relatives there?"

"That is true; I have a cousin." With Old Jules listening solemnly, an anxious expression on his face, she gave Philip the address.

She did not share Philip's hope that they would find the new government more moderate in the city. But she was willing to go there, or anywhere, on the chance of being able to help her father. In that effort she had nothing to lose.

Marguerite, a quiet and timid girl, expressed no wish to go with the party to Paris, and Philip thought that the girl's grandfather would have sternly discouraged the idea if she had.

In any case Philip packed essentials—blankets for sleeping out, powder and ball for his pistols, matches, razor, a change of linen, a little food and money, a clay pipe and some tobacco—in a couple of saddlebags, and tied the reins of his horse to the back of Melanie's light carriage.

Turning back for a last look, when he was already seated in the carriage with reins in hand, Radcliffe sighed. The house would have to be abandoned to its fate—there was no one to defend it, or the barns, which were now standing empty, prey to wind and weather, or any of the rest of the property. Besides, as an American in the revolutionary tradition, he was more than half-convinced that peasants who had been so long and viciously oppressed had some just claim to the land and other wealth of France. As for himself, he had no time or effort to spare in trying to assert a claim on property. He could expect nothing but more trouble if he stayed here, and therefore decided to evacuate the place while he still had a chance.

Once on the road, Philip and Melanie encountered little other traffic. They discussed the question of which revolutionary leader they should try to see first when they reached Paris. Tom Paine seemed a logical choice, though Melanie was doubtful about how much influence the American actually possessed.

Other possibilities were Robespierre himself, or the chief prosecutor, Fouquier-Tinville. A few months ago, Melanie would have chosen to put her case before Danton, but Danton himself had lost his head in April.

Another subject kept intruding: their recent strange encounter with the wounded man, now almost miraculously healed, who called himself Legrand. Melanie had an idea that this morning's change in the behavior of the servant girl, Marguerite, was somehow connected with the man's presence.

Radcliffe frowned. "But the fellow was three-quarters dead when he arrived. You don't suppose he—?"

"I don't know."

But never mind, there were plenty of other things to worry about.

Of course the main subject of the travelers' thoughts, whether they spoke of it or not, was the fate of Dr. Romain. As far as Melanie knew, her father was still alive, but he could easily have been beheaded this morning, or yesterday, or the day before, and she, at this distance from Paris, would be none the wiser.

"Philip, for the first time I am glad that my mother is dead. At least she was spared this torture." And with that, Melanie fell into a long silence.

Philip could only admire his companion's courage in bearing up as well as she did.

The more time Philip spent with Melanie, the more she intrigued and sometimes irritated him. She was of course vastly, delightfully changed from the child he remembered—yet in some delicious sense she was still the same girl. A remembered trick of tossing her hair to one side, with a quick motion of her head. His small female playmate of those days, now transformed into womanhood.

Melanie and Philip considered stopping at the house of Melanie's family in the nearby village to get some of her things, but she decided that would be taking an unnecessary risk; the local Committee of Public Safety might decide at any time to resume operations. The house in town would be deserted anyway. Her mother had died years ago, and all her other relatives were either dead or absent.

Melanie was reluctant to give a firm estimate of the number of days it would take them to get to Paris. In these troubled days, travel times were hard to estimate.

~ *16* ~

For some five years now, ever since the fall of the Bastille, Paris had served France and the rest of the world as a seemingly limitless source of news. Tremendous events were reported from the capital almost every day—and the passage of time proved that some of them, including many of the most improbable, had actually occurred. For example, it had to be accepted as a matter of sober, historical fact that the king and queen—or rather, the individuals who had formerly borne those titles—had indeed been arrested, bullied, and locked up by mere commoners. And that some months later, by decision of the people, the royal couple were both dead. Their heads had rolled into the basket as easily as those of ordinary criminals.

Yes, it was still hard to credit. Citizen Louis Capet—the man who had once been called by the title King Louis XVI, who had been the ruler of all France by divine right, anointed by the Church and all but worshiped by vast numbers of the people—that man had been beheaded, slaughtered in public like an animal, in January of 1793. His queen, Marie Antoinette, had followed him to the scaffold in October of the same year, after she had been proven (at least to the satisfaction of her enemies) to be in treacherous league with the rulers of her native Austria, sworn enemies of all revolutions.

Once everyone understood that those events were really true, it was hard to set any limit at all on miracles.

Other unbelievable stories, which it would have been easy to dismiss as wild rumor, were actually confirmed: The tide of war, the real war of armies, had turned again in favor of France, riddled though her armies were with desertions, political harassment, and executions. But meanwhile the majority of citizens, at least in Paris, were convinced that the most dangerous threat to their lives and happiness lay close to home. Wild rumors, heard everywhere, declared that bands of brigands, in the pay of royalists and foreigners, were scouring the countryside, raping and pillaging.

Still, according to the latest word from the frontiers, the Austrian and Prussian armies, commanded by the Duke of Brunswick, appeared able to make little headway against the armies of the people of France.

Philip's private opinion was that the war might now be going better for France only because her enemies, watching the revolutionary turmoil, were content to wait for her to tear herself to pieces.

In rapid succession, one generation after another of Revolutionary leaders had risen to power and fallen again. The time of turnover was now measured in mere months instead of years, and each new faction on achieving mastery exhibited more savagery than the last. Each was more fanatically dedicated to the ruthless repression of treasonous plots. And the more plots were discovered, and their fomenters executed, the more new examples of treason sprouted into light. Danton, once the unchallenged champion of the people against their aristocratic oppressors, more lately Robespierre's rival, had been arrested on March 30, 1794 (10 Germinal, Year Two, of the Revolutionary Calendar), charged with excessive moderation, and taken to the scaffold on April 5.

On May 7, Robespierre the Incorruptible, the newest

and seemingly invincible leader, disturbed by the atheistic tendencies shown by his colleagues and their spread among the people in general, had introduced worship of the Supreme Being. June 8 (17 Floréal, Year Three) was officially proclaimed the Festival.

On June 1, British warships commanded by Lord Howe defeated the French fleet in the English Channel.

Amid the strains and excitement of the journey, and the disturbing joy of Melanie's presence, Radcliffe almost forgot about the mysterious stranger, calling himself Legrand, whose life he had saved.

For several years now, the routines of planting and harvesting across much of France had been neglected, and the distribution of food had been disrupted, while armed peasants and other workers gathered to exchange inflammatory ideas, fears, hopes, and plans.

Lying athwart the travelers' most direct route to Paris were certain towns and villages around which Melanie thought it wise to detour, whole districts she preferred to avoid because of their reputation for fanatical enforcement of Revolutionary decrees upon strangers. The American deferred to her judgment in such matters. In one place, the sentry was asleep in his box, no doubt risking a grisly execution if his new masters should discover him thus. The travelers quietly rode on through the unguarded checkpoint.

A day or two later the trio, with Old Jules praying continuously to the Virgin, were forced to outrace in their carriage a motley band of unidentifiable pursuers—whether some self-constituted Committee of Public Safety or simple robbers was hard to say. More than once they saw in the distance, on town gates and walls, heads mounted on pikes, in provincial imitation of the now well-established Parisian custom.

It was the first time Philip had seen such a display, and

he stared in sickly fascination. The idea that the heads were artificial would not leave him, though he could see all too clearly that they were not.

"You seem upset," Melanie commented.

"I have seen hanged men, of course." The great majority of the citizens of America, as well as Europe, were no stranger to that sight. "But beheading . . ." Radcliffe shook his head. "That's something even more . . ."

Melanie appeared to be more thoughtful than shocked. "Yes, it is terrible. Though they say it is humane, more merciful than any of the older ways."

The travelers spent several days working their way through a countryside punctuated by the smoke of burning houses and barns. Enthusiasm for the Revolution was far from universal in the countryside. Black columns made ominous warning signals, visible for miles, at points spaced erratically around the horizon. When one fire died away, another sprang up somewhere else.

At night, the three travelers rested when and how they could. One midnight, on the verge of falling asleep in a haystack, Philip thought back to his recent stop in London, and told his traveling companions about his adventures there, where he had paused on his way from America to France. He told them also about his rough crossing of the Channel in a smuggler's small boat. England and France had been at war with each other for a year, but the secret commerce in goods and people was still thriving.

In a few days, after a journey that had afforded them no reassurance regarding the fate of France, Philip, Melanie, and Old Jules reached Paris. It bothered Radcliffe that conditions seemed no saner or quieter as they approached the capital.

Now Old Jules was rendered all but mute by unfamiliar wonders; and Melanie treated Philip like a visitor who had never seen Paris before. Indeed, his childhood memories of the great city were fragmentary and jumbled.

Of course the travelers' documents were examined at the

barrier before they were permitted to enter the city.

"Our capital, dear American, has been for many centuries the model for all Europe, the guide in all matters of taste and fashion.

"Here on the right, we now have the Faubourg Montmartre, and also the Temple; straight ahead is Faubourg Saint-Antoine."

Radcliffe turned to look where his guide had pointed. "And the address where I can reach you through your cousin—her name is Marie, right?"

"Marie Grosholtz."

"Yes." He nodded. "And the address, should something happen to separate us, is Twenty, Boulevard du Temple."

"That is correct—and over in that direction, across the Seine, we would find the Faubourgs Saint-Germain, Saint-Marcel, and Saint-Michel—all, of course, according to the old nomenclature. All names and titles connected with religion, particularly districts, have of course been changed. That was done by order of the National Convention, in 1792. But I'm afraid many people are like me, and keep using the old names, which no doubt is enough to get one arrested these days."

"But then one could just as likely be arrested for nothing at all."

"Very true. So be careful. Look, over there you can see the towers of Notre Dame. Of course now it too is supposed to be called something else, I forget what."

He gazed at the upper parts of the cathedral, visible above green summer trees and lesser buildings. "That I do remember." Here and there were a few such sights. Another was l'Hôtel Royal des Invalides, one of the largest buildings in Paris, a retirement home and hospital for veterans. On the high ground of Montmartre was a profusion of windmills.

Entering the Faubourg Saint-Antoine, one of the original hotbeds of revolutionary fervor, Radcliffe observed no great improvement. The streets were narrow and filthy, the dwellings wretched, the people dressed in rags.

*   *   *

The journeying couple—Jules, unless reminded, tended to tag along behind them, playing the servant's role in dangerously, conspicuously reactionary fashion—paused briefly to look at the Bastille. Or rather they stopped to survey the pile of ruins, inhabited by a few slow-moving workmen, that were now all that remained of that once forbidding fortress.

"So, this is where your Revolution had its beginning."

"Don't call it mine!"

"Sorry."

Melanie thought it over. She looked tired. "Yes, the thing began here, as much as anywhere. The nation, the government, all turned upside down. And it seemed necessary, and for a time I thought that we might really find a better way to live—as you did in America, without aristocrats or an established church. But soon . . ." Her voice trailed off, and she gave an expressive shrug.

"But what will they do with all the stones?" Philip gestured; the piles of disassembled masonry were impressive both in height and in extent. "There are certainly enough to do a lot of building. Schools? Better houses for the poor?"

Melanie shrugged. "No one knows. People argue about it. Construction is not one of the things that the new regime seems particularly good at. I have heard that the engineers in charge of demolition have sold many as souvenirs, and made a tidy profit."

Watching people coming and going on the city streets, Radcliffe observed that men generally wore red workers' caps, or tricorn hats with Revolutionary cockades of red, white, and blue paper pinned on them. Radcliffe was reminded that the *carmagnole* was a workman's jacket as well as a song, and the jacket had become part of the Revolutionary uniform.

In some ways the city showed itself about as Radcliffe had expected; in others it presented great surprises. Fascinating of course, but disappointingly unstable. On some streets people appeared to be going on with their lives, buying and selling, laughing and arguing and bargaining, as if things were normal after all. In other neighborhoods it was obvious that life had deviated a long way from its regular course. The slogans, and the scent of fear, were everywhere.

Melanie now guided Philip Radcliffe to the Jacobin club, a political organization so called because it met in a former Jacobin convent. Paine, whom they were hoping to encounter, was not there.

Philip was still puzzled. "Jacobin convent? I don't remember hearing of any such religious order."

"It is what the Dominicans are called in Paris," Melanie explained.

Radcliffe gazed around the large room furnished with desks and tables, and half-filled with men of a variety of ages and backgrounds—there were a few women present, seemingly as spectators—engaged in arguing pairs and groups.

Radcliffe overheard some fond whispers recalling Danton, who had so recently been guillotined. He had been loud, gross, and blustery, the very opposite of Robespierre in many ways. When Danton was holding forth, they said, one would require a very unusual voice to make oneself heard.

And then the voices cut off suddenly. Robespierre himself was approaching.

"It is Citizeness Romain. And how are you, my child?" The Incorruptible, his power now at its zenith, was holding a little nosegay of flowers. Not least among his achievements was the fact that he had been president of the Jacobin club since 1791. In that same year Robespierre had proposed that the death penalty be abolished. Since then he had changed his opinion, on that subject at least.

Melanie introduced her companion as the natural son of Benjamin Franklin, and an acquaintance of Tom Paine.

Radcliffe found himself face to face with a man of modest stature, thirty-six years old, wearing impeccably neat, jarringly aristocratic clothing, complete with powdered wig.

Maximilien de Robespierre had a small and somewhat cat-like face with greenish eyes. Green-tinted spectacles added a tint of that color to his sallow skin.

Robespierre's pair of bodyguards, armed with oaken cudgels, were large, fierce men, rudely dressed and with huge mustaches, seeming in every way a contrast to the man they served so loyally.

Radcliffe wondered if Robespierre was the only man in Paris who still wore the powdered wig and the fine clothes of a gentleman. The point of his doing so seemed to be that this individual stood serenely above all need to demonstrate where *his* sympathies lay.

In Paris the Incorruptible now maintained lodgings of becoming modesty, at 366 Rue St. Honoré, in the house of Duplay the carpenter and cabinetmaker.

Melanie said: "My father's life is dearer to me than almost anything else in the world."

Robespierre responded piously: "Nothing can be so dear to a good citizen as the Republic." The words were spoken with a terrible sincerity.

Standing beside the Incorruptible was a man introduced to Radcliffe as Louis-Antoine-Léon de Saint-Just. He was younger and taller than Robespierre, and classically handsome; Radcliffe had already heard him referred to in whispers as the Angel of Death.

Another man, eager and excited, broke into the conversation, challenging Saint-Just on the definition of a republic, and Radcliffe caught his reply: "That which constitutes a republic is the destruction of everything that opposes it!"

Meanwhile Melanie was doing her best to plead for her father, both with Saint-Just and his more powerful companion. She reminded them how Dr. Romain had always treated the poor in his district, whether or not they were able to pay.

The leaders looked momentarily sympathetic, but could not have been much impressed, because they promised nothing and offered no hope. Their response was restricted to a few more platitudes of Revolutionary morality.

"One moment." The Angel was holding up a pale hand. "I have seen that name . . ." Turning aside, he scattered papers on a table, then held up the one he had been looking for. "I am sorry to tell you, citizeness, that Citizen Romain, your father, deserved the full penalty for his crimes—and he paid that penalty this morning."

Five minutes later, when he and his disconsolate companion were back outside, Philip was muttering between clenched teeth: "I wanted to hit that man. I very nearly did."

Melanie, the tough young woman, had come near fainting at the news so brutally delivered, and Philip had to support her to the door. Her father's body—in two pieces—would now be in one of those anonymous mass graves inside the cemetery of the Church of the Madeleine . . .

Radcliffe embraced her like a brother, did what he could to comfort her. "The scoundrels! I am so sorry . . ." People walking in the street turned their heads toward him when his words fell clearly in the air. Well, he didn't care.

In an effort to divert her even slightly from the raw fact of death, he commented: "And so that is the famous Robespierre. He seems to make no effort to avoid dressing like an aristocrat . . . or behaving like one, either. I had no idea you knew the man."

"I have been present at a dinner or two where he was entertained, that's all." Melanie wiped her eyes. "But I don't suppose it would make any difference if I, or my father, had saved his life. Oh, Philip, it is horrible to think . . . of the grave."

"Of course it is."

"You will tell me my father died by accident? That someone was in a hurry and made a mistake?"

"No, I won't try to tell you that. Mistake or not, it's a damned outrage!"

"But one must go on." She wiped her eyes. "It is necessary to live for . . ." Her words trailed away.

"Yes, there will be a future for you someday. And for

France. What will you do now? And what about your cousin here in Paris? Are there any other relatives?"

"My cousin, yes," she murmured in a dazed voice. "Marie Grosholtz."

"I wonder if she has heard the news?"

Melanie made an effort to pull herself together. "Yes, I had better go and see my cousin."

"I'll come with you."

"No! That is, I think it will be better if you don't come just now. Besides, you still have important business that you must be about."

"You will be all right?"

"Yes!" And it seemed that, with a great effort, she had pulled herself together. She sounded almost normal. "I am sure."

The comment about his business was true enough. His meeting with Paine could be of some importance, and ought not to be postponed, even though Radcliffe had arrived too late to exert any influence on behalf of the Romain family.

Radcliffe reluctantly agreed to the temporary separation. But he insisted on arranging a rendezvous with Melanie, at the address she had already given him.

"Yes. Very well. We will meet there, and we will have . . . things to talk about, you and I. That is where my cousin is employed. Even if I should not be there, the people at that house will know where to reach me."

After being passed from one government official to another, most of whose names and functions he failed to remember, Philip told the last committee that he saw (whose title he never quite managed to find out) that, since housing seemed so difficult to obtain, he would appeal to his old acquaintance Thomas Paine, where he could be sure to obtain lodging for a few days at least. That seemed to solve the problem.

Meanwhile, Old Jules had kept tagging along with Philip. The old man was carrying his own identification paper, provided by the Committee of his own district, but he might as well have left it at home. With an American to question, a new set of foreign opinions to be sounded, none of the authorities seemed much interested in one more aged provincial.

Having given up on housing for the moment, Radcliffe set out to locate Tom Paine.

Again and again, as he sought to find his way to Paine's lodgings, Radcliffe's papers were checked by heavily armed and mustached men in workingmen's coats, with tricolor cockades on their red caps, who looked at the documents, and at him, suspiciously. He thought several of them were probably unable to read.

In fluent French he declaimed, so often that it began to seem like part of a ritual: "As an American, I am fully in sympathy with your wish to be rid of kings and queens."

Absent this almost regular interference, Paine would not have been hard to find. He was at his house.

Paine during much of his stay in Paris occupied a rented mansion at No. 63, Rue de Faubourg St. Denis. While still technically within the city, the area had a rural character, and seemed far removed from Parisian street life.

The house was separated from the street by walls and gates, and, isolated in a grove of maple trees, reminded Radcliffe of a farmhouse. Indeed the courtyard was like a farmyard, with geese and chickens scratching and waddling about.

Paine was a red-nosed man in his late fifties, a couple of inches under six feet tall, very nearly Philip's own height. When Philip caught up with him, standing in his courtyard, feeding his domestic fowl with handfuls of grain, Paine was dressed like many of the other Revolutionary officials Radcliffe had seen thus far in France: a blue coat over a red waistcoat, long hair pulled back and tied without wig or powder. And of course the ubiquitous tricolor cockade.

"I thought perhaps that I would find you at the Convention, sir," Radcliffe said in English. "Are you still a member?"

"Only nominally, I am afraid. I go but little to the Convention, and then only to make my appearance; because I find it impossible to join in their tremendous decrees, and useless and dangerous to oppose them."

The older American, having observed over a period of months and years how the situation was deteriorating, said he was half-expecting to be taken into custody himself at any time.

"Really, sir!"

Paine's smile was wan. "Really."

Not knowing how to respond to that, Philip got out his oilskin packet and handed over the confidential letter he was carrying.

Philip hadn't seen the letter open until now, and had only a general idea of its contents. Paine now enlightened him by reading the last part of the message aloud:

> . . . your presence on this side of the ocean may remind Congress of your past services to this country; and if it is in my power to impress them, command my best exertions with freedom, as they will be rendered cheerfully by one, who entertains a lively sense of the importance of your works, and who, with much pleasure, subscribes himself,
>
> Your sincere friend,
> G. Washington

"That is very welcome," Paine mused aloud, refolding the paper. "It seems that I—"

And then he suddenly fell silent.

An armed party of soldiers had appeared.

Their sergeant approached, grim-faced. "Philip Radcliffe?"

"Yes." *But this is some mistake . . .*

"In the name of the people, you are under arrest."

Philip was stunned. When a pair of men moved to seize his arms he fought back instinctively. Before the brief struggle was over, one of the soldiers had a bleeding lip, and the American had suffered a slight wound on the crown of his head. Meanwhile the voice of Thomas Paine was raised in crude and clumsy French, arguing with the soldiers to no purpose.

Blood trickling down his face, Radcliffe said: "If my father was living here, now, no doubt the Committee would find him dangerous too."

He was a block away from the gate of Paine's house, being marched along the street with arms bound behind him, before it crossed his mind to wonder what had happened to Old Jules. Certainly the old man was nowhere in sight now.

By the time I reached Paris again, I had more or less fully recovered my strength. Once more I was actively in pursuit of my brother, and I had in mind several refinements on the last cycle of punishment to which I had subjected him.

Meanwhile, Philip Radcliffe was not far from my thoughts. Given the young man's impulsive disposition, and the strange environment of Revolutionary Paris that he was about to enter, I thought it doubtful that he would be able to stay out of trouble very long.

It was Old Jules, of course, who brought me word that my recent benefactor had been arrested a few hours earlier, charged with aristocracy and other nonsense, and was now imprisoned, already under sentence of death—such speedy action by the Tribunal was by no means unusual in those days. Before leaving the chateau, I had privately arranged with Jules a means by which I could be summoned when the need arose. (His master, I was sure, was much too enlightened to take seriously the idea of burning a lock of hair in a candle-flame, whilst reciting certain words.)

When the occult summons came, surprising me only by its swiftness, I was annoyed by the distraction, but considered that my honor allowed me no choice. I must defend the man who had so recently saved my life. I would have to abandon for the time being my pursuit of Radu, and concentrate my energies upon the task of getting Philip out of prison.

Citizen Legrand received the news calmly enough from the old peasant. "Well, it did not take the young man long to put his head into the noose—or in this case under the blade. I am not much surprised. He seemed energetic and impulsive."

Old Jules nodded sadly. It was easy to see that he was more than half afraid of me, now that the bit of magic I had given him had worked, and would welcome the opportunity to spend as little time with me as possible.

Constantia, who happened to be on hand, remarked: "Is this American of such importance to you, then?"

I turned on her a look of cold surprise. "It is a matter of honor."

"Oh," she murmured. "Ah, yes. *That* again."

~ *17* ~

After his return to Revolutionary Paris in the last decade of the eighteenth century, Radu Dracula maintained at least two and sometimes three residences in the city, keeping no single one for more than about a year. He occupied each domicile under a different name, and of course lived in each in the guise of a breather. The metropolitan population was now swollen to more than half a million, and despite the determined efforts of the new government to keep track of everyone, one who knew how to go about such matters found it easy to dispose of one official identity and assume another.

He found it delightful to contemplate a world grown so crowded with breathing folk. The more of them there were, the more the beautiful youth of both sexes excited his sensuous cravings. And all his life, from his own youthful breathing years, he had preferred cities over the countryside.

While the hunting party composed of his associates had been out scouring farms and villages and forests, hot on the trail of his brother, Radu himself had remained in the city—which was, after all, a lot safer than trying to hunt down Vlad. He understood that fact much better than did any of the people he had sent out.

* * *

Endlessly fascinated by the Terror as it developed, the younger brother spent a great deal of time roaming about the city, usually after dark, dressed in sans-culotte costume.

Wearing his *carmagnole* and his red woolen nightcap with a jaunty tricolor cockade pinned on one side, in perfect accord with the latest in popular fashion, he joined hundreds of others in haunting the Place de la Revolution, waiting for the next batch of executions.

In such guise, he had taken a modest part, chiefly that of an encouraging observer, in the slaughter at the Palace of the Tuileries, in 1792; he never realized how narrowly he had escaped Vlad's efforts to find him there.

The sole survivor of Radu's failed war party returned to the city, bringing his master the story of the disastrous attack upon his older brother. The survivor for some reason believed that his making a thorough report entitled him to a reward of gold, or at least forgiveness, for his part in the fiasco.

When Radu was certain that he had extracted every bit of relevant information his informant could provide, he paid him instead in a different kind of coin. Then he made his own preparations to hurry to the scene of the reported combat.

Packing up one of his portable caches of home earth in a convenient traveling bag, and saddling a horse, the younger Dracula started out. He had a hidden earth or two of his own in the area that he was bound for, but Vlad had been there and might have destroyed them. Radu intended to take no chances.

Following with some difficulty the trail of his vanished posse, according to the best directions the unnerved survivor had been able to provide, he came in the course of two days to the rural site of the fight, a scene which had begun to regain its pastoral and peaceful character. Here the visitor from the city spent some time in observing closely the re-

maining marks on the ground and torn-up grass and shrubbery, reconstructing the event in his own mind. It appeared
that the failed assassins had almost succeeded in killing
Vlad before he could dig himself up out of his ravaged earth.
There, certainly, was the ruined grave, with a lot of French
dirt still scattered about, and the remnants of at least one
breather's body still lying where the crows and wild dogs had
let them fall.

Radu drove off the remaining scavengers, who dared to
clamor their annoyance at him. He even considered refresh-
ing himself with the blood of one of them. For some months
now all the blood, all the nourishment he had ingested had
been human. This rich diet sometimes began to pall a trifle
through the very sameness of its luxury; but now, after thinking the matter over, he decided to hold out for some finer sustenance than wild dog.

He was impressed anew, though not at all surprised, by
the evidence of his brother's ferocity and skill in combat.
These were matters that the younger brother knew and appreciated better than anyone else who was still alive.

With the experience of three hundred years to guide
him, Radu had little difficulty interpreting a number of the
surviving details of sign left by the fight. Scraping at the
ground with a booted foot, he unearthed more rat-gnawed
breather's bones, the last remains of another of his servants.

Served the fools right for bungling their job!

Until this moment he had at least allowed himself to
hope that his brother was truly dead. But he no longer
thought that there was any chance of that. Logically, of
course, there was still a chance that Vlad, injured and caught
out in the open, had died of his wounds, or succumbed to the
searing power of unshielded daylight.

Radu had chosen a strong, phlegmatic mount, and he went
riding languidly. Today it amused him to be brazenly aristocratic. Traveling by daylight under the shelter of a cloudy
sky and broad-brimmed hat, he found and followed the trail

left by his wounded brother in leaving the scene of the struggle.

He rode past one vulture, and then another, who from their perches on high dead branches regarded the journeying vampire with the air of amused spectators. He tried to find his own amusement in the fact, but failed.

One thing the cautious searcher knew he would *not* find was his brother's corpse; the old, old *nosferatu* did not linger on in any earthly form once they had expired; their bodies tended to vanish, quickly and rather spectacularly.

In good time the trail he was following brought him to a chateau, or manor, which now stood silent and deserted under the moon.

For a time Radu sat motionless in his saddle, probing the scene before him with all his senses. Only a few days ago, this house had been someone's dwelling, but now the subtle changes accompanying desertion had come over the place. Dismounting and walking forward, he found that he could enter almost without difficulty. Only a shadow of the habitation factor remained to slow him at the door, testifying to recent occupation.

If his brother had found shelter anywhere, the odds were overwhelming that it was here.

That feeling was soon confirmed when Radu sensed the presence of a vampire's earth. Alluring, like the faint aroma of baked bread to a breather. Radu had not known about this hideaway of Vlad's until now. There were no clues that a breather would have noticed, but undoubtedly there existed a flattened oval of Transylvanian soil under the paving of the floor in the oldest part of the house, beneath an odd irregular chamber now used only as a storeroom or shed.

The hideaway was now unoccupied, but evidence was not lacking that Vlad had been here, not many days ago. Wounded, but doubtless once he had reached this spot, he had been able to recover; ominously, there was no lingering psychic smell of vampire-death. A few small stains had been allowed to dry on the stone floor, and had since almost disappeared. But Radu could sense them.

Vampire blood.

The investigator was tempted to take advantage of the earth of his homeland to catch a daytime nap. But in the end he did not dare do so, thinking it quite possible that Vlad might be returning at any moment.

There might, he thought, be some advantage to finding out who else had been living here. Perhaps he would be able to talk to one of Vlad's active breathing helpers; there always seemed to be a few such folk around.

Prowling the deserted upper rooms of the house, he sought with no success for some evidence of the identity of the latest occupant. Well, there were other ways to obtain information.

At dusk Radu emerged from a doze on his portable earth, which he had tucked away inside the trunk of a fallen tree, to look for someone from whom he might be able to obtain more information.

The young girl appeared very conveniently, climbing a gentle path that led up to the rear of the house, obviously coming back from the stream, where she had caught a fish or two, now gill-looped on a string, to eke out her meager diet. She was as wide-eyed and innocent as her fish. Oh, charming, charming!

He stood beside the path, impeccably handsome, radiating kindness. "What is your name, my child?"

"Marguerite, sir."

And the girl, with her fond memories of Vlad, was easily seduced by this man who in some ways resembled his older brother.

In the farmyard, and later inside the house, in the small room off the kitchen where she slept, Radu petted her and interrogated her. The girl's cheeks glowed and her breath came faster, and her fish soon fell to the ground forgotten.

When he thought he had all the information he was going to get, had learned all he could about Vlad's stay in this house and the breathing folk who'd sheltered him, the game which had begun as a form of lovemaking quickly grew more intense. He began the leisurely process of killing the girl, paralyzing her early in the game, sipping blood, a little from here, a little from there, and inflicting mutilation.

I know, he thought, pausing, licking blood from his long nails, listening abstractedly to the sounds of pain. *This reminds me of a discussion I had once, with—someone, I forget his name. I know the very person with whom I would like to share and describe this adventure. Too bad that he is only a breather.*

Marguerite's body was still shuddering, still breathing, when Radu let it slump to the floor amid stained bedding. Sniffing fastidiously, he could easily sense the flavor and the scent of Vlad upon her. Even the two small puncture wounds his brother had left upon her shapely neck were still unhealed.

He tasted her in that very spot, and then, in slow succession, at several other places on her now fully exposed body. Experimenting, to discover how quickly he could locate the nerve centers that afforded the most exquisite pain. This gave her remaining blood a delicate flavor, which could be thoroughly appreciated only by the true gourmet.

To complete his enjoyment of the young peasant girl he decided to allow himself an hour or so longer, and during that time he put aside all problems, giving himself over entirely to the experience. Regretfully he concluded that he could not spare more time than that.

Casting the still-shuddering body aside for the last time, he stretched luxuriously, put on his clothes again, and let his mind go wandering. He had quite forgotten about Marguerite before her last thread of life quietly parted.

Radu, startled out a reverie by a slight noise behind him, out in the kitchen, jumped to his feet with a pang of fear, nerves twanging like plucked catgut, then jumped again, spinning around in his tracks.

Only a mouse. Yes, only a mouse, this time.

He stood there shivering and angry, suddenly a terrified vampire. For a moment he was convinced that *Vlad had lured and trapped him here . . .*

He even feared for his life, though he knew Vlad was not going to kill him. For Radu the true death was always— almost always—a terrifying prospect.

Radu, unlike his elder brother, was not immune to fear. Far from it.

That was one reason why he hated his brother so intensely.

Reason returned, and soothed him. Yes, someday—he could not escape the thought—*someday* he would turn around and Vlad would be standing there, staring at him. And there would follow another century or two of punishment, of mental and physical torture that only one Dracula could devise for another . . .

Yes, someday. But just now Vlad was nowhere in sight. Gradually his pulse returned to normal.

Radu supposed it likely that he was never going to hear the full story of how his brother had been speared in his earth and almost done to death.

Rather it was now up to Radu to be on guard against Vlad's inevitable counterattack.

Traveling most of the way on two wings, part of the way on four legs (all his own), making faster time than on his outward journey, he was soon back in Paris. Once there, he set someone to finding out more about the owners of the chateau.

Shortly after Radu returned to Paris, one of his people reported to him with great excitement a rumor racing through the vampire world that Vlad was dead; but the younger brother was far too canny to trust to the truth of any such tale without substantial proof.

He said: "It will take very persuasive evidence indeed to

convince me that he is truly dead. Never mind that for the moment. I want to know all there is to discover about an American named Philip Radcliffe and a young Frenchwoman, Melanie Romain."

Radu the Handsome considered it prudent to invent yet another new identity for himself, to use when he chose to walk among breathers as one of them. He changed his residence as well, moving to humbler quarters though he still remained within the city.

And now, for the first time in several years, he seriously considered abandoning France, even Europe, altogether. He pictured himself fleeing, to America, or the South Seas, some land in the remotest corner of the earth. Vlad would not kill him; no, Radu felt confident of that when he thought about it calmly. But Vlad was quite capable of inflicting truly terrible punishments, indeed was ingenious at devising them. The thought of another century of nightmares was enough to make Radu feel faint. Yet he never considered abandoning his schemes against Vlad; it was as if he really had no choice.

Then Radu heard, through one of his revolutionary contacts, that Philip Radcliffe, an American who was supposedly of an aristocratic family, heir to the very manor in which Vlad had taken shelter, had been arrested at the orders of the Committee of Public Safety.

Radcliffe was being held in prison, and had already gone through a form of trial on charges of being an aristocrat— there seemed no doubt of that, given his mother's family. He was also charged with plotting, a vague but generally effective accusation.

Radu's informant shook her head and muttered: "They say that he is Franklin's bastard son, but I doubt that will be enough to save him."

Radu continued to find out all he could about the condemned suspect Radcliffe.

* * *

Knowing Vlad as well as he did, Radu was not slow to assume that Vlad considered himself bound in honor to save Radcliffe.

The younger brother thought: "Surely I can turn that to my advantage somehow."

The more the younger vampire thought about this news, the more it seemed to open a great opportunity. Now the scheming younger brother determined to lure Vlad into a trap, force him to fail in something he had sworn to do, and possibly engineer his death. He knew how his elder brother driveled on and on about what he conceived of as his honor.

The first step was to make sure that young Radcliffe was indeed sentenced to death, despite any connection that might be shown to exist between the young man and Benjamin Franklin, and/or Tom Paine.

For his activities as far back as the 10th of August of 1792, and at a number of other times and places, Radu in one of his identities as a breathing Frenchman had even attained some minor status as a Revolutionary hero and leader. The hero had not been heard of for some time, and was now thought to be dead.

That was fine with Radu. Of course no vampire wanted to be subject to the intense scrutiny of a breathing public. More than very moderate success, in any breathers' enterprise, could draw a dangerous amount of attention to oneself, and awaken jealousy in potential rivals. Better to play the role of an almost-anonymous but recognizable and trustworthy *sans-culotte*. With that goal in mind, he had arranged to be signed up by Robespierre as a spy and special agent, reporting only to the Incorruptible himself.

Today Robespierre, cool as always, seeming impressively above most of the concerns of lesser men, was striking a pose of symbolic significance at one end of the green, cloth-covered table of the Revolutionary Tribunal, looming over everyone else including the judges, who were sitting.

The Incorruptible, chiding some judge for suspicious leniency, was saying calmly: "True innocence is never afraid of public vigilance." Then, glancing around suspiciously, he added in a private whisper to Radu: "See me later at the house."

The Tribunal met for most of its sessions in a huge, cavelike chamber with marble walls that in years past had accommodated the meetings of the Paris Parlement. Candles burned before the court clerk as he labored with a quill pen to keep up with the accusations made by the examining lawyers and the judgments handed down.

Frequently in attendance at the Tribunal, when bad weather or some other reason kept them from the guillotine, were Madame Defarge, and the rest of the bloodthirsty *tricoteuses,* the women who sat knitting through all the trials and executions.

(Narrator's note: "I don't see how those women can do that," Constantia once commented to me, when we were speaking of these women. "No?" "No; I hate knitting.")

Later in the day Radu, doing his best to fulfill his duties as a spy, showed up at the carpenter's house, bringing Robespierre, for his eyes only, a new list of suspects. Heading the list was a name often used by his brother as an alias—Corday. And a description of Vlad, in his frequently adopted guise of a young breather.

Then, into the ears of these dedicated, incorruptible defenders of revolutionary virtue, he whispered his poisonous advice, suspicions, accusations.

Many others were doing the same thing, or trying. But Radu had access to Robespierre in his private lodgings.

Everyone in the house had seen Radu coming or going at one time or another, and everyone thought he was there as a companion or associate of someone else. Therefore he could come and go pretty much as he pleased, enjoying the situation immensely.

Duplay himself seemed under the impression that Radu was a member of the secret police, coming in at all hours anonymously to give the Incorruptible his secret reports. And Radu, struck by an inspiration, gradually maneuvered Duplay into starting work on a wooden guillotine blade, precisely shaped to fit the grooves in the machine, the edge filed and sanded as smooth and sharp as wood could be. Radu wasn't yet sure just how he could possibly induce Vlad to lie down on the plank that fed the machine, but it would please him enormously to have some possibility along that line. He gave the cabinetmaker to understand that Sanson, the chief executioner, was eager to try out such a device.

"The danger of rust is eliminated, you see," Radu improvised. "Despite the constant wetting."

The woodworker frowned, picking absently at a sore on one of his own callused fingers, where the broken fragment of a wooden splinter was trying to work its way up out of the skin. "But the edge, citizen—surely a wooden edge will break and wear away much faster? One or two tough necks . . ."

"We will see; but they want to make a test using wood."

"I suppose, if you say so, citizen—but in the name of the people, why?"

Radu ignored the question. Looking around, as if to see whether they were being overheard, he let an ominous undertone creep into his voice. "If I were you, Citizen Duplay, I'd work fast, and say nothing of this to anyone."

Already the younger vampire saw several possible ways of turning these things to his advantage. If he played his cards right, it was not inconceivable that he should succeed in getting his older brother's neck beneath the heavy—in his case, wooden—knife.

At about the same time an elated Robespierre, who seemed totally convinced he had the perfect society now almost within his grasp, was driving everyone to prepare for the Festival of the Supreme Being, which he had decreed would be held June 8, 1794.

When that date came around, I, Vlad Dracula, made sure to be part of the audience in the cathedral. I was still stalking my brother, of course, and incidentally marveling at the blasphemy.

On 17 November, 1793, a week after the first great Festival of Reason, the Commune had ordered all churches in Paris closed. For the Festivals of Reason that followed, Notre Dame cathedral and a number of lesser churches had been turned, at least for a few days, into pagan temples. Stained-glass windows bearing religious images were draped with canvas until their final fate could be decided. The interim effect was to dim the interior enormously, even in broad daylight, incidentally making the place vastly more comfortable for the *nosferatu*.

Of course every trace of Christian "superstition," in the form of ornamentation, had already been expunged from the structure. Where the high altar had stood there now rose up an imitation of some Greek temple decorated with pikes and other weapons. The music which replaced the hymns may be imagined.

I remember hearing Hébert, one of the most vicious of the Revolutionary rabble-rousers, remark with a chuckle: "How angry the good God must be! No doubt the trumpets of judgment are about to sound."

But now Hébert himself was dead, reduced to the status of a headless corpse. He and eighteen of his colleagues and supporters had been fed to Moloch a few months back, on the 24th of March.

I remember Reason, sitting in her litter, borne by drunken men in what were meant to be Roman togas, swilling wine and brandy out of consecrated chalices.

I remember the burning of saints' relics, and ancient churchly books and documents, making a strange, rich incense. At such a time, I rejoiced that I was not compelled to breathe.

In the midst of all this sacrilege I moved, now wearing my own *carmagnole* as protective coloration, stalking my brother patiently, knowing that he would hardly be able to deny himself such sights and sounds as these.

Often I scowled at the blasphemous goings-on, and once or twice I came near doing violence. But in the end I made no move to interfere, thinking I could not allow myself to be distracted from my search.

On the 19th of the new month Prairial, all citizens had been invited to decorate their dwellings with flowers and live branches, a display of living things in honor of Robespierre's new friend, the Supreme Being. In the Jardin National, an amphitheater had been created, and in the most prominent place a statue representing Wisdom was temporarily camouflaged as the dingy, ugly figure of Atheism.

Toward the end of the Festival, someone ritually set fire to the straw man of Atheism, which, having been made for the purpose, obligingly burst into flames. The symbols did not quite all fall into place for Robespierre, though, as Wisdom emerged from the trial somewhat blackened and obscured.

A wax bust of Jean-Paul Marat, the martyred Friend of the People, was hauled around in a triumphal chariot, labeled:

TO MARAT, FRIEND OF THE PEOPLE
THIS IS HOW THE PEOPLE HONORS ITS FRIENDS

The vampire had never met the murdered man in the flesh, but if the Friend of the People had really been as ugly as everyone said he was, then the wax image, which must have been modeled by Marie Grosholtz, was impressively lifelike.

By now the Terror was in full stride and threatening to

consume Paris like a fire. The chief concern of many of the supposed leaders of the people was now nothing more than keeping themselves alive.

Indeed, I had begun to think that this Revolution of the French was something the world had never seen before, an event transcending ordinary wars, rebellions, and foolishness, far surpassing all the common outbreaks of bloodlust and madness. Casting my thoughts back through the three-hundred-plus years of my existence, I could come up with nothing very much like it. Mere horrors and blasphemies, of course, abound in every age. Wars come and go with the inevitability of thunderstorms, and rebellions and mutinies were not uncommon. But this . . .

Almost two hundred years earlier, at the court of Ivan the Terrible, I had seen horrors unbelievable . . . but no, that had been different; Ivan and his terror prefigured Hitler, a case of one man's madness infecting multitudes. This new French Terror had no such focal point. At the height of the infection, there was no individual, not even the Incorruptible himself, whose elimination would have broken the fever. Truly it seemed to swell up out of the People themselves. But it eventually proved self-limiting; the very individuals, the cells and organs of the body politic by which the game of guillotining was enforced, were the same ones on whom the blade fell with most dreadful frequency.

It is, I think, a significant fact that, as one historian has written, no high-ranking Revolutionary authority ever attended any execution but his own.

~ 18 ~

Sensing a great opportunity in the fact of Radcliffe's sentencing, though not yet sure just how to take advantage of it, the younger Dracula began a personal search of all the prisons within several miles of Paris, trying to locate the American. In this task he proceeded warily, wanting to locate Vlad also, but afraid of being seen by him.

In Radu's recent few years aboveground, it had become his habit, when things were dull, to cruise prisons and asylums in search of amusement. There was such a nice variety of such places now to choose from.

Anyway, the exquisite sufferings of . . . what had been the name of that last peasant girl? . . . of dear little Marguerite had put Radu in mind of a certain breathing prisoner he'd met, a year or two ago, in one of the asylums.

Radu, having identified the general character of the place from the outside, was not immediately certain whether he was entering an asylum or a prison; the clientele overlapped a great deal between the two kinds of institutions. Many of them were not really surprised to observe a man entering their rooms, despite locked doors and apparently solid walls, then later taking his departure by the same mysterious means. Nor would the authorities pay much attention when some inmates told them this had happened.

If Radu wanted to know about prisons, the former Marquis de Sade was the one to talk to—the man seemed to have spent most of his adult life in them.

Radu did not particularly wish to know more about prisons and asylums—only about certain of their clientele. Looking around him now, Radu noted that this place had the look of a converted convent. Religious images had been scrupulously torn down, in pursuit of Revolutionary orthodoxy. What had once been a well-tended garden was rapidly running to seed and ruin.

The man in the cell was of average height, about five and a half feet, and was now past fifty years of age. A rather jolly fellow, by all appearances. His light chestnut hair was thinning and going gray. His body was comfortably stout, his fair face marked by comparatively few smallpox scars. At the moment his pale blue eyes were wide with surprise under a high forehead.

Obviously the prisoner had been startled by the silent intrusion of an unexpected visitor. But he needed only a moment to recover.

"Welcome, Prince Dracula! Or is it Citizen Dracula now? It is more than a year since you have visited me."

Radu made himself comfortable, choosing the softest-looking of two available chairs. "Suit yourself as to the form of address; I am indifferent as to which my true friends use—and I certainly hope to count the Marquis de Sade among my friends. Or do you now prefer to be called citizen, along with everyone else?"

The Marquis was undoubtedly glad to see his mysterious visitor. At Radu's entrance to his neatly furnished cell, Sade had been seated (in his third chair) at a table, playing with a set of half a dozen little toys on the tabletop. Radu, looking at them with curiosity, observed that they were tiny waxen representations of human bodies, male and female, all naked, in various attitudes of fear, or menace. The two male figures, one a mere beardless youth, were both in a prominent state of sexual arousal. It was not the subject matter so much which interested the vampire—he thought that pretty tame—but the artist's skill at modeling on such a small scale. The whole body of each figure was no longer than a man's hand, and yet all the fine anatomical details were exquisitely rendered. Real, fine human hair had been affixed in little tufts in the appropriate places.

"You are interested in my little toys, prince? Ah, I yearn for the full collection I had with me when I was in the Bastille. There was a prison for you!"

"Not for me, thanks."

"They are frightfully expensive. But what is one to do? One must have amusement."

Radu observed him fondling the figures ardently. The pale fingers of the Marquis threatened to crush the wax, and must be heating it to slipperiness.

Radu raised an eyebrow. "I admit I am surprised that a man of your character must now content himself with wax images. Surely some of your fellow inmates here are women?"

"Ahh . . ."

"Or at least some of the visitors. And the men here must have sisters and daughters and wives. It would be easy to induce some of these fair ones to make themselves available for your enjoyment."

"Ah, one would think so! But no, prince, it is not that easy. Besides, as I am sure you would agree, one needs to be sequestered with the women to derive the utmost of pleasure from them—and nothing short of the uttermost in delight is worthy of a gentleman's devoted efforts. Do you agree, Prince?"

"The Marquis speaks wisdom, as always."

Radu's gaze returned to the little waxen figures.

"And who made these, my friend?" he asked. "They show great skill."

"Ah, yes." The former marquis gazed at the images fondly. "At the Cabinet du Cire, number twenty, Boulevard du Temple. You do not know the establishment? A man named Curtius is in charge—he runs it with a woman who is supposed to be his niece. Who models these miniatures I am not sure. Most of the waxen figures Curtius makes himself are lifesize, and, alas, fully clothed."

"I see. Yes, perhaps I have heard something." He suppressed a yawn; an affectation, now grown to be an unconscious habit, in one who was not required to breathe. In fact fits of yawning came upon him periodically. He supposed it had something to do with boredom; or possibly with his long sleeps and nightmares. Another thing he must remember to thank his brother for, as soon as the opportunity arose.

"Prince Radu?"

"Yes?"

The Marquis urgently, stumblingly, began to plead with the prince to arrange an escape for him. Radu smiled and nodded, and promised to see what he could do; but actually he had plenty of other things to think about just now, and foresaw that he would let the matter slide.

From the subject of escape and its difficulties, the conversation easily slid on to that of prisons. Radu was honestly curious. "But you have been in so many prisons! Are you able to keep track of them all?"

"Each has a different smell about it . . . It is totally unjust, of course, that I should be here at all!"

"Ah, but I have heard something about the case. The young woman *did* die, did she not, after you and your valet were through with her?"

"Which young woman?" Sade seemed affronted. "Not all of them died, by any means!"

Radu was ready to change the subject. "Comfortable quarters," he observed, looking about the room. "Of course it does not really compare to those you enjoyed in the Bastille, as a prisoner of the *ancien régime*. If memory serves me right, you had a desk there, and a wardrobe. Silk breeches, many shirts, coats, shoes, and boots . . . you had a fireplace, as I recall? Family portraits on your plastered walls, velvet pillows on your bed."

"Three kinds of perfume," Sade himself murmured in a husky voice. Eyes gleaming, he was caught up in memory. "All the lamps and candles that I wanted . . . but that was long ago. In 1784."

"Is it really ten years since you were first locked up in the Bastille? How time flies! For some of us, at least." Radu pretended to suppress a yawn.

Sade was staring at him, with a delightfully perfect expression of hatred and envy.

Radu went on: "You had quite a library there, too. More than a hundred volumes, wasn't it? And your poor, dear wife was allowed to visit you almost every week. Walking privileges in the garden . . . except that you *would* keep shouting your obscenities." Radu shook his head, chided his companion with a mock tut-tut. "Then they let you out. Then they locked you up again. That time—let me see—they put you in Charenton? The asylum."

"But they realized I was not at all mad, and they eventually let me go."

"And then—?"

Sade's voice had grown tightly controlled. His best courtroom voice. "Last year I was arrested again. As a former aristocrat, of course. Bah!"

"So, political reasons this time. Even you . . . now that you mention it, I seem to remember hearing that you were accused of 'moderatism' . . . one of the most unlikely charges that the Revolution has ever brought against any of its enemies—or do you count yourself among its friends? Has anyone ever died of 'moderatism,' I wonder?"

"Only when Doctor Sanson treats the disease! Ah, hah, hah hah!" A huge coarse laugh.

But de Sade was not minded to discuss that subject at any length. Instead, he began to talk of his present accommodations: "What more could I have wanted here? It was like a paradise; beautiful house, superb garden, exclusive society, wonderful women—when suddenly the execution grounds were placed absolutely under our windows and the cemetery for those guillotined put in the very middle of our garden."

Doubtless, Radu mused, Paris now produced too many headless ones for any one cemetery to accommodate.

His companion was becoming unreasonably excited. "I tell you, prince, there have been eighteen hundred executions under my window in the last thirty-five days. A third of them have been taken from this very building!"

"Eighteen hundred!" That really seemed an excessive estimate to Radu; he reminded himself that he was, after all, talking to a certified madman. Of course there might really be some auxiliary *mechanique* somewhere in the neighborhood. They were scattered all over France, after all.

Radu had not observed any such facility on his way in, or scented any nearby tract of blood-soaked earth. Now he went to the window and looked out, seeing only a garden. He concluded that his old associate was very likely genuinely deranged.

Meanwhile de Sade had let his outrage slide away and begun fantasizing about the young nuns who must have occupied this room before the Revolution.

"How many novices do you suppose slept in this little chamber?" Actually the room was generously sized indeed, compared to the vast majority of the prison cells Radu had seen. Sade seemed totally caught up in his speculations. "Three or four, at the very least. Maybe five or six. Do you suppose that it was necessary for them to share beds?"

Radu shook his head. "I too have slept in convents from time to time; but none of them were organized in any such fashion as that. But do go on. There is no reason why you should give up your daydreams."

"Daydreams, are they? Only daydreams?" De Sade's eyes flashed. "I should think that maintaining discipline in a convent would be one of the chief concerns of the authorities in charge."

"No doubt. You might have done well, I should think, as Mother Superior."

"Why do you say that? Women are more inclined to cruelty than we men are, and that is because they have a more delicate nervous system."

Suddenly the man sat back on his haunches and bellowed, a long, quavering note. *Perhaps he thinks he is a werewolf now,* thought his visitor, intrigued.

Then the crouching figure shouted: "Hear me, world! It is the Marquis de Sade, cavalry colonel, who is being subjected to such abominable treatment! Deprived of air and light! Rally round, my friends! To rescue me will be in the interest of all!"

Then abruptly de Sade fell silent, and went back to staring at his wax dolls on the table.

Already Radu was bored by the little figures. He picked one up, the blond girl-doll he thought the madman had been particularly admiring, and crushed it in his hand, reducing it to a smear of pink wax oozing between his fingers. De Sade made a sound like that of a victim under some probing stab by a torturer. Radu could derive faint amusement from the expression on de Sade's face.

~ *19* ~

*H*oping to discover the whereabouts of the newly arrested Radcliffe as quickly as possible, I stood before a Parisian wall which had been dedicated to the posting of Revolutionary news.

I had thought there might be a good chance of finding the name I sought on some freshly published list of those under arrest for crimes against the people—or under sentence of death, which now very nearly amounted to the same thing. But nothing on the board before me suggested that such lists were currently being displayed—if they ever had been. With the daily number of executions in Paris alone now in double digits and mounting steadily higher, perhaps the people in charge of the paperwork of terror were finding it increasingly difficult to keep up.

My weary gaze focused upon one of the placards on the wall. It was actually only one of a number of authoritarian proclamations, some of the older specimens overlapped and almost entirely covered by the new. Though they dealt with different subjects, all were similar in tone:

A portion of the treacherous suspects being held in our prisons have been eliminated by the people, vig-

ilant in the cause of freedom; and it is certain that
the entire nation, driven to desperate measures by
continuous conspiracies, will be inspired to pursue
the same course. All will cry out with one voice: Our
soldiers who go to fight the enemy must be secure
in the knowledge that they do not leave thieves and
murderers behind them, to prey upon their helpless
wives and children.

It was signed by Marat and others. The cardboard was
severely weatherworn in places, a reminder that Marat had
been assassinated almost a year ago, a long time indeed
when one was measuring the pace of Revolutionary events.
Many of the other signatures were illegible.

I felt a chill of foreboding on behalf of Radcliffe—and for
my vow that I would save his life. I would have to act with
dispatch to free my benefactor, who might well face not only
the threat of *la mechanique,* but the less predictable chance
of another wave of prisoner-slaughtering by mobs.

But of course my first step must be to learn exactly
where the unlucky wretch was being held. There were more
than a dozen prisons now in the metropolitan area of Paris,
with new ones being improvised, as it seemed, almost daily,
and prisoners sometimes shuttled from one to another. I
might conceivably search for days without finding the man
I sought.

It was one of those times when the demands of honor grip a
man like a migraine headache, an undeserved punishment
from which there can be no escape. I had as yet no evidence
that Radu was out to frustrate my purpose, or even that he
was aware of Radcliffe's arrest or of my commitment to the
American's welfare. But where Radu is concerned it is always
wisest to assume the worst.

Several hours passed before I saw the silver lining of the
cloud: It dawned on me that I might be able to use Radcliffe
as bait to trap Radu.

*   *   *

I had tried several methods, including hypnosis, of interrogating Old Jules. But even so the willing and faithful servant could do little more than blubber helplessly. I could not extract from him information which was not in his possession. He had no idea to which prison his newly adopted Citizen Master had been taken.

It began to look as if I might be forced to look through all of the rapidly proliferating Parisian prisons cell by cell, a procedure which would take days, days my client probably could not spare. Unless I could find some shortcut, magical or otherwise. I might have attempted some variety of sorcery, had I had in my possession anything—a piece of clothing, a lock of hair—which had been in close personal contact with Philip. But nothing of the kind was available.

My thoughts next turned to the young woman, Melanie Romain, who obviously had some fairly close relationship with the man I was determined to protect. I did not really believe that they were simply old friends, as she had claimed. And now I regretted my carelessness in failing to find out more about her when I had had the chance.

I thought about her. About Melanie Romain, the practical, kindly doctor's daughter, whose mysterious job required her to work in a churchyard in the dead of night, briskly doing inexplicable things with freshly decapitated heads. She had told me that the older woman who shared her midnight labors was her teacher, Marie Grosholtz . . . but her teacher in what craft or art?

Of one thing I was certain, having had my knowledge confirmed by Old Jules: Melanie had accompanied Radcliffe to Paris. And the elderly servant, after their party had reached the city, had heard Melanie give the young man the same Parisian address I had happened to overhear— Number 20, Boulevard du Temple.

Well, the key to what success I enjoy usually lies in instincts and hunches, not in logic. It is somewhere away from the paths of science and reason that I will find my salvation, if I ever do. I might have taken other pathways to attempt to locate my savior in his own hour of need; but somehow this one beckoned.

Looking for the address, I made my way on foot at dusk along the tree-lined boulevard, passing the building which had housed the once-famous English circus, now shuttered and apparently fallen on hard times. A number of theaters were in the same neighborhood.

The establishment I was seeking turned out to be a large house, three stories high, with a covered porch in front. The building fronted closely on the street but possessed spacious grounds in the rear. On the front of the house a sign, large and brightly painted but with a certain dignity, announced an enterprise headed by Dr. Curtius: a wax museum.

And at last, belatedly, comprehension came.

Not wishing particularly to be observed, since it was by then after public viewing hours at the Cabinet du Cire, I entered the grounds at the rear. The habitation effect proved too weak to prevent my uninvited entrance to the museum portion of the building, though no doubt the actual living quarters would have been denied me.

Moments later, rummaging about at random, I found myself inside a locked and otherwise deserted storeroom. Here light was almost nonexistent, yet for my eyes quite adequate.

There I paused, marveling. I had thought that, after three hundred years of life, there was no longer much in the world that could surprise me. But I had been wrong.

Of course, after only a moment's shock, I understood what the figures were. But still they were surprising. The lopped-off heads of Louis XVI and his queen, Marie Antoinette, were looking at me from a shelf. Some eyeblink fraction of a second passed before I was entirely sure that they were only wax, glass-eyed and painted with great realism.

The modeled heads of royalty, in keeping with the times,

were stored in an inconspicuous position on a low shelf. Other celebrities of the past, great and small, were stacked until their time should come again; and the elaborate costumes usually worn by many of these figures had, as I discovered later, been folded away and locked in trunks. A few were stored hanging up, and thus were easier to see. The most popular feature of the museum, to judge by the amount of space allotted, in notices and on the floor, was the Caverne des Grands Voleurs, a display of images of executed criminals.

A great many visitors of all kinds came through the museum every day that it was open. It was evidently nothing unusual for some of the customers to wander into the adjoining work areas and semidetached living quarters. None of the residents or workers were particularly surprised this early in the evening, so soon after closing time, to see a stranger poking about in their midst.

Politely I enquired of several workers for Melanie Romain, but for my trouble received only shrugs and thoughtful looks conveying cautious ignorance.

Attracted by a peculiar, small, mechanical noise issuing from a kind of workyard behind the house, I turned my steps in that direction. A moment later my eye fell upon the small form of a ten-year-old boy, raggedly clad in appropriate Revolutionary style, who was sitting by himself in a small veranda just outside the main building. I noted at once that the lad's features displayed an arresting resemblance to those of the woman I was trying to find. The likeness was so definite that I felt sure at once it was not accidental.

Casually I strolled in his direction, and observed what he was playing with. Or perhaps I should say, more accurately, what he was working on.

In the small model machine there lay a small wax doll, clumsily made from scraps by his own childish fingers, standing by in an attitude of sturdy indifference, ready to be beheaded. Whatever the lad's talents were to be in life, I thought, sculpture did not seem to be among them.

"What is your name, my lad?"

"Auguste." He was a dark and brooding child, evidently quite at home in this place.

Accustomed as I was to observing human faces change with age, and to observing several generations of a family in sequence, it was no great feat for me to convince myself beyond a doubt that small Auguste was a blood relative of Melanie Romain. My next thought was to consider whether this was likely to be her son. The age difference between them seemed not too small to make the relationship impossible.

"That seems an interesting game that you are playing."

He looked at me doubtfully—an enigmatic, dark-haired child with a pinched and gnome-like face, who as I later learned was not allowed to go to the cemetery with his mother, but spent most of his time at the museum engaged in building a toy guillotine out of some scraps of wood and a few bits of hardware.

I made my tone more businesslike. "Is your mother here, my lad?"

"I will see, citizen," the boy answered, politely enough, and got to his feet. "Who shall I say is looking for her?"

"Tell her her most recent patient is now quite restored to health; but even so, he wishes a consultation . . . never mind, tell her: Citizen Legrand."

Auguste gave me a strange look at that, then put aside his toy guillotine and arose to go and look for his mother.

As soon as he was gone, I picked up the toy and examined it. Ingenious, though not technically sophisticated. When the trigger was pulled, a brick fell on the poised blade, adapted from a broken pocketknife, giving it impetus enough to slice the neck of a tiny animal clean through. Maybe, I thought, a powerful spring would work better than a heavy weight, but such hardware would not be commonly available to children.

My brother, I thought, would be delighted to see this.

* * *

I waited patiently, and little Auguste was back in a minute or two. "Citizen, they tell me that her work has taken her to the cemetery this evening."

"Thank you, my lad—I know which one."

In the cemetery, many of the circumstances of our first meeting two years ago were now repeated, with minor variations. The trench, and the burial mound that marked where the trench had been, had moved on for a considerable serpentine distance. Again Melanie and her cousin Marie were at the raw end of this mound, where the latest burials were to be found. And they were hard at work, but now equipped with a smaller, better focussed version of the Argand lamp.

When I came upon them, Melanie was absorbed in the grisly task of looking for one particular head, while Marie held another in her lap, painstakingly coating the features with wet plaster. Now that I understood the point of the work, it seemed almost commonplace. The actual pouring of the wax, and the many remaining steps in creating the replica which was the object of all this labor, would of course take place back at Curtius's workshop, behind the museum.

Tonight the rats seemed bigger and bolder, more willing to interfere, than they had been on the occasion of my last visit.

The women took turns in interrupting their work, to try to drive away the annoying and dangerous rats by throwing pebbles. But mostly the beasts—arrogantly well-fed, confident clients of the Revolutionary state—ignored the ineffective bombardment and continued to pursue their own agenda.

With a slight bow and a polite murmur, I did the ladies a favor, or at least saved them some time, by driving off a whole swarm of the rodents with a great silent shout.

"I think they will not bother you for a while."

In response the two women gave me a strange look.

I wondered, aloud, if they ever had trouble finding the

head they had been sent to model, and decide to use a substitute instead? They could at least hope that no one would
be able to tell the difference. If so, they would not confess the
dereliction to me now, but only laughed at the idea.

To Melanie I said: "Your son told me where I could find you."
She paused in her work, and looked vaguely alarmed.
I hastened to be reassuring. "Pray do not be concerned;
he was quite safe when I saw him, at the museum. He seemed
a charming lad."
"Thank you, m'sieu."
"Who is his father? Excuse me, you may be sure that I
do not ask such a question out of idle curiosity."
"Then why do you ask it, sir?" Marie Grosholtz demanded.
Melanie shot her cousin an anguished look. "Oh, what
does it matter now? The gentleman is a friend of Philip's, and
has his reasons, I am sure."
While Marie, who had known about her cousin's troubles
for ten years and more, looked on sympathetically, Melanie
told me the story of how she had given birth to this child
about ten years ago, a few months after the kindly (in this
instance, anyway) Dr. Curtius, at the urging of his niece
Marie, had taken in a pregnant fourteen-year-old, and set her
to work at easy tasks in his establishment.
The father of Melanie's baby was, or rather had been, a
careless aristocratic youth named Charles Dupin, the scion
of a well-to-do family, who at first had declined to acknowledge his paternity of the child. Later, she thought, he might
have been inclined to do so, but before he had taken any definite steps in that direction he had allied himself with the
wrong political faction and been beheaded.
"I had thought it possible," I observed, "that young Auguste's father was Philip Radcliffe."
"No." Her fists clenched, and she stared at me. "Oh God,
do you bring me any news of Philip?"
I shook my head and gestured soothingly. "All I know

with certainty is that he has been arrested. I was hoping you could tell me in what prison he can be found."

"He is in La Conciergerie. We have been able to find out that much."

"Ah. That gives me a place to start. He is a foreigner, and I think that will give us a few days' grace at least, before they turn him over to Sanson."

Meanwhile, Marie worked on steadily, wiping dried blood and bits of bran from her subject's face. The baskets on Sanson's platform usually contained four or five inches of either bran or sawdust, intended to absorb blood. Having cleaned her subject as well as was practical, she then smeared it with a mixture of linseed oil and lead oxide, in preparation for the plaster of Paris, which when dry would make the mold.

With the rats held in abeyance for the time being, the three of us were soon chatting with something like a natural freedom. When I asked the two women why they had chosen this spot to do this work, they were ready with a simple explanation. If an impression of the face was made at graveside, there was no need to carry the head away. It could be tossed back into the pit.

The young women explained to me that if they did not make the molds at the cemetery, then, after finding the heads they wanted, it would be necessary for them to change their clothes, or put on clean garments over the bloodstained ones, and wrap the heads somehow or put them away in hatboxes. There would be nothing particularly conspicuous about the pair of women as, riding in a wagon or light carriage, they carried their finds back to the wax museum in the Boulevard du Temple.

But then, when they were through with the heads, they would be faced with the messy problem of getting rid of them.

"We might be able to bury one or two in our backyard, and no one the wiser. But with the numbers that we must handle . . . already there have been dozens, and there is no end in sight to what the Committee wants . . ."

As we conversed, Melanie had gone on crouching, digging, peering, up to her knees in muddy earth and decaying humanity, enduring the pervasive smell while going about her ghastly but (as I now realized) relatively innocent business. Meanwhile Marie, the more skillful modeler, went on using oil and plaster of Paris to make a mold in which the dummy head of the night's first subject would later be cast in hot wax.

Then the younger woman gave a little cry of triumph. "Ah, here he is!"

Melanie had found the head she had been looking for. There had been twenty-eight executed in the previous day's batch, and the search had not been particularly easy.

"But I think I recognize that face," I ejaculated suddenly. "Is it not Lavoisier?"

Yes, even I had heard of Lavoisier, the man who now, two hundred years later, is called the father of chemistry, and even I was shocked. Why should the artistic authorities, or the political, have wanted to execute a man of science and then immortalize their crime in wax? Of course the two fields of endeavor were still nowhere near as sharply demarcated as they have recently become.

It was Lavoisier who proposed the name "oxygen" for the dephlogisticated air required to support a fire. He had worked diligently for the Revolution in its early stages, perfecting its gunpowder and its cannon. But he had been overtaken by a period in his past when he had served as a kind of tax-collector for the old regime, and yesterday had received his reward.

Marie observed: "Someone pointed out his name on the list to Robespierre, and our leader said: 'The Revolution has no need of scientists.' "

And that, I thought, should have been chiseled on his tombstone.

I felt that Melanie deserved some reward for the assistance she had earlier given me, or attempted to give me, through her medical efforts. It was no fault of hers that those efforts were misguided. But I was not as greatly and as formally in her debt as I was in Radcliffe's.

"I understand now, Mademoiselle, the purpose of your work, and I find nothing discreditable about it. I regret having suggested—what I did suggest. My sincere apologies." I made a slight bow, including Marie, who nodded in return.

"Your apology is accepted, Citizen Legrand—and what of M'sieu Radcliffe? Is there . . . is there . . ."

"Is there any hope? I think so. You have told me where he is. Now we shall see what we can do."

"You mean . . . ?"

"I mean to help him. As to how, that has yet to be decided."

The prison called La Conciergerie, like most of the others in the city, was busy day and night during the climactic summer of the Terror. I think that not a single cell stood empty for more than an hour or two. The population fluctuated less than you might think, given the high turnover. On average the count stood at about three hundred souls, during the peak years of '93 and '94. The place stank, of course, of fear and sweat and unwashed bodies, though not as badly as most of the prisons of that epoch. An extra excitement seemed to vibrate in the air. I gathered that if one had to be in prison, this was definitely the place.

Conducting a preliminary reconnaissance on a rainy afternoon, I walked around the prison section of the Palace, or rather I covered three sides of it by this method, looking over the vast gray building from the outside.

I also made a flying trip, by night. Both methods of scouting had their advantages.

This prison formed part of the Palais de Justice, which stood on the same island in the Seine as Notre Dame, and at one time or another during the Terror its cells accommodated very many of the most famous victims, including Hébert, Corday, Robespierre, Marie Antoinette, and Danton—besides Charles Darnay, who later achieved a certain literary fame, and a few other foreigners.

Victims were brought in at all hours, while others were hauled away to attend their trials, most of the latter soon returning under sentence of death. Of the many who were taken from their cells never to return, all but a very few went to their executions. Also coming and going constantly were police and lawyers, along with members of the new hierarchy of bureaucrats, including some of the many priests who had sworn allegiance to the Revolution. As at any other institution where numbers of people dwelt, tradesmen came and went, food and other necessities were delivered.

I soon learned, somewhat to my surprise, that there seldom passed an evening in this house of horrors when at least one feast was not in progress. These banquets and parties were always rude and raucous but sometimes elaborate and expensive, hosted by one or more of those who were to lose their heads on the next day. Often these affairs were amazingly lavish. As a rule the guards and other officials, following a tradition established during the Old Regime, could easily be persuaded to go along with this practice, while maintaining the essentials of tight security. People who had experienced both prisons said that this one had a conviviality lacking in even the most luxurious quarters of the Bastille.

On occasion La Conciergerie even welcomed the efforts of musicians and other entertainers, hired by the more prosperous of the condemned at their own expense, to brighten the last days and hours of their impoverished comrades as well as their own. I wondered what success a fortune teller might enjoy. Dedicated atheists, of whom there were many among the Revolutionary theorists, would frown at the practice, and I supposed that for many other prisoners the idea would be too much to take.

Still, it occurred to me that this might be a good role for Constantia to play.

A gypsy singer and dancer might easily double as a fortune teller. Vague possibilities stirred, as is usual when I am making plans. She might specialize in telling happy fortunes for the prisoners' loved ones elsewhere.

I supposed I could, myself, appear as a gypsy musician. Sawing at a violin, or strumming a guitar. But there was not much time for elaborate schemes.

Radcliffe, like other prisoners, was at certain times allowed out of his cell to take part in at least some of these parties. It proved childishly easy to arrange for him to meet Constantia at one of them.

When it came Radcliffe's turn to hold out his hand to the fortune teller, she had solid information to convey to the prisoner. "I see a long life ahead of you, young master."

" 'Citizen,' " he corrected absently. He had never met Connie before, and had no idea that she knew his acquaintance M'sieu Legrand, or was anything more than the gypsy entertainer she appeared to be. And Melanie Romain was much in his thoughts.

But all the same, the gypsy wench was still impressively attractive. And what she told him proved to be of considerable interest too.

Through most of his life he had had nothing but contempt for superstition. But lately things had been very weird.

Well. Security was of course not as absolute as those in authority needed to believe. Three hundred years of experience had taught me that it never is; and nothing in the additional two hundred since then has caused me to believe otherwise.

A few prisoners were kept continuously confined in their cells. The late Marie Antoinette's cell (doubtless fancier than most) was a dark, almost unventilated chamber some twelve feet square, with an uneven brick floor, a narrow cot and a straw mattress, a few chairs and an old table. Wallpaper had been applied to wooden frames against the walls, but it was peeling off with the damp.

Meanwhile, as became clear later, my dear brother Radu was also attempting, rather cautiously, to keep some kind of watch on the prison. Mostly he tried to accomplish this through various breathing agents, despite the fact that they were so undependable. My younger brother at this point was chiefly concerned with staying out of my sight; he continually, and with some justice, suspected me of trying to set an ambush for him.

Radu's contacts with the authorities, direct or indirect, made it possible for him to know in just which cell any prisoner was supposedly being confined.

I needed no more than twenty-four hours to acquaint myself thoroughly with the details of the prison's physical construction, and of its daily routine. The latter tended to be irregular, a condition which has advantages as well as disadvantages for anyone who might be planning an escape.

Wanting to achieve Radcliffe's rescue as quickly as possible, and realizing that I had no time to waste, I swiftly worked out several possible plans of escape. I wanted to have a number from which to choose, in case whichever scheme I first selected should prove to have some insuperable flaw.

Bribery, that ancient and time-honored method of achieving almost anything in the scope of human activity, deserved to be considered first. But in this case there were reasons why I preferred not to rely on it.

My simplest and most direct means of locating within the prison certain men and women whom I could recognize would of course be to ghost in through one of the barred windows at any time between sunset and dawn, and take an inventory of its inmates, cell by cell. The place was crowded with wretched humble folk, along with a few who last year, or yesterday, had been among the leaders of society. Once on an earlier visit, many months ago, out of sheer curiosity, I had looked in unseen on Marie Antoinette.

Probably it is completely unnecessary for me to point out, to readers who have spent their entire lives in the second half of the twentieth century, that the vast majority of the victims of the Terror had never had any idea of committing the crime for which they died, never conspired in some way against the new republican government. Most were guilty of the Kafkaesque crime of being Suspect, and that is all. One could with perfect ease lose liberty and even life as the result of a chance remark, an anonymous denunciation by an enemy, or by simply coming under the eye of some police agent who was seeking to fill a quota—you who read will understand such matters, from your vantage point near the beginning of the third millennium, more readily than did I at the end of the eighteenth century.

Having located my benefactor and formed at least a preliminary plan, it seemed only reasonable to pay him a visit and offer him hope. Whatever method of release I finally decided on, his cooperation would be required.

I thought a prison cell would rarely if ever qualify as a legitimate habitation, in the strange calculus of possibilities that limit the comings and goings of the *nosferatu*. At least I had at that time never yet found one that I was barred from entering, be it occupied or not.

Radcliffe's cell was somewhat smaller than Marie Antoinette's, and of an unusual L-shape, with barely room for a small table and chair beside his bed. I came in quietly.

He started up from his mattress, where he had been

lying with hands clasped behind his head, and almost cried out at the sight of my shadowy figure, standing not much more than an arm's length away from him, my finger raised to my lips enjoining silence.

~ 20 ~

For a long moment the young American stared at me as if he thought I was the Angel of Death, whilst I stood waiting, wondering if I ought to have made a less dramatic entrance. But eventually recognition dawned in Radcliffe's eyes—and when it came, it brought with it a new astonishment.

"I did not hear you come in, M'sieu Legrand." In his surprise the young man spoke in English, but I answered him in French, my own English at that time being no more than rudimentary.

I smiled modestly. "I was rather unobtrusive about it."

"But I didn't see the door open either!" Leaping up from his pallet, shaking his head in growing bewilderment, he pushed past me to the door, seized it by the bars which almost filled the small high opening, and pushed and pulled some more, meanwhile trying to peer out into an empty corridor. The massive wooden construction remained closed. "Still locked!" he cried, now having switched to his excellent French.

I made no effort to quiet him. Actually there was little chance that an outburst of noise would do our cause any harm; in that world of confinement, strange and sudden outcries were as much a part of existence as were darkness and bad smells. In that prison there were always voices raised somewhere, day and night, arguing philosophy and other trifles, debating politics of course, pleading for life, or sometimes chattering in insane monologues, carrying on arguments with God or the devil; the guards made no effort to enforce silence, and a prisoner bellowing or raving to himself was unlikely to arouse any curiosity at all. The odds were very small that anyone outside the cell would be paying any attention to the sounds emanating from it.

Instead I remarked calmly: "I don't suppose you'd want it found standing open?"

"No—no, of course not." Turning his back on the door, he forced the fingers of both hands, front to rear, through his long, dark hair. That would soon change; all prisoners under sentence of death were treated to a haircut at state expense, on the theory that nothing, not even hair or a lace collar, ought to be allowed to restrain *la mechanique* from attaining its maximum efficiency.

I noted a small white bandage near the crown of his head.

Now he was facing me again. "But—what are you doing here?"

"You have saved my life, M'sieu Radcliffe. Now it is my turn to be of service to you." I bowed slightly. "In fact, I insist on doing so. What has happened to your head? I see that you are bandaged."

"A little scuffle when I was arrested." He shook his head, as if he found it hard to imagine what favor anyone could do for him in his present circumstances. But hope would not die in his eyes, and they stayed fixed on me.

"I had in mind revoking your death sentence," I offered modestly. "Unofficially, by means of escape. I take it you would not object if your stay in this world were to be substantially prolonged?"

My client stared at me incredulously, made a strange sound in his throat, and took a turn of pacing round his cell, which was inconveniently small for such activity.

In some other cell, far down the dismal corridor, some other prisoner chose that moment to loose a burst of maniacal laughter. Whilst my attention was thus drawn to the auditory environment, the thought crossed my mind that, if one closed one's eyes, it sounded very much like the interior of an insane asylum.

And that thought brought back an old memory, which I tried to retain in a place where I hoped it would be ready for use. I recalled hearing that my brother, since his last emergence from underground, had fallen into the habit of visiting such places as Charenton, amusing himself with the inmates. More particularly Radu had taken a special interest in one prisoner—what had his name been? A Frenchman, yes, and an aristocrat. The Marquis, marquis of something or other, and cruelly insane . . .

My client had given up trying to pace in the cramped quarters, and had found his voice again. He kept it low, as if by instinct, as he called me by the name I had given him at his chateau. Nervously casting glances at the door and its peephole, in an urgent whisper he repeated: "But what are you doing here, M'sieu . . . *Citizen* Legrand? How did you . . . ?"

"I have my ways," I assured him, in a normal voice. "Be of good cheer, Mr. Radcliffe. To get you out of La Conciergerie will be somewhat more difficult than getting myself in, but, believe me, it is well within my range of competence. Out from behind these walls, and then a few neatly forged papers . . . passage to the coast arranged, and then abroad. Three weeks from today you will very likely find yourself seated in some snug London tavern, regaling your friends there with some story explaining your improbable escape."

"Melanie," he said, making the one word a meaningful declaration.

"Very well, Melanie too. So, it is that way between the two of you. Well, why not?" And at that moment I was on the brink of trying to explain to him how his relationship with his beloved might be altered by the choice of means adopted to effect his release. But I let it pass. Everything I had told him so far was the truth. If not quite the whole truth, well—there would be time for that.

"Have you seen her? Is she well?"

"I have." I did not specify where. "And she is."

And all the time the rain was dripping, dripping mournfully somewhere outside. In the distance thunder grumbled.

Hope had now been born in Radcliffe's eyes, and I could see that his mind was racing to establish a basis for it. In the fertile soil of America, almost any seed could grow, and quickly. But he remained prudently wary of tricks and impossibilities. In his own fluent but accented French he once more demanded: "How did you get into this cell?"

"I have my own methods," I repeated. "Be reassured by the fact that stone walls and locks present small obstacles to me. As they would to you, if a certain transformation in your nature were to be effected."

"Transformation in my nature?" Radcliffe looked at the door and nodded sagely, as if he understood. Then he turned to face me again, and admitted: "I don't understand this at all."

"Nevertheless. If such barriers, and a few armed guards, were our only problems, you could be free already."

He stared at me, ready to dispute me. But here I was standing in front of him, in defiance of all logic, locks, and fanatical guards; evidently I could not be such an idiot as my claims made me sound.

He asked the question as if he hoped that I was not a madman: "What is it that truly confines me, then?"

"That is an intelligent question. The answer is: You have a very powerful enemy."

"Do you mean Robespierre? Or Fouquier-Tinville, the prosecutor?"

I shook my head. "I mean a man more dangerous than

either, hard as that may be to believe. A drinker of blood indeed, and one who does not mean to rest until he has drained yours to the last drop."

"And this enemy does not want me to get out of prison."

"Oh, on the contrary! Your most dangerous enemy will be happier if you are free to wander, out of my protection. We must consider carefully what we are going to do about him."

On my entry, my client had looked at me as if doubting his own sanity. But now his expression suggested that he thought I was the lunatic.

I gave up the task of explanation for the time being. "I bring you an interesting bit of news."

"Oh?"

"You are to have a visitor soon, perhaps within the hour. A woman named Marie Grosholtz will call on you; she happens to be the cousin of Melanie Romain."

His eyes lit up. "Marie—? Yes! Melanie has told me of her cousin Marie. I know her address here in Paris, though I have never met the woman. I thought she was some kind of teacher . . . but she comes to me on some official task?"

"Semiofficial, at least. As part of her regular employment, she calls frequently on people who are in your situation."

Radcliffe's perplexity was growing. "For what purpose?"

"I will leave that to her to explain. People in your position are usually willing to cooperate with her . . . I take it you were not many days, or even many hours, in Paris before your arrest?"

"Less than a day."

"Then I don't suppose you had time to visit the Cabinet de Cire of Dr. Philippe Curtius, on the Boulevard du Temple?"

"A wax museum?" He looked at me in utter blankness. "No . . . but that was the street where Melanie said I would find her. At number twenty."

"That is the very address. It has been a popular showplace for years, since before the glorious Revolution. I am told that for some time the most popular displays at that establishment—even more so than the effigies of the royal family—have been the modeled heads and busts of notorious criminals.

"In the eyes of the Committee of Public Safety, you now fall into the latter category."

On a whim I pulled from my pocket a small fragment I had recently torn from a Parisian newspaper, and read aloud the article it contained: *"Citizens may have their Portraits taken in the most perfect imitation of Life; Models are also produced from PERSONS DECEASED, with the most correct appearance of animation."*

Radcliffe hung on every word, trying to extract reason for hope. "I never heard of such a thing."

"It is an art form with something of a history." I did not mention that few citizens who were given a choice ever seemed to avail themselves of the opportunity.

The young American nodded at last. "But who wants my effigy?"

I shrugged. "Probably David."

"Who? . . . Oh. You mean the artist?"

I nodded. Jacques Louis David was a famous man in the field of art, where there was some justification for his being well-regarded, and also cultivated powerful friends in political circles. (As he had done before the Revolution, and as he continued to do afterward, when Napoleon and his whiff of grapeshot had swept the last red bonnet from the streets. Some people have the knack of survival.) "He is a member of the Convention, you know, and has a great deal of influence. They order wax replicas so he and other dedicated Revolutionary artists can use them as models, for accurate paintings and sculptures. A vast quantity of artistic work is planned, to tell the whole world the story of the glorious Revolution. Also the wax images themselves could play a part in festivals and parades."

Later I learned that it had been David himself who had commanded Marie Grosholtz to go to Marat's house when the

great propagandist was assassinated, and to make a cast of
the dead man's face, before the body was removed from the
bathtub where it lay in a rich mix of blood and water. The
fact of Marat's head not being detached (he had simply been
stabbed) only made the task a little harder.

David's own face, I have been told, was rather ugly, one
cheek disfigured by a huge wen. The main reason, I suppose,
why there were never many artistic representations of him.
And there are fewer now.

Radcliffe, thinking it all over, checked the door again, then
turned back, lowering his voice to a mere whisper. "I take it
this coming visit from Melanie's cousin may have something
to do with—my escape?"

"One might say so." Then, seeing a shade of disappointment cross his face, I hastened to add: "No, you are *not* going
to disguise yourself as Marie Grosholtz, and slip away while
she stays here. That would not be the act of a true gentleman, leaving the lady to face the music . . . and please give
me credit, sir, for a little more imagination than that.

"Besides, you will need forged documents, and they are
not yet ready." I did already have a worker started on them,
though; over several centuries of life, one picks up the knack
of doing many things that are not part of the daily routine,
such as recruiting forgers.

Radcliffe drew himself up. "The plan, whatever it is,
must not endanger Melanie, or anyone she loves. Otherwise
I shall refuse to go."

I intended to tolerate no rebellious behavior on my
client's part, whatever might happen. I knew what was best
for him, and I did not like to argue. "That is nonsense. You
will not refuse to escape. However important this Romain
woman may be to you, you cannot help her much while you
remain locked up—or if you find yourself a full head shorter
than you are."

Having said that much, I glared at him. God knew what

fresh villainy my brother might be preparing to launch against me, whilst I was entangled in these distractions. And, regardless of whether or not any of these breathers lived or died, I was determined to best my brother. He should not compel me to dishonor any of my vows.

Radcliffe met my gaze defiantly for ten seconds or so—it usually takes a strong-willed person to do that—then slumped and turned away.

"I could do with a drink," he whispered hoarsely, sinking back on his narrow bed.

Long experience brings foresight, and I happened to have a small flask of brandy in my pocket, which my client accepted gratefully.

"Then your feelings with regard to Melanie Romain are serious indeed," I remarked. And I wondered whether Radcliffe even suspected what I had recently discovered: the existence of Melanie's child. Melanie herself had assured me that he did not know.

He lifted his head. "They are. Unhappily, I did not fully realize how serious until I was locked up in here."

My next encounter with Melanie took place at a celebration in honor of the Supreme Being, a politically convenient deity whose existence had recently been discovered by no less an authority than Robespierre himself. Like a great many other folk, Marie was not attending by choice, but had been sent to look out for some of Curtius's wax heads, heroes and villains of the current political establishment, which were to be carried in a procession.

"You!" she breathed, when I silently confronted her. "Were you able to see Philip?"

"I was. He has asked me to convey to you his greetings—and his love." Perhaps this was not strictly true. I raised to her my glass filled with untasted wine.

"Ah! He used those words?"

"Just as I have said."

"But he does not know—you did not tell him—"

"About your child? No, that is your duty. No doubt some suitable moment will arise."

For a time Melanie continued to be suspicious, but I held forth the promise of Radcliffe's being rescued.

"How do you mean to accomplish that?"

"The final choice of means, from several alternatives, is what I have come to discuss with you. But rest assured that, one way or another, I intend to accomplish it. I am firmly determined that he shall regain his freedom."

"I bless you for telling me that, if it is true."

In the course of this conversation Melanie passed on to me a piece of news from the countryside that had only recently reached her ears: the murdered, horribly mutilated body of the servant girl, Marguerite, had been discovered in the grounds of the old chateau.

"Radu," I murmured. "In all likelihood, Radu."

In truth I believe that my vanity had been pricked, and I felt outraged that that slender girl whose veins had afforded me such delight and healing would nevermore embrace me, or any other, in the fashion of woman with man. Another score against Radu, for which due punishment would have to be administered.

After visiting Radcliffe in his cell again, to report to him on the status of his beloved, I made my exit from the prison before dawn, turning myself into bat-form before the moment of sunrise. Later than that, and I would be forced to retain that shape all day.

Of course I might if necessary have come to my client by day, approaching his cell door in the ordinary way, dressed in the clothes of a lamplighter or some other common functionary.

This time Radcliffe on recognizing me struggled to control his reaction. I could see him, this time, watching me carefully to see how I got in. He succeeded in this endeavor, at least to the extent that he could tell no deception was involved. I was outside the cell, and then I was inside, and neither lock nor bar nor door had moved by a hair's-breadth.

"I cannot believe what my eyes have shown me," he breathed, and rubbed at the organs mentioned. "You must explain it to me, somehow."

But I had decided to leave the bulk of that task to Constantia, who had a real talent for such matters, when she chose to use it properly.

Constantia was on hand and ready, more or less, to be of help. But, as the reader may already have deduced by now, rarely did I ever work with her in any important matter when I had any reasonable alternative. This was because of a certain lack of dependability which she was wont to demonstrate.

But it was she who had the brilliant idea (as it seemed to me then) of converting our client's cell into a genuine habitation, which would then be vampire-proof except by invitation.

"But how does one make a prison cell a home?"

"Maybe, Vlad—maybe if a loving couple were to inhabit it—even if only one of them was there most of the time—"

"It is worth a try. Do what you can. Philip Radcliffe must be protected at all costs."

As for myself, I was fully occupied with labors of a more aggressive nature.

After dark, Constantia and I ghosted together through the prison, melting into mist-form every time some guard, worker, or visitor approached, and in between such episodes regained a semblance of solidity, the better to read the labels on the cell doors or beside them. I wanted her to understand the lay of the land as thoroughly as I did. With this in mind I paused from time to time to read from the list I had borrowed of names and corresponding cell numbers.

"Whose cell is this?"

"Evidently what we have here is the foreigners' wing. The tag here reads CHARLES DARNAY. Not the man we want . . . here's Percy Blakeney, citizen of England . . . no . . ."

Forged papers, passport, and identity card would be vitally important assets to a fugitive. A majority of vampires kept up, as a matter of course, with dependable sources of such materials. Little birds had already whispered to me that Lepitre, a classics teacher who had become head of the passport committee of the Commune, did a superb job of providing what were in fact quite genuine documents, with names and descriptions to be filled in by the customer. Naturally such quality was expensive; but I was not poor, and would not be miserly with mere money when honor was concerned. I hoped to avoid the necessity of shepherding my client all the way to the frontier, and even beyond, though I had to face the fact that such a prolonged effort might be necessary.

It had occurred to me very early in the game that converting Philip to vampirism clearly offered the safest and surest means of saving his life, at least in the short term, by removing the immediate danger from Sanson and his machine. But in the long run, that conversion would do little to save him from an attack by Radu.

Ah, if only . . .

I had made my choice of means. Slowly, gradually, the final version of my plan for Radcliffe's escape was taking shape.

It seemed that I had now undertaken the protection of Melanie Romain as well.

Transforming Melanie into one of the so-called undead would somewhat facilitate the task of protecting her, also, from any effort Radu might make to get at Radcliffe through her.

Another objection loomed in the back of my mind: Converting Melanie would put an end to any possibility of ever establishing a romantic attachment between us; that is something I often concede, but never lightly.

Converting both Philip and Melanie to vampires would render their escape from prison impossible for the authorities to prevent; but it would also rob them both permanently of any possibility of bringing their mutual love to its natural conclusion. Again, that would represent a chance for my wayward brother to claim a kind of victory. And to deny him victory at every possible point, at almost any cost, had become my dearest goal.

Constantia needed but little persuasion to get her to visit the male prisoner in his private cell—in fact, as I now realized, my old acquaintance was already only too eager to do so. Constantia, whom I had known almost all her life, was, to put it mildly, a little flighty, and wont to act with dangerous impulsiveness. But I anticipated no difficulty in persuading her to make the acquaintance of a handsome and hearty young man.

I tried to talk over the range of possibilities with Constantia, before sending her to Radcliffe, to make sure my old associate understood precisely how I thought the matter should be handled; but, as the reader must have realized by now, it is sometimes difficult to hold a rational discussion with that dear girl.

Part of her assigned task was to convey the essentials of an escape plan to him, but I should have known better than to trust her with any mission of that kind.

It was my gypsy's own idea, and not a bad one I must admit, that she could talk to him more easily, and be more convincing, if she appeared in the guise of a fellow prisoner.

If she were in a cell next to his and could squeeze her body through a narrow opening or ventilator, much too small for him to pass, she could be something of a bodyguard against Radu. And perhaps establish the habitation defense.

Easy enough for a vampire to break open, by main force or other means, a prison gate or a cell door or window to allow some breathing convict to escape—but to get the escaped prisoner clean away in the midst of a fanatical manhunt would require at least moderate cleverness as well as force.

Any vampire could easily overpower any prison guard, or several of them, then open the cell door with the key and march Radcliffe out as if on some Committee business. It was not impossible for a woman to appear as a prison guard. But the pair almost certainly would be stopped and questioned at several points before they made it out of the prison. I, playing the role of escort, could probably bluff and bluster my way through such obstacles, but success could not be guaranteed.

And Radu might well show up, at the most inconvenient moment, to claim his prize.

Alternatively, a dead body, dressed to look like that of the prisoner in question, could be left in the cell, making it look as if my client had committed suicide. Perhaps by means of poison? Or with a gun, even a blunderbuss, which might make positive identification very difficult. Hanging, strangulation might well discolor and distort the face sufficiently. How would any prisoner have been able to obtain a gun? Of course it was not impossible, but finding one with his brains blown out would certainly have provoked a great investigation. Quite probably at least one guard would lose his head.

I thought I was on the right track with this idea, but did not yet see how to carry it far enough.

Clothes, rings, and so on would tend to confirm the presumption of identity. Radcliffe now had a partially shaved and bandaged scalp, which would be handy later on.

The body of someone freshly executed could be brought back a few hours later into the cell, but it would be hard to pass off decapitation as a suicide, no matter how dull-witted the investigators.

Any dead body found in the cell and accepted as the prisoner's would of course be carried out and guillotined—suicide does not save one's neck from that fate, once the People have commanded it.

~ *21* ~

Radu, counting on my fanatical attitude (as he saw it) in any matter where I considered that my honor was involved, was sure that I was going to try to rescue Radcliffe from the supposedly escape-proof prison of La Conciergerie. And of course he was right.

The obvious way for me to save my client from prison and the scaffold, and strengthen him against further attack, was to turn him into a vampire—and Radu, I was sure, would have no trouble deducing that that was my plan.

I felt confident of being able to follow my brother's thoughts—even though I was not yet aware that Radu already had the cabinetmaker Duplay secretly preparing a wooden guillotine-blade. That fact I learned later, when it was too late to do anything about it.

As I saw it, the main problem in rescuing Radcliffe lay in protecting him, indefinitely, against the evil machinations of Radu. In the course of nature, the young American might easily live another forty or fifty years. And if he were converted, Radu would be forced to abrogate his vow to drink the young man's blood—either that or poison himself. Radcliffe's blood would be safe from drinking, but the time in which I might be required to defend him from other forms of attack would very likely stretch out into centuries.

Another reason to simply kill Radu. But no, my oath blocked me immovably from that course of action.

Radu was ready to try any means by which he might succeed in catching Vlad in some kind of trap. Preferably fatal.

And yet, when he really thought about it, he wasn't sure that he wanted to kill Vlad.

He mused aloud: "No, I can be perfectly satisfied with less than that . . . no, rather, his mere death is not enough. I want more."

The more Radu thought about the situation, the more it seemed to him that he would derive greater satisfaction from forcing Vlad to break a vow than he would from killing him. *If only it were possible to torment him so that he would be driven to suicide . . .* that would be a perfect consummation.

But in his heart Radu knew that to be a futile dream. Even if he could somehow force Vlad to fail to keep a solemn vow. Neither brother was one to direct violence against himself.

My little brother had also, through frequent visits, acquired a better knowledge of prisons than almost any breathing person in the world, even among those whose daily work lay in the fields of torture and incarceration. Both my brother and I were well aware that such establishments in general were anything but escape-proof, no matter how they might be advertised. Escape-proof prisons, like unassailable fortresses, exist only in theory. In the real world, such institutions are never any stronger than the weakest human in possession of a key. Bribery was far and away the most common means of getting out of one type of stronghold or into the other.

But true fanatics were exceptionally prevalent among the guiding spirits of the Terror. Many of these revolutionaries qualified. Once a man or woman had fallen into their hands, bribery became much less dependable, and even dangerous. These *sans-culotte* jailers feared for their own heads, and spies were everywhere. Almost every official, high and low, was fearful of being charged with accepting the gold of Pitt, and being a part of the great ongoing conspiracy. There were a number of fanatics around who cared very little about money. A great many officials, fearing for their own necks, would refuse even to listen to business propositions, and even should they accept one they might think better of it and refuse to honestly stay bribed.

Radu had his minions on watch, vigilantly trying to detect any attempt by Vlad at bribery of prison guards and officials. If any such plot were hatched, Radu intended to make sure that it was betrayed.

Radu rubbed his bony hands together, enjoying the game immensely. He considered the possibility that he'd lose touch with Radcliffe, that Vlad could successfully get the young American out of prison and then spirit him away.

But the more Radu considered that possibility, the less he was concerned. He was very confident that he would be able eventually to catch up with his victim again, no matter to what lengths Vlad went to protect him.

It was at this time that Radu swore, or at least claimed to have sworn, his own great formal oath to drink Radcliffe's blood, and also to see that the American's head was cut off. How well he was able to keep it, we shall see. Oaths in themselves, of course, have never meant anything to that scoundrel; the only real purpose of this one, I am sure, was to mock me and irritate me further. Therefore he had to be sure that I knew about it. I could hear him in my imagination, expostulating in mock horror: "Do you want me to break my solemn oath, my brother? Whatever would our beloved papa say to that?"

Naturally any serious blood-drinking would have to be accomplished before Philip's execution.

* * *

Convincing the Terrorists that Radcliffe had been officially beheaded—with all the necessary paperwork in good order—meant that they would not be looking for him after his escape. He would still need forged papers, of course, but in a new identity.

"Do you suppose he could pass as a Frenchman?"

"I have little doubt of that."

I was discussing these matters with Constantia—because at the moment I had no more rational conversational partner available.

"Suppose that, once Radcliffe's been turned vampire, we were to let him be beheaded. No metal knife would be able to take his life; that has been already proven. Eventually—there need be no hurry—head and torso could be grafted back together. Long ago, as you may remember, I myself passed through much the same process; though my execution was not as clean as the one that Citizen Sanson will provide."

"A bit hard on his sensibilities in the meantime, though, don't you think?" Constantia often felt genuine sympathy for attractive people. "I mean, he'll have to ride the tumbril, mount the scaffold, have his hands bound behind him, look through the little window—then I suppose he'll be able to hear the blade, sliding in its grooves, as it begins to fall—" She gave a pretty little gasp of horror.

I studied her through narrowed eyes. "I understand your meaning perfectly, my dear. But I expect the real reason for your objection is that, once he is *nosferatu,* his blood will no longer be tasty in your mouth."

I had meanwhile considered and rejected another possible method of releasing a prisoner by trickery: I myself as a last resort might play the role of Radcliffe, and allow myself to be guillotined.

"Did you observe what happened in Darnay's cell the other day?" Constantia commented when I mentioned this. And she giggled at the thought.

"No, I did not. Does it have the least relevance to our own difficulties?"

"I don't know. Some stupid Englishman—Barton or Garton, some name like that—I suppose he was really tired of living—took the condemned prisoner's place—quite willingly!—without the guards catching on, and it seems they got away with it." She provided more details than I cared to hear. "Barton, or whatever his name was, said it was the best thing that he had ever done, or some such nonsense."

I thought it over. "It has seemed to me for some time that most English are quite mad; I really must visit there someday."

But the day for such a journey lay far in my future. At the moment, I had more urgent matters to think about. One trick could be to convince Radu that we were relying upon a stratagem similar to the one which had saved Darnay—ultimately, to convince my brother that Radcliffe, vampire or not, had had his head chopped off by a wooden knife, his blood perhaps already spoiled by death.

"So it will seem to Radu," I brooded, "that neither he nor I have been able to fulfill our respective oaths."

"I didn't know that you had sworn one."

"He will assume I have. And whether I have or not, it is still an affair of honor. *Unless* Radu's oath is limited to forcing me to go back on mine . . ."

Constantia, losing patience with what she called my Machiavellian habits of thought, flounced out, declaring she had more interesting things to do.

I had considered yet another plan: I might carry in the dead body of a man who resembled Radcliffe, waving an impressive-looking written order, announcing the necessity of a certain prisoner's identifying this body.

"And we cannot very well bring the prisoner out to do so," I would tell the guards. "Though if you would prefer that—?"

Of course not.

Then the dead body would be left in the cell, dressed in Radcliffe's clothes, and Radcliffe in the habiliments of the corpse would be carried out ... but there were too many things that could go wrong.

Suffice it to say that in the end there were many plans, and variations upon plans, but that necessity decreed that one be quickly chosen.

I decided that it would probably not be wise to fully explain the finally chosen plan to the man it was designed to rescue. In the first place, the most crucial stages of my scheme, as it was finally formulated, did not require any active, intelligent cooperation on his part. In the second place, I doubted there would be time enough to explain convincingly; and in the third, I could not predict the young man's reaction if he did understand. There was a possibility that he would even refuse to cooperate with any design so daring and outrageous. Rather I preferred to have him fed on vague reassurances in which the hope of salvation was emphasized.

With all these possibilities in my mind, my closing words of encouragement, on my last visit to Radcliffe's cell, were somewhat ambiguous.

"Listen to me—*do not despair*. Even at the last moment, when it seems to you that no earthly power could possibly help you, it will not be too late. Even when you hear the knife begin to fall, repeat to yourself: *In three weeks I can be in London.*"

No doubt Radu had also heard of the Englishman Darnay's escape. My brother could be counted on to block our move, if we should try something along the same line. Similarly he foresaw that the prisoner might be converted to vampirism, and he had his countermeasure ready for that ploy as well: his plan to arrange with the executioner Sanson, or one of Sanson's helpers, to substitute a wooden blade for the metal one.

* * *

Radu, unlike his older brother, generally enjoyed playing games, verbal and otherwise, with people he soon expected to kill, or at least to terrorize. Vlad as a rule obtained no intrinsic satisfaction from terrorizing anyone; it was basically the concept that justice was being done that gave him pleasure. Nor did he enjoy conversing with those for whom he felt contempt.

But Radu, irresistibly attracted by suffering and despair, which in a way drew him more strongly than mere blood, could hardly resist the temptation to sneak into the prison from time to time. He found the atmosphere there, of despair and fear and hatred, almost as much to his liking as the sight and feel of the sharp physical blade, redolent of raw blood.

Radu would want to drink Radcliffe's blood before the execution, if he was ever going to do it at all. Doing so immediately after death, in broad daylight, would probably be impossible to accomplish, and later the effort would be futile and disgusting; in fact downright poisonous. Would he be satisfied to see the execution without drinking the blood? Evidently.

Would he be able to distinguish Radcliffe's blood from that of some other man? Probably not.

Constantia, doing a favor for her old friend Vlad, and having some fun at the same time, announced herself ready to make repeated visits to the prisoner Radcliffe. Maybe even one visit would be sufficient to achieve his conversion, if it was handled properly. He would have to drink deeply of the vampire's blood, as she did of his.

No matter how strongly the breathing youth was devoted to someone else, Constantia considered that the task of seducing him lay well within her powers.

Connie was visualizing the scene for Vlad: "And when his dead-looking body was discovered—then excitement! Turmoil, uproar! The prisoner has taken poison, committed suicide in his cell. Unusual but by no means unheard of."

She began to argue for some form of the conversion sce-
nario. "A little searching by Philip's friends among the day's
fresh corpses in the cemetery, and his head and body could
be found and reunited, with the result that he's as good as
new."

"Some might say better."

"Should we try fitting his head on backwards? I wonder
what would happen . . ."

Vlad scowled. "My object is to repay a good turn, not to
confect a monstrous joke."

But maybe Radcliffe, on regaining his consciousness and
understanding, wouldn't look at it that way. If Constantia
had, accidentally or playfully, fitted the young man's head on
backwards, probably it would, in time, work itself around to
the proper position through the natural malleability of the
nosferatu physiology. Or could be put in place with a hearty
wrench exerted with the strength of some friendly vampire.
A temporary interruption of breathing would not matter in
the least.

Constantia and Vlad would no doubt feel insulted when
their client, for whom they were doing so much, complained
to them about having been converted, or protested that he
did not want to be.

Vlad might feel somewhat affronted, but at least he
would not be surprised to discover such an attitude in a
breather.

Vlad to Constantia: "You have told him too much, and
at the same time not enough."

She sulked. "Maybe you should do it then. Or get someone else."

"Come, come! No one can do such things any better than
you, if you will only concentrate on the job at hand."

Vlad and Constantia assured their worried client that a
man once changed to a vampire could never be changed back.

"That will not happen in this world."

Radcliffe, gritting his teeth and about to undergo his

fate, murmured some heartfelt prayers for the safety of his dear Melanie.

Did he fear that he, as a vampire, would be condemned, compelled by his own nature, to do harm to the woman he loved?

I considered one rescue plan after another, running each one through, in my imagination, to several possible conclusions. And then, when I felt that we were running out of time, I made my choice.

~ 22 ~

There came a time, on what Phil Radcliffe calculated was either the third or fourth day of his and June's captivity—they were beginning to lose track—a time when Graves had been gone longer than usual.

Philip had gotten nowhere in his attempts to guess or learn where the chief kidnapper went during these absences, or by what means of transportation. Vaguely the young man had the idea that Graves couldn't be going very far, for there were never any sights or sounds of vehicles departing or arriving. The small landing strip had remained unused since their arrival.

Of course he had tried asking. "Where does he go? Graves?"

"That's no secret." Connie tossed her head. In keeping with her seeming determination to keep people off balance by her behavior, she had just come in through the window, unlocking the barred grating from outside and then swinging it tightly closed behind her on its heavy hinges.

"Why don't you tell us, then?"

"He's looking for a way to save your little . . . *neck.*" The gamine smile again. "I almost said, save your ass. But in this case, 'neck' is really the right word."

Today Mr. Graves's chief assistant was carrying with her a plastic garment bag, too thin to contain more than a dress or other single change of clothing. It crunched and crackled faintly when she tossed it down on one end of the sofa. When she saw her captives looking at it, she smiled and told them it contained some of the earth of her homeland.

The couple exchanged looks.

"Why do you carry that?" June asked.

"It lets me sleep. I really can't sleep without it."

"Where is Graves today?" Phil tried again. "Come on."

This time the question was a little more successful. Maybe Constantia's thoughts, as usual, were tending to drift away from the matter on hand. "He goes out looking for his brother. He thinks Radu will be *not too far* from where you are!" And she giggled, touching the tip of Radcliffe's nose with a playful forefinger.

"Does he drive? I never see or hear any traffic, any engines starting up." In fact the silence here, after dark particularly, struck Radcliffe as eerie.

"Sometimes he does. Sometimes he flies."

"You mean a plane lands and picks him up? But we never hear that either."

No answer, except a smile.

"Have you ever met his brother?"

"Yes. I have." Connie gazed off into the distance. For the first time that Philip could remember, she looked sad.

Somehow Radcliffe hadn't been expecting an affirmative. "Well, is there any truth in what Graves says about him? I mean, what's this Radu really like?"

For once Connie seemed at a loss for words. "Please, stay here," she urged after a time. "Do what Mr. Graves tells you."

Shortly after dawn, Constantia's eyelids were evidently growing heavier and heavier. Looking more than ever the part of the gypsy girl, she slumped down with her crackling plastic garment bag beneath her slender body.

Looking as if she were about to yawn, but not quite doing

so, she closed her eyes, folded her hands across her denim-clad tummy, and announced that she was tired and deserved a rest.

Phil pointed toward the bag. "You say this is earth of your homeland? Where's that?"

"Far, far away."

"And your carrying this bag around is supposed to prove to us that you are a vampire?"

Constantia's eyelids opened halfway. Her voice was drowsy. "Oh, I could show you, sweetie. Trust me, I could show you very convincingly. But I'd better not."

"Show us?" June demanded. "How?"

But Connie only smiled and closed her eyes again, relaxing with a kind of snuggling motion.

As Radcliffe sat watching her, the idea suddenly came to him: *This woman's on drugs.* He whispered his insight to his wife, who nodded in agreement.

She must be, he thought to himself again. *Drugs, or simply booze.* Though, now that Phil came to think of it, neither he nor June had ever seen Connie or any of the other guardians drinking or smoking anything. Probably they were trying to keep alert while on guard duty, but now Connie had slipped up.

June, with her lips brushing her husband's ear, whispered her own discovery: "I don't think she's breathing."

Looking carefully, he couldn't tell. What, he wondered, were the infallible signs of death?

Moving carefully, he shifted his weight until he had brought himself into position to whisper an answer at the same level of volume: "We're not going to hang around and find out."

Philip felt confident of being able to overpower Connie if necessary—or at least he told himself that he did—but he didn't want to hurt this demented young woman.

It was June whose attention was first drawn to the window, by a new noise. It was only a little noise, hard to identify and locate at first, but every few seconds it was repeated: gusts of fitfully rising wind making the loose grate tap against its frame. By now, with nerves continually on edge, he was familiar with every creak and rattle of this dwelling.

Radcliffe realized with an inner thrill that there was nothing to stop them from getting out the window—the steel grill through which Connie had entered had been left carelessly unlocked, so it could be swung out on its hinges. Knowing Connie as well as he now did, he could believe it. A way of escape had been accidentally left open. And at the moment none of their guardians, masked or otherwise, were anywhere in sight.

Phil cast one more cautious glance toward Constantia before he stepped out through the window, and saw that she had not moved a muscle. Actually it was more like she was in a trance, or dead. Neither her eyelids nor her lips were entirely closed. He couldn't tell if she was breathing or not, and decided that he had better not wait to find out.

Before they made their move, June reminded Philip to bring water. He grabbed a plastic bottle from the kitchen; it was too big to fit into any of his pockets, but he could carry it in one hand. And Phil grabbed up from the floor beside the sofa the broad-brimmed hat Connie always wore during the day. It was a tight fit and lacked a chin strap so it tended to blow away, but it was still better than nothing as protection against the sun. June had her own hat.

Silently Phil swung back the grill-gate on its smooth new hinges and led the way out through the window. It was only a short drop to the dusty ground outside, which was only about a foot lower than the interior floor. June, having slipped on the hiking shoes so thoughtfully provided by their captors, followed close on his heels. What could be easier?

June was almost entirely out, when the unfamiliar shoe on her right foot seemed to catch on something. She tugged it free just as she began to fall, but came down awkwardly.

When June started to fall, Philip made a grab for his wife's elbow in an effort to save her, but he was off balance and her modest weight was too much for his extended arm.

Immediately she tried to regain her feet, but was felled at once by a lance of pain. Sharply she drew in a breath, and let it out with a whispered curse.

No alarms had been set off when Radcliffe and June went out through the window; no one seemed to have heard the light scrambling sound and sudden fall, the muttered curses. The day of broiling sunlight surrounded them with its quiet.

Their one chance, and they had screwed it up . . . but the small noise the two of them made in collapsing to the ground seemed to have gone unnoticed. The bright sun glared down like a merciless spotlight. Surely at any moment now someone would come out into the yard and see them, raise a general alarm . . .

But no one did.

"Come on!" Radcliffe whispered fiercely. With their lives at stake, he was going to be as tough as he had to be, on her and on himself.

June, gritting her teeth and clinging to her husband for support, tried bravely once again. But one second of frantic experimentation, groaning and swearing, was enough to make it plain that she couldn't walk on the injury.

Sure, he could carry her. But not for very far, or at any effective rate of speed.

In a desperate whisper June urged Phil to go on alone. "You're sure as hell not doing me any good by staying here. Will you get going?"

He glared at her as if he hated her. "Just sit there, against the building, and don't move. Maybe I can steal a car."

She started to argue and then thought better of it. She slumped back against the building, rocking, fighting to keep the pain inaudible, nursing her injury.

Still no one saw or heard them. By some heaven-sent chance, Graves's breathing helpers were all occupied with other jobs. Or one or two who had been up all night were sleeping their own exhausted sleep.

June held her breath as she watched Philip's figure recede from her in a swift walk. Hunched over to make himself shorter, less conspicuous, he was moving toward the nearest vehicle. From somewhere in the other mobile home a woman's voice was raised, as if for emphasis in some debate. Maybe June could have understood the words, but right now she couldn't seem to think coherently.

Their luck was still holding, at the minimum necessary for survival. But for how long?

There were two parked vehicles currently in sight, and Phil discovered, to his frustration, that neither of them had been left unlocked.

So far, unbelievably, the disturbance he and June had made in getting out had failed to draw the attention of any of their guardians.

He was going to have to get away on foot, or not at all. He waved and shrugged at June, and she waved at him, and made fierce shooing motions with both arms.

The silent message was plain enough: *Go on, get out of here! You're not doing me any good by staying.*

Before finally heading out, he ran back to where June was sitting, to get the plastic bottle of water they had brought with them from the kitchen. Had there been any time, he would have stuffed some food in his pockets—but there was no time for food. He knew enough about the desert to realize that water meant life and death.

He clutched her hand once more, exchanged with her a silent pledge of fierce intensity, and then was gone.

Watching, sitting huddled against the building, still clutching her ankle, June held her breath, her whole being tensed against the impact of an alarm that had not yet sounded.

* * *

Philip was on his way, running in a crouch at first, bending low until he'd put a rise of ground between himself and the mobile homes. Still there was no alarm.

He could get his overall bearings by the sun, but as he wasn't sure in which direction they had been driven to reach this place, knowing north from south was not immediately helpful.

Keeping to low-lying land as much as possible, he clung fiercely to the few remembered clues he had to determine by what road or route, from which direction, the van had approached the house on the night he was brought here. But the effort seemed hopeless.

Every few minutes he had to fight down a wave of frantic emotion, in which he wanted desperately to turn back, at all costs not to leave his wife alone. But each time he reminded himself savagely, with all the conviction he could muster, that the course he was following was the only sensible one. The only chance he had of doing June any good at all.

He trudged on across country. There was only one visible road, no more than a pair of ruts dead-ending at the front yard of the mobile homes, and he kept it intermittently in sight. But for the time being he avoided getting too close to the road. Any travelers on it might very well be some of Graves's people.

Before Phil Radcliffe had walked or trotted more than a mile, his heart gave a jump at the sight of a pickup truck approaching. Still almost a mile away, he could see the vehicle only by faint plume of dust raised by its passage in the hot dry air. The driver might, of course, be Graves himself. Well, he'd have to take that chance.

Long minutes passed before Phil thought he might be close enough to signal. Though he tried frantically waving his arms, the truck failed to stop for him, or even slow down. He thought he might not have been close enough for the occupants to see him. Anyway, who was going to stop in the middle of nowhere for a lunatic thrashing his arms about? Next time he'd make one simple, appealing gesture.

Philip trudged on, expecting at any moment to see signs of pursuit from the collection of mad people he had left behind.

The sun was already merciless, his hat was already saving his life, and his single bottle of water was not going to last him for many hours. Maybe it was just as well there weren't two people sharing it.

The good news was that no signs of pursuit had yet appeared. He trudged on, trying to turn up his speed a notch.

The fugitive consumed a little of the water he had brought with him. He tried to remember whether it was supposed to be better to drink your water freely or ration it out.

Soon he was close enough to the real road to see it quite plainly as a distant, whitish streak, marking the course of some kind of commerce between ranches or farms, he supposed.

More little plumes of whitish dust came into being, showing the presence of vehicles. First one plume, then ten or fifteen minutes later another, creeping in the opposite direction. Hiking that road, he wasn't going to have to worry about getting run over in the traffic. He wondered whether he should turn right or left (north or south?) when he reached it.

Even getting within shouting distance of potential traffic seemed to take hours. With every sloping of the land, the road disappeared and then rose again above the western-movie vegetation.

At last he felt he was so close to the road that the occupants of the next passing vehicle could not fail to see him.

But it turned out that seeing him and stopping for him were two different things. On the first try, and the second, waving and yelling did no good.

His heart leaped when the second or third vehicle he

tried to flag down, what looked like a converted school bus, repainted in military-looking camouflage, did stop for him, pulling an impulsive U-turn in the sand to do so.

A long-haired young man, dressed in baggy pants and a reversed baseball cap, opened the door and politely asked if he could offer him a ride. Three or four other faces looked out through a variety of windows.

"You can. You sure as hell can."

At first glance the people in the bus looked a little rough, perhaps, but at least none of them were wearing masks. They seemed reassuringly normal after Graves and his companions.

He got in with a great sensation of relief, slammed the door, looked at the expectant faces around him, and asked to be taken to the nearest phone because he had to call the police. "God, have I got a story to tell."

"Sorry, we don't have a phone in the bus. But we'll take you to a place where you can call."

Someone else said: "And we'd sure like to listen to your story." To emphasize his point, he was gesturing with a very real-looking automatic pistol.

And only then did Radcliffe notice all the weapons.

~ 23 ~

Within a few hours Marie Grosholtz, a woman in her early thirties, well dressed within the bounds of Revolutionary fashion, and attractive in her own way but bearing little personal resemblance to Melanie, appeared at the door of Philip's cell with a guard for an escort. When the door had been unlocked the guard performed brusque introductions, as of one citizen to another, and in the name of the Revolution thanked Radcliffe for so far repenting his aristocratic crimes as to consent to having his face modeled. The guard, in the manner of one dealing with a frequent visitor, took only a perfunctory look into the container Marie was carrying. She had brought with her, in what looked like a hatbox, the equipment she needed in her work.

Scarcely an hour before Marie's arrival, another guard had officially notified Philip that the model-maker was coming to take an impression in plaster of Paris of his living face. Radcliffe had taken care to look as if this coming of a visitor was news to him. No one was suspicious when he immediately expressed his readiness to cooperate. Most prisoners who were given the opportunity did so, because it gave them at least a few hours in which they were secure from a summons to immediate death.

Secretly, of course, Radcliffe looked forward with desperate eagerness to the chance of holding private communication with Melanie's cousin.

The guard soon left prisoner and technician alone. Marie had Philip recline faceup on his bunk, in a position which he could hold comfortably for an hour or so. She then set up a lamp on the small table, and began preparations to give him a close haircut and a shave. At the same time they began to converse in low voices about private matters.

The first step in the process, Marie informed him, would be the removal of most of the hair on his head, not sparing any beard or mustache. Any hair remaining on a subject's face would be smoothed down with pomade, to prevent it sticking to the plaster of Paris from which the mold-mask was made.

Naturally Philip was eager to hear news of Melanie. Marie immediately assured him that her cousin was in good health and seemed to be in no immediate danger of arrest. That was about as much as could be said for almost anyone in Paris. Still, Melanie was lying low as much as possible, so as not to attract the attention of the authorities. As the daughter of an executed man, she would fall automatically under a certain amount of suspicion.

As the conversation went on, Marie casually revealed that she was now engaged to be married.

"Allow me to offer my felicitations."

"Thank you, Citizen Radcliffe." Apparently that term of address had become habitual with many people, even when engaged in planning some action against the government. Marie, her hands busy, mused briefly in an abstracted voice about her own affairs. "There are certain difficulties, mainly financial, that must be overcome, as is often the case in these matters." On hearing this, Phil remembered being told by Melanie that Marie's Uncle Philippe, Dr. Curtius, was in poor health, and that he had declared his niece his only heir. "But if all goes well, next year I will be Madame Tussaud."

"Again, Marie, I wish you and your future husband every happiness. What is his occupation?"

"François is a civil engineer."

And now the preparations had reached the point where it was necessary for Radcliffe to close his mouth and keep silent while the technician put quills up his nostrils to let him breathe, anointed his face with oil, and then smeared and patted the wet plaster of Paris over his newly lubricated skin.

Marie continued talking to her subject as she worked. When a guard seemed to be loitering for a time close outside the cell's door, which had been left slightly ajar, she spoke of innocent matters, of the famous people whose likenesses she had already molded—some after their beheading.

What terror and loathing she had experienced the first time, and on several occasions since . . .

Marie reminisced about the king's and queen's heads, what their faces had looked like when she had worked on them. What the technician's thoughts had been.

"*Citoyen* Louis and *Citoyenne* Marie, both at peace at last."

She explained that by looking closely at one of the molds, you could tell whether it was taken from a living face or a dead one, because those taken from the dead have no breathing-tube holes at the nostrils.

Radcliffe silently wondered why any of the Revolutionary authorities would want his wax effigy.

She told Radcliffe also that eventually his image would probably go on display at Curtius's museum, and reminded him of where the museum was. He grunted an acknowledgment, deep in his unmoving throat.

As soon as the figure in the corridor had moved away, and there was no guard or other attendant standing by to overhear, Marie passed on to Philip, in secrecy, a further message of encouragement and hope from Melanie, who sent word that she loved him.

Philip groaned.

Marie lowered her voice, but spoke with an intensity of feeling. "You are not to abandon hope, M'sieu Radcliffe."

Someone else has told me that. The quick-drying plaster of Paris on his face kept him from saying the words aloud.

"You may believe it," Marie added. A pause. "When I am gone, yet another will come to help you. Now hold still, move not a single muscle. The mold will soon be dry."

Indeed, Marie was hardly gone, with her precious plaster cast packed in her hatbox, and the sun had hardly set, when there came a faint sound from the other end of the L-shaped cell, and—miracle of miracles!—a young woman appeared, wearing earrings of gypsy silver, peering with pretended shyness around the corner at him.

"The gypsy fortune-teller!" Radcliffe breathed.

She was dressed in a tattered costume suggesting gypsies, and in oddly accented French introduced herself as Constantia.

The L-shaped cell had an old ventilation shaft at the far end. Seemingly too small for anyone to pass through it; and yet . . .

Leaving his visitor behind him for the moment, Radcliffe went rummaging around in the angle of the cell where she seemed to have materialized. "There must be a loose stone somewhere. Or one of these window bars . . ."

But then he looked more closely at the smiling woman, and partial understanding came.

"Ah, perhaps I see. Or I begin to see. You, and Legrand . . ."

"Yes indeed, how clever you are!" Constantia clapped her hands, like a child. "He and I are friends, and M'sieu Legrand has asked me to look in on you."

Radcliffe was soon convinced that this woman was sincerely trying to help him.

"M'sieu Legrand also said that you might like some brandy." And with a conjurer's gesture, Connie produced a little flask.

Neither Legrand nor Marie had come back to see Radcliffe. The otherwise abandoned prisoner soon came to depend heavily on the comfort and hope offered by Constantia, who, once having introduced herself, stayed close to him as much as possible.

Connie could tell stories very amusingly when she made the effort, and Radcliffe was distracted and entertained by her tales of how she periodically adopted the role of the gypsy fortune-teller, and as such passed unchallenged among the other entertainers performing at the morbid parties.

Very early on in their acquaintance, Philip's new friend began to discuss with him the subject of vampires: their cravings, their powers, and even to some extent their weaknesses.

And their first meeting was not over before she had kissed him, putting a severe strain on what feelings of loyalty he had begun to develop with regard to Melanie.

From then on, whenever he was alone in his cell, which was very nearly all the time, Radcliffe kept expecting at every moment that the mysterious gypsy girl would join him. And frequently she did appear.

Her words of encouragement were along the same lines as Legrand's. "It will be possible for you to laugh at locks and bars and walls of stone, even as I do—even as the Chevalier Legrand. Possible to leave these walls behind you forever, and your jailers too."

"How can such a thing be possible?"

She began the incredible, truthful explanation, gradually filling in details. And when the young man did not at first believe the vampire story, she conducted another convincing demonstration: vanishing before his eyes, then reappearing in the corridor outside the cell, beyond its locked and bolted door. Then in another instant she was back inside with him.

"What is the secret?"

She laughed, a small musical tinkle. "Love is the great secret of life. It solves all problems—and laughs at locksmiths, hadn't you heard?"

"Love?" They were very close together now, sitting side by side on the narrow bunk, and he had become enthralled.

"It is at the beginning of everything, is it not, my tall American? Do you know what it is to love—?"

"I have loved. I do love."

"But you did not let me finish. Do you know what it is to love, in the way of the *nosferatu?* What you will call in English, vampire."

The prison around them was very dark, and howled its fear and madness in a hundred different voices, mostly very faint. Radcliffe whispered: "I have heard . . . only stories. Stories told by old women, to frighten their grandchildren."

"Stories, pah, they are nothing. Real life is everything." And Constantia, beginning by stroking his cheek with the seductive skill gained in three centuries of experience, conducted another demonstration, this one even more overwhelmingly convincing than the other.

"Philip, give me a kiss."

"I . . ."

"Bah, how can I show you, how can I do anything for you, if you will not do even that much when I ask it? Am I so ugly, then? You gave me a peck on the cheek before. But now I want a real kiss . . ."

Later, what seemed to Radcliffe hours later though it was only a matter of minutes, he asked: "How long have you known Legrand?"

"Ah, forever and a day! He calls me his 'little gypsy.' But there is no need for you to be jealous. For a long, long time now, for centuries in fact, we have been like brother and sister, because that is all that two of the *nosferatu* can ever be to each other."

"Oh?"

"Besides, he is very *old* . . ."

"Oh?"

"Yes. Let me tell you some of the facts of life . . ."

* * *

Ah, my dear little gypsy! Constantia though not very large was physically strong, and had been so even in her breathing days. In fact she was very nearly as old as my brother and I. Brave, ready to deal with the undead, those she called the *moroi,* for the sake of the magical power the body of such a one could confer—but she had never been known for her logic. The combination tended to make her an interesting ally; but I had no time to try to recruit anyone steadier.

The next time Connie came to visit our poor client, she brought with her another gift of brandy, this time a whole bottle instead of merely a little flask.

Philip grabbed it eagerly. Having momentary trouble with the cork, he was about to break off the bottle's neck in his impatience, but Connie intervened, using her long nails and remarkable strength of wrist to pull the cork out neatly.

When he put the bottle down to gasp for breath, she said: "Ah, Philip! Why should not the two of us seize a little happiness, in these last days of our lives?"

Connie's technique of lovemaking, which was certainly unique in Radcliffe's experience, confirmed her nature as something much different from an ordinary human.

Philip talked nervously to the new object of his passion. Sometimes he babbled. "Did I tell you I did much of my growing up on an island in the Caribbean? My mother is still there. On Martinique, it is much easier to believe in such things than it is in Boston or Philadelphia."

"I have heard the same thing from others. Someday, I think, I would like to see that part of the world."

There were moments when he knew strong guilt feelings for his behavior with the gypsy, when he saw it as a betrayal of Melanie. But as yet he and Melanie had made each other no formal pledge. There were times when she seemed very far away, a relic of his childhood—and other moments when all thoughts of her were wiped from his mind by a passion whose strength seemed born of the imminence of death.

Connie on her successive visits provided Philip with a

steady supply of strong drink. I believe that wine, brandy, and rum all appeared at different times. I had suggested a drop or two, to ease our client's anxiety, but in view of the result it seems plain that she overdid it.

Later, she admitted to me that she had added a few drops of some little-known aphrodisiacal drug. The Borgia pharmacy had not yet exhausted all its treasures.

Constantia, among her other achievements in our cause, succeeded brilliantly in her inspired plan of converting Radcliffe's cell into a genuine habitation, thereby granting immunity from vampire penetration except by the will of the occupant.

She knew she had succeeded when she discovered one day that she herself was unable to enter without asking permission of the inmate. Then, laughing and clapping her hands, she explained to Radcliffe what a good sign this was.

After Philip and Connie in the course of their lovemaking had exchanged a modest volume of blood, she told her handsome American explicitly that he was now liable to conversion. "If that should happen, you will have nothing to fear from Citizen Sanson."

"What do you mean?"

Choosing a time when there was no one in the corridor who might look in, Connie demonstrated on her own nude body how impossible it was for a metal-edged weapon to do one of the *nosferatu* lasting harm. She forced the sharp knife through her finger, through her hand, then in places that might have been expected to be more tender. She giggled and enjoyed her pupil's mixed reaction to the sight. Then she showed Radcliffe her skin undamaged.

Or almost. There remained on that smooth brown surface a single drop of blood, which she persuaded him to lick away. *A tingle of joy again, of pleasure that at the moment seemed worth dying for . . .*

"I say that if you become as I am, no prison will be able

to keep you in . . . and no metal blade will ever kill you. That would not be so bad, no?"

"Is it possible?" The words came out in a hoarse gasp.

She made an eloquent gesture. "If a king and queen can have their heads chopped off by gutter rats—then who is to say what is impossible?"

"You are saying that I would become like you and Legrand—and like the one who wants to kill me. Able to pass in and out of closed doors, and—and if I understand what you are saying—even able to withstand the great knife of Sanson's engine?"

"It would pass through your neck without killing you. Precisely, my friend. You would be in two pieces, no doubt, but you could be put back together."

"Two pieces."

"That is what I said. Head here, body there. Then, *zut!*— back together, good as new again."

He sat for a while on his bed in silence, trying to put it all together. Trying to make sense. "Why do you do this?"

"What?"

"Visit me, and give me back the chance to live."

"That is easy. I am Vlad's friend, and I want to help him save your life."

" 'Vlad'?"

"I'm sorry. I mean the man you call Legrand, my dear."

"I am not surprised to hear that he has other names. But . . . there is so much about all this I still don't understand. Two pieces, and back together?"

"Poof, why do you worry? What have you to lose, in your situation? You don't have to understand everything, just this: The man you call Legrand considers that his honor binds him to you in loyalty, simply because you saved his life when he was in most dire need. Believe me, he is not one to forget either good deeds done to him or bad." Constantia paused for a sigh. "The only problem is—"

"Yes?"

The lady looked wistful. "In earning the loyalty of Legrand, you have earned the hatred of his brother, who is almost as powerful."

"Yes, I have heard. The man who is supposed to want to drink my blood." He paused, rocking back and forth on his narrow prison cot, trying to get a grip on the short hair of his scalp, which was still bandaged, so he could pull it. "Which is what you do to me. And now you have me craving to taste your blood also. I think perhaps that I am going mad!"

His companion tilted her curly head on one side and considered him carefully. "No," she decided. "No, you are still a long way from madness. I know many people who are truly insane, and they are nothing like you." She paused, considering. "Well, not very much."

Spinning round, Radcliffe confronted her fiercely. "I tell you that I love Melanie!" And in that moment, when his passion for Connie had been momentarily satisfied, he experienced a burst of repentance, even of revulsion, for what he had just done.

Constantia smiled benevolently. "But I am not jealous of what you feel for your Melanie. Is that what worries you? I am simply enjoying a good time with you."

"What worries me is that—if what you tell me about you *nosferatu* is true—then, when I am changed—what will happen to her?" Philip in his desperation took another drink from the brandy bottle that was not yet emptied. "She is so fine, so pure—" Now tears were running down his cheeks. "Ah, I am not worthy of her!"

Connie tried to explain. But he was drinking—brandy, not blood—and not listening. And she has never been very good at explanations.

Philip's violent affair with Connie, indeed his whole acquaintance with her, lasted no more than a few days, but those few days were sufficient for our purpose. In them he lost track of time. More than enough happened, between him and Constantia, to teach Philip many things about the nature of vampires, and to afford him a real chance of becoming one.

Meanwhile Melanie was lying low, doing what she thought she could do to protect her son. She had no idea that Philip was being seduced in prison, or even that there were such creatures as vampires—except that she was ready to concede that Citizen Legrand, who had pledged his help, was no ordinary man, and in fact could do some quite extraordinary things.

Shortly after Marie had visited Radcliffe in his cell, Melanie at the museum received from the older woman a matter-of-fact report about the event. Melanie was able to take some comfort from it.

But the great question still tormented her. "Can we really succeed in saving him?" she demanded of her cousin. "*Can* there be a rescue, from that prison?"

"Why not? It is only a place, like other places. And Legrand has a scheme." Marie, whose eyes had seen a great many things in the last few years, nodded slowly. "I think I trust Legrand . . . whoever he really is."

"Yes, I know. He is an impressive man. But the situation still terrifies me."

Marie patted her sympathetically. "Let us each do our part. Then, it is in the hands of the good God."

The fate of the man she loved was not Melanie's only worry. She wondered also whether her young child, little Auguste, was ever going to bear a name other than that of a bastard. More urgently than that, she wondered whether she herself might be arrested on some charge and never see her son again.

Radu, knowing that patience and caution were essential in a conflict with his brother, made no real attempt to get at

Radcliffe in his cell. He approached no closer than was necessary to sense the habitation effect which guarded the occupant.

Something of the same caution kept him from trying to approach Melanie, whom he might otherwise have attacked just to get at Vlad even more indirectly.

And then, as almost unexpected as such days often are, came the morning when the stolid workmen came for Philip Radcliffe, without fuss or fanfare, just before dawn, and Connie had to fade into the stone walls and darkness to get out of the way.

Radcliffe was once more well-fortified with strong drink, a condition that had become chronic over the last few days; and he had been affected also by Connie's careless brush with converting him to vampirism. He could only stare around him stupidly. Where was she? But it was sheer fantasy to believe that they had done the things together that he remembered. It seemed to him that he remembered drinking blood from her veins; that she had tasted his was indelibly imprinted.

In the harsh glare of outdoor daylight, dazzling after days in his dim cell, it seemed to him that he had only dreamed the presence of the gypsy girl.

By the time Philip Radcliffe was hustled out of the prison into the light of day, he had more or less reconciled himself to his fate, whatever it was going to be—to everything, in fact, but the idea that he would never see Melanie again. Philip had no convincing reason to doubt that he was going to be guillotined. His knees felt weak as he was pushed, stumbling, this way and that.

The people who had come to load the tumbrils for the day were cursing and fretting over their lists. "Where is the Englishman, Percy Blakeney? Name of a dog, but he is not here!"

"But here is at least one of the foreigners, who will not escape us!"

The combined effects of seduction, alcohol, and anxiety on Radcliffe rendered him semiconscious before his trip to the scaffold actually got started.

The streets of Paris, and their jeering crowds, went by him as in a dream. Constantia had vanished, as dream-creatures were compelled to do in sunlight.

A wave of despair washed over him. Madness, all madness, and he had betrayed his true love, Melanie, for the embrace of a satanic enchantress. *Three weeks and I will be in London* . . . and he had allowed himself to be convinced. What hollow nonsense, before the reality of the tall cart, and his bound wrists!

He saw now, with unbearable clarity, that Constantia's pledges were fantasies, were lies, and he, Philip Radcliffe, had thrown away his life, clinging to a hope that could be no more than sheer insanity . . .

Radcliffe, mind spinning with the aftermath of brandy and exhaustion, jammed in among the sweating, trembling bodies of the other scheduled victims of the day, rode the jolting tumbril through the streets, with his hands already tied behind him, and his shirt torn open at the collar, and arrived at the Place de la Revolution to play his part in the great show.

The carpenter, Duplay, had only recently finished shaping and planing and sanding the wooden blade, of stout, tough oak, which Radu had ordered. Duplay had added a dark stain, which succeeded in making the finished product look almost like metal. The blades of *la mechanique* were changed fairly frequently, and it seemed unlikely that onlookers would pay this one any particular attention.

Radu had secretly arranged with one of the younger Sansons for its substitution in the death machine, on the proper day. And when that day came and the wooden blade was used, on a converted Philip or even a tricky Vlad, Radu was determined to be in the audience watching. The victim's

head, vampire or not, was going to come cleanly off, and
Radu would not have missed that sight for anything.

Philip Radcliffe thought that he and the Reaper had been on
intimate terms for some time now. He had a fleeting impression of familiarity when he looked into the face of Death,
in the form of Sanson's powerful assistant.

And Philip, his hands now tied behind his back, with no
sane reason in the world to expect anything but a dramatic
passage out of the world within the next few seconds, was
sent stumbling forward across the little platform. The long
arms of the taller executioner reached out, and his hands
seized Philip Radcliffe in a grip as tight as that of Death.

~ *24* ~

Where's your husband?" The questioning voice issued almost calmly from inside the monstrously lugubrious head of Frankenstein's monster.

June met the steady gaze of the almost invisible human eyes, inside the mask, with as much defiance as she could muster. "I don't know."

The man straightened, putting his fists on his hips. The voice from the monster's head was mild, conducting a casual inquiry. "Looks like you came out the window. I suppose he came out with you?"

June said nothing, but stared with as much courage as she could muster at the artificial face looming over her. At last she announced, in a tightly controlled voice: "I've hurt my ankle. Do you suppose you could help me get back inside?"

Reassuringly, the man's posture altered suddenly, as if he hadn't until this moment understood why she was sitting on the ground. His reaction seemed purely one of concern as once more he leaned slightly toward her. "Of course. Which ankle is it? But maybe you'd better just sit still for a minute. What happened?"

She pointed to the throbbing limb. "Twisted it, falling out the window." That one of the damned kidnappers should be concerned about her welfare seemed perversely offensive, and grated on her nerves. Baring her teeth, she indicated the exact location of the injury. "What do you *think* happened?"

"Sorry about that." The apologetic attitude seemed quite genuine. Then the mask turned, scanning right and left. "Where did Mr. Radcliffe get to?" But the question sounded casual, unalarmed.

"How should I know?"

Several other masks were now approaching, from different directions, and in a moment the newly formed group of rubber-faced monsters had begun a conversation among themselves. June, fearful but defiant, felt relieved and wept when her captors seemed to take the uncertainty about her husband pretty much in stride.

No one hounded her with questions regarding Phil's whereabouts. Presently two of the men, moving with the care if not the skill of ambulance attendants, picked June up and carried her solicitously back into the little house.

In the living room, Connie lay stretched on the sofa, dead to the world. Ignoring her, the volunteer medics set the injured woman in a chair.

June noted with mixed feelings that Connie was alive— the dark-curled head had turned a little to one side since the Radcliffes went out the window. But the gypsy woman slept on, her crunchy plastic bag beneath her as if she might be afraid someone was going to steal it. None of the renewed activity in the room disturbed her in the least, and the masked people in turn paid her no attention. If she had indeed fallen into some kind of coma, they evidently considered the condition in her case nothing out of the ordinary.

One or two of the masked guardians hastily searched through the other rooms of the small house. At last the group began to murmur among themselves on the subject of Radcliffe's absence. Then one hurried toward the other building as if to pass along the news.

The rubber images of Hollywood horror who remained in the room with June stood facing her in her chair, but the postures of their bodies gave no clue as to what they might be thinking.

Roused with some difficulty from his own trance in the other house, Vlad Dracula heard the news of Philip's escape. Obviously it came as no surprise.

"And the tracking device, Joseph?" he inquired.

"It's in place, and we're getting readings."

The almost microscopic transponder earlier attached to Philip Radcliffe's trousers was still faithfully emitting a signal when electronically prodded. A rotating antenna which had earlier lain concealed had been erected on the roof of the second mobile home. Inside, another breather, mask now off, was seated at a small desk, tracking Radcliffe's location on a green-tinged screen.

Among Vlad Dracula's breathing helpers, Joe Keogh, at least, would almost certainly be in on any trick that was being worked. Joe thought that over the years he had earned that right.

Joe Keogh on taking off his rubber mask stood revealed as a man in his mid-forties, his fair hair turned half gray. He was of average size, and sparely muscular, with a tough-looking face. Eyeglasses, acquired in the last couple of years, added a scholarly touch to his appearance.

John Southerland, missing the little fingers on both hands, was the same height as Joe, a little under six feet, but twelve or thirteen years younger. Maskless, John appeared strong-jawed and sturdy, with light brown hair beginning to be touched with early gray and showing a tendency to curl. John in fact looked slightly older than Mr. Graves, whom he once absentmindedly addressed as "Uncle Matthew."

Even while John had been wearing a mask, either of the prisoners might have noticed that the little finger on each of his hands was missing. John had considered wearing gloves to avoid that problem, but gloves could draw attention too, especially in hot summer weather, and stuffed glove fingers would not look particularly natural. So far the gamble had paid off; eyes drawn continually to the mask, neither of the Radcliffes had yet noticed his mutilated hands.

Everything in the conversation between Vlad and Joe Keogh, who now removed his mask and wiped sweat from his face, confirmed that it had deliberately arranged, with Connie's connivance, for Philip to get away and for June to be left behind.

Joe, reluctant to put on his rubber mummy-mask again after making his report—they were the devil to wear when it got hot—rubbed his fingers through his sweaty gray hair, and looked at himself in a nearby mirror—Mr. Graves did not object to the breathers' having them in their residence—and wondered whether he himself was maybe getting a little old for the rough stuff. The prospect of some very tough action indeed was looming ever closer.

Joe Keogh, out of curiosity and because he thought he had the right, dared to ask a question about Radu, and the origin of the bitter hatred between the brothers.

Vlad, reminiscing while they waited for other matters to be organized, recalled with bitter anger the circumstances of his own youth, his rivalry with his brother Radu, called the Handsome, their lives as hostages in the power of the sultan, and their early estrangement.

"Have I ever told you about my brother, Joseph?"

"Something about him, yes."

"A cautious answer to what was, I fear, a poorly phrased question. What lies between us began in the fifteenth century; and how many more centuries it will go on, I do not know."

Joe Keogh nodded.

But Vlad Dracula was not looking at him, only gazing into the distance. "I see two young boys, young princes, sons of old Vlad Drakul, or as the historians will call him, Vlad the Second. His two offspring held hostage by the Turks to guarantee their father's good behavior.

"Two princes in a tower that was very different indeed from the Bastille."

"Yes, I bet it was."

"My lifetime's allocation of fear was entirely used up, before I was old enough to grow a beard." Vlad was calmly stating a fact.

"I believe you," Joe Keogh said.

"Radu did not, does not believe me. He has always thought that I am lying about that, that my fearlessness depends on some hidden magic."

Vlad sighed, a faint reptilian hiss. "It was always so with him, I think. Determined that there must be some hidden trick in everything, a key of magic, available only to the elite. Radu the Handsome. Always he has welcomed men, as well as women, eagerly into his bed—in truth I believe that he prefers children, of either sex, to adults. Anything human, provided it is young, and . . . but in this case I accomplish nothing by becoming angry. I think perhaps that my brother was transformed into one of the *nosferatu* by one of his Turkish bed-partners, when he was hardly more than a child himself."

"It sounds like he's a sadist, then," said Joe. "I mean, a genuine, compulsive . . ."

Mr. Graves nodded. "Despite the common misconceptions regarding the *nosferatu,* this affliction is about as rare in vampires as it is in breathers. But I have no doubt that my brother is one."

Joe was silent, as often he was when in this man's company.

His companion appeared to be lost for a time in memory. Then he added: "Whether or not Radu ever became a Moslem is more than I can say. But I am sure that any oaths he swore in matters of religion were false, for the truth is not in him, and has never been."

Keogh, shivering as he listened to Vlad's smoldering anger, was extremely glad that it was not directed at *him.* Joe had now known this man for almost twenty years, and for most of that time had called him friend. But he had never entirely ceased to fear him.

June was once more left alone and with no one paying her close attention. Glowering at the peacefully sleeping Connie, she thought that she would try to take the shoe off the painful foot and see if that helped. It was a natural reaction. Though the ankle still hurt like blazes, at least it wasn't noticeably swollen. But she hesitated to try to take off the shoe. She feared that the ankle would swell and keep her from putting a shoe on again—damn it, she couldn't put up with being a helpless cripple!

Joe Keogh, masked again, came to see how the patient was doing, and looked carefully at the enchanted shoe.

"Let me help you get that shoe off; I think it'll feel better."

June winced involuntarily when the kneeling man gently began to take off her shoe. Once the laces were loosened and the innocent-looking encasement of leather and plastic was removed from June's foot, the pain disappeared with amazing rapidity.

Hesitantly June wiggled the foot, then stood up. She set the foot down flat on the floor, and then gradually shifted her whole body upon it. Hesitantly she took a turn around the room. The pain had vanished, like some kind of an illusion, leaving not a trace behind. Nothing was wrong now.

Her masked attendant, who squatted watching her, with his head a little on one side, did not seem at all surprised.

For some reason she felt defensive about the cure. "It really *was* hurt. But now . . ."

"I believe you." He nodded sagely. "I've seen things like this a few times before, when Mr. Graves is in action. Let me tell you, lady . . ."

"Tell me what?"

A benevolent chuckle came from inside the mask. "You ain't seen nothin' yet."

* * *

On the dot of sunset, the moment the last direct rays of the sun had vanished from the western windows, Constantia woke up, yawning and stretching catlike on the sofa in the mobile home.

"Good morning," said June, who was sitting in a chair nearby, there being not much of anywhere else to go. She threw down the magazine she had been trying to read.

The gypsy only looked at her sleepily, and murmured something about being afraid that she hadn't done her job well enough.

"What job was that? Guarding us?"

"Something like that." Connie sat up and looked around. "Is hubby back yet? No, I don't suppose he would be."

June stared at her. "How do you know he's gone?"

"Oops. Little Connie's talking too much again!" One red-nailed hand went up to Connie's mouth, covering an impish smile.

~ 25 ~

*T*oday's crowd in the Place de la Revolution, Radu noticed, was of only moderate size, no more than four or five hundred people. A few of them, mostly sitting or standing in the best locations, he could recognize from the numerous other times when he had attended. They were the regulars who did their best never to miss a beheading, rain or shine. A couple of the women, the notorious *tricoteuses,* who brought their rocking chairs and knitting to the performance, were as usual jealously occupying the very best spots close to the platform, on the head-side of the knife. There was Madame Defarge, who seemed to have made herself their leader. When she glanced in Radu's direction, he bowed lightly. She might someday have information that could be useful.

Too bad, thought the younger Dracula, that they would not hold these events at night . . . a few of those new Argand lamps would illuminate the scene well enough to satisfy the breathing rabble. He would have to try to find some way to exert influence . . .

Outfitted in a new disguise, one that as usual included a broad-brimmed hat, Radu had unobtrusively taken his place among the onlookers waiting to witness the day's official violence. He had already noticed that not all of the younger Sanson's usual assistants were on the job today, and in fact Gabriel had only one man with him on his high workplace.

But that was really nothing out of the ordinary; normally there was a heavy turnover and rotation among the crew, and some variation in their number. Nor did it seem so strange that a different set of workers, adopting a slightly different routine, had piled some extra baskets and other equipment about them on the platform.

Early this morning, Radu had received a short note scrawled by Gabriel Sanson himself, assuring him that the wooden blade had been installed and would be put to work today.

The sunlight, stabbing out with fierce intensity between rain showers, was bright enough to bother Radu more than a little, and to dull his senses somewhat, even to pose some danger. But he pulled his hatbrim down a little more and stayed where he was, in a good position on the head side of the lunette, the little window, despite the fact that he was not close enough to have an ideal position. Backed up to within a pace or two of the edge of the crowd, he had his line of retreat open behind him, should it prove necessary.

There was one beheading on today's list that for him was very far indeed from routine. One execution that he would not miss, not for all the sweet young red blood in the world. Because this one meant the humbling defeat of his arrogant brother.

The first tumbril had arrived, stuffed with more than a dozen arm-bound, crop-haired men and women, and the day's work for the crew on the platform got briskly under way. Radcliffe was not in this shipment. Well, then he would be in the next.

Radu turned frequently from side to side, shooting suspicious glances into the crowd in all directions. He was considering several possibilities regarding the present whereabouts of his brother. Of course Vlad was not going to give his enemy the satisfaction of being here to experience his humiliation at first hand. That Vlad was dead had to be counted a remote chance. More likely the elder was preparing some truly monstrous counterstroke of punishment for his rebellious little brother. But even if Vlad should succeed in that, there was nothing, nothing in the world that he could do now to prevent Radu from savoring this triumph.

Still, it bothered Radu that he had no way of telling whether Vlad might be nearby, concealing himself among the crowd.

He was not surprised to glimpse Constantia in a distant part of the crowd, and beckoned to her. But the gypsy only looked flustered, and tried to pretend she had not seen him. Which again was not surprising.

One or two of Radu's other associates, lesser vampires, were at no great distance, and he allowed himself to take some comfort from their presence. Not that anyone at whom Vlad's anger was directed could really feel safe anywhere.

Again a feeling of uneasiness returned to nag at him. He would not be free of it until he knew exactly where his brother was . . .

Meanwhile, up on the platform, matters seemed to be proceeding according to the somewhat variable routine. Everyone was now accepting as standard practice the absence of the patriarch of the Sanson clan. The chief executioner's health had been failing for some time. Radu remembered hearing that the old man, Charles, had not long to live—his difficulties being purely natural, not political. Over the centuries Radu had noted that if any class of people were truly safe from changes in political leadership, it was that of the executioners and torturers. Their jobs were secure no matter what.

Today's session was one of those when the crowd's view from the sides, on the "body-side" of the little window, was partially screened off as if by accident. Today the executioners, as they sometimes did, were arrogantly refusing to heed the occasional shouted demands for a better view. They had, no doubt inadvertently, created obstructions by piling a couple of extra body-baskets, along with spare parts for *la mechanique,* on either side of the platform.

But Radu, along with the great majority of the audience, was not in the least inconvenienced. As the tumbrils began to unload, and the slow one-way parade started up the stairs in single file, he still had a perfectly clear view of one head after another, coming through the lunette, then rolling, with no more dramatic flourish than a potato dropped by a kitchenmaid, into the waiting basket. No doubt even a breather would soon get used to it, if he were here every day attending the show. And yet, where else in Paris, or in the world, was there anything like this to be seen? One raw neckstump after another spurted blood, then was pulled away to make room for the next, all to the accompaniment of raucous and rhythmic cheering by the crowd.

Had Radu been writing a critical review of the event for the newspapers (he had considered doing that, if the business could have been managed anonymously), he would have been forced to inform his readers that today's level of technical skill was not of the highest. The two workers on the high stage mishandled more than one of their victims, depriving each of whatever last moment of dignity he might otherwise have been able to attain. And here came Radcliffe at last, face pale with prison and the terror of death, hands bound and collar torn open like the rest, short dark hair surrounding a small white bandage, clumsy and stumbling in his terror— or quite possibly, thought the observer, he had been given strong drink as he climbed into the tumbril, in an effort to numb his awareness. A petty effort to spoil Radu's triumph, perhaps—and now the man in his fear, or his drunken stupor, had fallen to the platform—but the two workers, demonstrating strength and dexterity for once, had their client up again in a moment, and were putting him on the plank.

Radu's pink-lipped mouth hung open in anticipation, as

if he were about to kiss some morsel of human flesh. His eyes drank in his triumph as Radcliffe's dark hair, showing the little bandage in the midst of the close-cropped scalp, was pulled and pushed through the little window. For a moment, regrettably but inevitably, the body of the assistant who was pulling on the ears largely cut off the audience's view of this process. Then the wooden lunette slammed closed, and the executioner moved out of the way.

As always, the machine was disconcertingly quick. Whoever was ultimately in charge of these events, the original designer no doubt, had really little sense of drama. The peak of Radu's triumph came and went so swiftly that if he had blinked, he might have missed it.

But of course he had no need to blink. He heard the usual double-thud, of falling knife and head, and he saw the head go tumbling into the wicker basket.

The executioner's tall assistant lifted it out carefully, by the short dark hair; the red flow drained out visibly for the crowd to watch.

The raw neck spurted red, adding its stain to the day's previous spatterings, before the headless body was withdrawn.

Radu, looking on, had to squint into uncomfortable daylight. But he was focusing his entire attention on that face, and had no trouble at all in making certain that it was Radcliffe's. Unable to contain his joy, Radu spun round slowly, once, twice, performing a little dance of triumph.

Since yesterday Melanie had known, through a certain private line of communication, that this was the day when the man she had come to love must escape, or perish in the attempt.

Today Philip Radcliffe, following in her father's unwilling footsteps, was to be taken to the scaffold. But she did not go, could not have forced herself to go, to the place of execution. Legrand had assured her that her presence there would be neither wise nor useful. And to be there, a witness, watching the worst happen, would have been unbearable.

Instead she put in another day of waiting at the museum, spending part of the time in the modest living quarters she shared with her son, part in the workshop where there was always plenty to keep her busy. She waited under the greatest tension imaginable. Someone had promised to bring her a report.

But before any report could reach her, there came a warning.

Men, armed soldiers, agents of the Committee of Public Safety, were coming to the museum to arrest her. She had barely time to hide.

Quivering with fear, cowering in a storeroom among wax figures and listening from her improvised hiding place to men's raised voices only a few steps away, she heard that they were going to look for her in the cemetery, too.

Eleven years ago, in 1783, at a time when the childhood playmates Melanie Romain and Philip Radcliffe had already been separated for about eight years, Curtius had modeled a life-size figure of Benjamin Franklin, who had then been in residence on the edge of Paris. The effigy had been placed on display with those of other celebrities in his museum. And Melanie Romain, grown woman and mother, found herself hiding behind it now.

Melanie, fourteen years of age at the time of Franklin's sitting, had been an assistant to the artist, beginning to learn the art and craft of modeling, at which she was later to excel.

And the young girl had received some grandfatherly attention from Franklin, who would have expressed his sympathy on seeing that she was in a family way. *And* especially when she introduced herself as the childhood playmate of one of his favorite illegitimate children, the old man, with his lifelong susceptibility to feminine attraction, was said to have, scattered around the world, more than one or two offspring who were not openly acknowledged.

She would have appealed to Curtius to use whatever influence he possessed to free Franklin's son. But by the time Radcliffe was arrested, Curtius the good republican was much too ill to help, or even to understand.

When the men who had come to the museum to arrest her had given up and gone about their other business, calling to each other in loud voices and stamping their boots, she remained prudently in hiding and did not emerge until after the museum had closed for the day, when Marie signaled her that it was safe.

This new threat meant that Melanie would have to move on, earlier than planned, to where the next step of Legrand's plan called for her to be—move on, and hope for the best.

"What word of Philip? In God's name, tell me!"

But there was no word as yet. Meanwhile, where was little Auguste? Melanie could only hope that her son had gone ahead of her, following Legrand's instructions, and that the hunters were not after him as well.

Making hasty preparations for her own flight, she asked Marie: "And how is Uncle Curtius today?"

"Too ill to know or care much about the affairs of the world. I think maybe he suspects something out of the ordinary is going on, but he doesn't really want to know about it."

Radu, pleasurably reliving over and over again the memory of Radcliffe's head falling into the red wicker basket, had immediately taken himself away from the place of execution, out of the bright morning sun and into the deepest shade that he could find, savoring what he thought to be his triumph.

Exhausted by strain, weakened by sun-glare, he went into what he considered the best-hidden of his Parisian earths, meaning to rest until sunset, or even later. He had won, he had beaten his hated elder brother. Whatever happened now, there was no hurry about taking care of the details.

* * *

Emerging from his earth near midnight, Radu took time to go and sit on the frame of the now otherwise deserted guillotine. The night had turned chill and rainy, after the bright, hot day, and all the crowds had gone.

Radu sat there apostrophizing the death machine, from which he had pulled back the oilskin cover. Tenderly he stroked the heavy blade. He murmured, in one of the old languages that he had learned in childhood: "It almost breaks my heart to see so much blood going to waste. To decay, and the breeding of flies in the hot sun."

With a little moan of satisfaction, he leaned forward and ran his tongue over the blade—yes indeed, it was still the wooden one, he noted. And no one had got around to cleaning it as yet. Old Sanson would be angry if he knew of such abuse of his equipment.

This, Radu would be able to tell anyone who asked, was how he fulfilled, at least symbolically, his vow to taste the blood of Philip Radcliffe.

There was an aftertaste of something strange, mixed with human blood . . . orange juice?—something like that. More likely some kind of vinegar, blended with unidentifiable substances and used as a cleaning fluid. Some attempt at cleaning had been made, then, but an abysmally poor job. The vampire spat.

Now it was the middle of the night, and Radu felt well rested and wide awake. He would sit here and gloat a little longer, and then make his way to the wax museum. Vlad, evidently devastated by defeat, was keeping out of his way; and Radu had an idea as to how he might improve upon his triumph.

He strode forth this time with a confidence that even prompted him to sing in his beautiful voice. Even if Vlad caught him again, and defeated him, there was no way the older brother could wipe out what he must see as a stain on his honor brought on by this defeat.

He remembered something one of his aides had asked him, before that last fight in the countryside: "Why is your brother's honor of any importance to you?"

And Radu had replied: "Because it is of the utmost importance to *him.*"

Philip Radcliffe was not awake, and he was dreaming.

He had just been decapitated—and yet he hadn't.

In his strange mental state, he could, for the moment, consider dispassionately the fact that the blade had inexplicably failed to whack off the vampire's head—or almost failed.

Somehow, in Radcliffe's feverish dream, only a thread of neck still held. This strand of tissue was broken manually, by one of the new vampire's enemies, and the victim's head was thrown at last into the coffin with his body.

There he soon recovered consciousness, and he understood that reunion was quite possible—after all, other vampires had been decapitated before him, and had survived.

It seemed to Radcliffe in his dream that the heads and bodies of a whole day's output of victims had been thrown indiscriminately into a giant tumbril, and the whole bloody mess hauled away for burial. By now the medical schools of Paris were sated with disconnected heads and bodies, and could be prevailed upon to accept only a few choice specimens, those with something extraordinary about them.

The body's hands went on patiently groping for and trying on one head after another.

Meanwhile, the vampirish brain lived on, thought, raged, experienced pain and sometimes pleasure, while still connected to the senses of sight, hearing, taste, and smell. The eyes could turn in their sockets, blink, and change their focus. Breathing was never a necessity for him. Meanwhile, as he had hoped, the trunk and limbs retained enough affinity with the disconnected brain to take the necessary actions.

Groping through the charnel pit, the strong white hands

at last found the proper head, only after rejecting several, and with an awkward movement lifted and tugged it into place . . . and the head had been put on backwards . . .

. . . and with that extra touch of horror, the nightmare was finally over, leaving its victim sobbing, cold sweat mixing with the cold rain that fell from heaven on his face.

Philip Radcliffe was finally, thoroughly, waking up. He had no trouble now distinguishing dream from reality, and he knew that his trip to the guillotine had been no dream.

~ 26 ~

J ouncing along inside the gutted and rebuilt vehicle, Radcliffe tentatively decided that it must once have been a
school bus. He couldn't be absolutely sure, because about
half the seats had been ripped out, as if at random, and the
interior, like the outside, had been repainted in a dull camouflage pattern, mostly olive drab.

The best thing Philip could find to hope for at the moment was that he was being taken back to Mr. Graves—but
he knew that wasn't what was happening.

Every look these people gave him, every word they said,
every nightmarish minute that passed seemed to bring some
new confirmation of Graves's warnings. These people, with
their foul language and their waving weapons, fit to perfection the role of friends and helpers of the mysterious Radu,
the shadowy monster against whom Graves, on tape and off,
and Connie had so often and so solemnly warned their cod-
dled prisoners.

The cruelty of these people, to him, to animals, to each
other, was a continuing shock.

Now he remembered, in bitter contrast, how patiently

and persistently Mr. Graves and Connie and the others had kept trying to convince him that their fantastic tale was true.

Over and over Phil now kept telling himself that there was at least one bright spot in the situation—at least June hadn't fallen into this horrible mess with him.

Someone across the aisle between seats offered him a drink of water, then as soon as he reached for the canteen, pulled it away with a giggle, continuing to watch him with bright speculative eyes.

When chance brought about a pause in the steady drum-fire of cursing and taunting, most of it not directed at him, in what seemed to pass for conversation in this group, he spoke up to demand: "Where we going?"

The old bus lurched along at a good speed, bouncing, roaring as if at the injustice of its fate in being slowly beaten apart by the rough road, which alternated with intervals of roadless land. No one bothered to answer Radcliffe. It was as if they had already disposed of him and he was dead.

After a minute or two of silence he tried again: "It's all right, you can just let me out here. I'll hitchhike."

"Sure you will," said the woman who was sitting next to Radcliffe, in a remote voice. Another man and woman showed their crooked teeth.

Another minute or two went by before Radcliffe, licking his dry lips, gave way to a wholly unreasoning impulse and suddenly lunged at the nearest door handle. Half the people in the forward seats did not even bother to turn their heads. His arm was caught and pulled back. Weapons were once more displayed.

One of his fellow riders, who a moment earlier had been whistling a cheery tune, suddenly broke it off and began muttering obscenities, whipped out a pair of handcuffs and manacled Radcliffe's hands behind him.

One of the rattier-looking villains abruptly astounded him by starting a song, in which about half the others promptly joined in. They were singing in French, of all things—the *ça ira?*

> *Ah! ça ira, ça ira, ça ira,*
> *Les aristocrates à la lanterne . . .*

Years ago, Radcliffe had memorized the song for one of his language classes in college. In the present situation it was so incongruous that he wanted to laugh. But who had taught these donkeys French? The singing was raucous and out of tune. Though Philip would have felt helpless if required to conduct a conversation in the language, his memory retained bits and pieces of it from his classes in high school and college. Enough to derive the sense:

> *That's just the way it is,*
> *We're going to hang all the aristocrats . . .*

Still uselessly erupting with sporadic protests, Radcliffe was driven a few more miles, up a winding road and into a narrow valley in the foothills.

It was around mid-morning, with the sun definitely getting warm, when the driver pulled onto a patch of bare, rutted ground before the house, and stopped.

This time no one had made any effort to keep Phil from seeing where they were going.

Their destination turned out to be an old two-story frame house, starved of paint and maintenance for years, probably once some rancher's home. The dwelling seemed miles from any other house, and was almost hidden in the midst of a small grove of cottonwoods and Russian olives. A barn a little bigger than the house, standing some twenty or thirty yards behind it, had fallen even more completely into disrepair.

A battered pickup truck and a late-model sports car with a New York license were parked near the little cluster of buildings. A small stream, temporarily a small torrent fueled by spring snowmelt in the high country, came thundering down past the cluster of buildings, making a steady background noise, a lot of racket for a small amount of water.

Philip was dragged out of the converted bus, and shoved stumbling into the house. People who had been in the house greeted those returning in the van. The latter were crowing and babbling, suddenly moved to boast in triumph of their capture. Radcliffe wasn't at all sure why, but it seemed he was considered something special, more than just a chance acquisition.

He was roughly searched by several people in succession, as if none of them trusted the others to do a proper job, and his valuables confiscated.

The place was a mess, and it seemed that a sustained effort had been going on for some days to turn it into one. The walls were stained by unknown causes and daubed with graffiti. The windows were dirty, with a third of the glass knocked out, and much of the furniture was broken. A woodburning stove, iron door open and housing a summer population of carefree spiders, stood in the middle of the main room.

Radcliffe's latest set of captors spoke among themselves in awed tones of someone they called the Master, whose arrival they were awaiting eagerly, but with some trepidation. But the Master would surely be pleased to see who they had captured for him.

Judging from what Radcliffe was able to overhear, one or two of the Master's devotees had never actually seen him yet, but they knew every detail of a largely fictitious reputation that had grown up around him. And they were looking forward to meeting him, as to the high point of their lives.

So far Phil had encountered only about half a dozen members of this gang. But judging from certain clues dropped in their conversation, more were coming when the Master did, and they might well have the band of Mr. Graves outnumbered. These people gave the impression of being less competent than the rubber-masked league of the Radcliffes' original kidnappers, but far more dangerous.

On the heels of that thought followed the discouraging one that maybe Graves's people weren't really as competent as they seemed. Otherwise they wouldn't have let him get away.

"What'll we do with him?" one of the more frightening men asked another, nodding at Philip.

"Do with him? Nothing." The speaker seemed vaguely horrified at the thought. Then he seized on the one idea that had evidently been firmly impressed upon him. "We keep him safe until the Master comes back."

"How soon is he coming?"

Two or three of the gang were ready to offer their opinions on that subject, but it soon developed that no one really knew. Obviously they were a little worried about the Master, whom they all feared, whoever he might be. The possibility of his quick return seemed in a way as disturbing as that of his continued absence.

One of them asked Philip, in an offhand way, where he had been for the last few days.

He gave the first answer that came into his head. "Resting up."

"That's good, 'cause you're gonna need it. We were looking for you on the road a couple days ago, sonny. We was driving all over hell, sniffin' round after you, but you didn't show up. Where were you, anyway?"

Still it seemed that none of them really cared about the answer. Philip got away with letting the question slide.

"The Master sure wants to see you."

"We been looking for you a long time already."

"Where've you been the last few days?" This was a different questioner, who seemed not to have heard what the first one had just said.

This time Phil didn't bother answering.

"Cat got your tongue? No, not yet. Soon, though, soon." That evoked a widespread tittering of laughter.

* * *

This house, with its two floors plus attic and basement, was obviously much older and several times larger than the mobile home from which Radcliffe had escaped. This habitat of Radu's servants was also dirtier, grimmer, and much less hospitable. Grease-stained pizza boxes still holding decayed remnants of last week's meals lay scattered about, along with an extensive menu of paper wrappers, attracting energetic flies. The whole fast-food litter suggested that some place where a lot of people lived was not that many hours away. A frightened and dazed-looking cat went wandering from room to room, ignoring the garbage as if it had smelled it all before.

The kitchen sink gave evidence of a contest among inmates to see who could go longest without washing dishes. At least one wall in each room had been defaced with obscene pictures and scribblings, some of which Radcliffe took to be gang symbols.

The one class of objects the group did not seem to be careless with was their collection of firearms and knives.

At the sink he helped himself to water, taking a long drink directly from the faucet. He expected at any moment to be stopped, but no one tried to do so, or even seemed to notice.

Philip, listening to a renewed debate as to whether to tie him up, found some abandoned detergent and a scrubber under the sink and adopted the job of washing dishes. Under the circumstances he had no objection to making himself useful.

There was no hot water from the faucet, but he soon had a pot heating on the propane stove. Meanwhile Philip was thinking that if these people could be persuaded to let their prisoner cook, he might have some hope of poisoning everybody. But there didn't seem to be any rat poison available, and mighty little detergent.

Two gang members, a man-woman couple who had been sent to town to buy supplies shortly after Phil's arrival, came back after an absence of four or five hours with a weird variety of canned goods, beer and wine, boxes of crackers, and a greasy bagful of Big Macs.

"Anybody follow you?"

"No way." The couple gave contemptuous reassurance.

The incoming cargo included a couple of heads of lettuce, looking incongruous among the other stuff. Philip had no suspicion at this point of the reason for their purchase.

Scattered here and there through the big house was considerable evidence of drug use: discarded syringes, a smell in the air—actually, in certain rooms, a clinging haze. Half of the inhabitants were coughers, smoking tobacco cigarettes.

Rock music, alternating with rap records of a particularly debased kind, was playing more or less constantly in the hideout. The prisoner listened dazedly to one performer after another declare at great length what he was going to do to the next ho and bitch that he encountered. Certainly there were at least two radios; no one ever listened to them or turned them off.

Half a dozen cans, containing substances more or less edible, and brought in by the recent shoppers, were opened—the litter on the floor testified that a great many had been emptied over the past week or two—and food of a kind offered to Philip when some of the others sat down to eat. He settled for a bag of Pop Tarts. The cat, with the air of a gourmet, was sorting through the garbage in a corner.

At this point someone had the idea of searching Radcliffe all over again. Naturally enough the results this time were disappointing. His money had already disappeared casually into people's pockets. And the argument over what to do with his credit cards had evidently been settled somehow; certainly the bits of plastic had vanished also. His watch was taken.

"The Master won't be interested in this. We can have it."

*   *   *

They left him his recently acquired wedding ring, because even in a few months it had become a very tight fit, and it soon became obvious that they didn't want to risk spilling any of Philip Radcliffe's blood, even scraping the skin of his finger, without the Master's permission.

"*He* owns your blood," one of them explained to Radcliffe, seeing the prisoner's uncomprehending look.

He didn't argue the point.

The discussion as to whether to tie Radcliffe up, or lock him in the cellar, or both, rambled on inconclusively.

While the crew were still waiting for the Master to come back—though no one seemed really to expect his awesome presence until after dark—someone suggested that they show their unwilling guest the guillotine. Immediately the others cried approval.

They were sadistically eager to observe Radcliffe's reaction to the machine, and dragged him out of the house, across a yard where he was beset by snarling dogs, and into the barn.

Most of the space inside the barn formed one large room, as big as the interior of a small house, with a few disused animal stalls at the farther end and a dangerous-looking built-in ladder ascending to an open hayloft above. There was a lot of space available, and the bulk of it had been converted into a kind of workshop. There was one electric wire, a long shop cord strung carelessly over ground and floor, but it had probably been used only for power tools. After-dark illumination was going to be provided by two or three self-fueled Coleman lanterns.

Bats, small motionless dark pods, small bulges suggesting the shapes of folded wings, were hanging by their feet under the high, peaked roof. A couple of pigeons cooed sleepily.

There in the center of the open space, on a floor of decades-old concrete, stood what was undoubtedly a guillotine. The unique shape, immediately recognizable, stood some fifteen feet tall, and most of it, at least up to the level where a tall man could reach with a paintbrush, had been painted bright red. The lower surfaces, up to a little above the level of the plank and the lunette, bore brownish stains that might have been old blood.

"What'd you think of that?" The questioner really wanted to know.

It was hard to find an answer . . . *a man who wants to cut off your head* . . .

One of Radcliffe's captors, one of those who seemed to have comparatively little trouble in speaking in coherent sentences, told him that the machine before him was an exact replica of the one used in Paris, France, during the Terror. Someone else broke in to argue that no, this was the original, the very one that had taken off the heads of the king and queen and pope.

The bandit looked at Radcliffe anxiously, with the air of one who was proud to show off his intellectual attainments to someone who could understand them—but at the same time he wasn't quite certain that he'd got it right.

To Radcliffe the machine appeared amazingly tall, and quite authentic. This was the very instrument, one character solemnly affirmed, with which their Master had vowed to chop off his, Philip Radcliffe's, head.

A tall young woman, tattoos on her bare arms, told him: "After that, the cats will probably have your tongue. Your blood, though, that's another matter altogether." She squinted at him judicially. "I think that most of your blood will be out of your body before your head comes off."

"What's your Master's name?" the prisoner asked on impulse.

"None of your business."

He thought of mentioning it—Radu—but then decided that there was nothing to be gained by doing that.

Radu's assistants fussed over the solidly built, authentic-looking guillotine, and again expressed their hopes of pleasing their demanding Master.

"He'll be real happy when he sees what we built for him. All the care and effort we put into it."

They bragged of how they had made all the parts of the guillotine somewhere (they were coy about revealing exactly where) and trucked it here, disassembled. Then they had set up the device in the old barn. Signs of fresh repair work suggested it had been necessary to patch the roof and run in a long power cord from the house.

All of them were eager now to give their prisoner a demonstration of how the machine worked.

For some reason it was thought necessary to tie Philip into a chair first. He didn't protest; certainly this was better than being strapped to the plank and tilted into the guillotine. Then an inspiration came, and he persuaded his keepers to untie him, by complaining that the cord was so tight that his arm was bleeding inside his shirtsleeve. He'd observed that these people were very worried about the chance that even a drop of his blood would be spilled.

The complaint brought him immediate attention, and a loosening of the rope. The villains stripped up his sleeve as far as it would go, then sliced it very carefully with a surgically sharp knife, and looked at his arm. Then they looked at him, in outrage because he'd lied. Actually the bonds had been tight enough to leave marks, though there was no real bleeding.

For all their feverish anticipation of the Master's arrival, every one of his disciples missed the event when it took place, a few minutes after sunset. As had been the case earlier with the comings and goings of Mr. Graves, Radcliffe had been able to hear no sound of aircraft, motorcycle, car, or even horse. There was just the sudden presence, standing in one of the barn's farthest recesses, of a remarkably handsome young man wearing a Greek fisherman's cap and a dark suit jacket over a dark T-shirt.

"Radu," said Philip Radcliffe, aloud and quite involuntarily. Half-untied as he was, he started. He was the first, or very nearly the first, to notice who had just come in.

Radu was simply standing there, hands down at his sides, looking at them all. When his followers finally noticed his presence and began a murmuring movement toward him, he raised one pale hand in a curious gesture that seemed half warning, half benediction. The advance stopped instantly, and silence fell.

"Philip Radcliffe," said the beautiful young man, as if simply returning a greeting, and smiled his winning smile.

Casually he approached the place where Philip sat half-bound before the guillotine. The people who had been arguing and fussing over his bonds stepped back.

Philip looked up into eyes of gentian blue, under hair of raven black. The man smiled, revealing frankly pointed teeth, a jarring note like something out of Hollywood.

"I knew your namesake, long ago," said Radu. His voice was gentle, almost whispering. He put one finger under Philip's chin, and raised it gently. "I thought that I had seen him dead, and tasted of his blood, in 1794 . . . but it turned out that I was wrong about that. So now I must have yours."

He shifted his position by a step or two, so that now he was looking down on Philip from a different angle. "You do not seem surprised. Someone has been telling you the story." And he raised his eyes to his supporters, seeking information. The looks he got back were blank, or frozen with fear and fascination.

Once more the vampire dropped his gaze to Radcliffe's. "To settle the vexing question of your ancestor's fate to my own satisfaction, I investigated the genealogy of your branch of the Radcliffe family during the nineteenth and twentieth centuries."

It had taken Radu some time and effort to make sure, he explained now, but in the end there could be no doubt— somehow the beheading he'd thought he'd witnessed had been a fake. "And I think I know now how that was accomplished."

Philip Radcliffe, bastard son of Benjamin Franklin, had survived the Terror in France, and—as Radu's subsequent research demonstrated—had returned to America with his French bride, Melanie Romain, to settle in the state of Virginia, where he founded a substantial family and eventually died in 1861 at the age of ninety-two.

Radu's words trailed off slowly, and he fell silent. He was looking at the guillotine.

The world seemed to be dissolving in horror and unreality around Philip Radcliffe. Tied down, unable to move more than one hand, he was surrounded by smiling and giggling enemies, all their attention now focused for a moment on the object they had brought him out here to see. The full-scale instrument of two hundred years ago, or so nearly so that it made no difference. Spruced up with a fresh coat of bright red paint.

"Demonstrations," said Radu at last, stroking a pale hand up and down one upright of the massive frame. "I wish to see how well it works. Just how reliable it is."

Murmuring their eagerness, his slaves got busy. The heavy blade, sharpened edge gleaming a little in the lantern-light, was hauled to the top of its track on a new rope. On the first trial, with nothing in the lunette, the blade fell with a startling crash, to be caught by the slot in the lower frame. The fall of the knife had a distinctive double sound, because the heavy metal bounced up and fell again.

On the second trial it became evident that parts of the death machine were not always going to work smoothly. When a head of lettuce, recently brought from town, was set in the lunette, the blade when triggered began to fall, then heart-stoppingly became stuck halfway down. As soon as someone touched the machine with the idea of making an adjustment, the blade recovered itself, plunging the rest of the way at the impulse of a very slight vibration. The jarring impact sounded just as heavily as before, and the lettuce fell in two, divided as neatly as if by some fine kitchen tool.

The second subject of the day's demonstration—Radcliffe was not sure who had made the choice—was the live cat. Sensing evil intent, the beast clawed and bit one or two people before they could get it under control. Two or three of Radu's breathing acolytes, ignoring their bleeding scratches—it seemed that no one, including themselves, placed any value on their blood—held the animal's four limbs in a practiced way, as if this were not the first time they'd done this trick, and pushed its snarling, screeching head in through the little window at the front end of the machine.

Once more the blade came down, putting an abrupt end to living noise. The sound of its fall was only subtly different than before, but it was to stay with Radcliffe for a long time. Somehow the smallness of the jet of blood was a surprise, a mark of the pettiness of evil that would spend its energy to kill a cat.

Someone at once snatched up the fallen head from the barn floor, and tossed it into Radcliffe's lap. Another apprentice vampire, heedless of crimson splashes, held up the dead cat and tried to drink the blood which had not yet entirely ceased pumping from the vessels in its neck.

Philip felt a wave of dizziness, gray faintness threatening to blot out the world, amid the sound of laughter. Coming and going, like the pulsing roar of blood in his own head, there came from outside the steady noise of the swift white water of the mountain stream.

But no, he wasn't going to faint, not quite. No such luck. He raised his eyes, trying to look anywhere but at the machine, or at the man who was chewing on the dead cat's neck—and had to bite his lip to keep from crying out.

Because at the nearest of the barn's high windows he could see, in outline against the darkening twilight sky, the head and shoulders of a human figure. The figure was holding some kind of tool or weapon in one hand, and the watcher held his breath, for now from some unknown outdoor source there came a tiny flash of light, revealing the familiar features of Mr. Graves.

~ 27 ~

At some time around midnight, on the night following his helpless journey to the scaffold, Radcliffe regained his senses.

He was roused from a state of nightmares and stupefaction by several unpleasant stimuli of increasing urgency, among them a brisk shower of cold rain.

Struggling to sit up, he discovered that his limbs were stiff, and the grass that had been beneath his body pressed down and dry.

Now in a seated position in the grass, grimacing with the pain of his pounding headache, he fought back a wave of dizziness and nausea. *Where in hell or on earth was he . . . ? What was he doing here?*

He was in the open air, and the world around him was very dark and wet. The fact that he was still alive seemed to indicate that he had been turned into a vampire—he could think of no other possibility. But the evidence of this tremendous transformation aroused in him, at the moment, no particular emotion. It was as if he had none left.

Groaning, he made a great effort and stumbled to his feet, staggered a few steps this way and that, everywhere encountering more long, wet grass. Thunder grumbled somewhere overhead; clouds dripped. Well, a few things were obvious, giving him a kind of foundation from which to start thinking about his situation. It was near midnight, by the look and feel of things, and he was in a cemetery. The rows of graves, dimly perceptible, stretching away through darkness, the tall church in the middle distance looming against clouds and sky, testified to his location. It might well be the very cemetery where Melanie worked. The burial ground where the Revolution sent its dead, when Sanson was through with them . . . like Melanie's father, like . . . Philip Radcliffe, too?

The thought of Melanie drove even his own immediate problems momentarily from his mind. Oh God . . .

He rubbed his face with both hands. Was he ever going to see her again?

As her image rose before him in imagination, Radcliffe found that his feelings for her were stronger than ever. But when he imagined his beloved in his arms again, he was faintly surprised to discover that he experienced no special craving to bite her neck or taste her blood.

What his body wanted now, of hers, was much more commonplace.

Standing in the wet grass, he turned around, shifted his weight from foot to foot, and tentatively waved his arms. The power of flight did not seem to have been given him. Nor had he the faintest idea of how to turn his body into mist, nor did he enjoy any sensation of augmented muscular strength. In fact he felt weak after his ordeal, stumbling every time he moved.

But as horror began to recede, a great mystery took its place—*somehow* he had survived the guillotine. He came to a halt, rubbing the back of his neck where the muscles seemed to have clenched in a reflex bracing, still anticipating the impact of that razored weight . . . if he was *not* a vampire—and the transformation seemed at least doubtful—then the blade ought to have done the job with no trouble at all.

But here he stood, miraculously still in one piece. He began to tremble. What in the devil *had* saved him?

Dazedly, he seemed to remember Connie telling him that the transformation from breathing man to vampire, and all the changes which must accompany it, took a little time.

Oh yes, Connie. Oh God . . . how could he have done the things he did, with her? But there was no question that he had.

Maybe it was the brandy. He could try to blame his behavior on the drink.

However miserable his regrets, simply groaning over his situation was going to be no help. He was, or had been, under a sentence of death, and he had to find some practical answers to what seemed a hundred urgent questions. Shivering with the chill of rain (his trousers and torn shirt, almost his only garments, were soaked through, he made an effort to pull himself together.

Try to think! The last thing he could remember was . . . yes, of course, the scaffold. Oh God, yes. That would be the last thing he would ever forget.

The city streets were a good distance from him in every direction. The cemetery contained a large expanse of open ground, and no doubt that was the chief reason it had been chosen to meet the needs of the People for burying-space. Those needs had turned out to be enormous.

The summer night was not really cold, and Radcliffe's shivering soon ceased when he forced his body into a regular walk—not that he knew yet where he was going—waving his arms and beating them against his sides. His legs woke up and started to perform more normally. But his body still ached in every bone, and his head throbbed.

Only now did Radcliffe realize that the piece of cord that had secured his wrists behind his back had somehow been removed. He ceased thrashing his hands around for a moment and gazed at them in puzzlement. Did the gravediggers routinely perform that service for their customers? He doubted it. Phil wondered dazedly if he might have broken the cord, without realizing the fact, in an access of that new vampirish strength Connie had so vividly described and demonstrated with her own body. His wrists were still chafed from being bound.

The bell of a church clock was striking somewhere in the distance, but Philip was too muddled to count the strokes. Stranger sounds drifted to his ears from somewhere else, also far away—it sounded like some drunken mob, singing the *Ça Ira.*

If only his head would stop aching—not the least of Radcliffe's practical problems was an ugly hangover.

And this time the usual ghastliness that a hangover left in a man's mouth was compounded by an unmistakable aftertaste of blood—he remembered all too well that it was a woman's blood. Vampire blood, if the one who had called herself Constantia had been telling him the truth about anything. The thought of the gypsy woman, the vivid memories of what he and she had done together, now sent shivers of mixed repulsion and attraction along his spine.

The gall and wormwood in his mouth had subtle but important differences from the taste of his own nosebleed or knocked-out tooth.

There was also the savor of remembered ecstasy. But at the moment, all recent memories were predominantly horrible.

He spat. God, but he was thirsty. All this rain, and no water anywhere to drink—

Again the combination of taste and recalled experience provoked him to nausea, and his empty stomach retched.

But to hell with blood, and to hell with gypsy women, whether they were vampires or not. The fundamental fact that Philip Radcliffe had to bring himself to face was that he knew his head had been cut off.

He could *remember,* damn it! They had dragged him up there on the scaffold, and . . . he could almost remember the impact of the falling blade . . .

All right, everything wasn't exactly clear, just at the vital point. Go back a little farther. Far enough so that memory was plain and unequivocal. Somewhere sense and sanity must be attainable.

Very clearly the young man remembered having his hands bound by one of the jailers before he'd left the prison. Even now his wrists were sore, in evidence of that. Then he remembered being in the narrow courtyard where the great carts were loaded with the condemned, its stone walls seemingly threatening to crush him. No doubt about that either. Then the ride to the scaffold, in a large cart pulled by a team of horses and crowded with his fellow victims. There had been jeering crowds along the way.

Very little time had elapsed between the termination of that ride and the moment when the lights went out for Philip Radcliffe. It was the events just before the end of consciousness which were hard to pin down—like trying to remember the exact moment when you fell asleep. But yes! With a little effort he now clearly recalled being half-marched, half-carried up the steps.

The fierce, dark eyes of the executioner, the great shock of the falling knife—and also the sharp tug on his recently shortened hair, as the executioner displayed his head—or someone's—to the routinely cheering crowd.

. . . *the great shock of the falling knife* . . .

But wait a minute! He could not possibly have watched, looking on as a spectator, seeing from the rear his own head being held up for display. Oh yes, he'd recognized his head; there was even the small white bandage on the crown . . .

Whatever the answer, however the mystery of what had happened on the scaffold might finally be explained, here he was now, alive—yes, alive—in what was certainly a cemetery.

Peering around him in the darkness, he at last made out,

at a distance of some thirty or forty yards, the raw earth mounded beside a trench.

At least the gravediggers had not ripped the clothes from his body. That, he had learned in prison, was what those predatory vultures often did.

The clothes Radcliffe had been wearing when he was arrested, and while he was in prison, had been only ordinary. His coat had been taken from him when his wrists were bound, and the collar of his shirt had been ripped open. Small wonder that the petty thieves in the cemetery had not bothered with what was left, if they'd had the chance. There had lately been no shortage of finer garments for their selection.

If he'd had a hat, they'd certainly have taken that. Hats must be one item they very seldom encountered in the course of business. The idea of a man wearing a hat to his own beheading suddenly struck Radcliffe as tremendously amusing, and he began to chuckle, an ugly sound. But of course he'd been hatless when his would-be murderers had dragged him from his cell to have his head cut off.

While these thoughts were running through his mind, unconsciously he had started walking again, toward the pale blob that he thought must represent a mound of raw earth.

In prison he'd also heard the gruesome details about the burial mound, the endlessly long mass grave whose active end was excavated every morning for the day's harvest of bodies, and filled in every evening—that was the place where Marie and Melanie sometimes came to do their work.

His feet slowed to a stop, dragging through the grass. Suppose, just suppose, he'd never been in the hands of the gravediggers at all.

Slowly Radcliffe came to realize that some clue to the solution of his mystery might lie in the fact that he had come to himself lying perhaps forty or fifty yards from the place where the bodies were routinely dumped—and where the gravediggers had been, or ought to be, industriously at work.

He wanted to see the place where the latest crop of bodies had been dumped. He set out to reach it.

When he had covered half of the remaining distance to his goal, stalking stiff-legged toward the mass grave, a pair of young lovers burst up from the ground like startled birds, almost at Radcliffe's feet. Tripping on their own half-shed clothing, they ran away screaming through the darkness when he came toward them. Alarmed by this eruption, he almost turned and ran in the opposite direction.

In his imagination, recalling his nightmare, Radcliffe pictured his headless body separating itself from the jumbled, gory pile, finding his head and putting it back on. Then his reconstituted self had tottered away, under his own power, before the gravediggers had been given a chance to do anything at all with him. The shadow of a nightmare, already almost forgotten, came to plague him again.

He shuffled slowly forward.

Yes, damn it all, his head *had* been cut off. He could *remember* the event . . . or at least parts of it, a moment here and there. But no, he couldn't actually remember his hands groping for his head, pulling it into place.

But now his head was definitely on his shoulders, as firmly attached as it had ever been.

If Sanson and his great machine hadn't been able to kill him, that meant, according to all Connie had told him, that he, Philip Radcliffe, had become a vampire. What other possible explanation could there be?

The marks left on his throat by Connie's fangs—*they* had been real enough—were genuine. They didn't hurt, but he could locate them with the sensitive surface of a fingertip, like tiny pimples.

He drew a deep breath of pride. Pride more in his own sanity, in the integrity of his memory, rather than on the occasion of his joining a gloriously different race of men. Connie, as he remembered her, was real.

But in the next moment, drawing a deep breath, he realized that everything wasn't settled yet. Ought he, as a vampire, still to be breathing?

What might have been the basis for an alternate explanation loomed in his exhausted mind: Were all his recent memories, including his trip to the scaffold, only the fabric of a hideous dream? But maybe all of life was one great dream; that answered nothing.

In Radcliffe's current mental state, only one thing seemed incontestably true: He was no longer in prison. And for that he could be devoutly thankful.

At last approaching closely the mound of fresh earth, Radcliffe was afforded his first good look at the Revolution's most recent crop of corpses. Tonight's shift of gravediggers had not yet finished their job. Now he could hear their voices rising from a little distance and see the indirect glow of a small light, where they had taken shelter under an awning stretched out from the side of a wagon. They were distracted in some dispute among themselves, perhaps over some clothing or other valuables taken from the latest batch of victims.

But it was the silent victims, or their bodies rather, most of their arms still bound behind their backs, that drew Philip with a sickly fascination.

He shuffled toward them to take a closer look.

He recoiled from their staring eyes, reflecting faint gleams of stars and moon, or distant torches.

Some of the mouths in the head-pile were open, and their eyes indifferently looked at him, and at each other, like the eyes of dead fish. Dazedly, feeling that what he did was no more than was now expected of him, he picked one up. This, Marie had told him, was what Melanie did, helping out her helpful cousin.

He maneuvered his hands carefully, to avoid touching the raw neck-stump (odd, but most of the neck seemed to have disappeared) and to touch the face as little as possible.

If Melanie could do this, he could too.

The hair offered the easiest and surest grip. The weight was not surprising, seeming neither too little nor too much.

He threw aside the peculiar object. The modest weight went bouncing, rolling, across the muddy and uncaring earth.

Someone, he supposed, would pick it up again and bring it back.

The rain was slackening off.

There was a burst of laughter from where the gravediggers had gathered. Now their meeting, whatever it had been for, was breaking up. They were grumbling and laughing, and he could see their lantern bobbing toward him.

How long he stumbled to and fro in the long grass around the border of the churchyard, making his way from one tall fence to another, looking for a gate, anxious to do something but not knowing what to do next, he was never able to determine. When the sky in the east began to brighten, behind clusters of leaden clouds, he remembered certain promises that Legrand and Connie had made, warnings they had given him while he was in prison. And Radcliffe expected that the morning sunlight when it appeared was going to kill him.

Suddenly the wonder concerning his own miraculous survival was overridden by an obsessive urge to locate Melanie. In his shock and amazement he had almost forgotten the plan of escape Legrand had outlined to him. There were certain things that he, Radcliffe, was required to do once he had left the prison walls behind. Somewhere he would be given forged papers, providing a new identity for himself . . . though whether a vampire would need papers or not . . . and Melanie would be given hers . . .

He shook his head in an attempt to clear it. Yes, Melanie. Once he had found her, everything else could be made to come out all right. And Philip clearly remembered the address where she was to be found. And the directions for getting there.

Rain fell intermittently throughout the remainder of the night, keeping Radcliffe's short, raggedly cut hair wet, and running down his face.

Running his hand through his hair at one point, he noticed vaguely that his bandage was gone. It must have finally come loose somewhere.

. . . then there was no getting away from it. Crazy or not, it had really happened. Or most of it, the key parts. *He had survived the guillotine.* He was a vampire now. Brother to Legrand, and sister, no longer lover (the thought brought a pang of sharp regret) of Constantia the gypsy.

At last finding a gate that he could climb, he trudged away from the cemetery, moving in the direction where the city lights glowed brightest. Putting a finger in his mouth, he tested the sharpness of his teeth. Still one missing, ever since that brawl years ago in Philadelphia. The others' shape had not changed one iota, as far as he could tell. Not a bit pointier than they had ever been.

As he stumbled into a puddle it occurred to him to wonder why, if he had really undergone the tremendous transformation, he could not see better in the darkness?

He had walked a quarter of a mile from the cemetery, through darkened and almost completely deserted streets, before he found water in a drinkable form. Rainwater standing in a barrel, beside one of the outbuildings of a small church.

He drank and drank, slaking a terrible thirst, then plunged his whole head into the water, and pulled it out. Now, for the first time in days, it seemed, he began to feel completely awake. Brandy and vampire blood were slowly being purged from his system.

The rain had stopped again, and the unaccustomed shortness of his hair gave him a sense of coolness, and of liberation. Where his bandage had fallen off he could feel a tender scar.

But he had seen the bandage on that detached head, his own head, as it was held up by its hair . . .

Another sensation was finally becoming identifiable. He was desperately hungry.

So, I am one of them now. Or am I? Still he could not settle the matter, one way or the other, with any degree of satisfaction. He raised his arms, feeling his head with his fingers, testing its connection to his body. He seemed to be as
totally in one piece as he had ever been. With tongue and fingers he once more tested the sharpness of his teeth. His skin
flowed without interruption, smoothly from jaw to throat to
chest—except for Constantia's tiny fang-marks—and save
that he once more badly needed a shave; Marie's visit to his
cell had been days ago.

The aftermath of brandy, seasoned with a few drops of genuine vampire-blood, was still throbbing in his head. Yesterday's unsurpassable delight still lay as this morning's cold
nausea in the stomach.

*There, for an hour or two, he had known beyond all doubt
that he was a vampire . . .*

With the directions for reaching Dr. Curtius's museum
fixed in his mind, Radcliffe plodded doggedly on his way.

~ 28 ~

R adcliffe, moving with a strange sense of freedom, even a growing (and dangerous) perception of his own invulnerability, found his way to the Boulevard du Temple with only a couple of wrong turnings. Once he asked directions from a streetcleaner, and the man, assured by his provincial accent that he was from out of town, gave him directions willingly. Fortunately no one bothered him about papers.

Philip had never before visited the House of Wax. In prison he had heard from Marie Grosholtz herself that she expected soon to inherit the property and the business from Dr. Curtius. It stood on a broad street that must be briskly busy in the daytime.

A prominent signboard, and now just above that a painted banner, faced the street, each declaring that this place was the Salon de Cire.

The sun was not yet quite up when Radcliffe arrived, but every minute more people were stirring in the streets, and soon traffic would be heavy. Not wishing to be conspicuous, he paused outside the first side door he came to in the big building and uncertainly experimented, half-willing himself to pass through the narrow crevice. He was not really surprised to find himself unable to pass through knife-edge cracks beside doors, or melt his body into mist. But maybe, he thought, this whole structure counted as a dwelling.

In keeping with a growing sense that things were being made easy for him this morning, his way somehow smoothed, Philip found a door toward the rear of the main building standing slightly ajar, as though someone had forgotten to close it.

Listening, he could hear faint snores from open windows in the upper stories, where he thought there must be living quarters.

He entered through the door he had found open and quietly pulled it shut behind him. He was standing in a dim, drab corridor, more closed doors on either side. The first one he tried showed him a broom closet. The second, a kind of storeroom, very much larger.

Led by his instincts, and a growing curiosity, he went in.

Working his way silently into the large storeroom, Radcliffe moved among the silent and unmoving shapes of lifeless kings and queens, prelates and murderers, admirals and generals.

The first bright glow of the morning's daylight caught his eye, entering the room through a high window. Looking where that light fell upon a set of shelves, Philip Radcliffe came face to face with his own severed, lifeless head.

When the world had righted itself again, he approached the shelf and helped himself to another, closer look. He had needed only a second to realize that this must be the model made by Marie Grosholtz. Now he could appreciate her artistry.

There was the white bandage, stuck on amid the short, dark hair which was indistinguishable from his own hair . . . because, Radcliffe realized with sudden insight, raising a hand to his scalp, it *was* his own, trimmed from his head in his prison cell by Marie herself on the day when she had made her plaster cast.

Other details besides the bandage distinguished his simulacrum from all the others present in the room. The glassy eyes were half open, the coloring a muddy pallor. Shading on cheeks and chin suggested the growth of a few days' beard.

With an effort he put out a hand and seized the thing by its—no, by *his own* hair—and tilted it. The raw neck-surface now exposed was mottled red, and from it protruded narrow tubes of rubber, their ends stained brightly in the color of fresh blood.

Radcliffe was still pondering his discovery, when some subtle sound, a change in atmosphere, informed him that he was not alone.

He turned to confront a figure, which was much more than a mere image, though it was standing as motionless as the surrounding shapes of wax and wood and cloth.

Monsieur Legrand, smiling faintly, bowed to his young friend in silent greeting.

Radcliffe felt a sudden surge of anger, born of the memory of terror and despair that could never be forgotten. "So, the sentence has been carried out, has it?" he blurted. "Perhaps you didn't notice. I've been beheaded!" The young man spoke through his teeth in a strained voice.

Legrand, blinking, seemed utterly taken aback. At last, his own anger stirred, he got out: "What is this idiocy?"

The young man took half a step toward him. "Have you forgotten that I was taken to the guillotine? . . . My head has been . . ." Radcliffe's hands flew through a sequence of shaky and elaborate gestures. Meanwhile he continued to glare at Legrand, as if daring him to confirm or disprove his claim. "The gypsy told me. She told me what you were going to do! To change me into a—a—" He struggled and failed to name the object of his scorn, but it was plain from his tone that the idea now aroused his disgust.

* * *

Upset at what seemed to me a profound lack of gratitude, I glared back at him without sympathy, but rather with a full measure of contempt. "I shall tell you what has happened to your head: It has been filled with brandy and with nonsense!" After venting my annoyance in a string of oaths in antique languages, I seized him by the shirt-front and shook him— still rather gently.

"You have not been decapitated. Nor have you yet been honored with induction into the illustrious ranks of the *nosferatu*—though I fear," I added as I peered into his eyes, "that Constantia may have brought you rather closer to that goal than I intended. Yes, I see. Never mind, now I begin to understand. Where is she, by the way?" And I glared around angrily in search of my sometimes deranged assistant.

"How in hell should I know?" Radcliffe stared at me. Then his voice began to break, with the relief of strain. "But I *remember*—the scaffold—"

When I thought about it, the way my client must have perceived the process of his rescue, I had to admit to myself that he really had been under a tremendous strain, that all the details of my plan had not been executed to perfection, and that he was perhaps entitled to some consideration on that account. I launched into a hasty explanation of the key points of the seeming miracle:

"You remember that you stumbled and fell, even as you stepped up onto the platform?"

"I . . . yes." His hands were trembling now, and he was looking for a place to sit down.

"You fell because you were tripped. You tumbled into one of the long baskets, which was practically concealed from the onlookers behind another basket whose lid stood open."

Radcliffe, who had found a stool, was listening, openmouthed.

"The body that was lifted out of the basket, slammed on the plank, and bound in place, then shoved into the machine, was not yours. It was one of *these!"* And my open hand thumped one of the anonymous dummies standing nearby. "To which *this*"—a long forefinger stabbed at the ghastly head on its low shelf—"had been attached."

At the museum, Marie and Melanie had done all the work on Radcliffe's head with their own hands, pouring the molten wax into the plaster mold Marie had brought back from the prison. Then, knowing that the young man's life depended on their skill, they had painstakingly attached some of Radcliffe's own hair, inserted the glass eyes, and administered the final touches with shaping tools and paint. None of the other workers in the shop had questioned Marie's orders or concerned themselves with her behavior. They were perfectly willing to take orders from the woman who was about to inherit—dare I say it?—the whole ball of wax.

In the museum storeroom the young American was beginning to weep—tears were somewhat more common then— with the relief of strain. "But I felt someone pulling on my hair—lifting my head—"

"You are confused," I explained in a soothing voice. "That was a little earlier, when I tripped you and threw you into the basket."

"You!"

The intricate performance on the scaffold of course had required the secret cooperation of the whole crew of executioners who happened to be present on the platform.

"But there were only two of us, as you undoubtedly remember." I smiled modestly, proud of what I still considered a well-nigh perfect stratagem.

"You—!" He repeated, staring at me.

"Yes, of course I was one of them! You had not seen me in daylight before, and you certainly were not expecting to see me there, in that costume. Also I had allowed myself to age a couple of decades in as many days—we have that privilege, you know."

"And the other executioner?"

"Oh, that was Citizen Sanson, right enough. One of

them—a member of the younger generation, who have now completely taken over the family profession. One of them and one of us. Once Constantia and I hit on the proper sort of bribery, he proved quite susceptible—much easier to deal with than the elder head of the family would have been."

And in fact poor Gabriel Sanson had been quite madly in love with Constantia by that time, ready to risk everything for her, as poor foolish breathers so often are. Radu's people, his spies, for all their cunning efforts, did not get wind of the great plot involving a key person in the matter of executions: the executioner himself.

Methodically I provided my trembling client with more details of the deception. My vampiric strength had enabled me to handle the box containing his live, unconscious body as if it were empty. To prevent onlookers from noticing that Radcliffe's "corpse" still had a head, that wicker box was transported with its contents directly to the cemetery rather than being dumped into a cart at the base of the guillotine, where its contents would have been exposed.

The cart driver, who was partially in on the plot, had dumped Radcliffe's body, still living and intact, in a place somewhat apart from that where he conveyed the quieter majority of his load.

"I suppose you may have been starting to come round by the time they put you in the tumbril, or maybe even a little before that. My intention was to spare you that, but . . . I suppose Constantia failed to give you any clear explanation of our plan."

"You mean I'm not a . . . a . . ."

I bowed to him slightly. "I trust you will survive the disappointment. You have not yet been honored with the opportunity to join the illustrious race of the *nosferatu.*"

The plan as designed had called for either Melanie or Marie to pick up the wax head in the cemetery, as well as seek out Radcliffe there, and, if he was in sufficient possession of his wits, give him his forged papers and some new clothes. But the panicky wagon driver, working in darkness, had dumped him in the wrong place. Then Philip, on recovering his wits, had taken himself away, and Marie, arriving an hour or so late, unavoidably delayed, hadn't been able to find him.

Radcliffe, listening in the storeroom, was not yet wholly satisfied. He kept feeling his neck, turning and nodding his head, as if he feared they might still somehow come apart. "But . . . there was blood spurting, gushing . . . I remember that."

"Your eyes were easily deceived; and so were my brother Radu's, in glaring daylight and at a little distance. What you saw was not exactly blood. Just now when you were looking at your head, there on the shelf—no doubt you took notice of the tubes."

They had been fabricated from what was then called caoutchouc, an early form of industrial rubber. With such tubes and a couple of bladders inside the dummy, it had proven eminently possible to create the appropriate brief jets of "blood."

And of course the wax model of Radcliffe's head had been provided with an internal cavity, filled with a liquid having much the appearance of fresh blood. So that when the executioner's tall assistant lifted it out carefully, by the short dark hair, the red flow drained out visibly for the crowd to watch.

"Real blood of course would have coagulated and changed color long before we were ready to use it. Coming up with a good substitute required some effort, but Constantia and I know something of the subject. We settled on the reddish juice of blood oranges, darkened with a little something else."

I thumped the wax head familiarly on the temple. "Now that this object has served its primary purpose, and perhaps after it is carried in some parade as an illustration of Revolutionary justice, there seems no reason why it should not go on display along with the others in the museum. Perhaps as the head of some minor anonymous figure in one of the groupings. But I believe Marie will wanted to do some retouching on it first. The tubes, of course, should go. They might make someone suspicious."

Today, as on most days, the museum opened early in the morning, and already there were customers out in the public rooms. Radcliffe, listening to them from the storeroom, thought it plain that they took seriously their concerns about whether the wax effigies were really up-to-date and accurate. The political correctness of the display was of perhaps vital importance to the proprietors.

"The day quickly grows bright, and it is time for me to seek a deeper shadow—where I can wait." I looked about thoughtfully.

Radcliffe was on the point of asking, but did not, just what his mentor was intending to wait for.

Before dropping into obscurity, I reminded Radcliffe of the next step in the plan, and handed him some money and a set of beautifully forged identity papers; he was now Citizen Joseph Tallien, a native of Martinique. A wardrobe in the storeroom provided him with a change of clothes.

The young man's eyes grew wide as he looked at the money—gold coin, as well as Revolutionary *assignats;* the latter were almost worthless, but good Revolutionary patriots carried them about. For the purpose of bribes, the old gold coin was much preferred—even though possession of it was seriously illegal. Only precious stones were more readily accepted.

"Sir, this is very generous."

"Tut tut." I waved a hand dismissively. "I am not a poor man—and there is nowhere I would rather spend my money than in the game of discomfiting my brother. Now, you will find the lady you are seeking at Tom Paine's house—or, if not there, at another house nearby, whose address I have jotted down. If you must go to that neighboring dwelling, ask for Citizen Gabriel Sanson."

"Gabriel—?" Radcliffe recoiled slightly. "You are joking!"

"Not a bit. It should be obvious that our little show on the scaffold depended utterly on that young man's cooperation."

"Will he be at home?"

I shrugged, and squinted at the sun-bright window. "It seems more likely, at this hour, that he is at work."

Several hours later, secure in his new identity and boldly asking directions of passersby as he entered the quiet suburban neighborhood, the American found himself standing before a neat little cottage on a quiet, tree-shaded street. There were no street signs near, no clamoring crowds, no walls screaming with inflammatory placards. Like the house where Paine was lodging, this anonymous dwelling stood amid its own fenced grounds.

According to the dictates of the Committee, each place of residence in Paris, including houses and apartment buildings, was now supposed to have the names of all the inhabitants clearly posted on the door. But evidently this one was an exception.

At the door a colorless servant said that Master (". . . er . . . Citizen") Gabriel was expected home early today. And yes, Citizen Gabriel was expecting Citizen Tallien to call. The servant led the visitor around the house to a quiet garden in the back.

This was the place where the elder Sanson still liked to tend his flowers, and now and then some vegetables as well. Plump geese in their separate enclosure greeted the strangers with a hospitable flurry of honking.

And the venerable gentleman himself, patriarch of the clan of executioners, glad to see a visitor, put down his pruning shears and began to talk of gardening with Citizen Tallien.

Time passed, pleasantly enough, except that Radcliffe was on tenterhooks waiting for Melanie to arrive. Where could she be? Of course there could be a hundred harmless causes of delay.

When the man of the house arrived home from work, Philip could not help noticing that the new chief executioner's clothing was quite clean—he must, of course, have changed somewhere before leaving the Place de la Revolution. His wife had his pipe and slippers waiting.

When they went indoors, the senior Sanson petted his dog, smiled at the cat, and invited his guest to choose between a brandy or a glass of wine, which his wife had waiting for him. Meanwhile the ormolu clock on the mantel ticked on, in a perfect image of bourgeois domesticity. Small children, the patriarch's grandchildren, came running to rejoice that Papa had come home from work so early.

Their mother chided the younger children for bothering Papa now, when he had a visitor; later on Papa would tell them a story.

And Gabriel protested, in a way that seemed a matter of family ritual, that he knew no stories. But after making a brief excuse, he went off with his children anyway.

Old Sanson, puffing on his pipe, frowned slightly as he regarded Radcliffe, now seated in a chair opposite. "Citizen Tallien, was it in the course of business that you became acquainted with my son?"

"Yes sir. In a manner of speaking it was."

"Ah. Then in Martinique, you are—?"

Radcliffe did his best to think fast. "I have a connection with the authorities there, sir. With the system of justice. Though mine is not precisely the same profession that you share with your sons." After a pause he added hastily: "And which is an admirable profession indeed."

The old man nodded. Suddenly he looked grim. "Though

some will dispute the fact. Of course it is a great benefit to society."

"Of course, sir."

"Have you seen my machine in operation?" Then, before Radcliffe was compelled to find an answer, he pressed on: "A vast improvement over the old ways! In the old days, at best, the sword—and with the sword, even if the victim did not resist, even if he was perfectly composed, the executioner had to be very skillful, with steady nerves and hand. Otherwise— dangerous accidents!" Old Sanson shook his head and puffed his pipe, evidently recalling some examples.

"Yes," said Radcliffe. "I'm sure the new way is much better."

"The sword quickly grows dull; it has to be sharpened and whetted often. If there are several to be executed on the same day . . ." Again the patriarch shook his head and muttered darkly. "The guillotine is much better—I see the newspapers have begun to call it the guillotine now."

"So I have heard."

The old man's old wife came bustling by, testing furniture to see how well the maid had dusted. "Papa, Papa, the young people don't want to hear about such things."

"Nonsense, of course they do. The young man here is in almost the same business. Besides, everyone should hear them."

People in this respectable if somewhat isolated household were looking askance at Radcliffe's clothing. Only the coat he had taken at the wax museum made him look at all respectable; his other garments still bore noticeable traces of the scaffold and the grave. Well, these days poor clothes could be taken as a sign of Revolutionary fervor.

Gabriel came back into the room, having finished for the time being playing with his children.

Old Sanson looked at him from under heavy brows. "What is this, Gabriel, that I hear about a wooden blade?"

The young man blinked. "Yes, father?"

"Someone told me that yesterday you used a wooden blade in the machine. Well, never mind it now—but when you have finished with your guest, I want to talk to you about it."

"Certainly, father. We were trying a little experiment. The idea is to prevent rust."

"Citizen Tallien," said the young maid from the doorway. "Your wife is here." And it was at that point that Melanie came in, well-dressed and looking radiant.

At the end of the 18th century, coffee was still something of a novelty in Europe; Gabriel Sanson's wife was soon offering some to her visitors.

"Have you ever tried coffee, citizens? It is all the latest thing."

"I have heard that it is also Citizen Robespierre's favorite drink by far." But then, despite the hopes of Citizeness Sanson, the Incorruptible had never come to call on the executioner.

Melanie was introduced to the old people as a young relation of old Curtius's.

The patriarch appeared interested. "Eh? Yes, I know the man. And how is he?"

"Feeling better." There seemed no reason to burden one ill old man with the troubles of another.

Radcliffe, when presently he had a chance to take Melanie aside, embraced her feverishly. "My darling Mellie, if you will have me, we will be truly married the first chance we get. Perhaps at sea."

"Oh, Philip. I want nothing more!"

"But something's wrong. I can tell. Are your new papers in order?"

"Everything has been taken care of, thanks to Legrand—except—one thing!"

"It must be very important if it is going to delay us here!" She was having a hard time finding the right words.

"Philip, I told you that I had met your father."

"What has my father to do with this?"

"It is just that . . . in fact I met M'sieu Franklin at his rented estate at Passy—that's just outside Paris . . ."

"I didn't realize you met him there. But what does it matter?"

". . . where he was living then, when I was a fourteen-year-old apprentice to my cousin. Oh, there was nothing wrong about that! I just didn't want to tell you . . . because of something else."

"What?"

"Because of the reason for my coming to Paris, alone, at the age of fourteen."

"Ah." Something was coming; whatever it was, she must not be allowed to fear that it was going to matter to him. "Go on, Mellie."

"Well . . . it was years after you and your mother had departed for Martinique . . . there was a young man who loved me—yes, he truly did! Even though he was only sixteen at the time, and I was even younger . . ."

"I think that I begin to understand."

"You do? Philip, I have a son, ten years old."

"My poor dear—you could have told me—"

~ 29 ~

*T*he figure of Mr. Graves (what could he be *standing* on to look in that high window?) now raised one finger to its smiling lips, enjoining silence.

Radcliffe complied. He even held his breath. But then, with the desperate certainty that silence wasn't going to be good enough, that the figure at the window was likely to be soon discovered by those inside, he tore his gaze away, lest the people around him should begin to wonder what he was staring at. What he ought to do, inspiration urged, was to create some distraction so that the villains in the house with him would have their attention diverted away from the intruder, at least for a critical few seconds.

When Philip had complained that his arm was bleeding, the knots on the cord that had bound his arms were undone, and his right arm completely freed. Now he should be able to untie and unwind the cords holding his left arm and his legs, but he would need at least several seconds to do so.

He started to untie himself, but the heroic distraction proved unnecessary. A moment later, the glass in three windows simultaneously came crashing in.

*   *   *

The crucial phase of the break-in, which involved getting all the attackers into their chosen positions, had been timed for the moment when the attention of everyone inside would be on Philip and his horrified reaction to the beheading of an animal.

Vlad Dracula had delayed his assault until Radcliffe was brought out to the barn; but he would not have delayed it much beyond that, even if Radu had been late in coming.

It was also exquisitely timed with regard to Radu, to catch him just after his arrival, when he was gloating over his prisoner Radcliffe, at a moment when he'd be relatively off guard.

A moment later, one door of the old barn burst in as well.

People were screaming, roaring, in what sounded like more different voices than there were people present. All of the figures breaking into the barn, through several doors and windows at the same time, were masked—no, all save one.

Neither Radu nor Mr. Graves were any longer to be seen. Instead there were two wolves, two great beasts locked in a snarling, sparring swirl of fur and teeth and glowing eyes.

One mask-face standing in a doorway raised a shotgun, and an instant later a double blast tore splinters from a roof-supporting beam standing ten feet from where Radcliffe sat tearing frantically at his bonds. The body of the man standing beside the post, he who had been drinking cat's blood a minute earlier, was flung violently away.

Moving in ones and twos and threes, the masked breathers on Joe Keogh's combat team were forcing their way in. Vlad Dracula's entry, too, came with smashing force; and he was immediately occupied in a one-on-one struggle with the minor vampire.

The majority of Radu's associates in the barn had carried weapons with them from the house. Despite being taken by surprise, some of them fought back fiercely; one even had an assault rifle within reach.

All of the enemy fought desperately; not one, apparently, thought only of getting away.

The instant the last loop of cord fell free, Phil rolled out of his chair, and continued rolling across the floor. Meanwhile bullets were pounding into the barn's walls above him, loosing a hail of splintered wood . . .

His progress was not unopposed. One of the villains moved to intercept him, aiming a pistol at his midsection. Moving without thought of either fear or bravery, Phil flung himself forward, grappling for possession of the firearm. When he suddenly found he had control of it, he raised the metal weight and used it to hit his opponent over the head. The man slumped down, and Phil ran on.

The twilight, inside and outside the barn, had now come alive with gunfire. Muzzle flashes spasmodically brightened the dimness inside the barn. It seemed that several members of each force were armed with automatic weapons.

First one and then another Coleman lantern was shot out. Glass shattered and fuel spilled, but no fire caught on the stone floor.

Someone or something tripped Radcliffe, and he went down hard. He realized that a woman had tackled him, and now a man was coming to help her out—the effort still seemed to be to capture Phil rather than to kill him. In the midst of his own struggle, Radcliffe caught a freeze-frame impression of Graves, in a form half-man and half-wolf, still grappling with his major enemy. The brothers seemed oblivious to the combat among lesser beings that raged around them.

The acrid smell of burnt ammunition drifted in the air, a haze of wood-dust, and the residue of smokeless powder.

The woman had let go of Philip's legs; he saw her writhing on the floor and realized that a bullet had likely hit her. The man fought on doggedly but lost ground, gasping, lungs wheezing with the burden of a carload of cigarettes.

Phil at last got a good grip on his throat and banged his head against the concrete floor.

Then he was on his feet again. His own lungs were gasping now, but he wasn't going to stop for breath. One more human obstacle loomed up. Radcliffe ran into a small man with his shoulder, ramming his foe with all his force, and knocked the villain sprawling.

At last an open door was just ahead, and Radcliffe went out through it as if all the devils in hell were after him. He wasn't armed or trained for combat, not this kind anyway, and he had no heroic notion about hanging around to claim a bigger share.

There were several vehicles parked nearby, the same ones that had been parked here at the time of his arrival. Fighting down the nightmarish feeling that he had been through this before, he thought that if he could get to one of them, and then get to June—

Before he had taken more than a couple of outdoor steps, a car he recognized as belonging to Graves's faction came roaring up and screeched to a halt in a cloud of flying gravel. From the driver's seat a figure beckoned to him—he recognized Constantia.

Philip ran for the car, had almost reached it, when the woman inside reached out a powerful hand that swept him off his feet and pulled him in. A moment later they were roaring away, bouncing down the pitted and eroded road.

I believe it necessary to report to the reader that one of my gallant breathing allies was killed in the gunfight in the barn, and two more were wounded—professional help was standing by to give them care. At this writing I am not at liberty to name names. As victors we carried away with us our dead, as well as our wounded, when we withdrew from the field.

The habitation effect prevented my getting into the

house. There was no compelling reason for my presence inside; I simply set fire to the building, and waited outside to finish off the small handful of Radu's breathers who had been in the house when we attacked, and who preferred encountering me in the open air to burning to death. The inmates were about evenly divided in their choice. Ruthlessly—and why not?—I exterminated all who came to light. I suppose that one or two might have remained hidden in the basement of the house—to which the fire had soon spread—and come through alive. But I considered that the time and effort necessary to dig them out would have been a poor investment.

Eventually we considered it best to burn the barn as well. But I made sure that the guillotine was carried to safety first. My brother had been taken alive, and the machine was going to be needed.

Joe Keogh commented that when law enforcement eventually reached the scene, which might not be for many days, they would readily enough account for the killings by the presence of drug paraphernalia—another deal gone sour, nothing too much out of the ordinary, except for the numbers involved. In a house of drugs and violence, some overtones of satanism would be no great surprise to the investigators either.

Again Radcliffe was driven across several miles of desert, including a stretch or two of offroad travel. Connie at the wheel chattered brightly through most of the journey.

Once again on this ride, as on the first one he'd taken with these same people, the last embers of sunset were fading. How many sunsets ago was that? He couldn't remember.

The fight, which had seemed to go on forever while it was in progress, had actually taken only a few minutes.

Inside the vehicle, the atmosphere was upbeat but still tense. Connie, looking in her driver's mirror, murmured to Radcliffe: "You're not safe yet. You won't be, as long as Radu is still alive." She sounded dead serious for once.

"At the moment, this feels like being safe."

"Something of a rough time, huh? Sorry about that."

My own fault. Maybe he thought the words if he couldn't yet bring himself to say them. "What's happened to June?"

"Little wifey is just fine."

"Thank God for that!"

Gradually giving way to the shock of all that had happened to him, Philip clung to his wife when they were reunited in the mobile home that once had seemed a prison. At one point he blurted out to the masked Joe Keogh: "I thought—I thought I saw a—a guillotine just now. Set up right outside the window."

"Oh?" Joe sounded only mildly surprised. "I wouldn't worry about it. I expect it won't be there when you look out again." And he reached out and closed the drapes.

The Radcliffes listened to an explanation of how Mr. Graves and his associates had induced him to run away by leaving the window grill unlocked, and how they had kept June with them by working a little mild magic with a shoe. Tracking Phil had been easy, thanks to the wonders of modern electronics.

Gradually, after sleep and food, he got up the nerve to look out of the window again, June standing beside him.

The guillotine was gone, if it had ever really been there. In its place sat their own car.

~ *30* ~

Radu, still gloating over the delicious memory of Philip Radcliffe's decapitation, decided that it might be very amusing to look up Melanie Romain, Radcliffe's lover. He knew the young woman was employed at the wax museum. Perhaps she would be in a mood to accept the kind of consolation he might offer; and today, properly clothed, under what appeared to be a dependably cloudy sky, he felt secure in going out.

He knew that Curtius maintained one exhibition, or museum, at the building which had once been the Palais Royal. But far bigger and more important was his main establishment on the Boulevard du Temple. He had read one of the advertisements:

A collection of wax figures representing famous personages, living and dead, attired in their everyday costume, and exhibiting their usual pose and attitude . . . known as a "Cabinet de Cire."

For all Radu knew, the relationship between Melanie Romain and Philip Radcliffe might have started years ago, and the child she was so concerned about now might well be Radcliffe's.

That was of interest, too. Radu was fond of children.

*   *   *

Turning over in his mind various plans for amusing himself with Marie and her small son Auguste, the younger Dracula approached the museum at No. 20, Boulevard du Temple.

At this hour the place was busy with people engaged in various activities; but a child who wishes to be alone, to play a game that is not approved by the authorities who rule his life, will find a place where he can be alone.

In the rear of the property at No. 20, Boulevard du Temple, stood a kind of shed, almost abandoned, and enclosing a small deserted yard once used for repairing wagons and the like.

Radu took his time, and looked things over. Then he decided that he should first take a look through the museum.

The latest exhibits currently showing, along with several of those which had recently been dismantled, were being considered as items to be sent on a grand tour of India, where interest in such matters was currently very high.

Some work in preparation for the voyage (Marie was going to have to decide whether to risk sending her valuable property halfway around the world as scheduled) had been done within the last few hours.

After inspecting the regular exhibits—the skill of the artist was intriguing, if the subject matter was not—Radu surreptitiously made his way into a storeroom. Here, lined up or piled up for inspection were likenesses of all the villains and heroes—which was which depended of course upon one's point of view—who filled the ranks of the Revolution and made up its rapidly changing leadership. Wave after wave of them came to power, and in a matter of months, or only weeks, were denounced and carted away in batches of ten and twenty to the cemetery—pausing only briefly en route to have their heads chopped off. Folk rested more contentedly in the cemetery if that was done to them first . . .

In 1778 Dr. Curtius, exerting his masterly skill in modeling, had done several studies of Voltaire, posing perhaps the most famous man in Europe as *The Dying Socrates.* Now, the dying Curtius was still justly proud of the fact.

Another group in storage showed the late Royal Family dining in public, a ritual they had engaged in on occasion. Here were Voltaire, Rousseau, and dozens of lesser lights, including members of the first National Assembly. Some were clothed in garments worn by their originals, while others, according to no plan that Radu could make out, had been reduced to a crude and sexless nudity.

The fact that the figures were standing or lying in close proximity to one another seemed to make them all more meaningful. As if they were engaged in dialogue . . .

Standing in the lifeless room, he wondered briefly what famous man or woman might be the next unwitting recipient of this waxen, sham immortality. He was not impressed. The horrors depicted were such feeble, melancholy shadows of the real thing that Radu took no pleasure from them, but rather found them quite depressing.

The younger Dracula's ears brought him confirmation that his instincts had been correct: He could hear, proceeding from the disused shed and courtyard in the rear, the small click and minor thud that the toy guillotine made in its operation. He had seen and heard other Parisian children engaged in similar games, and recognized the sound. It seemed to him as he listened that the little blade was not falling uselessly, but encountering living flesh and blood.

Radu knew a pang of resentment and envy that his own childhood had been deprived of any such toys. Yes, it still rankled that Father had always favored Vlad.

Well, the world made progress, at least in the types of toys that modern youngsters had available.

And there was nothing wrong with the itch of resentment—he, Radu, had discovered centuries ago that it could always be scratched, quite satisfactorily, on the tender skin of someone else.

He had no indication that Vlad was anywhere nearby.

One could never be sure about that, of course, but a great part of the joy of life lay in taking chances.

He would be in no hurry to kill either Melanie or her son when he caught up with them. He intended to savor the sweet child-blood for a long time, before the boy's heart could pump no more . . . yes, ten was an interesting age. The endurance, as Radu had proven to his own satisfaction on many occasions down through the centuries, was much greater than at only five or six, for example.

The pleasure to be obtained from two breathers who were closely related to each other, if one could use them together, was more than twice as great as that to be had from what the total of the two might be in separation. Ideally the mother would, of course, be encouraged to watch what was happening to her baby. And then the mother's turn would come . . . or he could do it the other way around . . .

The trend of Radu's thoughts made the roots of his fangs ache in anticipation, and also brought back the Marquis de Sade into his thoughts. The sight of the wax figures he had just been looking at reminded him of the madman's pathetic, small collection. But he, Radu, had more pressing matters to think about just now . . .

In a way it was too bad that Radcliffe himself had died so quickly. It would have been an interesting refinement to have him available now, to compel the breather to watch what now was going to happen to his woman, and to the child. But, alas, one could not have everything. And the guillotining itself had been supremely satisfying; once the man was dead, there was no way that even Vlad could bring him back.

Ke-chark. There went the model guillotine again.

Slowly, moving only when he was not observed, Radu made his way toward the rear of the establishment. Just before entering the deserted yard he paused once more, relishing the moment. His ears brought him the sound of a single set of childish lungs, breathing quite easily. Now and then a voice, readily identifiable as that of a little boy, murmured something. The judge and executioner of birds and mice was talking to himself, rehearsing for an adult role. Already passing sentences, no doubt, with the supreme self-satisfaction of the head of a tribunal. Somehow it must be instinctive in the race . . .

Entering the courtyard, he set the hook and eye that served as crude lock on the door by which he'd just come in. There was a good bit of shade inside the gloomy shed, and with a little luck he might hope to pass the remainder of the daylight hours here quite undisturbed.

I can call up some mice and birds to feed his guillotine, thought Radu suddenly. Hastily he began to revise his plans. First I shall speak winningly to the child, gain his confidence, and perhaps the two of us will be merry playmates for an hour. I will teach him the thrill of power, and the taste, the real taste, of blood, and then how to skin a small animal alive, so that it still breathes and suffers when its skin is almost entirely off. So that he shall be no longer merely innocent when the game is suddenly transformed . . . so he will understand his own fate when his own skin begins to disappear, a little patch at a time . . . when the smaller extensions of his own body begin to be tried, as to whether they will fit into his toy . . .

Ke-chark.

At last, smiling silently, Radu stepped out into the courtyard. The child, all alone and absorbed in his game, was raggedly dressed in approved Revolutionary fashion, and dirty with the neglect of these last few hectic days. No doubt Mama had been thinking of other things.

On bare feet the small boy crouched before his ingenious toy, rapt over his small institute of slaughter. On the executioner's left, an array of headless mice and birds were laid out on a plank. On his right, half a dozen other shivering small animals, still intact, awaited their turns.

Radu's thoughts were elsewhere than on the animals,

and several seconds passed before he noticed that those arrayed on the right of the miniature scaffold were in no way confined or bound, but only mesmerized. Their small hearts hammered rapidly, their little lungs kept laboring, but their limbs that might have carried them to safety were quite immobile.

Several additional seconds went by before the significance of this fact struck him.

Someone, no doubt to make friends with the apprentice executioner, had mesmerized the animals.

The smile froze on Radu's face, even as the boy, unafraid, looked up to take note of the man's presence.

Radu knew what had happened, he understood what his own fate was to be, before he heard another sound.

There elapsed what seemed to Radu a very long time indeed, in which he tried without success to nerve himself to turn and look.

But he remained staring straight ahead. Because he knew, perfectly well, that whether he turned around or not was going to make no difference.

"I am glad to see you, my brother." Vlad's deep voice was unmistakable. It addressed itself to Radu in a language he understood very well, centuries older than the French of 1794. And it was very close behind him.

Radu's beautifully shaped lips twitched in a faint smile. Whatever was going to happen to him now, at least Philip Radcliffe was dead, and he had tasted Radcliffe's blood. By no punishment could his brother ever deprive him of that triumph.

~ *31* ~

*I*n 1996 Radu's head and body, separated by the latest technology of the end of the eighteenth century, quick-frozen by the most up-to-date equipment of the twentieth century, were shipped to a region of the world very distant from the American Southwest.

On the day Vlad Dracula said good-bye to the twentieth-century Radcliffes, he had something he wanted to show them. He had only borrowed it for a while, for this very purpose.

"So, that is what he looked like," the modern Philip Radcliffe said, when he had gazed for a little while at the object in his mentor's hands.

Vlad nodded. "Originally, of course, the appearance was much more natural. The models in the galleries can last for more than twenty years. Eventually, however, the wax becomes discolored, it dries and crumbles. And the hair wears out; of course it has to be periodically brushed, combed, and washed."

June looked away from the ancient model. Her eyes fell on the rubber masks, discarded days ago by Vlad's modern helpers, now lying in a row on a shelf like so many decapitated heads.

The thought occurred to Mrs. Radcliffe that on the day Vlad Dracula and Gabriel Sanson had worked their trickery on the platform of the guillotine, the two of them must have actually beheaded more than a dozen victims—the savior of her husband's ancestor must have played perfectly his role of assistant executioner.

She looked up to see him smiling benevolently at her, and knew a shudder of fear that he perhaps could read her thoughts.

Both Radcliffes in 1996 wanted to know more about what had happened to Philip's namesake and ancestor in the summer of 1794.

In that year I once more forced Radu into a trance, then beheaded him with the same guillotine he had planned to use on Radcliffe—with a spare metal blade carefully substituted for the wooden one.

I did not bother to tell the modern Radcliffes that it had amused me on that earlier occasion to have Radu's head modeled as a keepsake—I advised the technician to handle the object with great care, lest it stir in the midst of trance and bite her fingers as she worked on it. There was of course no need for breathing tubes in Radu's nostrils. But I do believe she sewed his lips shut, with a special cord . . .

One more job for Marie, and the most difficult and dangerous of her career. But I assured her that she was quite free to reject the job if she had wished, and she was well rewarded indeed for its successful completion.

Within a year of Radu's last visit to Citizen Louis Sade in his cell, the former marquis was released from prison. In 1801 he was rearrested, by yet another French government, charged with obscenity, and locked up again in the Charenton asylum. There he spent the thirteen remaining years of his life.

* * *

Melanie's child by a previous relationship, little Auguste, accompanied his mother and her new husband to England in the summer of 1794. That same season saw the fall of Robespierre, who was shot in the jaw before being carried to the scaffold. Before her marriage, Marie Grosholtz held in her lap the Incorruptible's lacerated head, and did her routine work with plaster and with wax. By that time, the job had become only a job.

In London little Auguste fell in with his paternal grandfather, himself a successful refugee. Old Monsieur Dupin conceived a liking for this youngster, wanted him to bear the family name, and more or less adopted him. I have heard that Melanie's child, like many another exile, returned in a few years to France, at a time when Bonaparte promised glory, and that in later life he formed some vague connection with the Parisian police.

Melanie was saddened by the separation from her son, half-brother to her other children who were to be. However, her new life in America as Mrs. Radcliffe, wife of a successful young lawyer, brought her considerable happiness. And in any case, there was nothing she could do about Auguste.

The Philip Radcliffe who so narrowly escaped the guillotine lived on another sixty years and more. He was eventually brought down by a stray cannonball in one of the early battles of the American Civil War, as he tried stubbornly to work his Virginia fields, meanwhile cursing the authors of yet one more rebellion.

Sanson's eldest son and chief assistant, Gabriel, one of dear Constantia's many lovers, died unexpectedly in 1795, in an accidental fall from the platform of the guillotine, whilst displaying his last severed head. It is possible that his foot slipped in a smear of blood.

I have heard it whispered that the head he was holding

moved in his hands and startled him, which would seem a certain indication that it was that of another vampire. I offer no explanation.

Before bidding farewell to the modern Radcliffes, I assured them that the odds were very small that they would ever have to worry about their family nemesis again. I had to admit, though, the real possibility that their grandchildren would encounter some such difficulty—probably some time in the vicinity of the year 2090.

   If it should prove to be so, I trust that their descendants will feel free to call on me for help. I will grant it willingly, if I am still alive to do so—and I have every intention of being as fully alive as ever. The matter will still be a matter of honor, no less than ever before.